Lion in the City

Allan P Smith

Richard,
Thanks for the happy childhood memories of playing together. I admire and am proud of the man you are. You remind me of Dad.
   Love Allan

Copyright © 2019 Allan P Smith
All rights reserved.

ISBN 9781689783675

For Madeline, my muse.

Acknowledgements

I would like to thank my wife, Madeline, for her unwavering support and encouragement, and for her endless proof-reading and editing.

I would also like to thank my writing group in Washington, D.C. for their always useful feedback: Wendy Lynch, Cynthia Folcarelli, Len Kruger, Carrie Morris, and Katie Steedly.

I would also like to thank April Bodie, Stephanie Schlick, Karen Page, and my mum, Molly Smith, for reading early drafts of the manuscript.

"It's not a good idea in the town to rear a lion cub, but if you do, make sure he is happy when he grows up and not liable to run amok."
(Aristophanes, *Frogs*)

Character list

*Characters based on historical personages are indicated by the symbol (H)

Alkmaeonids and their associates

Alkibiades (H): son of Deinomache and Kleinias (deceased)
Andromachus (H): slave of Alkibiades
Ariphron (H): brother of Perikles; ex-guardian of Alkibiades and his brother, Kleinias
Axiochus (H): uncle of Alkibiades; brother-in-law of Deinomache
Deinomache (H): mother of Alkibiades and Kleinias
Hipparete (H): wife of Alkibiades; daughter of Hipponikus; sister of Kallias
Hippokrates (H): son of Ariphron
Kleinias (H): brother of Alkibiades
Maria: maid to Hipparete
Megakles (H): uncle of Alkibiades; brother of Deinomache

Characters associated with Plataea

Alexias: son of Stephanos and Khara; grandson of Lakon
Ammias (H): soldier in Plataea
Arkadius (H): general in Plataea
Astymachus (H): orator in Plataea
Eupompides (H): general in Plataea
Hybrias: friend of Sémon and Mikos
Khara: wife of Stephanos; mother of Alexias
Lakon: elder brother of Sémon; father of Stephanos
Mikos: slave freed by Sémon
Sémon: brother of Lakon; uncle of Stephanos; husband of Ana (deceased)
Skopas: friend of Sémon and Mikos
Stephanos: son of Lakon; husband of Khara; father of Alexias

Nikias' family

Aristeia: daughter of Nikias
Armina: Persian maid to Aristeia
Eukrates (H): brother of Nikias; uncle of Aristeia
Glukera: aunt to Nikias; great-aunt to Aristeia
Hiero (H): servant of Nikias
Nikias (H): a leading politician and general; father to Nikeratus, Strettipus and Aristeia; husband to Agné (deceased)
Stilbides (H): Nikias' diviner
Theodora: sister-in-law to Nikias; aunt of Aristeia; mother to Isias and Nikolea

Alkibiades' associates and their families

Antiphon (H): oligarchic associate of Pisander; a speechwriter
Demosthenes (H): Athenian soldier
Elené: wife of Pisander; mother of Nikolas
Hipponikus (H): father of Kallias and Hipparete; father-in-law of Alkibiades; general and politician
Kallias (H): son of Hipponikus; brother of Hipparete; brother-in-law of Alkibiades
Kleon (H): leading politician in the Assembly
Leaina: sister of Timokles; daughter of Nikopatra
Nikolas: son of Pisander and Elené; a friend of Alkibiades
Nikopatra: mother of Timokles and Leaina; friend of Deinomache
Orontas: Persian slave of Timokles
Pisander: husband of Elené; father of Nikolas; oligarchic associate of Antiphon
Samias: Timokles' lover
Sellene: prostitute under the protection of Simaetha
Simaetha (H): mistress of Alkibiades
Timokles: childhood friend of Alkibiades; son of Nikopatra; brother of Leaina

Chapter 1

Summer, 431 BC

Stephanos knew the town had been betrayed. He cracked the door open again and peered into the muddy street. Soldiers still jogged past, rain drumming on their bronze helmets and shields. To Stephanos, it was a dirge: the shields bore club emblems, the device of Theban soldiers, and for a Plataean it was hard to imagine a more hateful sight.

He closed the door and uncovered the lit oil lamp. His three-year-old son lay sprawled on a straw mattress in the corner, Stephanos' armour hanging on the wall above him. The wispy curtain that separated the bedroom from the family room parted and his wife squinted at him.

"What's the matter?" Khara whispered. She was bundled in a blanket and cloaked in sleep.

Only a mud-brick wall separated Stephanos' wife and child from enemy spears, and images of slaughter, rape, and slavery seared his mind. "Quickly. Take Alexias onto the roof."

"The roof? Why?"

"We've been betrayed. Theban soldiers are here."

"Betrayed?" Khara froze as Stephanos climbed the ladder and opened the trap door to the roof. She was still motionless as Stephanos eased Alexias from his bed and carried him onto the flat roof, where he laid him under the shelter, still asleep.

"What shall we do?" asked Khara when Stephanos returned.

He wrapped himself around her and buried his face in her cheek. When he released her, his glance towards his armour told Khara all she needed to know.

"Come back. Promise by Hera of Marriage you'll come back," she whispered as tears welled in her eyes.

"I promise by every god and goddess on Mount Olympus." He kissed her, then gently disentangled himself, donned his breastplate and helmet, and seized his spear and shield. "Stay on the roof. Keep the door bolted."

The narrow street was now deserted, and rain hammered the mud as he crossed to his uncle's house and rapped on the door. Sémon was a bear of a man whose laugh could rock the streets and whose loyalty and bravery were as powerful as his physique. Stephanos adored him.

By the time Sémon had roused himself and put on his armour, other neighbours had risen, and they crept together towards the heart of the town, the agora.

Plataea had become a menacing spider's web: streets in which Stephanos had played as a boy now threatened an ambush at every dark turn. More men joined at each corner, urging one another forward. When they reached the agora, they halted. The square glowed with torches, and the steps of the Temple of Athena and the colonnade of the East Stoa swarmed with Theban hoplites.

"Come! Come," bellowed the Theban leader, Eurymachos, holding his arms wide as if he were Athena's priest welcoming them to her temple. "We are here by invitation. We wish you no harm."

The Plataeans slipped into the agora from every side, huddling together around the towering statue of Zeus the Liberator, which dominated the centre of the square.

"How many do you think?" asked Stephanos.

"A few hundred," said Sémon. "But how many goat shaggers are on the walls?"

Stephanos looked around the growing mass of his townsmen. They could normally muster six hundred men at best, but how many of them were outside the town on their farms, like his father?

For generations the city of Thebes, only eight miles from Plataea, had struggled to control its smaller neighbour, salivating over its manpower and rich farmland. Plataea's alliance with Thebes' hated rival, Athens, had stoked Theban anger, but the town's walls had so far confounded Theban ambition. But Stephanos knew that the strongest of walls could not protect against betrayal. Someone must have opened the gates.

When the last cluster of Plataeans had gathered in the agora, the

Theban leader invited them to revoke their alliance with Athens, to dismantle their democracy, and to place leadership in the hands of a few Plataeans whom the Thebans trusted. Stephanos had suspected what their demands would be, but to hear them still felt like a sword to the gut. It would be virtual enslavement to Thebes. He could see in his neighbours' eyes that they had no wish to abdicate their rights or to desert Athens, but nothing persuades like the point of a spear.

Negotiations began in the rain, and rumours rippled through the Plataean ranks that the traitors were certain wealthy men whose oligarchic ambitions had long been suspected and who would expect to rule under Theban protection. Whispers began to circulate that there were no Thebans on the walls, that their entire force of hoplites was in the agora. The mood of the Plataeans hardened. Eurymachos sensed the danger and ordered them to return to their homes until further notice. The crowd dispersed in knots of angry debate.

"What's happened?" whispered Khara from the roof as Stephanos and Sémon splashed along the street. She let them in and Stephanos lit the oil lamps.

"That pompous prig, Naukleides, has made a gift of us to Thebes," growled Sémon.

"Will it be peaceful?" asked Khara.

A troop of Theban soldiers marched past the open door. "That remains to be seen," said Sémon. "No doubt their entire army will turn up tomorrow to make sure we're sewed up tighter than Artemis' arse."

"They're not here now?"

"Seems not. I'd like to crack a few of those Theban skulls," said Sémon. "Guarantee they're as empty as my purse."

Another squad of soldiers jogged past.

"They're making sure we can't organize a resistance," said Stephanos. They fell into silence and stared at the rain pounding the street.

Khara started at a thud on a wall they shared with a neighbour. She frowned at Stephanos, who turned to investigate.

"Don't go outside," said Khara. "The soldiers."

The plaster crumbled and a spear poked through the wall. The hole enlarged, and their neighbour's panting head appeared. "Hey,

Stephanos. What say we get those bastards?"

Around Plataea, adjoining walls were being torn apart, and men began to infiltrate the houses nearest the agora. During the last watch of the night, the Plataeans prepared to reclaim their town. Stephanos stood beside Sémon in a room crammed with hoplites, his heart racing, praying to Zeus the Liberator that the fighting would not spill into their homes, into their families.

A whistle sounded and the men exploded into the agora, Stephanos roaring his anger to battle pitch. The main Theban force was lounging in the stoa when the Plataeans burst upon them. Stephanos saw their surprise, but even in the midst of his furious charge he admired their disciplined response as the Thebans quickly locked shields, forming a wall in front of the columns at the top of the stoa's steps. The Plataeans were forced to attack from below. They hurled themselves at the massed Thebans, shields crashing into shields, spears jabbing, arrows thudding, the agora boiling with yelling and screaming.

The Thebans held their ground. Stephanos pressed against the comrades in front of him as they strained to push the Thebans back. He thrust his spear repeatedly between the heads of his friends, aiming at the faces of the helmeted Thebans as shields from behind tried to drive him forward. The roar around him was a storm.

After five minutes of shoving and stabbing, Stephanos felt the pressure of the ranks behind him slacken and then disappear. His comrades were fleeing, and when the Thebans began to surge down the steps, Stephanos turned and fled with the rest of the Plataeans. He ran as if chased by the Furies until he reached the rest of the Plataeans on the opposite side of the agora, crowded against the walls of the Council chamber and the Assembly. The Thebans had not followed them, but laughed and jeered from their position on the steps.

Stephanos was sick. They had run away so easily. He had run away. His home and his family were in mortal danger, yet his courage had fled like a startled deer.

"Come on, you bunch of cow turds!" yelled Sémon. "Are you going to let those goat shaggers steal your town? Rape your women?"

Anger surged again within Stephanos, and he gripped his spear more tightly and swung his shield back in front of him. All around him the Plataeans planted themselves into ranks facing the Thebans. There was no command to charge, yet the Plataeans hurtled forward as one. Stephanos' eyes burned, his ears filled with his own battle cry. He was a ravenous wolf again.

He crashed into the Thebans with a surge from the ranks behind him, glaring at the enemy only a foot in front of him, but Stephanos' long spear could only strike those in the third rank. He took half a step forward. Then a step up. He was on the stoa, level with the Thebans, his muscles quivering with the strain.

Suddenly the resistance in front weakened and the Theban ranks splintered and broke. They bolted down the narrow streets, but in the dark Plataea was a labyrinth and they became hopelessly lost. Behind them Plataean hoplites hunted; from the roofs wives and slaves launched tiles. The Theban hoplites stumbled into traps, careered into spears.

Stephanos flew at the backs of men who had cast aside their shields with thoughts only of escape. His spear ripped a neck, showering him in a fountain of blood. He splashed through mud and entrails and leapt over ravaged bodies. He turned a corner and burst upon the massive town wall, where a handful of Thebans were cornered.

"On your knees," someone shouted.

"Let's kill the bastards!" cried another.

The soldiers knelt; one blubbered, "For the love of Apollo, mercy!"

Mercy? What mercy would you have shown my wife? thought Stephanos.

The Thebans removed their helmets, and Stephanos was startled by the young faces. One had eyes just like Alexias'. *They're just boys*. Stephanos felt ice water quench his fury, and he suddenly felt nauseated at the smell of the blood that cloaked him. "Wait," he shouted. "Let's take them prisoner."

"There'll be no prisoners today," growled Onasos, whose legs were splattered with faeces, blood, and lumps of intestine.

"Don't you think that boy on the right looks like your son, Onasos? And Phanias, that one has your curly hair, as if he were your child." Onasos and Phanias frowned, relaxing their spear grips slightly. Stephanos pressed his advantage. "They'll be more useful alive than dead. We can ransom them, earn some silver."

Slowly the bloodlust ebbed, and the Plataeans shepherded the prisoners back to the agora, where they were penned with one hundred and seventy of their comrades. One hundred and twenty Thebans lay dead in the streets of Plataea.

At sunrise the full Theban army marched on Plataea, but was forced to withdraw to Thebes when the lives of the captured men were threatened. Negotiations began for the prisoners' return, but once the Plataeans had rushed their families, livestock, and goods from the countryside into the safety of the town, their anger was free to lash their captives. Wives demanded that husbands punish potential rapists; mothers demanded that sons avenge fathers killed in past battles. Flames of vengeance stoked the town.

Deliberative assemblies served only to release the wrath of the Plataeans, despite the impassioned pleas of Sémon. The town gathered in the agora to celebrate their salvation, cheering as the bound prisoners were executed, the men taking turns to hack off heads and send them tumbling down the steps of the stoa, then dipping their hands in the bloody necks and daubing their faces.

Stephanos had made Khara and Alexias stay at home, but had felt he had no choice but to attend the barbarity. He looked around the crowd, but instead of seeing friends and neighbours, he saw monsters.

A chorus of jeers greeted the Theban leader, Eurymachos, who struggled to break free of the men who led him forward, and exuberant cheers accompanied the cart-wheeling, blood-spraying head. The steps were mired in blood, fragments of bone, and chunks of brain matter by the time the crowd encouraged a slight fifteen-year-old boy to sever the head from a victim. It took three blows.

Stephanos could bear it no longer. "This is an offence against the gods," he hissed. "Unarmed men."

"Yes," nodded Sémon slowly. "This is a day the Thebans will never forget."

Stephanos turned to meet his eyes. "Or forgive."

Chapter 2

Three years later

For Khara, the new moon heralded the day when she would discover whether her husband still lived. She was indifferent to the day's propitiousness for trading and to the incense being offered on the altars of Athens. Like her fellow exiles from Plataea, she dreaded and yet lived for the news this day would bring.

She peered out into the darkness, which seemed to creep into her small kitchen and threaten to extinguish the oil lamps. She half expected to hear the tramp of enemy soldiers, to discover that Athens had been betrayed, too. But it was silent. Khara ached for sunrise, for a distraction from the Furies who galloped in her chest and chased away the gods of sleep.

She huddled into her blanket and stirred the watery pot of leeks and onions on the glowing charcoals. A lamp guttered, a shadow died on the roughly plastered wall, and Stephanos' absence knifed her. It had been three winters since the raid on Plataea that had helped spark another war between Athens and Sparta, Thebes' ally. The women, children, and old men of Plataea had been shepherded into Athens for protection. Khara had seen her husband only once since then, almost two years ago, and the last night of that blissful month was etched in her memory. Stephanos was to return to Plataea the following morning and had struggled to placate their four-year-old son, Alexias.

"Why can't we come with you?" Alexias had demanded, brushing his hand across his runny nose.

Stephanos met Khara's gaze across the fire in the heart of the family room. His face was solemn, his usual warm smile missing. Khara knew he was arming himself for the wrench to the fields of war. "I need you here to look after momma and pappu," he said.

"I can look after myself," snapped Lakon, Stephanos' father. The deep chasm between the old man's eyes gave Lakon the appearance of perpetual ill-humour, an appearance not without foundation, in Khara's opinion.

"But they can come, too," said Alexias.

Stephanos opened his arms, and Alexias accepted the invitation to sit on his poppa's lap. "Sparta and Thebes are still angry with Plataea because we're friends with Athens," began Stephanos. "When people are angry they sometimes do bad things, so we think it's best that you stay here."

"But aren't they angry with Athens as well?"

Khara exchanged a proud smile with her husband: it was hard to get much past their son.

"They are," said Stephanos. "But the walls around Athens are so huge that even the Titans couldn't climb them."

Alexias frowned, swinging his legs back and forth under the chair, watching a spark escape the fire and flee like a shooting star to the low ceiling. When he spoke again, his voice was soft. "Could the Titans climb the walls around Plataea?"

Stephanos hugged his son and kissed his curly hair. "The Spartans are like old Drool. Remember him? He could growl and bark, but he never bit anyone. All he did was cover you in slobber. The Spartans make lots of noise and then go home to their farms. The war won't last long."

"Don't count on it," said Lakon. "There's a prophecy that this war will last thrice nine years."

"Thanks, poppa," said Stephanos.

"Just being honest. You shouldn't mislead the boy."

"I'm not misleading him. Whoever heard of a war lasting twenty-seven years?"

Khara had eventually settled Alexias on his straw mattress, and then spent the night in her husband's arms, memorizing the feel of every muscle, every tone of his voice. He had a sturdy, farmer's body and rough hands, but his words were tender and his caresses gentle. For a few blissful hours his leaving was forgotten as they clung to each other, hoping that Apollo would fail to harness his chariot, that the night would last forever. But the sun had risen, and Khara had hung a charm of Apollo around Stephanos' neck as a parting gift before standing sentry on the city walls, watching him disappear towards the mountains of Aegaleus.

She remembered that night as rushing past, but every darkness since then had lasted a lifetime. Khara shivered and looked beyond the bubbling pot at the crude wooden statuette of the goddess Hestia, Protectress of Homes, which stood on a rickety table. Its paint was fading and flaking. *Much like myself,* Khara thought with a sigh. She knew she had been a beauty. Her black hair was long and luxurious, but she was now twenty-five and her face had begun to acquire a slave's olive hue, and lines like dry streams had sprung around brown eyes that had lost their sparkle. Would he still think her beautiful?

A bubble broke the surface of the stew, and Khara felt sobs fighting to be released. She surrendered to the tears, allowing her grief to wash over her. She longed to hear his laugh, to be held, to feel safe. She took a deep breath and glanced at Hestia. Why had the gods not acted? Why had mighty Athens done nothing? Where were their friends now?

She wanted to scream at the gods, but she could not, nor could she shed her tears except at night. She had to be strong for Alexias. Her son was now six, her sunshine. He was confident that his heroic poppa was safe, never doubting that he would return. Khara was determined that her son's wall of hope would not be breached, but this was always the most difficult day of the month, when the scouts returned to report on the status of Plataea. The town had now been besieged for well over a year, and it was possible that it had been stormed weeks ago, that Stephanos lay dead and unmourned without her knowing. Today she would know.

A cockerel announced that the night was retreating at last as birdsong welcomed the grey light. Khara heard her father-in-law hack in the neighbouring room, and she roused herself to wash away her tears in a bowl of cold water, finding solace in the routine of making preparations for the morning sacrifice. She dragged Alexias from his mattress, and he soon stood in his short sackcloth tunic alongside Khara before the stone altar in the centre of their earthen courtyard.

The cramped yard was gripped on three sides by the cracking, whitewashed walls of their single-storey house, beyond whose orange-tiled roof rose the second floors of their neighbours' houses. A narrow wooden door gave access to the outside world through a mud-brick wall. Their house was squeezed between the abodes of noble families, but Khara remained grateful to their neighbour, Alkibiades, whose shared trials with Stephanos at the siege of Potidaea four summers ago had persuaded him to rent them an old servants' quarters. Other Plataeans had not been so fortunate and lived in wooden huts erected around temples. Nevertheless, Khara refused to accept that this was their home. She had hung weavings in only the family room and had not adorned the courtyard with plants, leaving it a patch of dirt punctuated by the altar.

Lakon hobbled from his room, glowering. He had grown frail, and Khara thought his unkempt hair and greying stubble made him look like an angry stoat. But he was Stephanos' father, and she remembered him as he had been before the death of his wife, so she loved the man hiding behind the gruff exterior. She raised the folds of her sea-blue himation to cover her head, and Lakon grunted a greeting as he reached the altar, before raising his hands to the heavens.

"Mighty Zeus our Protector, God of gods, hear our prayer," he began, hurrying through the ritual. The patriarch lowered his hands, lifted the beaker of wine from atop the altar, and poured the liquid over the weathered stone. "We honour you, son of Kronos, with this libation." He replaced the beaker and raised his hands to the dawn again. "Protect my brave son, Stephanos, and my brother, Sémon, as they defend Plataea. Grant them your shield and fill them with your courage." He lowered his hands, and Alexias stifled a yawn.

Khara pretended not to notice her son's guilty glance, but raised her arms and focused on the brightening, cloudless air. "Gentle Hestia, protector of our home, we give you this cake in thanks for your sustenance," she said, placing a small corn cake on the altar. Alexias shuffled his bare feet, and Khara smiled as she guessed his sacrilegious desire to transfer the offering to himself. "Save my husband and Theo Sémon and make our home complete." She wanted to stretch her arms and grab the goddess, to shake her into doing her bidding. Instead, she removed her head covering and walked towards the kitchen. "Get washed, Alexias. We're going to the Heroes today."

Alexias dashed to the clay pot of rainwater in the yard, and after a perfunctory exposure to the frigid liquid, was soon ensconced beside his mother around the glowing hearth in the family room. Geometric weavings adorned the walls, a memorial to Khara's beloved mother-in-law, Eiréné. A short prayer was the prelude to Alexias wolfing his share of the remains of the previous day's stew, along with stale chunks of barley bread, a handful of olives from Attika, and a cup of heavily diluted wine from Aegina. Lakon picked at his food, refusing to meet his daughter-in-law's eyes.

"Come with us," said Khara. "It'll make you feel better."

"I feel fine," growled Lakon, scratching his bristles.

"Just come to hear what they have to say."

Lakon almost choked on his bread. "What's the point? What can they tell me that I don't already know? Can they tell me my son and brother aren't still trapped because Plataea refused to surrender? No. Can they tell me Athens is going to send an army to save Plataea? Artemis' tits can they. They have *commitments* elsewhere. Or too many have died of plague. Or there are too many Spartans. And of course, Zeus hasn't farted for a month. Excuses, excuses."

"You never know," said Khara. "If we are good to the gods, they may rescue them."

"The gods?" spluttered Lakon. "You mean the same gods that sent the plague? The gods that consume Stephanos and Sémon in war while imprisoning me in this decrepit body so I can't fight alongside them? The same gods who no doubt started this war for their own amusement and killed my wife?"

Khara remained quiet, allowing the tempest to blow itself out. She glanced at Alexias, who was watching them with wide eyes but without pausing in his eating. Eiréné's graceful image floated into Khara's consciousness. She had been a remarkable woman, loving, kind, and able to run a household and a farm seemingly effortlessly. Khara had worshipped her. She remembered walking beside her as they fled for Athens, both of them looking back at each step to wave to Stephanos on the stout walls of Plataea. She recalled little Alexias jumping up and down, his arms above his head like the branches of a mad tree, as they reached the rise of land beyond which their home would dissolve into memory. Eiréné had held her as they drank one last look at the plains of Plataea, at the deserted farms, at the procession of carts and people heading for the mountain pass towards Athens. It had reminded Khara of flocks of birds fleeing in the moments before Poseidon pounds the ground in anger. And yet, with Eiréné beside her, she had felt strong.

Plataea had been evacuated before, during the Persian invasion in the time of her grandfather. The barbarians had destroyed the town, but it had been rebuilt after the Greek victory over the army of Mardonius on the plains before Plataea. Even so, Khara had shared the sense of foreboding that had settled on the refugees as they streamed towards the pass. Their livestock had been taken to the island of Euboea for safety, but they had had no choice but to abandon the fertile soil to the ravages of war. And then the three-day journey in the heat of summer had ended in despair. Eiréné had sliced open her leg on a bush on the first morning, and by the time they reached Athens she had been feverish and the wound had begun to smell.

They had rushed her to a visiting priest of Asklepios at the Temple of Apollo, where she had been purified with water and dressed in a white robe and an olive wreath. The priest had led her to a bed of twigs where she was to spend the night, in the expectation that the gods would visit her dreams and reveal a cure.

Khara and Lakon had paced the night away outside the temple as Alexias slept on a cloak, and in the first light of morning the priest had come to them, unable to meet their eyes. Khara had sprinted into the temple and on to the inner sanctuary. She had paused, breathless, at the sight of Eiréné's unseeing eyes, and then sank to the ground and hugged the cold body to her.

The image of Lakon balled up in the dust outside the temple, sobbing, was one she would never forget. Alexias had been comforted by Khara telling him that his yaya was smiling in the happy fields of Elysium. For Khara, Eiréné's passage to Hades had left the family rudderless.

The exiles had arrived in Athens like aliens, in houses yet homeless, uprooted from the land and planted in foreign soil. They had left a small town and found themselves in a loud, bustling city, where rumours suggested that Perikles' mistress, Aspasia, had goaded the Athenian leader into the war with Sparta and Thebes. Others declared that Corinthian anger over Athenian aggression had been the cause, and yet others that Sparta was jealous of Athens' empire. Khara did not understand the reasons, nor did she really care. All she knew was that Stephanos and Theo Sémon had been forced to garrison Plataea, leaving their family without protection. But she had coped. She had bought food from the stalls in the agora; she had mended clothes; she had prepared meals; she had sacrificed to the gods. The pain of separation gnawed at her, but her determination to provide for Alexias had dragged her onwards.

"Look," continued Lakon, jolting Khara back to the fire and Alexias' slurps. "The Athenians allow their enemies free rein to destroy their own land here in Attika, so why should we expect them to lift a finger to save ours? How can there be any good news? The only news we're likely to hear is that Plataea has surrendered." He paused, and added softly, "Or fallen."

Khara envisioned Stephanos marched from their home in chains, shipped to a foreign land, never to see his family again.

She noticed that Alexias had halted his breakfast and was staring at his elders with frightened eyes. Khara brushed a tear from her cheek and kissed him on the head. "Zeus the Liberator will save Plataea, we need have no fear." She motioned towards the open door. "It's going to be a beautiful day."

"Humph. Why hasn't Apollo got out of bed? Where's the damn sun?" said Lakon.

"I'm sure the sun is shining, if we could only see above the roofs. In the agora, you'd be able to see the sun."

"I can wait for him here. The streets are fit only for rats. Full of noise and filth. They stink. Give me fresh country air."

Khara shook her head and returned their bowls to the kitchen. Ever since his wife's death, Lakon had been vanishing, as if he were already half way across the River Styx. She did not know how to rescue him. If only Stephanos were here.

She crossed the hard-packed earth of the courtyard to the store-room in the corner, ignoring Lakon, who watched her surreptitiously as he positioned a couch outside with Alexias' help. She stroked a jar filled with water, seeds, and olive oil that represented Zeus of Property, and she prayed for her home's protection.

A loud crash from their neighbour's house cracked the air, followed by the roar of Deinomache, Alkibiades' warrior-like mother. Alexias appeared in the doorway. "Do you think Hipparete is in trouble?" he asked.

"No, I'm sure she's fine. It's probably just one of the slaves." Hipparete was Alkibiades' young wife, and Alexias liked her, which was not difficult. Khara felt the same way.

A rap on the outside door constricted Khara's chest. She hurried out of the store-room and, with a pretence of composure, opened the door.

"Master asks if you're ready." It was Andromachus, the youthful slave from next door. He reminded her of a temple column: slim but strong, tall but graceful.

Yet it was the imprint of an owl burned into his forehead that always ensnared Khara's eyes. Bile burned her throat at the prospect of Stephanos enslaved, branded. She looked away. "We'll be right there." She shut the door and glanced down at Lakon, who lay on the couch with his eyes closed as if unaware of the disturbance. "There'll be lots of your friends there," she said. "A chance to catch up and talk about the old days."

"Hades!" exclaimed Lakon without opening his eyes. "What makes you think I want to talk about the old days? To remember what I can no longer do? People I can no longer see and places I can no longer go? Just leave me alone, woman." As an afterthought he added, "Bring me back a cheese and barley bread roll."

"Fetch it yourself, you old piece of cheese." A smile twitched Lakon's face as he scratched the grey stubble on his cheek. "I hope Apollo stays in the agora," she added, annoyed that she would, of course, do as he asked. She pulled up her himation to cover her head, leaving only her face exposed. "Come on, sweetheart." She opened the door and Alexias followed her into the dirt street.

Andromachus led them around the extensive walls of Alkibiades' house to the entrance, through which the slave disappeared. Unlike the white walls of his neighbours' houses, Alkibiades' were painted red. Beside Athenian entrances stood stone herms, carved figures of a grinning Hermes with an erect phallus, which brought the protection of the god to each house, but there was no such statue outside Alkibiades' home. Khara shivered at her neighbour's ostentatious neglect of the gods. She feared some terrible punishment would descend on this family, and she trembled for her friend, Hipparete.

"Will poppa be coming home this time?"

Khara grasped Alexias' hand. "I don't think so, sweetie. He still has to protect our home."

"So when *will* he come and get us?"

"Soon, Alexias. Soon."

Over a year ago, the Spartan-led Peloponnesian army had attempted to storm Plataea, but had failed. At the insistence of their Theban allies, the army had built a besieging wall around the town to starve Plataea into submission, leaving a garrison to man the wall. Since then, the only news of the town that reached Athens was gathered by scouts, but Khara needed no scout to tell her that the food in Plataea was running out, that Stephanos' time was short. Athens *must* go to his rescue.

She had urged Alkibiades to help her, to help his friend, to make Athens send an army. But he was ambitious, and Khara felt that he was losing interest in such an unpopular cause. He was her only lever; without him she was powerless. She had trodden carefully with him at first: they were dependent on him, after all, for their house. But she had discovered that he found her attractive and seemed to enjoy her anger, so she exploited these assets when she could.

The door opened and Hipparete launched herself into Khara's arms, gushing, "Today is going to be a good day for you, Khara. I know it." She released Khara and grabbed Alexias' hands, kissing him on the cheeks. "Alexias, my darling boy! Let's dance."

Khara smiled at Alexias' laughter as Hipparete twirled him around the street. Alkibiades' wife was seventeen, with lustrous black hair hidden by her himation, and with a moon-face that radiated warmth. Her smile reflected a naiveté that Khara loved. She appeared nervous and restrained when she felt scrutinized, but at other times she exploded into a laughing young girl.

"Good morning, neighbour," smiled Alkibiades, as he stepped through the doorway, followed by Andromachus.

"Good to see you back, Alkibiades." Khara bowed her head slightly at the young god recently returned from cavalry duty. He was a strikingly handsome man, adored by both men and women, and himself. His flowing dark hair framed a smooth face that seemed an anatomical perfection, and his mouth was never far from smiling. It was easy to understand why people believed his family to be descended from the gods, but Khara never felt comfortable before his blue eyes, which seemed to burrow into her. She had heard the gossip at the fountains, the whispers around the agora, but she wanted to disbelieve them, and those eyes, for the sake of Hipparete.

"Alexias, my friend," grinned Alkibiades, lifting the boy and tickling him.

"Stop it. Stop it, goat breath," giggled Alexias, struggling to escape.

"Alexias! Don't be rude," said Khara, despite Hipparete's squeal of delight.

"No, no," said Alkibiades, lowering Alexias but threatening to attack him again. "I don't mind what little weasel-face says."

Alexias slapped Alkibiades on the leg. "I'm not a weasel-face, dung-head."

"That's enough, Alexias," said Khara. "We should go. I don't want to miss the announcement."

"No Lakon again?" asked Hipparete, taking Khara by the arm as they started for the agora. Hipparete's support was a comfort, even though Khara knew it was not totally selfless. Hipparete had been married a year and there was no sign of pregnancy. Only a son would cement the alliance between the Alkmaeonid and Kerykes families, and Khara was aware of the family pressure and bullying to which her friend was subjected, particularly from Hipparete's mother-in-law, Deinomache. Accompanying Khara to the agora was therefore a welcome escape for her.

They turned a corner, and a girl just escaping puberty strolled towards them. The wispy drapes that veiled her body were disordered, and on her shoulder she carried a twin-cylindered aulos, which she had played at a party last night. She flashed a smile at Alkibiades and swayed her hips. Hipparete glared at the temptress. The girl laughed and swept her hair. "I'm free tonight, tiger. Two drachmas for a night your wife can never give you." Hipparete's eyes bored into the girl's head as she passed.

Alkibiades turned to his wife and whispered, "She could never please me in the way that you do, my little dove."

Hipparete glowed.

"What was two drachmas, momma?" asked Alexias, staring after the girl.

"Never mind," said Khara, grabbing his arm and turning him back around.

"She looked like a nice girl to me," said Alexias.

Khara silenced him with a look.

When they reached a crossroads, Hipparete raised her hand to her lips before touching a stone herm and praying for the god's protection. They passed the open-fronted workshop of Kastor the shoemaker, who was pounding leather; Khara sympathized with the animal skin.

The street widened, and the smell of sewage from a walled-in stream assaulted them. A woman in sackcloth passed, bearing a hefty amphora on her head. Khara bumped into the back of Alkibiades, not realizing that he had been stopped by his wife, and mumbled an apology.

"A rat just crossed our path," explained Hipparete, kissing the gold figure of the goddess Kore that hung around her neck. "It's an unlucky sign. May the Twin Goddesses protect us." Alkibiades and Alexias competed at kicking stones down the street as they waited for someone to pass them to break the omen, while Khara prayed to Demeter and Kore that the sign would have nothing to do with Stephanos.

When the omen had been broken, they joined the herd on Piraeus Road, where trusted slaves marched boys to their lessons and athletic young men, with the first spring of manhood on their faces, strode alongside older companions, heading to the agora for the day's business and entertainment. The young men reminded Khara of the first time she had noticed Stephanos, at the Festival of Zeus the

Liberator, eight summers ago. She had been struck by his ready smile and found herself staring at him. She would have been Hipparete's age; an age of hope. Khara shook herself mentally: this was *still* an age of hope.

To draw near the agora was to approach the hum and hurry of a beehive. It was the beating heart of the city where trade, government, and entertainment collided. The cries of shopkeepers, the painful squealing of pigs, and the nervous clucking of poultry emphasized that Khara's destination was near. Her dread mounted.

Oxen ate straw as bare-chested slaves unloaded marble from an oxcart into a workshop. Beside the road, a woman laid an olive branch at the feet of a statue of Apollo, but her prayer of supplication was lost in the noise of Athens. The crowd's jostling was oppressive, and Khara drew a deep breath and clenched Alexias' hand.

They passed the agora's stone boundary marker, and the mass of people split into diverging paths. Alkibiades was momentarily distracted by a bookseller, whose scrolls filled hide buckets on a wooden table. The smell of cedar oil, used to protect the precious papyrus from worms, wafted from the stall, triggering Khara's memories of her father reading stories, over dying charcoal embers, of the adventures of Odysseus. Happy days. It had been six years since her parents had died, but she still thought of them every day.

They joined the crowd of Plataean exiles gathering before the Monument of the Eponymous Heroes: ten bronze, life-size statues of the Athenian legends who had given their names to the tribes of Attika. There was no statue for the Plataeans – they were merely allies, not citizens, of Athens. In this city the Plataean men were just another set of foreigners, ineligible to participate in the people's Assembly where citizens could vote on every issue. The Plataeans' lack of influence made Khara feel that they were less than the people around them: not slaves, but not free, either.

"There's Jason's momma," said Alexias, tugging at Khara's drapery. "Where's Jason? Do you see him?"

Khara eased Alexias through the throng to Diokleia, an efficient, matronly woman whose leathery skin bore witness to her days in the fields, and tight mouth to the anxiety she shared with her neighbour.

"How are you, little man?" said Diokleia, smiling at Alexias as she released Khara from her hug. "Nice to see you, Hipparete. Alkibiades. Come to enjoy the show?"

"Show?" said Alkibiades.

"Some men enjoy seeing women suffer."

"Indeed?" said Alkibiades.

"You must have seen your fair share of broken hearts in your time," said Diokleia.

"The death of my guardian caused widespread grief," said Alkibiades, referring to the great Athenian leader, Perikles.

Khara realized that Diokleia's frustration was uncorking at Alkibiades and worried that her friend might say something indiscreet. Khara squeezed her arm. "Zeus the Liberator," she murmured.

"Zeus the Liberator," sighed Diokleia.

An Athenian general climbed onto a short platform in front of the statues. A bald, over-fed man, he adjusted his white cloak over his arm and held up a hand for silence. Khara held her breath.

"Citizens and friends. It is now the third month of the archonship of Diotimus, the tribe of Pandionis holding the presidency." He had a forceful voice, and Khara wanted to urge him to bypass the formalities. "I can tell you that the Council has had the latest reports from our scouts on the situation with regard to our noble allies in Plataea." The air seemed to freeze. Alexias squirmed under his momma's crushing grip. "There has been no attempt to storm the town. The army that recently invaded Attika has begun its retreat across the Isthmus in response to our fleet's devastation of the Peloponnesians' own land. Only raiding parties from Boeotia remain. The grape harvest approaches, so we believe that there will be no attempt to storm Plataea before the spring."

The winds sighed, and relief surged through the Plataeans. Khara knelt and grabbed Alexias to her.

"Momma, momma. You're hurting me."

"Sorry," said Khara, easing her grip and fighting to stop the tremors.

"What is it?" said Alexias. "Is poppa hurt?"

"No, sweetie, no. Poppa's safe. He's safe, Alexias." She brushed a hand through his hair and planted a wet kiss on his forehead. "Safe." Khara felt her shoulder squeezed and glanced up at Hipparete, who was smiling through her own tears.

"I'm so relieved," said Hipparete.

Khara struggled to her feet. The news was as good as she could have expected. She had hoped for a miraculous escape, of course. But safe was something, a piece of driftwood to cling to.

"What about the supply situation?" A lone voice cried out.

"We have no new information," said the general, smoothing his bald head. "Based on what we know, we estimate they can hold out for another six months to a year."

"And what happens then?"

The general shifted uneasily. "Athens has many commitments. In order to win the war, we must choose our battles carefully. You know the plague has robbed us of many men. We cannot risk a major land battle. One defeat could destroy our entire army."

"What about all the service Plataea has done for Athens?" shouted a grey-beard whose angry looks were starting to spread through the exiles.

"Yes, remember Marathon," cried a neighbour. The crowd rumbled its agreement. Plataeans had been the only Greeks to stand alongside Athens in its battle against the Persians on the plain of Marathon over sixty years ago.

"Athens owes us," yelled Diokleia.

"Friends. Friends," said the general with a strained smile. "Plataea has ever been our greatest ally. The special relationship that has existed between us since the Persian Wars means that the interests of your town are always in our minds. Our navy is inflicting ruinous losses on the Spartans and their allies, and we believe they will soon see that they cannot win this war and will sue for peace." Further cries of frustration and anger showed that he had failed to convince them. "Trust us, my friends. With the help of God we will prevail and you will return to your homes before a year is out."

The general and his attendants hurried from the scene and the Plataeans drifted away, but Khara remained staring at the Heroes, with

Alexias drawing patterns in the dirt beside her.

"Perhaps the general is right," said Alkibiades. "Perhaps the war will be over in six months, and you will be able to farm your land with Stephanos again."

Khara turned to Alkibiades, her eyes dripping anger. "How can you say that? You of all people? You don't believe it any more than I do. Spare me your lies and *do* something."

"It may have escaped your attention, but I am too young to be eligible for general," smiled Alkibiades.

"Excuses. My father-in-law is right. You're all full of excuses. Gushing friendliness when you're in trouble, but like marble when your friends need help. Where's your honour?"

"Khara!" cried Hipparete.

Khara wondered if she had gone too far, but she felt absolved from her indebtedness to the young man before her. Too much time had passed.

A touch of colour had risen on Alkibiades' cheeks. "I have done what I can. You know I have."

"Not enough, Alkibiades. Not nearly enough. You have the ears of the young men of this city. You have your family's influence. Who hasn't heard of the Alkmaeonids? You're practically gods. Yet you say you've done enough." Khara noted his eyes drinking her anger.

"The city is ruled by factions, Khara. Families form alliances," he said, glancing at Hipparete. "They protect one another and push their agendas in the Assembly. But I am not even the senior member of my own family. I cannot force a policy even my family has no faith in."

"Your guardian was Perikles, may he dwell in the Elysian Fields. Would *he* have lain down so readily?"

Alkibiades' lips tightened, his light smile evaporated. Khara saw she had struck a blow. She was glad. She wanted to sting him, to set a fire under him that would consume all obstacles that stood between Stephanos and his rescue. Alkibiades was ambitious, and Khara was determined to channel that ambition to save Plataea, but she was losing hope. Time was running out for her husband as inexorably as Plataea's supplies were diminishing, and it seemed her one point of influence had conceded defeat.

"Come, Khara." Hipparete took Alexias by the hand and drew Khara away from Alkibiades. The owl-branded slave followed at a discreet distance, as Hipparete added, "Let's go home."

Chapter 3

Alkibiades watched his wife's little party leave. He was still smarting. How dare Khara question his honour? She was just a woman, and not even an Athenian one at that. Beautiful though, especially when she was angry; those eyes flashed like the lightning of Zeus. But he could not think of that now: he had a meeting with men who he could use to launch his fortunes. But they were dangerous, and if he was not careful they could destroy him.

He strode towards the heart of the agora, where the plane trees shivered to the excited songs of sparrows, and shoppers browsed the traders' stalls of vegetables, amphorae, fish, spices – the bounty of the Athenian empire.

Alkibiades acknowledged the respectful greetings that were his due as an Alkmaeonid, descended from profligate Zeus. The common people were dazzled by such nonsense, even believing his beauty a divine sign of virtue. These were political assets, but Alkibiades needed more than good looks and a god for a forefather if he was to raise his sails in the storm of the Assembly, where ruthless but senseless men bullied the citizens to adopt policies that were destroying the city. Their determination to avoid a land battle was bleeding the city to death. He felt his anger rise. His youth was a barrier. Only twenty-four, he had to be thirty before he could aspire to generalship. Athens was losing the war, and he needed to save it, for only in a great city could a man achieve immortality.

His plan to save Athens would even please Khara. Almost thirty years ago Athens had seized control of Boeotia, carving the beginnings of a land empire to match its maritime one. But after only ten years the Athenian army had been defeated at Koronea, and Alkibiades' father, Kleinias, had been killed in the battle. Four years old, Alkibiades had been transferred with his brother to the guardianship of Athens' great statesman, Perikles. Alkibiades was determined that his father's death would not be wasted. Boeotia was the door to destroying Sparta, saving Athens, and securing his own greatness.

Plataea was the key. Its position just across the border from Attika, and only eight miles from Thebes, the dominant city of Boeotia, was an ideal stronghold from which to foment rebellions against the oligarchs that ruled the hostile towns of the region. Democrats would seize power, and the Athenian army would keep them there. With Boeotia taken, the Spartans would be deprived of cavalry, without whose protection their invasions of Attika would be untenable. Athens would be safe.

But the snivelling cowards who controlled the Council and the Assembly were blind, hiding behind Perikles' old strategy of avoiding land battles. The man was dead, for Apollo's sake. The war was three years old and showed no sign of ending, and maintaining a fleet on a wartime footing was emptying the Athenian Treasury. Even if the navy controlled the sea lanes and islands, it could not harm the Spartan-led Peloponnesian army. Alkibiades knew that had Perikles lived, he would have altered his strategy. But the lion had died, succeeded by a pack of pups vying for a power they were incapable of wielding. It was time for a new lion to rise.

Why was he so young? *Time had no mercy*, he thought, as he kicked a pebble down the slope. He needed this meeting to bolster his influence. They were important men, after all. And dangerous.

He manoeuvred through the stalls, ignoring the cries of, "Buy my charcoal," and, "Best oil in Hellas here today," but paused at a table loaded with thrushes, ducks, and cages of pigeons. He was attracted by the tasty finches tied to short wooden stakes. The alert shopkeeper noticed his interest.

"Stick of seven for three obols, my friend. No 'aggling."

"Three obols?" said Alkibiades. "You cannot be serious."

"'Fraid so. It's the bloody war. Closed the Boeotian market so they're damned 'ard to get. I swear by 'Ermes, God of the Market, you won't get a betta' price round 'ere."

Alkibiades grimaced and moved on. War or no war, there was no way in Hades he was going to pay three obols for seven finches. He smiled. What were three obols, after all? Half a day's wage to an artisan, but for him, with his estates throughout Attika, his stake in the silver mines, his investments with the prosperous merchants of Piraeus, three obols was an acorn on a hillside of oaks: nothing. It was his mother's doing. He could hear her now. "Why waste an obol you can use to buy a vote?"

A dispute erupted at a cart surrounded by amphorae of wine, the market inspector accusing a trader of diluting his product, vehemently denied of course. Alkibiades grinned: he would think nothing of spending thirteen drachmas, more than twenty-five times as much as three obols, on an amphora of fine Milesian wine for a party. Perhaps it was more about not being overcharged than the actual price. It was the justice of the thing.

He dodged a garland seller wafting a wreath of flowers in his face and heard a familiar voice break through the market banter.

"Alkibiades! Over here."

Alkibiades knew well the attractions that the croaky voice portended, and notwithstanding his appointment, he wandered over to the canopied table of a withered log of a man who had a broad, toothy smile. "Hello, Praxas. How are you today?"

"Oh, can't complain. If I did, who'd listen?" The old man broke into a breathless laugh.

"Looks like you have quite a selection today," said Alkibiades, surveying the bowls of tuna steaks and plates of sole and mullet. Ignoring the cheap sprats, he peered into a clay pot of water and discovered an eel, a great delicacy.

"For sure. My son bargained with Poseidon himself for these this very morning. And if I may say so, he was 'specially considerate of your tastes, my friend. See? This is perfect for you, don't you think?" Alkibiades examined the potted eel in Praxas' hands. It was a good size and still frisky.

"Are you sure Poseidon did not empty his rubbish onto your son's boat a couple of days ago?"

"Are you suggesting I'd sell fish that's not as fresh as an unplucked girl on her wedding night? Look, come closer. If you put your ear to its mouth you can hear it singing."

"Hmmm...smells a bit rank to me," muttered Alkibiades.

"Rank? Are you crazy? This eel has a smell that could give a nose a hard on." They both laughed and Praxas set down the pot.

"Alright. I will help you out and give you six drachmas to take it off your hands."

"Six drachmas?" Praxas threw up his hands. "Do you want my family to starve? Do you want our ship to fill with holes and sink? Six drachmas wouldn't buy this eel's eye. It's an insult to Hermes is what it is. Come on, let's be fair. 'Coz you're a good friend I'll let you have it for sixteen." Praxas picked up his wax sale tablet as if confident his client would accept his most generous offer.

"If sixteen is your price for a good friend, it would be better for me to be a bad one. Nine drachmas and I will remove this eyesore from your stall."

"Eyesore indeed! Let me tell you, I have it on good authority that Poseidon held a beauty contest in the ocean deep and this eel won it!" Alkibiades fought to hide his amusement. "For a looker like this," continued Praxas, "I'm tempted to divorce my wife. Surely my wife is worth thirteen drachmas?"

"I will give you my final offer of ten drachmas just so your wife can buy something that makes her a little more attractive to you than an eel."

Praxas leaned forward conspiratorially to whisper, "Because you're such a considerate fellow, I'll give you my best price. Eleven drachmas." He looked around to ensure they were not overheard. "But don't let anyone know, I'll be out of business in a week. Hermes my witness, I can't possibly sell it for less." Praxas leaned back again and crossed his arms, as if certain they had a deal.

Alkibiades studied him, and then said, "Ten drachmas, take it or leave it."

Praxas threw up his arms again and shook his head. He muttered to himself, mumbling about what would happen to his business, his wife and daughters, his poor son, his ship. Finally, he sighed dramatically. "Okay, ten drachmas, you thief." They shook hands on the deal.

The usual price.

Praxas produced a wax tablet inscribed with markings to which he added a few more and passed it to Alkibiades, who pressed his signature ring into the wax.

"I will send Andromachus for it."

Praxas nodded. "Escorting the neighbour back is he? Bad business, Plataea. Such loyal allies. But what can be done?"

We could save them, thought Alkibiades. "At least they are safe for another winter. See you next week."

"May Athena watch over you."

"And Poseidon continue to throw eels your way." Alkibiades left the area known as The Fish, musing on the fact that he had just spent considerably more than the finches would have cost and had delayed a crucial meeting. But they would wait for him; everyone did.

He paused and looked back up the agora towards the hill of Ares and beyond to the great rock of the acropolis, home of the gods and the envy of Hellas. The statue of Athena rose above the acropolis wall, the bronze tip of her spear glinting in the sunlight. He savoured the spectacular Propylaea, the monumental entrance to the temples of the acropolis. The acropolis' display was a testament to the power that his guardian, Perikles, had exercised over the people, who had followed him as if to the magic of Pan's pipes. *This was Athens*, thought Alkibiades. Not the petty squabbles and jealousies that ruled the Assembly, but the glory laid down by his ancestors and picked up by each succeeding generation. Now it was his turn.

His city's rise to greatness had been an unlikely one. Athens had been destroyed by the Persians when his grandfather was in the prime of life, but the city had risen again, becoming the saviour of Hellas as Athenian ships chased the Persians from the Greek islands and cities of the Aegean. Those grateful communities had become Athens' allies. It was then a mere stroke of an oar from alliance to empire, a subjugation fully deserved, in Alkibiades' opinion. Perikles' policies had led Athens to such glory. Policies that he had enacted, not as a tyrant, but as a leader the whole city followed willingly because of his genius. A kinsman worth outshining.

For more than a year, Alkibiades had struggled to persuade Athens' noble families of the need to rescue Plataea and use it as a base from which to wage a land war. Many men of his own age supported him, eager for the chance to prove themselves in battle, but their fathers did not. Alkibiades had harried these family patriarchs at parties, in the stoas, in the agora, but he had failed to move them. The old men seemed content to follow General Nikias, content to allow the city's treasury to evaporate and ensure their poverty, their defeat, their enslavement.

Alkibiades could not stand aside and watch his future, his city's future, be destroyed, and so as a last resort he had approached Pisander, one of the leaders of a wealthy faction in the city known to have oligarchic sympathies, and who were thus suspect to the government, to the people, even to Alkibiades, whose Alkmaeonid family had been instrumental in the establishment and growth of democracy. If they ever came to power, the oligarchs would be a mortal threat to Alkibiades and his family. But he was desperate, and so the risk of working with them was worth taking if it could save Athens, and indeed they had listened respectfully to his initial proposals. Today he would discover if they would support him.

He hurried from the agora, crossed the narrow Eridanos River, which bore the city's waste, and strode along the stone-paved road past neat, white houses and on to the Sacred Gate. He joked with the guards on duty as he left the city through the heavily fortified structure, and found his spirit lighten at the sight of green fields and the distant peaks of Mount Aegaleus. His pace slowed as he breathed the clean air; they would wait, and it was unwise to appear too eager.

The Akademy gymnasium, named for the hero Akademus, was a refuge from the city, a release from the oppressive cloak of haste worn by the crowds. Less than a mile from the impregnable walls of Athens, its groves of poplars, maples and elms gazed upon athletes training in the grassy open spaces. The smell of honeysuckle mingled with the chorus of willow warblers and the iridescent voice of a song thrush. The place seemed blessed by Zeus, protected by the chief Olympian himself from the ravages of the Peloponnesians.

Alkibiades wondered why they wanted to meet him here, in a public gymnasium, which attracted men from many stations in life. Why not meet in one of the private gymnasia? What did they gain from meeting here? Perhaps he was overanalysing, but he doubted it –

these men calculated every step. They had to: citizens known to hold opinions unsympathetic to the democracy trod on thin ice, as did those who walked with them.

"Where have you been?" demanded Nikolas, materializing before Alkibiades. He was a short young man with angry eyes, whose black hair, black brows and black stubble gave him the appearance of personal assistant to Hades.

Alkibiades had fought alongside him and they were, he supposed, friends. There was only one person he completely trusted, and she was not amongst his "friends". But Nikolas had his uses, and he had been a conduit to his father, Pisander.

"I was buying fish," said Alkibiades.

Nikolas' mouth opened, then closed, eyebrows raised. "Father is waiting," he replied eventually.

"Is Antiphon with him?"

"Yes. I think that because of my vouching for you, there's news worth hearing."

Alkibiades rewarded him with a smile to melt icicles. They walked past the javelin throwers and on to one of the larger open spaces, which was surrounded by a low grass bank. In its heart was a rectangular running track on which naked young men spattered the thin layer of sand as they hurled themselves towards the finish line. Watching from the near bank were Antiphon and Nikolas' father, Pisander.

"Good morning, gentlemen," said Alkibiades on reaching them.

"Still morning is it?" said Pisander, his piercing blue eyes searching for the sun's position above the horizon. What remained of his grey hair had been cropped, and a small tuft was marooned on his jutting chin, but it was the crooked nose escaping his narrow head that dominated his features. He was known as Pisander the Hawk.

"I was buying an eel," said Alkibiades.

Pisander grunted and shook his head.

"It is good to see you back in one piece, young man," said Antiphon, a stocky man whose balding head was covered by a straw hat. His bushy black beard was known to mask a sharp wit that had poked a stick up the backside of many false accusers. He was a man unable to hide his disdain for the "little people", and so his support for democracy was suspect, forcing him to operate away from the showmanship of Assembly politics. He reminded Alkibiades of a stalking mountain lion. "Your reputation for bravery grows faster than barley," added Antiphon.

"I am simply a citizen doing his duty," replied Alkibiades.

"Of course. But remember: today's hero is tomorrow's exile," said Antiphon.

"With my family history, how could I forget?" said Alkibiades. "But you are right. The people are fickle, jealous, and capricious. Just like a woman." Nikolas laughed; the two older men twitched smiles.

"Speaking of the little people," said Antiphon, scanning around them, and reminding Alkibiades of how exposed they were, "while you were with the cavalry, the city has grown more restless. There was another outbreak of plague, and the city is bursting with scrounging refugees."

Their attention was drawn away by the shouts accompanying the start of another race. Four men hurtled over the sand, their large round shields pumping back and forth with their arms, the red crests of their bronze helmets streaming.

"The manpower shortage caused by the plague," continued Antiphon, adjusting his hat, "has meant that fine men such as these," he indicated the runners, "men of the hoplite class, are forced to serve as rowers in the fleet. *Rowers*. Sweating alongside the scum of the city."

"And then there's this damn tax the all-wise Assembly has imposed on us," said Pisander, glaring down his beak. "People are losing patience, Alkibiades. People who matter."

"Some might say it is about time," said Alkibiades. "You know my opinion on how the war is being waged."

"We do," said Antiphon. "And that is why we are here."

Alkibiades' heart skipped, and he allowed an eyebrow to rise.

"Your arguments have convinced us," continued Antiphon. "The strategy of inaction espoused by General Nikias is going to bankrupt us. We cannot allow that to happen. We have no desire to work as slaves in Spartan fields."

"Do you speak on behalf of yourselves only?" asked Alkibiades.

"No, we do not," said Antiphon, fingering his beard. "The rumblings in Mytilene have persuaded many that something has to change. If that city rebels against us we could lose the whole island of Lesbos, and with it our grip on the Aegean. The empire could vanish in a breath. Mytilene supports your argument that our allies are losing confidence in our ability to control the sea."

"Let us hope the Council's negotiations with Mytilene's leaders succeed," said Alkibiades.

"Unlikely," spat Pisander. "As long as we have this mass hysteria we call government, there's no hope."

Antiphon glared at Pisander, and Alkibiades knew that the Hawk had let slip more than he intended. Alkibiades hid a smile. Did they think he did not know where their sympathies lay?

"What my friend means," said Antiphon smoothly, "is that our allies will think we are weak as long as Nikias and his cronies control the Council and the Assembly and refuse to do anything meaningful. We will not stand by and watch our beloved city destroyed by incompetence. We must defeat Nikias, and your ideas regarding Plataea may help us do this."

Despite their unsavoury views on government, Alkibiades was unable to refrain from smiling. A year of fruitless endeavour and suddenly the first shoots of spring had arrived. "And rescuing Plataea is the honourable thing to do," he said.

"Yes, well, honour *can* be a useful commodity," said Antiphon. "But if the Assembly agrees to rescue Plataea, Nikias' position would be undermined, and we would be freed to fight an aggressive land war. The only way we can win."

"Of course," added Pisander, launching a withering stare, "our support assumes the full co-operation of your family."

They know I have failed to win over my family, thought Alkibiades. "My family supports me," he stated calmly.

"I am sure they do, Alkibiades," smiled Antiphon. "I am sure they do. But we will need yet more friends to defeat Nikias."

"Others will flock to us," said Alkibiades.

"Perhaps. But we need to think more radically. Turn everything upside down." Antiphon's eyes blazed.

"Do you mean revolution?" said Nikolas.

"Revolution?" hissed Pisander. "Don't be foolish, boy."

"What *do* you mean?" said Alkibiades.

"Working with Kleon," grinned Antiphon.

"Kleon?!" Alkibiades was aghast. "*Kleon?*" Kleon was the son of a tanner, risen to great influence in the Assembly since the death of Perikles by ranting against the aristocrats, blowing the horns of war, and pandering to the mob, which adored him.

"That piss-breather," said Pisander, spitting into the grass. "A wolf who whips the people to a frenzy, playing their greed and fear like a damn lyre."

"Precisely," said Antiphon. "And who is an expansionist."

"And so would support the relief of Plataea," surmised Alkibiades.

"Yes. Plus he gives us credibility with the little people," said Antiphon. "You know how they view me. Sometimes one must hunt with wolves to bring down a deer."

It was a radical suggestion, and his family's likely aversion to it appealed to Alkibiades. "Why talk to me again?" Alkibiades asked. "Why not approach the more senior members of my family?"

"Because your uncles are either drunkards or self-obsessed, and we're not sure of your father-in-law's sympathies," said Pisander.

"And besides, you sold us the idea. You are the future, Alkibiades," said Antiphon. "The Alkmaeonid family is revered, people adore you, you are quick-witted and brave, handsome and wealthy. You were born to lead, Alkibiades. You are the hope of your family, the hope of Athens."

Alkibiades nodded. He knew how to project an image of self-adoration, as if owed such flattery. But the question was – why were they flattering him? They seemed as desperate for him as he was for them. Why?

"Anywhere else you'd already be a leader and statesman," added the Hawk. "But not here. Oh no. Here ability counts for nothing when a host of damned empty-heads controls policy. If the right people ran the city, you can be sure *you'd* play an important role."

Alkibiades maintained his face, but he was surprised by the

blatant hint at overthrowing the democracy. Would they really expect the Alkmaeonids to support such a scheme?

"The time is coming, Alkibiades," said Antiphon, "when one's choice in friends may be the difference between salvation and ruin. Remember, 'Beside the wine cup many are friends, but in important matters there are few'."

Alkibiades laughed. "I know Hesiod's warning. My companions and I enjoy a drink or two, but I know my real friends. After all, I have Nikolas here."

"And a damn good choice he is," said Pisander.

"Think about what we have said," continued Antiphon. "If we are to use Plataea, we must strike quickly. And as for your friends, people will judge you by them. Rumour is they are drunken, godless gamblers. So be careful, young man."

"I am always happy to take advice from my betters, when I can find them."

Antiphon and Pisander bowed slightly and Alkibiades strode away from the racetrack, his fists clenched. *Why do men of years always assume they have wisdom?*

He passed young men gathered among the trees to hear the ruminations of the sophists, while their elders scouted the perfectly toned boys in their late teens enduring their military training. It had been four summers since Alkibiades' own training had ended. The old men may insinuate his youth as much as they wanted, but they had backed him. It showed that aristocrats believed in him, even if they thought they could use him for their own purposes. He would outsmart them.

But it would be for nothing if he failed to get his family's support.

***

"What do you think?" asked Pisander, watching Alkibiades' retreating back.

"He is sharp and ambitious," replied Antiphon, removing his hat to scratch his balding head. "Aggression suits his appetite for glory. But we need to be careful."

"I think he'd favour getting rid of the democracy," said

Nikolas. "It would allow him to fulfil his destiny as a leader, as he sees it."

"Perhaps," said Antiphon. "But the Alkmaeonids have always supported democracy. It is how they have exercised their muscle and stroked their vanity. I doubt any of them will be rushing to replace it. However, he does seem susceptible to flattery."

"His ego could fill the city," said Pisander.

"Or enslave it," muttered Antiphon. "What of his companions, Kallias and Timokles?"

"Kallias is just a beard," said Nikolas.

"Rich family, though, and Alkibiades' brother-in-law," said Pisander.

Nikolas nodded. "Timokles... Timokles is an idealist, loyal to the democracy, and would follow Alkibiades to the River Styx."

"But would he cross it?"

Nikolas shrugged. "I'm not sure, father. But Timokles may be susceptible to financial pressure. His stepfather drank away several estates."

"Kallias' family may be useful," said Antiphon, "but we do not want Timokles' idealism to influence Alkibiades. You should try to undermine Timokles."

"I'm trying, but they have been friends since childhood."

"Try harder," growled Nikolas' father. "Alkibiades will destroy this idiotic democracy, whether he wants to or not."

***

Alkibiades wandered towards a cluster of sandpits surrounded by giant elms, where naked wrestlers grappled. The sand sprinkled on their oiled bodies allowed them to grip one another, and their grunts encouraged the chorus of onlookers. Alkibiades paused beside the pit where Timokles was locked in battle with his young lover, Samias. If Alkibiades had a friend he supposed Timokles was it. Their fathers had died at Koronea, and the two boys had stood beside one another at the state funeral. Alkibiades felt a bond to Timokles that he felt with no one else, and in return Timokles worshipped him. And yet he was no sycophant. Idealistic and naive Timokles might be, but there was only one person Alkibiades trusted more.

He smiled as he watched the wrestlers' legs try to kick and trip, their hands to grasp and throw one another. Alkibiades enjoyed such contests: it was easier to determine who had won than it was in political battles.

"Who do you think will win?" asked his brother-in-law, Kallias. Kallias' unkempt auburn hair sat on his head like an overgrown bush, but it could not hide his lascivious grin, no more than the money his father had spent on sophists for him could suppress his idiocy, in Alkibiades' opinion. But he was from one of the most respected and wealthy families in Athens, which had not escaped Alkibiades when he had chosen Kallias' sister as his wife.

"I suspect young Samias. Timokles will be too soft-hearted to beat him," said Alkibiades, as he watched his friend try unsuccessfully to sweep the leg of his opponent.

"You are probably right. Timokles *is* too soft."

"Maybe, but Samias dotes on Timokles and it can be very difficult to defeat a lover."

"Yes, yes," agreed Kallias. "So Timokles to win, then."

"Or perhaps neither can bring himself to beat the other."

"Hmm. Yes, a draw does seem likely."

Alkibiades considered whether he could convince Kallias that the sand might win, but his thoughts were interrupted by dark Nikolas' sudden arrival.

"Haven't they finished yet?" said Nikolas, breathing heavily.

"We think it is going to be a draw," said Kallias.

"By Prometheus' fire, I think not," said Nikolas. "Timokles doesn't have the heart of a fighter. I'll wager five drachmas that Samias wins."

Kallias pondered the confident looks of the short man, noticed Alkibiades watching them, and declared, "I will take that bet."

The wrestlers' faces were flushed and taut as they gripped one another's shoulders, their feet jockeying as if they were dancing. Samias lunged and twisted, depositing Timokles on his back with Samias' arm wrapped around his throat. Timokles banged the sand in submission and Samias rose to receive the congratulations of his audience.

"Ha!" cried Nikolas. "Timokles, you couldn't wrestle a chicken to the ground that's already had its neck wrung."

Timokles struggled to his feet and clasped the victor. "Well done, Samias. I'm proud of you."

"You taught me well," replied Samias, blushing.

Timokles' damp curls swirled towards his broad shoulders like breaking waves and gave him a gentle appearance, but Alkibiades knew his friend was no weakling. Timokles was passionate and loyal, and he could be relied upon in a fight.

"A loser, just like his stepfather," muttered Nikolas as the sandpit's audience dispersed.

Alkibiades flicked a smile toward the dark one. Nikolas seemed to dislike everyone, but he was useful.

"Scrape us down," called Samias, and slaves immediately began to scrape the sand, sweat, and oil from the two men. The virile mixture would be sold for its medicinal value. Samias was twenty, had only recently finished his military training, and had a sculpted, bronze body. He had been imprisoned by shyness when Timokles first met him; the boy's father was a shield slinger, a coward for whom Samias had to make amends. In the three years Samias had been with Timokles, the boy had blossomed.

"I thought you were well matched," said Kallias, brushing aside his unruly hair. "It looked as if it were going to be a draw."

"He's getting too good for me," said Timokles.

"I'll never be too good for you," said Samias.

Timokles laughed and stroked Samias' cheek. "How are the oligarchs?" he said to Alkibiades.

"My father is not an oligarch," snarled Nikolas. "He loves the city as much as you do."

"No doubt," said Timokles, raising an arm so the slave could scrape it. "But if *you* are anything to go by, I'll bet he hates the Assembly."

"You're trying to label me falsely, Timokles. I've simply pointed out its shortcomings. You don't understand how dangerous a time this is. We're at war and the city's funds are disappearing quicker than Kallias' thoughts." The young man in question frowned, but appeared unsure as to whether a rebuttal was necessary. Nikolas continued,

"You're blind, Timokles, when it comes to the Assembly. A mob cannot take the tough decisions necessary for our survival. Do you *want* to be a slave?"

Timokles grimaced. "The city has flourished in dangerous waters before. In Perikles' time the city rose to great power against all odds, and yet the 'mob', as you call them, was in power."

"Even Perikles had to bow to the whims of the people," pressed Nikolas. "Is your brain as pickled as your stepfather's was? Don't you remember how they forced Perikles to send that disastrous expedition to Egypt? Men shackled by elections can't govern."

Timokles' eyes narrowed. "And you wonder why I call you oligarchs?"

Nearby, a pipe player accompanied discus throwers practicing rhythmically. Nikolas glanced at the slaves and continued anyway. "Look, the founders of our democracy had no intention of the city being subject to the base desires of every lowborn citizen. We must restore a property qualification so that those most invested in the state, run the state. Give leadership to those most able to exercise it, like Alkibiades."

Alkibiades raised an eyebrow and smiled at Timokles.

"You assume, Nikolas, that the richest are the most able leaders," said Timokles as the slave scraped his thigh.

"I understand why you wouldn't want to make that connection," said Nikolas, smiling as Timokles flinched at the reference to his diminished financial status. "But do you really think that elections give us the best leaders?"

"Perikles was elected," said Timokles.

"True," interjected Alkibiades, whose quiescence seemed to have encouraged the disputants. "The people voted him into that position, and then in a fit of pique they voted him out. But that is past. Theo Perikles is dead. In his absence, have we elected the best generals?"

Timokles paused as the others stared at him. This was a common discussion among them these days: Nikolas arguing for a reduced form of democracy; Timokles defending the current system; Alkibiades guiding the debate; and Kallias listening but generally not participating without a strong lead from Alkibiades.

Timokles scratched his forehead. "The generals chosen were perceived to be most trustworthy."

"Give me a general born in poverty and I'll show you a corrupt one," said Nikolas.

"Corruption is not the possession of the poor alone," responded Timokles.

"They do not even have their fair share in it," smiled Alkibiades. "But do you think the generals always act in what they believe to be the best interests of the city?"

"I assume that's rhetorical," said Timokles. "But I *prefer* them to be afraid of the Assembly's disapproval."

Nikolas jumped in. "How can the little people know what's best? They are a tide, swayed by their emotions. Decisions are made based purely on the quality of the speech, not the issues. *There's* your government, Timokles."

Timokles grinned at Nikolas' intense glower.

"It is true," said Alkibiades, "skilled orators may wield more influence than men of strong character. Just look at Kleon."

"I agree," said Kallias, oblivious to Nikolas' disdainful glance.

Timokles smiled. "We've talked of this before and you know I'm not as pessimistic about the Assembly. If we bypass it, where is our freedom? If Nikolas has his oligarchy, I'd be deemed traitorous for even raising the subject of democratic rule."

"Ha! You don't think I'd be flung into the pit if I declared I supported oligarchy?" said Nikolas.

"Maybe," said Timokles, tempted to do the flinging himself. "But I prefer our imperfect freedoms to living like a slave in a state dominated by a few men."

"Your idealistic freedom is an illusion, Timokles, and would condemn us all to slavery," spat Nikolas. "We can be the freest men on earth, but if the Assembly's idiocy destroys us, we'll be conquered and enslaved. Where's your freedom then?"

"Well, all I can say," said Timokles softly, "is that oligarchy would be like having a tyrannical stepfather. I've experienced that once and I'd rather not again."

Alkibiades intervened. "I believe the great Athenian character will save us no matter what. Just remember the feats of our fathers."

"You're right, Alkibiades," said Nikolas, "but we're still stuck with a bunch of ancient leaders more terrified of the mob than they are of Sparta. They wouldn't recognise a winning strategy if it were shoved up their collective arse."

Alkibiades' smile broke through the clouds. "Well, the current strategy *is* cowardice dressed as prudence. This should be a time for us to show our worth. All heroes are famous for their exploits in war. Peace breeds tortoises; only war can raise an Achilles."

"As for me," grinned Timokles, "I like a cosy shell, but I recognize the greatness that beckons you."

"I know you do, Timokles," said Alkibiades. "We have a duty to ourselves and to Athens. We may be too young to be generals, but we can still save the city."

"Talking of duty," said Kallias, "we have a family gathering tonight, Alkibiades. Remember? Dull, dull, dull."

Alkibiades remembered. He exchanged a glance with Nikolas: tonight he must cement his family's support for Plataea. He must finally convince his father-in-law.

Chapter 4

To Alkibiades, his father-in-law, Hipponikus, was a relic, but not because of the grey that littered his dark beard, or the furrows that bit into his forehead. General Hipponikus, like many of his age, was conservative, superstitious, a firm believer in duty and discipline. Alkibiades disliked him, but Hipponikus' wealth, derived largely from the silver mines of Laurium, was a powerful asset, and his influence over the rest of the family was decisive. If Alkibiades could convince Hipponikus to rescue Plataea, the family would follow. So far, he had failed.

Hipponikus had seized leadership of the family after Alkibiades' marriage to his daughter, Hipparete, and the death of Perikles. Hipponikus had used their network of influence to get elected general, and his position seemed secure.

The dining-room glowed with a hundred oil lamps, and Alkibiades' uncles and cousins, reclining on couches, had created a jumble of thrush bones, half-eaten onions, and fish heads on the sunken rectangular floor they surrounded. Slaves bustled around the diners, whose laughter and good humoured conversation animated the room.

To Alkibiades' right Demosthenes guffawed and slapped the arm of General Hipponikus. Demosthenes was not family, so why was he here? His daring in battle was already legendary, but Demosthenes only led by example and had little political influence, returning Alkibiades to the vexing question: why was he here? What was his father-in-law scheming, and was it something he could exploit? Alkibiades knew that he could outwit that dullard: rich Hipponikus may be, but sharpness of intellect was not a family trait.

Alkibiades threw the remnants of a lark's leg to the floor and looked round expectantly. A well-groomed boy appeared from the corner of the room and handed him a hunk of bread. Alkibiades wiped his hands in the bread and then tossed it over a tall lamp stand and into a corner, where two Spartan hounds devoured the offering.

By rights, after the death of Perikles and his sons, Ariphron, Perikles' brother, should have taken the initiative and assumed leadership of the family, but therein lay the problem: grief had dumped a mountain of weariness upon Ariphron. Though an intelligent man, he had lived his life in the shadow of Perikles, and had been happy to do so. By contrast, despite what Alkibiades thought of him, Hipponikus was vigorous and ambitious, determined that his first term as general would not be his last.

"Gentlemen." Hipponikus' deep voice rolled around the room. "If I can have your attention, please." Conversations halted and the host held centre stage. He sat upright on his couch and raised a kylix of wine. "Demeter and Kore, who watch over this house, we give you this offering." He poured the wine onto the floor at his feet and replaced the cup on his table, before picking up a delicate flask.

"Demeter and Kore," continued Hipponikus, "grant us your wisdom. May our words be as wise as this offering is sweet." He dripped a little frankincense from the flask, replaced it, and then resumed his reclining position on the couch. "I imagine you have been wondering why Demosthenes is here," he began with a smile. He gave a curt command and the room emptied of slaves. "The city is in danger."

It has taken you three years to realise that? thought Alkibiades.

"Too many politicians sit on the board of generals," continued Hipponikus. "We need men who know how to fight. General Nikias is a useful voice for us in the Assembly – the people trust him. But I am beginning to doubt his ability to direct strategy. The Treasury is emptying, and when the money is gone, we lose, and if we lose, our positions, our wealth, probably our lives will be gone. We must change the trajectory of the war. Men such as Demosthenes, here, are fighters. If we can place two or three of them on the board, I believe we could implement a more coherent plan."

Alkibiades' heart raced. He spied a glimmer of light for his plans amidst the general's rambling.

"What do you mean by a more coherent plan, Hipponikus?" asked Ariphron. He had flaxen hair swept back to his shoulders, a broad forehead like a beach at low tide, and black eyes that seemed focused inwards. Alkibiades retained a soft spot for him from boyhood summer days spent on his farm.

Hipponikus coughed and shuffled on his couch. "Well, something different. We know something has to change, and the first step is to place real soldiers in positions where they can influence things."

"So you plan to reduce Nikias' influence amongst the generals," said Alkibiades. "And increase your own. But to what end?"

Hipponikus' black brows closed like city gates. "I am talking of saving Athens, young man. Given your wishful thinking regarding Plataea, you should welcome some grown-up analysis."

"Plataea?" said Demosthenes, his alert eyes flicking between Alkibiades and Hipponikus. "What about Plataea?"

"Young Alkibiades seems to think that Plataea is the key to the war," said Megakles. Alkibiades' uncle radiated health: his cream chiton off one shoulder exposed a bronze chest crowned with a golden necklace, and he smoothed his dense hair like a cat preening itself. A winner of the chariot races at Olympia, he bore his self-satisfaction as a trophy. Alkibiades shared an understanding with him: mutual contempt. "His drinking has fuddled his mind," continued Megakles, "and he has forgotten that the town is besieged." He bestowed a smug smile on the room.

"Have you been spending too much time in the Prytaneum again, Theo Megakles?" responded Alkibiades, his eyebrows raised. "All those free meals distracted your poor little head from the fact that only a small force guards the town?"

Megakles' eyes narrowed, burying themselves in the upstart.

"We have a guest," muttered Ariphron, scratching the expanse of his forehead.

Silence glided around the room and dared each man to spurn her. Alkibiades was not surprised that Kallias was unable to resist. "Ooo, it is so quiet," said Kallias. "Hermes must be passing through the room." His father frowned at him, and Kallias' grin was swallowed by embarrassment.

"My brother Perikles' strategy appears to be in need of modification," said Ariphron. "Perhaps Demosthenes has some ideas he can share with us, of how he might change it if we help him become general."

"Of course he has," said Hipponikus. "That is why I chose him. Why don't you tell us your thinking, Demosthenes?"

Known as The Hammer to his men because of his brutal effectiveness in battle, Demosthenes was built like an oak, but his face could light with joy or empathy at a moment's notice, endearing him to his soldiers. He glanced around the illustrious company and cleared his throat. "It's a pleasure... er, no... an honour, to dine with you today. Don't know much about money or politics, but I know fighting. The Assembly's been convinced, by the likes of Nikias and Perikles..." He paused, running a hand through his curly locks, chuckling as he glanced around Perikles' relatives. "Er, I mean, by the likes of Nikias... that we can't match the Peloponnesian army. That we can only fight at sea. Now there's some truth in that. Our ships dominate the seas, but they can field a far larger army than we can, especially after our losses to the plague. But theirs is a disjointed army from many cities, cities that we could pick off one at a time. For example, if we can split off the Boeotian League led by Thebes, we deprive the enemy not only of manpower but also of most of their cavalry, which allow them free rein to devastate our land."

Alkibiades smiled on hearing ideas so similar to his own.

"Something amusing, Alkibiades?" snapped Hipponikus.

"No, not at all. It sounds very interesting, Demosthenes. Please continue."

Demosthenes fidgeted on his couch and continued. "Anyway, as for the Peloponnesian allies, if we knock out Sparta, the alliance will disintegrate."

"Oh, is that all?" laughed Alkibiades' permanently drunk uncle, Axiochus. "Beat the Spartans in a land battle where they're invincible. Zeus' dick. And I thought it was going to be hard." He quaffed his wine and burped.

Demosthenes glared at him. "I know Sparta's not lost a set battle in living memory, and their military training is the best in Hellas. But we don't give them a classic battle; we employ the same piecemeal tactics we'd use in Boeotia. We know the Spartans are scared shitless of their helot slaves rebelling, so we create a coastal stronghold from which the enslaved Messenians can fight to win back their land. Sparta's army would be tied down restoring order. Meanwhile, if we can also ally with the democrats in Argos the Peloponnesian League will collapse."

"That is good. That is very good," exclaimed Alkibiades. "You take out the Spartan army risking almost none of our own forces."

Demosthenes nodded and eased back onto his cushion.

"Our strength is in our fleet. I fail to see much of a role for them in your scheme," said Ariphron.

Demosthenes shook his head. "Our ships will help establish and supply a stronghold for the Messenians, but it's true I'm not much of a sailor. Never have been. But I understand how to fight on land, and our only way of ending this war is to beat them on land."

"I believe he is right," announced Hipponikus. "Our ships control the seas, but our situation only gets worse. The Treasury empties to pay for the fleet's maintenance, whereas the Spartans can maintain their army indefinitely as long as the Messenian helots remain slaves. And if our opponents on Lesbos have their way, Mytilene could rebel, making matters even worse. We cannot afford another siege like Potidaea."

"Such grand visions are all very well," said Ariphron, "but how do you propose we set about your first step, separating the Boeotians from the Peloponnesians?"

"We use Plataea as a base, as I have argued before," said Alkibiades.

"Not that old acorn," said Hipponikus. "Everything comes back to Plataea for you."

Alkibiades met the general's challenging stare with a sympathetic smile.

"Actually, Alkibiades' idea could work," said Demosthenes, deepening Hipponikus' furrows. "Plataea would be the ideal base, properly garrisoned. It's only half a day from Thebes, and its resistance shows how well fortified it is. We could destroy the besieging force by taking them by surprise, attacking out of the campaigning season when the Peloponnesians are at home."

Alkibiades wanted to kiss him, ugly as he was. Why had he not thought to approach the likes of Demosthenes before? Because they had no power, of course. There had seemed no point in gaining the approval of those in no position to do anything. Happy though Alkibiades was to have Demosthenes on his side, when the votes in the Assembly were counted, Demosthenes could only influence one man: himself.

"I hope you are not as reckless as my son-in-law," said Hipponikus. "If we tried to rescue Plataea, the Thebans and their Boeotian allies would be on us faster than Apollo's chariot."

Demosthenes shrugged. "We take our chances. You can't win a war without risk."

"A victory against their army could knock the Boeotians out of the war in a single day," said Alkibiades.

"Possibly," said Demosthenes, "but it's more likely they won't offer battle without Spartan support. With Plataea firmly in our hands, we can raid, disrupt communications, and undermine the leadership of Thebes in Boeotia, as we did in the past."

Hipponikus scowled. It was clear that this was a proposal he had not expected from his protégé. "Well, that may be interesting in theory," he said, "but I cannot see it gaining any support."

"That is not true," said Alkibiades. "I had an interesting conversation today at the Akademy."

"We do not care about your conversations with your drunken friends in the gymnasium," snapped Hipponikus.

Alkibiades smiled at the older man. To soothe him or to tease him? To tread like a mule or a mountain goat? "Antiphon and Pisander came to me to discuss the state of the city."

"They came to talk to *you*?" exclaimed Hipponikus. "Why did they talk to *you* of such things? They have not talked to me. Have they talked to anyone else here?" The others shook their heads. "It is nothing to be proud of, young man. They probably think they can manipulate you more easily."

"Whatever the reason, Hipponikus," said Ariphron, studying his former ward, "they did choose my nephew. What did they have to say?"

"They want a more aggressive war strategy, too, starting with the relief of Plataea. For the moment it is clear we can work with them and their followers for a common goal. I am sure I could persuade them to support Demosthenes' candidacy for general, for example, if they thought it would precipitate action on Plataea. And your candidacy, as well, general."

Hipponikus scratched his chin, glaring, but Alkibiades knew he had found a key to unlock his father-in-law's obstinacy; the man wanted to be re-elected in the spring and would need all the support that he could muster.

"Why do they want a more aggressive policy? And why start with Plataea?" asked Ariphron.

"I am unsure," admitted Alkibiades. "They say for patriotism."

"Patriotism?" said Ariphron. "There is a word to conjure many meanings. They are clever men, Alkibiades, and ambitious. Ambitious for their own power more than for Athens', and people distrust them. I am not sure their support is necessarily a good thing."

"You may be right, Theo Ariphron," said Alkibiades, "but we are smart, too, and our family made this city great. It is our right to lead Athens. Theo Perikles would have used these men for his own purposes. Is it not worth the gamble to save the city?"

Ariphron pursed his lips and did not answer.

"We should proceed cautiously," said Hipponikus. "It is in the family's interest, obviously, that I remain general. And I think we can all agree that Demosthenes has at least one promising idea, though nothing will come to fruition unless we have generals elected with more soldierly appetites."

"And how exactly do you plan to accomplish that?" Ariphron asked Demosthenes.

"Don't ask me," laughed Demosthenes. "That's not my area."

"No, it is not," agreed Hipponikus sharply, causing Demosthenes to redden. "That is where we come in. We must use the family's political influence to get me re-elected together with Demosthenes. We will need to muster all the usual resources." He glanced at Alkibiades. "And perhaps we can use Antiphon and Pisander."

"That is fine, but it will not be enough this time," said Alkibiades. All eyes focused on him, and Olympian Megakles in particular seemed prepared to enjoy the putdown coming his arrogant nephew's way.

"I beg your pardon?" said Hipponikus.

"I said it will not be enough this time."

"I heard very well what you said, young man, but perhaps you might want to be a little less absolute until you have the experience to know what you are talking about."

Alkibiades ignored his father-in-law's comments and addressed Demosthenes. "You are from the tribe of Aiantis, are you not? I thought so." He turned back to the room in general. "Paches holds the generalship of Aiantis and he is closely associated with Nikias. Our own faction is not strong enough to unseat him, even with the help of the oligarchs. At the moment we have no one in the family who can replace Theo Perikles in swaying the will of the people." He glanced at Hipponikus, whose eyes narrowed. "No one will be elected this time simply because they were connected to Theo Perikles in the past. The politics of the Assembly have changed in the year since he died, and you do not seem to have noticed."

"Listen to me, boy," growled Hipponikus, stabbing a finger in Alkibiades' direction. "I was in politics when you were still pissing in the plant pots in Perikles' yard. I understand how the Assembly works. By Zeus, you have never even spoken there. Your only contribution to an Assembly was to cause chaos by losing your damn quail when you were pledging money. How can anyone take you seriously after that?"

"People always take wealth seriously," said Alkibiades. "That little incident just ensures everyone remembers that I contributed my own money."

"Are you suggesting you let go of it deliberately?" said Hipponikus, his face the colour of a Spartan cloak.

Alkibiades smiled and looked away. "Does anyone remember who else gave money on that occasion?"

"You would reduce the Assembly to the clownish antics of that fool, Kleon," blustered Hipponikus. "Have you forgotten your illustrious family name?"

"We are getting off the point," responded Alkibiades, a slight flush dawning on his cheeks. "Perhaps you can explain to us how you expect to circumvent Nikias' supporters, many of whom you will need to win to your side to elect Demosthenes and yourself."

Hipponikus adjusted his himation and cleared his throat. "Nikias is a reasonable man. We must convince him of the necessity of our plans. Then his followers will support us."

Alkibiades gripped the gold-embroidered mattress that covered his lion-footed couch. He had heard this argument before. *'Nikias is a good man. We can persuade him.'* Nikias was a coward: afraid of the people; afraid of war; afraid of risk. There was no persuading the man. The only way he would possibly support them was if he were family.

Alkibiades jolted. Family. Could he become family?

Marriage.

Why had he not considered it before? Nikias was one of the wealthiest men in Athens, but he had no name, his ancestors being mere mortals. It was likely he would buy a connection to one of the noble families, and he had a daughter to bargain with. But marriage to whom? Kallias? No. Too close to Hipponikus, too stupid. Alkibiades' brother, Kleinias? Too wretched. Alkibiades needed someone desperate for money, whom he could control. Whom he could trust. What about... Timokles? He was not family, but he was as loyal as a brother. Alkibiades would be doing his friend a favour by securing his financial future, and in the bargain he would have a voice, and an ear, inside Nikias' family. Timokles and Nikias' daughter. Was it possible?

Possible or not, it could have no impact on their immediate political problems, so when no one contradicted Hipponikus, Alkibiades resumed the conversation. "Nikias is a timid man and his policy suits him perfectly: do little, risk nothing. He lacks Theo Perikles' strength and fails to understand the need to change tack. I think it unlikely that you will convince Nikias to adopt a policy he thinks threatens the city's safety and his own position."

"He is right, Hipponikus," said Ariphron.

"I think he has read Nikias accurately," said Megakles, his shoulders sagging with the effort of agreeing with his nephew.

"So," said Hipponikus, "does our self-proclaimed genius have another idea?"

Alkibiades picked an olive from the short table before his couch. "We can do without Nikias. We make common cause with others." He placed the olive carefully in his mouth, rolling it around his cheeks, holding it between his teeth and squeezing gently before releasing it again for another trip around his tongue, toying with it.

"Well? Spit it out," said Hipponikus. "Who did you have in mind?"

"A belligerent man who could almost assure us of electoral victory." There were blank looks around the room. "Someone able to bring the little men to our side with his rhetoric."

Recognition began to whisper in the ears of his listeners. "You cannot possibly mean... *Kleon*?" asked Hipponikus, as if the name were poison.

Alkibiades' nod was the signal for an explosion of outrage. Hipponikus stood and roared verbal abuse, gesticulating wildly. Axiochus and Megakles thundered about dealing with such a lowborn creature, and Axiochus upset his table and sent his wine cup crashing to the ground in a dozen pieces. Kallias gawked; Demosthenes seemed to wonder if he would need his sword; Ariphron gazed into his kylix and smiled.

Eventually Hipponikus resumed his place and managed to hiss a coherent sentence. "We are not going anywhere near that scum. His family's perfume is dung and urine. Let him stay in his tannery where he belongs."

"He is dangerous, too," said Megakles. "He likes nothing better than to lick the wine from other men's cups."

"I know all that," said Alkibiades. "It is true that he has little family background and entered politics using money from his father's tannery. No doubt it is also true that he has connived in the confiscation of the properties of wealthy men on dubious grounds and then pocketed some of the profits. But that shows he is creative, ruthless, and effective. Qualities we need. In the absence of Theo Perikles, Nikias and Kleon battle to rule the Assembly. Kleon stirs the people to vigorous action, so why not support him if he wants the same things as we do?"

"Because he is not one of us," declared Hipponikus. "He is dirt, a scoundrel. He struts before the Assembly waving his arms like branches in a storm. We cannot trust him."

"His vulgar style works and we cannot compete with it," responded Alkibiades. "He would give us credibility with the people and remove any suspicion regarding our co-operation with the oligarchs. Consider this. If Kleon were to propose the plan to take Plataea, then if it succeeds, we win. If it fails, he is discredited. We still win."

"But if we take Plataea, he will get the credit," said Hipponikus.

"Let him. Plataea is just the ant hill to start the mountain. Once a land strategy is in place there will be far greater glory for us to win."

"An interesting analysis, Alkibiades," smiled Ariphron. "Like the excellent food we have eaten, perhaps we need time to digest it." He glanced at Hipponikus, who looked away angrily but then nodded in agreement.

"Perhaps, Theo Ariphron, it would be easier to swallow in my absence," said Alkibiades, winking at his uncle.

Chapter 5

The question plagued Alkibiades again as he stared out of the sunlit doorway. A scroll of Euripides' play 'Hippolytus,' winner of that year's City Dionysia, lay unread on the oak table, and lion-headed paperweights defied the breeze that wandered through the window. His misgivings had risen with the sun, and his attempt to distract himself had failed: his eyes had scanned the dialogue, but the ink might as well have been ant trails. Instead, the words of Antiphon and Pisander blew a gale inside his head.

His uncle was right: they were dangerous men, but just how much could they put him and the city at risk? The oligarchs' only path to power in Athens lay in destroying the democracy, but Alkibiades could not see how the rescue of Plataea was a threat to it. And yet it must be. And a threat to the democracy was a threat to his family, to him.

He surrendered to the inevitable and jogged down the wooden stairs from the balcony to the ground floor; he needed to talk to his mother. He passed through the sturdy door that protected the women's area of the house from the outside world and entered the sunshine of the courtyard. The two-storey construction on all sides was a stadium in comparison with other Athenian houses, although Alkibiades, like most men, spent little time at home. Elegance pervaded, from the marble columns supporting the balcony to the geometric patterns of brown and white tiles on the floor. Busts of his ancestors sat atop the chest-high columns lining one side, a constant reminder that he had not yet surpassed the past. Alkibiades had erected a colourful figure of a cavorting Dionysus in the centre of the yard, and had moved the marble altar out of the way, into a corner. His mother still liked to observe the formalities of sacrifice.

His mother, Deinomache, reclined on a couch in the shade of the balcony, absorbed in a papyrus of the previous day's news. Athenians had lived in this land as long as the grasshopper, and so she wore a gold grasshopper clasp in her golden hair. Rivulets of curls tumbled over her shoulders, and her cheeks glowed with the perfumed oil she had rubbed into them, but it was the quick, flinty eyes that demanded attention. They showed a sharp intelligence and a hardness born of survival. At forty-six, her body had started to reflect her taste for fine food, but she was still a great beauty.

"Do you believe this story of grain ships lost in the Hellespont?" she asked without looking up.

"No." Alkibiades sat on a low stool beside her.

"The price of bread will still go up. Hades take them, damn thieves." She mashed the papyrus and threw it on the floor, and a teenage boy in attendance dashed to remove the discarded item from view. "So," Deinomache continued, "how were the old coots? Was your idiot brother there?"

"No, Kleinias did not make it, though Axiochus managed to drag himself from their latest debauchery." After Kleinias, fired with drink, had brutally raped a visiting cousin, Deinomache had banished him to his uncle Axiochus' house. It suited all parties: Deinomache could pretend she did not know of her son's degradation; Kleinias was free to pursue his interests; and Alkibiades could float between the two depending on his mood. Alkibiades picked a fig from the low table between them. "Theo Megakles implied that I drink so much that I am blind to what is going on."

Deinomache snorted. "Just because my stupefied brother won an Olympic crown he thinks he is Herakles. Well, he was always a snivelling little coward in my presence."

"He still is, Mother."

She chuckled. "Still, he will play the hero as long as no one else surpasses him. Your great-grandfather and grandfather both won the Olympic chariot race, and now your uncle." She allowed the statement to hang in the air and to settle with its own imperative on her son.

Alkibiades needed no reminding and let it pass. "Hipponikus thinks I am an undisciplined drunkard."

"I wonder if that is better than a disciplined one," smiled Deinomache, smoothing her finely woven red peplos, which was embroidered with gold. "It does no harm if he underestimates you. Soon enough they will recognize that the family's future lies with you. Cousin Ariphron has quality but no drive; the others are worthless. You are the heir of Cousin Perikles. He recognized it himself. The gods have blessed you with extraordinary gifts, and you are the one that will champion the Alkmaeonid name."

Alkibiades nodded without embarrassment, accepting the mantra that was as familiar as his mother's face. "I was approached by Antiphon and Pisander yesterday."

Deinomache was raising a ruby-encrusted gold cup, but paused, then slowly replaced it on the table. "And what did they want?"

"The rescue of Plataea. I have been trying to understand what they gain from it. No one at the meeting knew either."

"Hipponikus must have been pleased they came to you."

"He was." Alkibiades took a taste of water from a finely worked silver cup. "There was something else as well. Something about Mytilene. Almost as if they knew the city was going to rebel. Pisander hinted that Mytilene would only remain loyal if we overthrew the democracy."

"Really? He went that far?"

"Yes. If they encouraged Mytilene to rebel, an expensive siege would empty our Treasury; the city would be unable to pay its officials, forcing the nobles to take over. They will have achieved a mild form of oligarchy, although it is hard to imagine them risking the empire like that."

"There is no knowing what men may do to satisfy their ambition and ego." She chewed a fig as she gazed at the bust of her father. "Three years after your grandfather fought at Marathon he was ostracized and sentenced to a ten-year exile. Mother used to talk about how bitter it made him, but he still returned to fight against the Persians, at Salamis and at Plataea, alongside the same men who had plotted his downfall. Other exiles preferred to see their political enemies crushed, even if it meant the city was destroyed. They sided with the Great King in the hope that, when the fighting was over, they would hold power in the enslaved city. Men will do what men will do."

"Perhaps. But what great grievance can Antiphon and Pisander have?"

"Well, Antiphon's estates have been ruined by the war, so now he must write speeches to earn a living, and it's so vulgar to have to work to eat. Besides, there have always been those who believe Cousin Perikles gave too much power to the little people. They want a return to the moderate rule of the aristocracy, as in the old days before Pisistratus. It is not an unreasonable position."

"Perhaps, but the people are used to ruling. It would be difficult for them to relinquish power. It always is." A robin alighted on the head of Perikles, perused its surroundings and flew off again. "They hinted that I should be among the city's leaders."

Deinomache's eyes narrowed. "What did you say?"

"I pretended to enjoy the flattery but was noncommittal."

"Good. You must be careful. Remember, in Athens what you hear can be as dangerous as what you say."

"Perhaps I should have been more receptive. I might have discovered what they really want with Plataea."

Deinomache pursed her lips. "It is not clear to me, either, what they are up to. Maybe you can use Nikolas to find out. What did Hipponikus say to all this?"

"I only told them about Plataea. I did not mention Mytilene or their hints about me."

"Good. It would have scared them."

"Antiphon had another idea that I told them about. Collaborating with Kleon to promote the rescue of Plataea."

Deinomache's eyes stared into the distance. It was clear to Alkibiades that his mother's mind was humming. It was a sight he enjoyed. Eventually she nodded. "I can see the logic, distasteful as it would be. Hipponikus must have burst a vein."

"He was still bubbling nicely when I left. I think the family will collaborate with Antiphon, but I am not sure about Kleon. I am uncertain myself, actually. It makes sense politically, but he is just a tanner, after all." Alkibiades glanced at his mother, whose unblinking eyes were fastened upon him. He felt exposed, as he often did with her. It seemed that she knew he was about to suggest something he would rather hide from her. He took a deep breath. "I wonder whether it is possible to get Nikias' support instead. With a marriage alliance."

His mother's face retained its regal aloofness, but he knew she was calculating, weighing the possibilities. He doubted she would consider his friend. "Who?" she said.

"Timokles."

Deinomache's head fell back as she burst into laughter. Alkibiades had half expected this and so he was not dismayed. It was whether she would be ruled by her competitiveness with Timokles' mother, Nikopatra, that concerned him. The two women had clawed at each other since they were girls.

"Timokles? Really?" she said as her laugh faded.

"Yes, Timokles."

She stared at him and her smile dissipated. "Timokles. Hmmm... Nikopatra will be insufferable."

Alkibiades relaxed. How could he have doubted her? The trees never distracted her from the landscape. "Timokles will not like it, even though it would be good for him. I do not want him to know that I am involved."

"That is easily done," grinned Deinomache. "I will make sure Nikopatra thinks that it is her idea."

Footsteps on the balcony above heralded the approach of Hipparete, who skipped down the stairs and then threw her arms around her husband's neck from behind, nuzzling his cheek. "Good morning. Did you have a good evening?" A gold band held her long black hair in place, and her face was alight with the reflection of her husband's presence.

"Yes, I did, thank you," said Alkibiades, recalling the party at Nikolas'. "It lasted longer than I had expected," he added, pre-empting the line of enquiry that he knew would follow.

"These things always do," said his mother, raising an eyebrow at him.

"I'm glad you had fun with your friends, but I missed you so." She blushed as she whispered, "I waited up a long time hoping you'd join me."

"Yes, yes. These things cannot be helped," said Deinomache. "Tell us, son, about the party." She sank deeper into the pine green cushion, ignoring her daughter-in-law's pouting as Hipparete plopped onto a chair beside her.

"What can I say?" said Alkibiades as he rearranged the night's events into a more innocent narrative. "Firstly, Nikolas was drink master, the immediate effect of which was..."

"He chose a dilution of three to one," burst Hipparete, forgetting to pout.

Alkibiades smiled at his teenage wife. "Nearly. Two to one."

"Two to one?" she murmured, her eyes wide.

"What a rascal," said Deinomache. "I bet Timokles did not last long, then."

"And that was the next effect," said Alkibiades. "He managed to head-butt a statue."

Hipparete giggled; his mother shook her head. "That boy has never been able to hold his wine. You made sure he got home safely?"

"Tell us about the dancers," said Hipparete. "What instruments did they have? What did they play? Did they go down well?"

Alkibiades pictured again the voluptuous lead dancer inviting him onto his bed. "Oh yes, I believe they went down very well."

"Oh, I would so like to have seen them. How was their hair done? What did they wear?"

Alkibiades tried to recall the images from earlier in the evening, when clothes had mattered. "I did not notice. Perhaps Andromachus will recall."

"It's a shame they weren't more memorable," said Hipparete, although she did not appear overly disappointed. "You could have visited me afterwards." She leaned over and whispered in his ear, "I nearly came to your room."

He smiled as if he were disappointed that he had missed her, safe in the knowledge that she would not have gotten past Andromachus. "I am sorry, I was feeling tired."

"Perhaps tonight? I really feel as though a baby is near," whispered Hipparete, but not quietly enough to escape the Hera-like hearing of her mother-in-law.

"Ha! I will believe it when I see it," said Deinomache. "A year of marriage and still no sign of a child. What is the matter with you girl?"

Hipparete lowered her eyes and clasped her hands. Alkibiades knew that she was desperate to fulfil her duty to her family and the gods, that the jibes of his mother were like daggers to her, and that she could not bear the idea of failing him. He had tried to encourage her to be strong and to stand up to his mother: it was the only way Hipparete would grow up. But she was still a child in many ways, a kitten with big, sad eyes. Alkibiades squeezed her hand and released a sublime smile. Hipparete's clouds dissipated. He kissed her cheek and stood. "Please excuse me, I have a marriage to promote."

Alkibiades strode from the courtyard towards the wider world.

***

"You can lose the tears now that he has gone," muttered Deinomache.

Hipparete's eyes snapped to her mother-in-law. "What do you mean?"

Deinomache took a fig, a smile hovering near her lips. "I knew your grandmother, Elpinike, a real Athenian woman. I cannot imagine her crying so easily."

Hipparete recalled the gaunt woman who had terrorized her into the open arms of her mother. "My mother was nicer."

"Nicer? Nice does not raise great Athenian men, Hipparete."

"She raised my brother, Kallias." Deinomache arched her eyebrows; Hipparete flushed. "My mother was the best of women."

"Cousin Perikles had hoped so when he married her."

Hipparete's mother and Perikles had divorced before her marriage to Hipponikus, releasing Perikles to live openly with Aspasia, a former prostitute from Miletus. "Perhaps he was too distracted to realize how good she was," said Hipparete, and she immediately felt a twinge of guilt for such a remark.

Deinomache smiled as if she had won a victory.

Chapter 6

They had seen no enemy patrols, but Timokles remained tense and alert, fidgeting on the back of the tan horse beneath him. He wondered again how Alkibiades had persuaded him to ride in the wooded mountains, along a dirt road bejewelled with weeds, when Boeotian cavalry were still in the area. He held the reins loosely to allow the horse to set its own pace alongside his friend. An urgent tapping plucked Timokles' nerves: a woodpecker, or a signal? *Don't be as witless as a Boeotian*, he thought, *of course it's a woodpecker*. He focused again on the track and tried to ignore the army of trees and boulders that whispered danger.

Timokles glanced at Alkibiades' handsome features, and the confidence he saw there settled his own anxiety. He really knew why he had come, of course. The same reason he always trailed behind Alkibiades: Timokles loved him. Not in the way he loved Samias, but as a brother, as a father, as a best friend. Ever since they were boys, Alkibiades had singled him out, making it clear to all that no-one was to mess with Timokles. The god's lovers may come and go, but Timokles the Friend remained, protected by a special favour he had never understood. Other than Timokles' sister, Alkibiades had been his only spring of encouragement during the desert years of his stepfather's rule.

Timokles smoothed his dark, swirling hair. "I still don't understand why we have no weapons."

Alkibiades grinned. "Do you not trust me?"

"Of course I do," though Timokles' frown belied his words.

Alkibiades reined in his horse. "Timokles, do you really think that the two of us could fight off an enemy patrol?"

"Yes. No. Maybe. We might make them think twice."

"Believe me, no Boeotian horses can catch the ones we are riding. Better to be unencumbered and let our friends here do the work."

There was a hole in the argument: Timokles' horsemanship. His horse may be as fast as those of Apollo, but could he stay on it? Alkibiades hungered for danger with the lust other men had for women, but it was an appetite they did not share. Timokles had known the maniacal exultation of battle, but the faces of young boys ravaged by spears haunted his dreams, and the memory of the sickening smell of the aftermath could still churn his stomach. He forced a smile and said, "You're right."

Alkibiades seemed satisfied and flicked the reins. It was clear that he revelled in the controlled power of his horse.

"How was your family meeting?" said Timokles.

"Oh, you know. Families." Alkibiades glanced across at Timokles and continued. "They bring to mind one of Solon's sayings: 'I turned around like a wolf among many dogs'. Their senseless yapping drives me mad."

"Let's hope the wolf wins in this case," smiled Timokles.

They rode on in companionable silence, Timokles grateful for the shadows that made the heat bearable. When they emerged from the pass, a landscape of undulating farmland lay before them, beyond which, less than two miles away, slept the sea. Several miles across the bay rose the headland of Eleusis, a sight familiar to them both from the annual pilgrimage to celebrate the Mysteries. Timokles felt his tension ease as the woods released them onto the plain. An ambush seemed less likely here.

They cantered through a deserted village, the ruined houses and burned olive trees testament to the ongoing conflict.

"Your estate in Acharnae must look similar to this mess," said Alkibiades. "How will you afford to rebuild and restock?"

"Don't know. I heard someone say there are more olive trees in Hellas than people. Do you think that's true?"

"Enough to make an army large enough to fight the gods, I bet."

"They're Greeks. They're more likely to fight each other."

"True enough," chuckled Alkibiades. "You know, you need to find yourself a rich wife, like I did. Then you would not have to worry about your farms, and you could afford to join me in the cavalry."

"A wife?" said Timokles, immediately picturing Samias. "She'd just get in the way."

"Only if you let her."

Timokles glanced at his friend. He knew that Alkibiades had continued his affairs after his marriage to Hipparete. Not being family, Timokles did not know her, of course, but he could not help wondering how the young girl felt about it. Did she even know? And if she did not know, could it hurt her?

"A wife," continued Alkibiades, "is to create heirs and alliances. You know that. Your family name could buy you a rich little thing that would ornament your house and give you the freedom you deserve."

"Perhaps. I'm a little young to be marrying, though," said Timokles.

"Same age as me. And anyway, money is blind to wrinkles, or lack of them." Alkibiades pointed to a grassy square a few hundred yards ahead. "There it is." It was a small sanctuary, demarcated from the track and the surrounding groves of olive trees by a wooden fence. At its heart rose an elongated mound marking the tomb of the Homeric hero, Aias[1]. Beyond the tomb squatted a building that housed the offerings of countless generations. Alkibiades and Timokles dismounted, tying the horses' reins to a burnt tree away from the sacred olive trees around the sanctuary.

An old man in sackcloth emerged from a hovel across the road, leaning on a stick seemingly to prevent himself from folding in two. On reaching the visitors, he stopped and examined the two men, reaching out to feel the richness of their chitons and the smoothness of Alkibiades' beardless face.

"What is it, old man?" asked Alkibiades gently as he pulled his face away from the bony fingers.

The man jolted in surprise and stroked his grey beard. "You be Athenians," he said. "Not expect any of you for a while."

Alkibiades glanced at Timokles and grinned. "We are the advance party."

---

[1] Ajax.

"You be wanting to talk to 'im, I expect," he said, indicating the sanctuary.

"We'd appreciate that," said Timokles.

"Hmm." The old man scanned the visitors. "Can't let just anyone in, you know." He licked his lips as Alkibiades lifted a cloth bag from his horse and extracted a jug of wine and a loaf of bread.

"We have an offering for Aias. Perhaps you would take care of the remainder when we are done," said Alkibiades.

The old man bowed – or was he just standing? – and swept his arm towards the shrine. Alkibiades and Timokles entered through a gap in the fence and walked over the carpet of grass to the altar before the tomb.

"Do you really think Aias is buried here?" asked Timokles.

"Who knows? But his name still lives."

"Perhaps his shade is quickened here by all the prayers that have been offered through the generations."

"Perhaps." Alkibiades removed the stopper from the jug and poured a little wine onto the altar, before making a token offering of bread and leaving the remainder beside the unused wine. "Mighty Aias, son of Telamon," he began, his palms facing the Underworld. "Your name echoes through the ages for your greatness in battle. Share with me your peerless courage that I, too, may claim a name that reverberates forever. I am Alkibiades, son of Kleinias, an Alkmaeonid, your descendant."

The offering over, they climbed the three stone steps of the ancient Treasury, entering between two worn columns. In the cool chamber, incense overwhelmed their nostrils and they squinted to penetrate the gloom. A life-size statue of a soldier wielding sword and shield dominated the space; ancient weapons and helmets hung on the walls. Alkibiades left a coin at the foot of the statue and stared into its dark eyes. Timokles watched, conscious that his friend had to outshine even the likes of Aias.

They left the sanctuary, giving a nod to the old Guardian, and as they mounted their horses, Alkibiades said, "Athens needs leaders with the cunning of Odysseus, the leadership of Agamemnon, the bravery of Aias, and the daring of Achilles, do you not think?"

"If you want to follow their example, you'd better be careful your wife doesn't scheme to stab you in the heel." Timokles laughed at his own joke – someone had to – and they rode away from the Guardian and his sacred olive trees, following the road towards the sea, a flock of seagulls squabbling overhead.

Alkibiades seemed distracted, and eventually he said, "You know, Timokles, sometimes I think it may be best for our survival to run the city differently. The Council and Assembly are too easily swayed. They make compromise decisions at the expense of what is best. In times of war, perhaps extreme measures are justified."

"But when are we not at war? Government matters, Alkibiades. The people feel they have a stake in it. It's what's made Athens great."

"Individuals like us make a city great. Did Aias or Achilles care whether they served a king or the people?"

"I'm no Achilles, but..." Timokles started, gaping at the shore less than half a mile away. Ten riders had rounded the foothills and were galloping in their direction.

"Theban cavalry! Go! Go!" cried Alkibiades, wheeling through one hundred and eighty degrees and unleashing the power of his horse.

Timokles followed, leaning forward, his body close to the horse, gripping it with his thighs, the ground rushing by in a whirl of dust. His heart pounded with the hooves, the horse's panting deafening, its smell assailing his nostrils.

Alkibiades, several lengths ahead, repeatedly glanced over his shoulder to check the position of their hunters. "They are trying to cut us off," he shouted. "We have to cut across the field." He swung his horse off the winding track and into the uneven field.

Timokles followed, wondering how the mare knew where to tread as it crashed through the undergrowth. His chest constricted at the thought, and he banished such fears from his mind.

Alkibiades continued to look back and Timokles heard him laughing. Alkibiades' eyes were aflame, and he looked around again and shouted, "Hades! We are losing them. I think they are about to give up already."

Timokles looked over his shoulder. His horse stumbled and suddenly Timokles was on the ground, gazing at the sky, dazed and uncertain what had happened. The smell of thyme filled his nostrils, and a seagull laughed at him. He lay for an age, immobile, imagining death approaching but unable to do anything about it. He had not even thought to call out to Alkibiades. Too late now; his friend would be safely away.

He eased himself up and saw the cavalrymen arrowing towards him. It would not be long now.

A shadow passed over him.

"Come on, let's go." Alkibiades jumped down from his horse, and Timokles tried to respond but only managed a feeble nod. "Here, let me help you." Alkibiades yanked his friend to his feet, where Timokles wavered for a moment. "We need to move. I will help you on to your horse the Persian way."

Timokles noticed that Alkibiades had both horses by the reins, and over his shoulder saw the armour and helmets of the hungry patrol. Alkibiades boosted Timokles onto his horse and then leaped onto his own. Death was less than a hundred yards away as Alkibiades encouraged both horses to show their breeding. "Hang on for your life!" he cried, as the horses exploded and the fields fled beneath them. Alkibiades stayed alongside his friend's horse, keeping a close watch on him, never looking behind, making a direct line for the pass. There was no laughter now, no indulging his excitement.

Timokles' head thudded. A javelin landed in the dirt a few yards away. Timokles bent closer to the horse, acutely aware of the large target the animal made. At the periphery of his vision, he saw another missile land a little behind them. Muffled shouts taunted him. His knees hugged the mare's flanks like a lover; his hands crushed the reins.

By the time the pass narrowed among the trees the horses were lathered, the white froth spreading like breakwater across their necks and sides. Alkibiades reined in and let the horses breathe as he scanned the slope for signs of pursuit. "They have given up. You okay?" he asked as he dismounted.

Timokles nodded; the scratches and bruises would heal. "That was a close one."

"Yes. Fun though, eh?"

Chapter 7

An arrow sang past Stephanos' head and disappeared into the darkness beyond the moonlit battlements of Plataea's southern walls. He snapped his attention to the enemy wall, which stood less than a hundred yards away and encircled the town. On one of the imposing towers that punctuated the crenallations, a bowman jeered at the target he had missed. Stephanos glared from within the protection of his helmet, gripped his shield closer to him, and admonished himself for his lapse of concentration.

Weeks of guard duty would pass without incident, and the enemy wall would blend into the background: bricks, mortar, plaster; part of the scenery that familiarity makes invisible. Then an arrow out of the darkness would remind him that the town was being choked, that it was only a matter of time before... what? Surrender? Conquest?

There was another possibility, of course: betrayal. How many traitors were left in Plataea, waiting for their opportunity to strike? Besieged for so long, how many men felt abandoned by Athens and were ready to trade their comrades' lives for their own? These questions haunted him during the treasonous night hours. He would find himself staring over the fires at his fellow soldiers, imagining he could detect duplicity in their faces, and when they left for guard duty Stephanos would feel certain that he would not see the morning. Yet most of these men were his friends and neighbours, people he had lived among all his life. How could he be so twisted as to imagine them enemies? But then again, such people had betrayed Plataea to Thebes three years ago. The tortuous battle between distrust and guilt at times consumed Stephanos more than the war.

The full moon gazed at the distant mountaintops, which ensnared low-lying clouds that tumbled down the slopes like waterfalls before settling in the rolling plain below Plataea as a mist, shimmering like liquid snow. Khara would have loved such a spectacle. Stephanos sighed and wondered if she, too, were gazing at the moon this very moment. He drew comfort from this link to his wife in Athens whom he had not seen since his visit two years ago. She rose from the mist with her shy smile, and he could hear her giggles and smell the roses of her perfume. The vision tantalized and pierced him.

He shook himself, kissed the clay charm of Apollo that hung around his neck, and scanned the town below him. Plataea clung to the slope of Mount Kithairon like a sentinel above the plain. Its immense walls had defied the entire Peloponnesian army, but the serpentine streets in the area near Stephanos were black and lifeless: collapsed walls, missing roofs, and blackened beams were testament to a ravenous fire in the early days of the siege. Three hundred yards down the hill the glow of cooking fires hovered above the public buildings of the agora, and occasional laughter escaped to break the isolation of Stephanos' patrol. He glanced at the moon again and judged that his watch was almost over. The old joke of Greek parochialism sprang to mind: a young man asking his friend if they had a similar moon in other cities. Stephanos smiled and started walking once more.

The dark mass of the mountain loomed over the south of Plataea, and the peaks' outlines against the stars were as familiar to Stephanos as his own hand. He lowered his gaze in the direction of the cemetery, hidden by the besieging wall, where his grandparents waited, expecting libations and prayers that he was unable to give. It reminded him of his mother, buried in Athens, far from home. Anguish and frustration burned within him. He felt his anger focus yet again on his prison wall.

The bustle of its construction fourteen moons ago still lived in his mind. The Plataeans had struggled for three weeks to prevent the Spartan-led Peloponnesian army and its Theban allies from capturing Plataea's walls, and then the attacks had ended. The land around the town transformed into a building site, and the besieging wall had arisen. No one had expected the siege to last long: either the war would end or Athens would rescue them. Now, when Stephanos looked at the wall that separated him from the cemetery and from his family in Athens, he felt that a cord connecting him to the past and to the future had snapped, marooning him in an endless present. He longed for the release of one decisive fight. It was easier to gird himself for battle than it was to endure the empty days of waiting.

Footsteps approached. "Time for some food, Stephanos," a voice boomed.

Stephanos nodded his thanks and jogged to the nearest tower, skipping down its stone steps to the level of the town. He started for a deserted street once popular with blacksmiths and bakers, but movement by the postern gate fifty yards along the wall froze him. It was a secure gate, so no guard was posted there. His heart quickened as he peered into the moon's shadows. The guard above him had begun to pace the wall. Stephanos stared at the gate, but he could see no one. Had he imagined it? He inched forward. He glanced at the broken houses along the road, the burnt echoes of people's lives, shook himself and pulled his cloak more tightly around his neck, even though it was not cold, and quickened his pace towards the lights.

A two-man-high stone wall, constructed from the debris of fallen houses, enclosed Plataea's agora, and the soldier guarding an entrance smiled at Stephanos as he passed. It was the place where the Plataeans would make their last stand if the goddess Tyche desired. It was an additional protection, but for Stephanos it was an irritation: even in the agora he could not escape imprisonment and pretend he was just passing time with friends.

The towering statue of Zeus the Liberator dominated the agora, its bronze armour reflecting the cooking fires that ringed the centre of the square. The statue commemorated the Greek victory against the Persians sixty years ago, and was a reminder of the god's favour for the Plataeans. Hope lingered because Zeus the Liberator was with them.

Stephanos laid his weapons and armour on the steps surrounding the Temple of Athena, whose Ionian columns dominated the northern side of the agora, and he hurried to the nearest cooking fire. He was dismayed to face a broad woman, a head scarf framing her scowl, one of the hundred slave women remaining in Plataea to cater to their needs. She stirred the contents of a pot suspended above the fire, and Stephanos glanced at the unappetizing mixture, trying not to grimace or show any sign of weakness that could provoke the lashing that this

Medusa's tongue was wont to bestow. She plopped the sludge into a wooden bowl and handed it to Stephanos, glaring at him, daring him to make some criticism.

"Is there any bread?" he asked sweetly.

"Coming."

Stephanos thanked her and escaped, passing the colonnade of the East Stoa where groups of soldiers marked time. "Hey, Stephanos," called a pock-faced man from the midst of a dice game. "How's it hangin'?"

"The nights are long," smiled Stephanos, and continued on to the steps in front of the imposing law courts, where he saw the well-loved faces of his bearish uncle, Sémon, and his friend, Mikos.

"Where have you been?" cried Sémon as his nephew approached. "Did you get lost in this enormous town of ours? Was the moon not bright enough to light the way? Perhaps you need Apollo to guide you?" Sémon was a powerful man in his mid-forties, overgrown with black hair, Stephanos' light in Plataea.

Sémon's slight companion, Mikos, twenty years his junior and quiet as the moon, tilted his head to one side and closed his eyes. Sémon's laughter rivalled Poseidon splitting the earth, and Mikos' shoulders betrayed his own enjoyment of the joke.

"Yes, that's right, Mikos. I'll bet his relief spent a water clock trying to wake him up."

Stephanos sat on the steps below the pair, the columns of the law courts rising above them. "You're supposed to wait for your relief to arrive before leaving your post, you know. I believe the promise of food does not make a valid excuse in the eyes of the generals."

Sémon laughed again, slapped his nephew on the back and resumed the attack on his meal. These two kept Stephanos sane, and his uncle's passion for food, any food, made the contents of his own bowl more appetizing.

"How does that woman get away with treating us as if we were the slaves?" asked Stephanos, indicating the cook he had encountered.

Sémon shrugged. "She brews wonders out of nothing and organizes the other cooks. A good cook can be forgiven a poisonous tongue."

"I'm not sure I'd call this good," said Stephanos as he stirred the contents of his bowl, a roasted acorn the only item that he could recognize. "Anything happen today?" he asked. Conversation was a distraction from taste.

Mikos made a bouncing movement with his hands. "Oh yes," said Sémon, "we saw some rabbits. That was the pinnacle of our excitement. The fools had burrowed their way from freedom into the prison between the walls. Anyway, we decided to kill them and have them for dinner." He stared at the remains of his food. "So here we are, eating our delicious, stewed rabbit in wine."

"It's the funniest tasting rabbit stew I've ever had."

"I tell you, it's lovely rabbit stew." Sémon closed his eyes and savoured another mouthful. Mikos tapped Stephanos on the shoulder and raised his eyebrows.

"Me? My high point was a Theban and a Spartan fighting."

"Really?" said Sémon. "What happened?"

"I only caught snatches, but I gathered there was disagreement over a dice game. The Theban was getting a good beating until a couple of guards separated them."

"The spoil sports. Perhaps we should encourage them to gamble more and they'll all end up killing one another." Suddenly there was shouting in the East Stoa, and two men tumbled down the steps to the agora, fists flying, legs kicking. "Fight! Fight!" shouted those nearby as they gathered around the show. "On the other hand," continued Sémon, calmly regarding the chaos of an overturned cooking pot and its tripod as the fighters crashed through one of the fires, "give us long enough and we'll probably all kill each other."

A couple of men, under instructions from the austere General Arkadius, dragged the combatants apart, and the spectators dispersed to their normal monotony.

"I got shot at tonight," said Stephanos.

"Yes?" Sémon glanced at his nephew. "A good shot?"

"Passing good." Stephanos smiled at his uncle's chuckle. He did not mention the movement by the gate: perhaps they would think he was going mad. After all, the thought had occurred to him. "The moon is clear tonight. Made me wonder what Khara's up to."

Sémon and Mikos exchanged anxious looks. Stephanos' bronzed face was half in shadow as he stared into space. He had retained the body of a farmer in his prime, and though his dark hair was receding, when lost in reflection he had a boyish countenance.

"I imagine she'll be sleeping soundly, probably having had real rabbit stew," said Sémon, twirling his beard.

Mikos shot an invisible arrow, and Stephanos nodded. "I can imagine Alexias catching the rabbit, as well. He'll be six now. I wonder what he's like." It was the familiar introduction to a hundred conversations, but Stephanos never tired of them: talking about his family quickened their spirits within him.

"His pappu will be lecturing him on when to plough, when to plant and when to reap," said Sémon. "Lakon always did to me."

"How's Alexias going to learn that properly, stuck in the middle of Athens?" asked Stephanos.

"True. Well, what do you think he'll be like?"

"I think he'll be a rascal. Neither Khara nor my poppa has the heart to punish him, so I suspect he's tearing around Athens causing havoc. At least, I hope so. When we have a daughter..."

"Ho! Wait a minute. A daughter? What makes you think your next child will be a girl? Perhaps you'll have another strapping boy," said Sémon.

"Khara was sure the next one would be a girl, and women seem to know these things." Stephanos noticed a shadow pass across Sémon's face, and suspected that he had stirred his uncle's memories of his own children dying at birth, and of Theo Sémon's darling wife, Thea Ana, his sun, going to sleep in his arms for the last time, another bloody stillborn beside her.

The shadow faded and Sémon's face was alight again. "Well, far be it for me to argue against the wisdom of women. So what will your daughter be like?"

Mikos held his hands to the sides of his face and fluttered his eyelids.

"Yes," agreed Sémon. "Given your wife's beauty, Stephanos, your daughter'll have the face of Aphrodite, even if she does have an ox for a father."

"That's right," smiled Stephanos. "With the advantage of her momma's looks, it wouldn't matter if her poppa was a Cyclops. And if she takes after my momma she'll be running the household by the time she's three." He paused, watching the slave women bustling around the cooking fires, remembering his mother's industry. "I hope... I hope my poppa's helping."

Sémon's brother, Lakon, was old enough to be his father, and the death of their mother three days after Sémon's birth festered like an open sore between them. "Lakon will rise to the challenge of life in exile, I'm sure," said Sémon, punching Stephanos on the arm. "I'll wager Khara has even more friends than she had here."

Stephanos wanted to say that Sémon's wife, Thea Ana, had been Khara's closest friend, but they had not spoken of her for four years. Not since that bloody day and Theo Sémon's disappearance into the mountains for three moons, leaving Mikos to run the farm. Stephanos recalled his uncle's bedraggled return, when Sémon had seemed his jovial self, but he had never mentioned Ana again.

"I hear they're negotiating to hold the Freedom Festival," said Sémon.

"Yes. Seems risky to me," said Stephanos.

"Why?"

"Many more Thebans than Spartans out there now. All of us standing unarmed between the walls, the Thebans above us? We'd be target practise."

"Even those grass-munchers wouldn't dare break a truce and upset the gods," said Sémon.

"Maybe," though Stephanos suspected that the Thebans could find a way around such a technicality. After all, they hated the Plataeans with a ferocity that only neighbours could incite. "I wonder how many more festivals there'll be?"

Sémon laughed. "Come, come, you pessimist. It'll continue as long as Zeus the Liberator is here."

Stephanos nodded; he was right: the siege would end some day, and in the worst case they would be prisoners to be exchanged at the end of the war. Plataea would survive and he would see his family again. That *was* the worst case, wasn't it?

"Your problem," Sémon continued, "is that you're in love with a good woman. Me and Mikos, we're in lust with some very, very bad women. It lightens the spirit."

"You're incorrigible, Theo Sémon," said Stephanos, "and if I'm not mistaken, one of your bad women is on her way over." He indicated the crowded stoa from where two women headed in their direction, one carrying an amphora on her shoulder, the other a basket in her arms.

"Welcome, my lovelies," called Sémon. "We were quite desolate at the ugliness everywhere, but here come jewels to adorn the night."

"Oh, you're a devil. You've the silver tongue of Hermes, you do," said the basket woman, Rebia, as she lowered her burden to the floor so that she could reveal the ample fullness of her figure, which threatened to break free from her tunic. Her younger, slimmer companion stood behind her, shooting flames at Mikos.

"There's nothing so exciting at night," said Sémon, "as your coming." He twitched his eyebrows, and Rebia shrieked with laughter.

"You boys, what am I going to do with you?"

"What, you mean you'd like me to draw a picture or something?"

"I can't imagine what you mean," said Rebia. "Me and Mila came over here, all innocent, to fetch you bread and water. And what do we get? Coarse lip. Here." She shoved a long piece of bread into Sémon's mouth, and then honoured Mikos and Stephanos with bread and clay cups of water. When Rebia turned her attention to Sémon again, he elevated the bread in his mouth until it was pointing skywards. Rebia's giggles erupted despite herself. "Something on our mind this evening, is there?"

Sémon removed the bread. "Well, it's hard to say. It's something that keeps raising itself in my mind."

"Is that the best you can do, dear?"

"When I see such beauty as yours, it's difficult not to think I'm in the presence of Aphrodite herself, and it's a religious principle of mine to give myself to the gods."

"That's a bit better," she said, swaying her wide hips.

"Anything else?"

"I beg the honour of showing this goddess of love the extent of my devotion. Tonight. Right now." Sémon stood and grabbed her to him. "What do you say?"

Rebia made a feeble attempt to escape his clutches. "Well, I don't like to disappoint my worshippers. Meet me at the villa in a couple of minutes."

She waddled towards the nearest exit from the agora, leaving Sémon with a flushed face and his companions with silly grins.

"How about you, quiet boy?" asked the water girl. "Would you like to come with me?" Mikos jumped up and hurried with her towards the temple, leaving the amphora behind.

"Hades! How does he work so fast?" said Sémon. "I have to carve words out of the air, and he just nods his head. I guess there are advantages to having no tongue, eh?"

"It might have something to do with the fact that he looks like Apollo and you look like a bear," said Stephanos.

"Ha! You have a point. I assume you can't be persuaded from your abstinence?"

Stephanos shook his head. "There's only one woman for me, and I made a vow to Hestia as well."

"Oh, come on. Men need exercise. It's expected. You've been going without for nearly two years. It's going to fall off if you don't use it. Khara and Hestia would understand." Sémon paused as he looked into his nephew's eyes, and then smiled. "Yes, yes, I know. You don't need an excuse. See you at Assembly." He patted him on the back and marched towards his night's carousing.

Stephanos gazed towards the raucous groups in the East Stoa, wrestling with the urge to discern the traitors. He finished his food and wandered over to join them.

Chapter 8

The Plataean army waited in silence, filling the steps of the law courts. There were no fires, the only light coming from the sparkling stars. There was no noise, except for the occasional cough, the shuffling of a colossal bull, and the awakenings of birds. A chill breeze, a prophet of autumn, penetrated the men's white chitons. Zeus the Liberator, symbol of Hellas' victory against the Persians, stood at their head: they had assembled to honour the Greeks who had died in that battle for freedom.

A week earlier, a rowdy Assembly had debated whether to proceed with the Freedom Festival. Plataeans such as Stephanos expressed their suspicion of Theban treachery. Some thought that the Spartan offer of wine and a bull for the sacrifice was a trap: the Plataeans had not tasted meat or felt the transport of wine for more than a year, and their mere promise was intoxicating. Although betrayal was never voiced, the fear of it wove itself into their arguments. The generals exhorted them to remember that Spartans, who had sacrificed a king in the war against Persia, still commanded the surrounding garrison and would honour the ceremony. But the Thebans had sided with Persia in the struggle for Greek survival, and the rituals were a reminder of Theban faithlessness.

However, the Festival was a sacred rite to honour a generation that had risked everything, and its observance was also a matter of respect for Zeus the Liberator. Stephanos was unsure whether fear of the gods or wine lust had won the day, but the final show of hands was decisive. Now they waited as a grey light leeched into the darkness, and eyes turned to the brightening sky.

A trumpet shattered the stillness, signalling the beginning of the procession. Two men jerked the black bull forward, its horns gilded in gold foil, red ribbons fluttering from its tail. The garrison followed, crowned with garlands of myrtle. Stephanos' stomach clenched: Thebans should not be trusted. This must be a trap.

The procession eased down the slope and out of the agora towards the North Gate. The trumpet assaulted their ears as they shuffled past the whitewashed houses. Memories of his grandfathers' stories transported Stephanos to the clamour and fury of that famous battle. He saw his grandfathers glaring at the Persian army across the plain beyond Plataea, sure that this was their last day. He felt their fear and anger, the imperative to flee and the determination to fight. As the two forces clashed with demonic savagery, amidst the chaos he heard the wild screams, stared into eyes filled with hatred, and shuddered with the crash of weapons. The Persian features of the enemy mutated into the snarling faces of Thebans as Stephanos approached the gate.

The North Gate swung open and the prisoners of Plataea advanced to celebrate the freedom of Hellas.

Marble funerary monuments lined one side of the dirt road, and the procession formed ranks facing them. Stephanos' breath caught as he noticed that the enemy wall bristled with soldiers. He turned, ready to rush back to the town and grab his weapons, but reluctantly he obeyed the herald's instructions, and started a new row twenty yards from the enemy wall, followed by Sémon and Mikos. As he glanced at the brutish faces above him, rope ladders suddenly clattered over the wall.

We've been betrayed again, thought Stephanos as the enemy slid down the ladders. His heart pounded and he reached for his sword, but the rite forbade them to carry weapons. He glanced at Sémon and saw his own alarm in his uncle's eyes. He turned around to face death, but instead the garlanded Spartans lined the wall in weaponless silence. Thirty men stood at the wall and met the hundreds of hostile stares, until the tension ebbed away as it became clear that the Spartans were joining the ceremony. Stephanos glanced again at the battlements, where Theban soldiers scowled their disapproval.

The trumpet blared once more, and stillness blanketed the valley as General Arkadius filled his urn at the sacred spring. The general's grey hair and gentle eyes gave the appearance of a benign grandfather, but he was a proud, stout-hearted man. He poured a handful of water over his head, then sprinkled the myrrh-bearers with the purifying water. Arkadius stepped to the bull, and Stephanos tensed. It was a crucial part of the rite: the bull must accept his sacrificial role to be acceptable to Zeus. Arkadius poured water onto the bull's head, and the beast nodded, spraying the men around him. Stephanos relaxed. The bull had accepted its fate.

The general cleansed the first monument with sacred water before pouring myrrh over it to arouse the nostrils of the gods. He faced the assembled soldiers and proclaimed, "We honour the brave citizens of Corinth who stood against the enemies of Hellas on the plains of Plataea. We thank them for their sacrifice, that all Greeks may be free."

Arkadius repeated the ritual for each of the city monuments in turn, and finally, as the first cranes of the season flew overhead, the bull was coaxed towards the altar. A torch bearer lit the pile of oil-soaked twigs assembled on top of the altar, and the general threw a lock of hair from the bull's forehead, together with a handful of barley, into the flames on the altar. Raising his arms to the sky, Arkadius prayed.

"Mighty Zeus the Thunderer, Liberator, god of gods, accept our sacrifice. You gave the Greeks, led by brave Pausanias of Sparta, courage and strength to defeat the forces of the Great King and the traitors to Hellas."

Stephanos flinched. He had no need to look up at the watching Thebans to know the reaction the end of the general's prayer would provoke.

Arkadius lowered his arms and turned his palms to the ground. "We implore you, Pluto, master of the dead, to grant respite for the brave souls that are with you, and to allow their shades to taste the sacrifice we make in their honour."

A giant Plataean from the front row stepped forward and launched a blow to the bull's head with an axe. The animal staggered, and a knife flashed across its throat. Blood spurted in long bursts, painting the earth and filling a basin. The bull collapsed. Arkadius poured the blood over the altar as butchers carved up the carcass. The general offered the thigh bones, wrapped in fat, on the altar fire, and poured a libation of wine into the flames. He mixed the remaining wine with the holy water in his urn, offering a little of the liquid to the dusty road before drinking. "I drink to the men who died for the freedom of Hellas!"

The wine carriers hastened to mix their wine with water from the sacred spring, and cups passed along the rows of patient men, each taking a sip and proclaiming, "I drink to the men who died for the freedom of Hellas!"

Stephanos received the cup, recalling the destruction of Plataea, the devastation of Athens, the death of Sparta's King Leonidas. It had been a moment when all Greeks had stood on the precipice of slavery, but they had prevailed. He repeated the formula he had heard from boyhood, but which was still a heartfelt prayer. He peered at the quiet Spartans nearby. They had led the Greeks; they had lost a king. He broke away from his comrades, his heart thumping, and walked to the nearest Spartan. Stephanos offered him the cup, and felt the sting of hundreds of eyes buried in his back.

The handsome young Spartan regarded him with surprise before accepting the cup and breaking the silence that had returned. "I drink to the men who died for the freedom of Hellas!" He handed the cup to his neighbour, who repeated the ritual, and in a heartbeat other Plataeans crossed the short distance to share their drinks, the ordered ranks dissolving, the Spartans and Plataeans mingling freely. The ceremony was over; the celebration had begun.

The meat was boiled, the entrails roasted, the wine inhaled. Sémon and Mikos joined Stephanos beside the young Spartan in the shadow of their prison wall. "We were a little surprised when you climbed down," said Stephanos. "That didn't happen last year."

The soldier nodded. "New garrison commander. Wanted to show our respect."

"Even for an enemy?" said Sémon.

The Spartan frowned. "Our King Leonidas at Thermopylae, and Pausanias here at Plataea: we revere those who fought the Persians. And I mean all Greeks. Plataea is a by-word for freedom. To view it as an enemy now is..." He shrugged his shoulders.

Mikos saluted, waved and pretended to march away. The

Spartan raised his eyebrows.

"I think what Mikos said," began Sémon, "is that we want to simplify your life. Let's be friends again and you can march back to Sparta with lighter spirits."

"We know that won't happen as long as there is war with Athens. Why does he not speak for himself?"

"Our friend here is the perfect companion. Absolutely loyal, an attentive listener, and totally silent. A mighty relief from a nagging wench." Sémon laughed, but it faded quickly. "But seriously, perhaps you should remember who your real friends are."

"A friend of Athens is no friend of Sparta."

"Really? We've honoured the graves of your ancestors for fifty years," said Sémon.

"Athens threatens the freedom of Hellas as Persia did."

Sémon's laughter was a roar. "That's nonsense, my friend. It's Thebes that wants to enslave Plataea, not Athens."

"Athenian greed has enslaved many cities."

"Enslaved?" said Sémon. "Athens protects those cities from the Persians. Those cities are her friends."

"Which Athens crushes if those cities want new friends."

"Perhaps Athens suspects that such new friends would destroy her if they had a chance," said Sémon.

"Athenian excuses to keep their feet on the necks of fellow Greeks."

"In the way Sparta does to the Messenian helots, you mean?"

The Spartan's face flushed at the mention of the neighbouring people the Spartans had enslaved. "The Messenians are dogs, not Greeks," said the Spartan.

"Ah, yes. I forgot," said Sémon. "Funny how that works, eh? But I think on that note, my friend, it's time to go and find out what's happened to the wine." He strode towards the wine bearers congregated near the monuments, with Mikos on his heels.

The Spartan cleared his throat. "One speaks too much, the other not at all. Why is your friend silent?"

"He has no tongue," replied Stephanos. "Cut out in his youth by a former owner."

"He is a slave?" His boyish features displayed his horror. "It is sacrilege for a slave to participate in such a rite."

"He's not a slave anymore. Theo Sémon bought him from a trader about ten years ago. He freed him at the start of the war, but Mikos chose to stay with him. Theo Sémon has that effect on people." The Spartan frowned, as if unable to comprehend why anyone would free a slave.

The sun climbed, and wine played the good host. The besieged soldiers wolfed the meat, and in late afternoon the Spartans staggered back to the ladders and bade farewell. Sémon and Mikos had rejoined Stephanos near the wall. "Take care, young friend," Sémon shouted as their Spartan companion clambered onto the wall. "I hope to see you again in happier times."

The Spartan waved and disappeared from view. A one-eyed Theban, who had watched the proceedings, spat over the wall and called down to them. "Oy! You won't see no happier times, mate. You better make the most of how you feel right now."

"I assure you," replied Sémon, "that better feelings are yet to come tonight. While you're pounding the wall, I'll be pounding softer things. Think on it!" Sémon wheeled and strode towards the town gate, accompanied by Mikos.

Stephanos chuckled and made to follow but turned around at another shout from the enemy above. He looked up as the Theban raised his head, slowly drew a finger across his throat and shouted, "Think on it!"

Chapter 9

Even in his befuddled state Timokles sensed danger marshalling in the dark street. A threat was growing, but what was it? He leant on Samias: his own legs were defective.

"You should be more careful how much you drink," smiled Samias.

Timokles burped. A dog started barking in a nearby house. "Shut it," he shouted. Alkibiades had given them Andromachus to light their way from the party, but Timokles found little comfort in him. What was it that threatened him? Robbers? Cutthroats? Fog shrouded his mind.

"What do you think Nikolas was up to tonight?" said Samias as they twisted down another street. "Don't you remember? He said that a true Athenian doesn't get drunk so quickly, and a man who can't hold his drink can't be trusted, that he's of no use in trying to free Plataea."

Timokles sniggered; he was unsure why. He hugged Samias and kissed him on the cheek, wondering why the symposium's wreath of flowers still sat prettily on Samias' head, when it drooped over his eyes on his own. The need to sleep descended like a boulder, and yet he was pricked by the threat that hid in the shadows of his mind.

They reached Timokles' house and Andromachus stood aside, holding the torch aloft as Timokles pushed on the door. It was bolted from the inside. The threat flooded the street, urging him to flee. He scratched the door in the hope that no-one would hear, but it was immediately unbolted and opened, and the threat became flesh.

"I should've expected nothing better than for you to come home drunk at this time."

"Hello, hic, Mother."

Nikopatra filled the torch-lit doorway as Timokles disentangled himself from Samias. Andromachus slipped away, rather too quickly in Timokles' opinion, given that he had instructions to keep him safe. Samias started to greet Nikopatra but withered before her glare and fled, his crown of flowers falling to the ground behind him. Timokles tumbled over the threshold, landing on the stool where she had kept watch. Nikopatra huffed and then waddled across the courtyard carrying a torch, not deigning to look back as Timokles meandered after her into the dining room, where she set the torch in its stand and eased herself onto a chair. Her son collapsed on to a couch and lay down, sinking into the cushions like they were the Fields of Elysium.

"Your father would never have gotten drunk like this. Oh, no. And in a time of war, too. How do you expect to marry into a respectable family if this is your behaviour?"

Timokles' ears received, but his mind was in meadows of grass and flowers. He smiled and nodded like a tree brushed by the wind, falling asleep to the lullaby of his mother's scolding.

***

Timokles' escape was disturbed by the sore-throated cry of a rooster, a monster banned in Sybaris to allow revellers to sleep late; he decided to move there. He slipped into a fitful doze until the sunlight accused him through the open door. Someone was drumming inside his head, and he groaned. The scrape of a stool nearby propelled him upright, but the pain levelled him again.

"Hello, Leaina," he mumbled.

His sister's thin, pretty face beamed at him. "Good morning. What a lovely day it is. Don't you just love the sun in the morning?" She was a rose in spring, and Timokles held her gaze for a moment before closing his eyes. Leaina laughed. "I see you had a good time last night. Let me guess. You were with Alkibiades and someone set an unforgivably strong dilution." Timokles defied the thumping and raised a thumb. Leaina tossed her dark hair from her eyes. "No surprise you came home in such a state then."

Timokles opened an eye, and Leaina grinned. "Mother has informed the entire household of your late-night entrance. I believe she's frustrated that her prepared speech failed to receive its due attention." There was no reaction from her brother. "Well, I'm glad you had a good time, but it's time to get up now, I'm afraid."

Timokles recognized the playful tone of voice too late, and he cried out at the shock of the deluge of frigid water as Leaina doubled up in laughter, holding an empty jug. Timokles spluttered, wiping the water from his eyes as he sat up. "Was that really necessary?"

"Oh, yes." She wiped the wet hair from his face, kissed his forehead and sat beside him on the damp couch. "I think mother's unhappy."

"There's a surprise." Timokles glanced at his sister's gentle, smiling face. She was only twenty-one, but her eyes betrayed the grief of last summer. He stroked her shoulder-length hair; it was good to see her laugh. They had always been close, childhood confederates in a war of abuse and neglect by a drunken stepfather. Timokles was happy that she was back home, but why under such circumstances? The plague had taken her husband and both young sons within a few days of each other. But she had survived, and he thanked Apollo every day for sparing her. "I doubt mother will ever be happy with me until I get elected general, beat the Spartans single-handed, and supplant Zeus on Mount Olympus."

"That would satisfy her?" They both laughed. "She loves you really, Timokles. She wants the world for you. She's buried two husbands. She wants you to live the lives of three men."

"Only three?" Timokles wondered when Leaina would be ready for another man of her own. He prayed that the scars of the past would not paint her future. He would let Time sleep on her awhile.

He looked around the dining room – not his usual sleeping place. His mother's chair was empty, a carved wooden throne awaiting its monarch. The black and white floor mosaic portrayed the story of the Amazons. Timokles was convinced his mother was their descendant.

"Did you hear any news yesterday?" Leaina was a sharp commentator on the city's politics. The family's Persian slave, Orontas, had given her almost as good an education as Timokles himself, rare for an Athenian woman.

"The negotiations with Mytilene broke down. Their rebellion looks inevitable."

"That's terrible," said Leaina. "To have one of our strongest allies desert us in the midst of war. What if others follow suit? It could finish us."

"Yes. The Assembly has ordered General Paches to raise a force to 'restore their loyalty'. They want to set an example."

Leaina nodded, but her hands played with her white peplos, her frown telling Timokles that her thoughts were flying in another direction. "Paches is one of the generals Alkibiades wants to replace," she mused.

"Yes. With Demosthenes. Paches being out of Athens for a while will give us a good chance to undermine his support."

"Not if he covers himself in glory at Mytilene," said Leaina.

"True, but Alkibiades felt that, one way or another, such an appointment would provide opportunities to bring Paches down."

"Alkibiades arranged Paches' assignment?"

Timokles chuckled. "Alkibiades is gaining influence all the time." He glanced at Leaina, who widened her eyes to prompt him. "He didn't exactly arrange it, but he did promote it."

"Still, a campaign against Mytilene will make it harder for him to win approval for the resources to rescue Plataea," she said.

Outside, two slaves exchanged a joke in the sunshine, and a mule brayed in the street beyond the courtyard. Leaina stepped to the open door and leaned against the wall, watching the bustle of the slaves. Timokles could tell she was carrying a burden. "What is it?"

She turned to face him, biting her lip. "We know, Timokles. About *The Patroklus*."

Timokles flinched. To regain some of their losses caused by the war and his stepfather's excesses, Timokles had invested in the voyage of *The Patroklus* to the Chersonese, but on its return journey, the captain had dumped much of the cargo overboard to outrun pirates. Far from making money, Timokles had lost it. He had hidden the debacle from his family, but he had no need to ask how they had found out. The slave gossip network was a great revealer of the city's secrets.

"Don't worry. Your dowry is safe," he said.

"Timokles!" cried Leaina.

Timokles blushed. "Sorry. I didn't mean it. I know you're not worried about that."

Leaina sat beside him again and held him to her. "I'm supposed to be bringing you to mother."

Timokles grimaced, but after drying off, he allowed his sister to drag him outside and through a door into the second courtyard.

"Ah, so it's true, the dead do walk the earth." Nikopatra's voice reverberated around the yard as Leaina led her brother towards his verbal execution.

Their rotund mother sat on a low stool in the shade of the balcony, grappling with a wicker basket of sewing. Her obsidian hair and eyebrows gave an absoluteness to her face that brooked no opposition. Timokles sat on the ground against a stone pillar, at a distance bordering on rudeness.

"I suppose he thinks it's perfectly normal behaviour to carouse drunkenly through the city at night?" she asked Leaina.

"Mother, you know perfectly well that Timokles rarely drinks." Leaina paused and winked at him, "And I'm sure he wasn't carousing."

"Hah!" burst Nikopatra, no doubt recalling the pretty youth draped around her son. "Young men these days, what do they know of discipline? Orontas should have taught you some Hesiod. 'At first you drink to a friend, then for a bet, another for the gods, and then – because it's in your hands and you can't say no'." She looked down at her basket again, shaking her head. "*There* was a man who understood discipline and respect. Who understood 'everything in moderation'. These days all they care for is wine, young boys, and two-drachma women."

"Timokles is an honourable man and a good Athenian. And you know it," said Leaina.

Nikopatra stole a glance at her daughter that expressed agreement, without letting Timokles see it. "It would be difficult to tell from the godless company he keeps." She paused, waiting for her son to take the bait, but he did not. "It's Alkibiades' influence. Alkibiades used to be such a good boy. Polite, respectful...sober. Now look at him. He thinks the world owes him anything he wants. He's as arrogant and ambitious as his mother."

"Mother, how can you speak so badly of him when you only knew him as a boy?" said Timokles. "He's always been a true friend to me and our family." Timokles took the cup of water that his mother's pretty slave had poured for him. He had expected her to launch into a denunciation of his investment, but the fact that she seemed to be sailing on a different course did not deceive him. He knew where her anger was really directed and that a painful tack was yet to come. "I'm sorry for making you stay up late. Please forgive me."

"Forgive? Forgive?" Nikopatra adjusted her ample figure precariously on the stool. "It's not a matter of forgiveness, is it? It's a question of respectability. We're an ancient family. What will your sons inherit? How will we live?"

"We're far from destitute, Mother," said Timokles. "If your husband had been more circumspect we'd be very wealthy."

"Don't criticize your elders so readily, the men who built the empire. *He* didn't fritter away his money on some half-brained scheme."

"No, he drank it instead."

Nikopatra's face reddened, and Leaina rose quickly. "Would you like to hear some music?" she asked.

It had been many moons since they had heard Leaina play, and the shock of her suggestion produced an uneasy truce. Leaina retrieved her lyre from the dining room, her fingers caressing the tortoiseshell instrument as she returned. She plucked the strings with a bone plectrum as she restored the tuning, and then she played. Her body swayed with the music, and Timokles was transported to rushing streams and towering mountains. Nikopatra even laid aside her sewing. When Leaina finished, the thrill of the music still coursing through her body, she looked up expectantly at her brother, but he felt unable to speak, as if the notes had bound him.

Their mother broke the spell that hung in the air. "That was quite nice, dear. You should practice more."

Timokles saw the disappointment spread its icy hand across Leaina's face. "I thought it...magical." It seemed he had found the right word, and Leaina sparkled.

"How long is it since you played the pipes?" she asked Timokles. "It seems a shame that you gave them up."

"My efforts sound like the breathing of a winded horse next to your playing."

"Might your description may have something to do with your

close encounter with Theban cavalry?" said Leaina.

Timokles laughed. "Perhaps. It was as scary as my music."

Leaina clapped her hands in delight.

"Good Athenian men don't get scared," said Nikopatra.

"Believe me, Mother," began Timokles, "I know plenty of Athenian men that spend as much time as possible away from home because they're terrified of their wives."

"Well, at least they have such an opportunity," she responded. "At least they have fulfilled their duty to their families. Unlike some I could mention."

Timokles kicked himself for giving her such an easy opening, but chose not to respond, hoping she would drop the subject. He should have known better.

"One thing I'll say for Deinomache," continued Nikopatra, "is that she has Alkibiades married into a wealthy family. They have no financial worries. Does his example mean nothing to you?"

"Kallias' sister came with a huge dowry and important family connections. It would have been unwise of Alkibiades to ignore such an opportunity, despite his youth. There's no-one as eligible now, and I'm only twenty-four. I have plenty of time."

"That depends on how many incompetent captains you trust."

Timokles battled to hold his peace, but his heroics failed to restrain his mother.

"It's a man's responsibility to provide for his family. Both security and a legitimate heir."

"Alkibiades hasn't managed that yet, Mother," Leaina pointed out.

"Maybe not. But at least he has the chance to do so. If we wait around for your brother to sort things out, we'll end up working in the fields and I'll never have a grandson." Timokles and Nikopatra were too distracted to hear Leaina's sharp intake of breath, or to notice her suddenly pale face.

"It's not a good time to marry," said Timokles. "We're at war. Who knows what will happen?"

Nikopatra exhaled dramatically. "We're Greeks, we're always at war." She stared at the brown tiles of the courtyard, towards the altar against the wall. "I've decided that this family can't afford the luxury of your dithering. I've talked with your uncle, and he's going to approach General Nikias with a proposal for you to marry his daughter, Aristeia."

Leaina's jaw dropped; her brother exploded to his feet.

"What?! You went behind my back? Without asking my permission? Or my opinion?"

"What's to ask? It would be impossible to find a more appropriate match."

"I'm not a child anymore, Mother. You can't just arrange things for me without my consent."

"I'll do anything I think necessary to make sure this family has a future. Someone must take responsibility."

"I can't believe you." Timokles stormed into the outer courtyard and slammed the door on his way into the street, raging through the winding alleys, oblivious to the greetings of neighbours. She was unbelievable, treated him like a little boy. Why should he marry? His father was thirty-five when he married. Thirty-five. That would give him eleven more years, eleven more years with Samias.

He halted. Slaves chattered at a fountain, and a spherical man emerged from a tavern, coughing up phlegm. Children laughed as they played knucklebones in the dirt, and Timokles wanted to shout at them. A vision appeared of his lover's earnest young face, his innocent eyes, his wavy hair, his smile, his laugh. Where would that laughter go if Timokles married? He could not give up his friend, his love. He would *not* marry yet.

The decision made, he calmed himself to search for weaknesses in his mother's scheme. He knew nothing of Aristeia other than that she was the daughter of Nikias, Athens' leading general and politician. A very wealthy man. Many had tried to win Nikias' approval for marriage and had failed, a good omen. Timokles knew that Alkibiades disliked the general, that he saw him as weak, a danger to Athens. He would enlist the support of his friend, whose family's influence would no doubt dissuade Timokles' uncle from making such a match. Relieved, Timokles marched to the agora where he was sure to find Alkibiades.

The pointed roof of the Temple of Hephaestus peeked above the houses, and as he turned the corner he passed the busy Stoa Basileus, its colonnade crammed with wooden tablets mounted on revolving cylinders, each inscribed with the laws of Athens. Timokles wondered if there was a law to deal with interfering mothers.

The agora opened before him, breathing with the usual crowds and noise, and he jogged across the stone slabs covering the sewage-bearing Eridanos River, and up the slope towards the Eponymous Heroes. The statues of the lovers Harmodius and Aristogeiton dominated the heart of the agora, in memory of their assassination of the tyrant, Hipparchus, but Timokles doubted they would have had the bravery to stand up to his mother.

Alkibiades was listening to a group of old men when he caught sight of Timokles. He waved, but his smile faded when he saw Timokles' face more closely. He excused himself from the Plataean grandfathers and turned aside to his friend, putting his arm around his shoulders and leading him away from the Heroes. Alkibiades had his brother-in-law, Kallias, and the dark little oligarch, Nikolas, in tow.

"I apologize. I didn't mean to make you break off your conversation," said Timokles.

"My dear friend," said Alkibiades, "do you really think I would rather talk to some old moaners than to you?"

"I thought you had some sympathy with their complaints."

"Indeed I do, but talking with them feels like having your head held under water. But enough of them. What is the matter with you?"

Timokles grimaced. "My mother is being... mother."

"Ah." Alkibiades squeezed his friend's shoulder, releasing him as they approached the South Stoa, which rose like a crown above the agora. They sat on its steps, listening to the clamour of the makeshift market amongst the trees as a stream of people visited the small shops and public offices within the colonnade behind them. The young men were sombre: mothers were a serious matter. "So," continued Alkibiades, "what has she done now?"

"She asked my uncle to make a marriage proposal on my behalf without consulting me." Timokles waited for his companions' faces to reflect his own outrage, but after a momentary pause and quickly exchanged glances, they burst into laughter.

"Little Timo's up for auction," roared Nikolas.

Kallias stood and proclaimed, "Timokles for sale! Timokles for sale! Any takers?"

"Sit down, you fool," laughed Alkibiades. "Sorry, Timokles. I am surprised she has not tried this before. She has been at you long enough."

"She has, but I never thought she'd resort to this. I don't want to get married."

Kallias raised his voice several octaves. "Want? Did I hear you say 'want', young man? Let me hear you say 'duty', 'responsibility', 'legitimacy'. No one cares about 'want'."

Alkibiades bestowed a smile on his brother-in-law. "Who is the lucky girl?" he asked.

"The daughter of Nikias." Here, at last, was the reaction Timokles had expected. Kallias and Nikolas were clearly stunned, knowing Alkibiades' opinion of General Nikias. Their eyes turned to Alkibiades, who stared over the trees, his hands clasped under his chin. He had not reacted with the horror Timokles had expected. Instead, a calm, calculating aura had settled upon him, and Timokles' stomach began to writhe.

Alkibiades seemed to become conscious of his friends. "Timokles, I have no doubt of your love for me and your loyalty to me. Nikias may not be my favourite Athenian, but he is one of the wealthiest and most powerful men in Athens. Your chances are good. Your sister was married to a distant cousin of his, after all. It would be a good match for you and your family, and it would not change the esteem in which I hold you."

Timokles stared open-mouthed at his friend, an axe buried in his chest.

"Just think of the dowry she would come with," chimed Kallias. "You could keep us in wine and women for the rest of our days."

"But I don't want to get married," said Timokles. "I'm only twenty-four. I'm not ready. I won't betray Samias."

"I understand," nodded Alkibiades. "I was overly young to

marry, and so are you. Neither of us can be expected to give up the pleasures of youth while our beards are still fresh."

"Neither of you has one," pointed out Kallias.

"It was a figure of speech," snapped Alkibiades. "So why give up Samias? I fail to see why your relationship with him should not follow the normal course of things."

"Everybody knows," said Nikolas, stroking his dark stubble, "that the best age to marry is thirty-five. By then you've tired enough of your lovers to make the break natural. You'd be justified in continuing with Samias if you married now."

"Age is unimportant," said Kallias. "Dowry and family are what count. Do you not agree, Alkibiades?"

"I cannot argue that I did not receive a worthy reward for my sacrifice from Kallias' father. But Nikolas is right. Why should you lose those years with Samias just because you are a worthy prize for a sapling family?"

"You really think I should marry but continue as if it never happened?"

"Why not?" said Alkibiades. "Look, you will have to marry someone, and given the city's losses from the plague, the sooner the better. You owe it to your family and you owe it to Athens. You do not need me or your mother to tell you that." Timokles felt his hope shrivelling like the leaves on the trees in the agora. "But you also owe it to yourself," continued his friend. "You cannot choose your wife's character or looks, you can only choose her family, and there are few more wealthy families than that of Nikias, even if they do not have an ancient name. Is not this a choice you may have made for yourself anyway? You are just annoyed that your mother took the decision out of your hands."

Timokles threw a pebble down the steps, staring vacantly into space. Alkibiades was making a reasonable case, but what of Samias? Would he understand?

"I think our friend needs a distraction," said Alkibiades.

"Let's go to Keramikus tonight and console him," said Nikolas. "Simaetha has a new girl, Sellene, who I'm falling in love with."

"Come on, Timokles," said Alkibiades, "this is not the end of life, believe me. It can be the very beginning. New experiences for you." Timokles was unconvinced. "Right, that's it. Tonight we are all going to Simaetha's. Neither you nor Kallias have been there before. You will have fun, and you can bring Samias if you want. We will eat and drink, talk and sing, and you will forget about bossy mothers. Agreed?"

All eyes turned to Timokles. Marriage was a hunting pack of wolves. His life was about to be torn apart and he was powerless. He sighed and said, "Fine."

Chapter 10

"Why do you think prostitutes hang around potters?" asked Kallias with a stupid grin, as the young men approached the potters' quarter known as Keramikus.

"Perhaps because of the skill potters have with their hands," suggested Alkibiades.

"Yes! Excellent," said Kallias.

The potters' workshops had closed for the night, but men bustled in the dark, narrow streets, which twisted like a confused serpent. Oil lamps threw light through open doorways into the streets, beacons of honey illuminating half-naked women and pretty boys waiting for customers. Colourful advertisements decorated the walls: three obols for "bent over"; two drachmas for "the racehorse". These places were nothing like Simaetha's, but Alkibiades enjoyed the atmosphere, a festival of human nature. The thought of the old prigs, Pisander and Antiphon, walking through the area on their way to meet him tonight, amused him.

His entourage turned into a quiet street that seemed a different country. An oil lamp hung above a stout door, on which Nikolas banged. "Let us in. It's an emergency. It's Nikolas the Long." He strained to increase his short stature beside the stone herm whose genitalia, it was to be understood, bore no comparison to his own. A peephole opened above their heads. The disembodied eyes grunted, and the peephole slammed shut.

"It seems your reputation here isn't quite what you thought," said Timokles.

Nikolas shook his head in smug expectation, and sure enough, the door opened and a monstrous, bald, bare-chested man gave them entry with menaces. They stepped into a bright courtyard lit by torches mounted on the columns supporting the upper storey. A statue of Eros rose from a pool in the centre. Alkibiades felt the dirt of the city wash away.

"I'll tell my mistress that Nikolas the Short's here," growled their chaperone. Nikolas was a gathering storm amidst his companions' laughter. Alkibiades eased his way to the front, and the monster's countenance brightened. "I'll inform the mistress immediately, master." He hastened to a room in the far corner.

Young Samias muttered, "Is he going to crush us?"

"Only if we don't pay," said Kallias, pleased with his witticism.

Aphrodite burst into the yard, twittering welcomes like a song thrush. Simaetha's black hair emphasized startlingly blue eyes that fired thunderbolts at the young men. She floated towards them with the folds of her wispy peplos hovering above painted toenails. When she opened her arms in welcome, the fabric extended like wings, fastened at intervals along her bare arms in the Ionic fashion.

"Gentlemen," she cooed, her gaze lingering on each one of the group. "Ah! I see my own Ganymede is here," she said as she took Alkibiades by the hands.

"You know I am unable to stay away from such beauty," he replied, bowing slightly. "I see you received my gift," he added, noticing the gold necklace that graced Simaetha's neck.

"It's beautiful, no? So pretty. An excellent choice, Ganymede."

"I am glad you like it."

Sadness shadowed her face. "Such a shame I have no earrings to match it."

"Well," said Alkibiades, kissing each of her hands in turn and suppressing a smile, "we will have to see what we can do about that."

"He's an excellent Ganymede, no? Please. Follow me."

Alkibiades had been a frequent visitor here for two years. It surprised him, as a single season was usually enough to feel the barnacles latch on and drag him down. But Simaetha was different. Beautiful and witty, she continued to delight and amuse him. He was accustomed to being the Siren himself, so the little gifts for her were a fair price for a place where he had no need to perform.

Simaetha led her procession into a room that caused Timokles to choke, his eyes pinned to the graphic paintings that adorned the walls. "Close your mouth and grab a couch," smiled Alkibiades.

Timokles dropped onto one of the luxurious, red-cushioned couches arrayed in a square. Samias grabbed a cushion and jumped beside him. Alkibiades, Nikolas and Kallias staked out their own couches, with room for visitors.

"The girls will be here in a moment," said Simaetha. "In the meantime, enjoy the wine. It's Lesbian."

"Did you receive the supplies we sent earlier?" asked Kallias, planted on his couch like an overgrown bush.

"Yes. So thoughtful of you all. My cook is preparing them. We'll have a delightful evening, no?" She frowned at Samias, who was stroking Timokles' exposed calf. Alkibiades had known that she would be annoyed: if they didn't intend to use her offerings, why were they here? But he was sure she would say nothing. After all, had he not kept his promise? A new fly in her web from one of the wealthiest families in Athens.

She left the room, closing the door behind her as a handsome Ethiopian slave served wine, amidst laughter at Timokles, who seemed incapable of ripping his gaze from the wall paintings. To Alkibiades, the depictions of outlandish sexual feats were mere background, and he was more amused than aroused by the images of ecstatic women serviced by clients who, judging from their ridiculous grins, were not averse to the task.

"Timokles!" Kallias raised his shallow kylix of wine. "May your wife bear you sons, but no grudges for your mistresses...er, or boyfriends."

Timokles glanced nervously at Samias, who smiled and raised his kylix with the others. Timokles lifted his own as if it were Sisyphus' rock and drank with them.

The door burst open and a torrent of giggles flooded the room. A dusky Persian girl and two pale Thracians bunched on the same couch, laughing at one another's appraisals of the men drooling at them. Two Milesian girls in sunset chitons glided in with a bronze harp and an aulos, and began to play soft, soothing music. Simaetha rejoined them, followed by a young goddess with hair like fields of barley in the dawn, and luminous lips asking to be kissed. Her shapely legs caressed the air as she walked, in a way that appeared innocent, yet was highly erotic.

"Gentlemen," said Simaetha, "not all of you know my good friend, Sellene." Captivated stares indicated that they wanted to know her. "A fire killed her parents when she was nine, and I found the little thing wandering the streets, starving. Well, I was just a girl myself at the time, making my way in the world, but how could I just abandon her? I've brought her up as my own sister, and now it's time to share my friends with her, so please, for my sake, be kind to her, no?"

"She's the very image of Aphrodite," said Nikolas, his darkness melting in beauty's fire. "And she must know from our previous meeting that I worship at her shrine."

"Thank you, kind sir," said Sellene. "And thank you for the generous gift you sent." She fingered the silver serpent coiled around her wrist.

"How could I fail to offer gifts to such loveliness?" said Nikolas, trapped by the gentle, pretty face.

"It's so beautiful," said Sellene, "though it doesn't shine as much as Simaetha's necklace." Simaetha gave her a fleeting glance of approval as she took her own place beside Alkibiades.

"Someone of such beauty," cried Kallias, bursting into flower as he brushed the hair from his face, "should be decked only in gold."

The dawn faded from Nikolas' face. "I could only find it in silver," he said. "I thought you'd like the design. It's supposed to bring good fortune."

"And so I do," said Sellene as she settled like a snowflake on the end of Kallias' couch, between the two men.

The little charade amused Alkibiades. He knew that Simaetha had plucked Sellene from a neighbouring brothel two years ago and coached her to hook a rich squeeze. The three of them would share the profits. For Sellene it was an opportunity to earn a future that did not include the depths of poverty and degradation that were likely to follow on the heels of fading beauty. But Alkibiades enjoyed the way the young girl moved, and the sly, sultry looks directed his way. "Having loyal friends is so important, no?" asked Simaetha.

"I agree," said Nikolas, tearing his eyes from Sellene. "Loyalty to your friends trumps everything." He glanced at Timokles, who was lost in earnest, whispered conversation with Samias. "One wonders about those lost in love. Where does their loyalty lie?" Nikolas added this softly, looking at Alkibiades, who satisfied him with a smile.

"Family is the foundation of loyalty," declared Kallias, unable to avert his stare from Sellene. "Did you know that my family is one of the richest in Athens?"

"Really?" said Sellene.

"We are torchbearers for the Mysteries. My grandfather was an ambassador to Persia, my father is a general, and Alkibiades is my brother, married to my sister." Kallias diverted his focus to Nikolas for a fleeting moment. "Family always comes before friends."

"A man chooses his friends," said Nikolas, darkening. "Alkibiades and I have fought side-by-side with death all around us. No bond is greater than that formed in adversity. And as for Kallias' wealth," Nikolas turned back to Sellene and lowered his voice, "his father keeps it close by. He wouldn't trust a drachma of it to his son, so if I were you I'd ask him whether he has his pocket money with him this evening."

Sellene cast her eyes down and appeared to be upset.

Kallias took her hand. "Forgive Nikolas for speaking so coarsely. He is more at home with three-obol whores than with such a fine lady as yourself."

"Go to the crows, Kallias," snapped Nikolas.

"A friend you can love as yourself brings the greatest joy in life, no?" said Simaetha as her fingers played with the folds of Alkibiades' chiton. "To have someone totally on your side."

"I agree with you," said Timokles, awakened from his conversation with Samias by Nikolas' outburst.

"Someone to love you is a gift of the gods," said Sellene, her head tilted as she smiled at Kallias. She looked across at Alkibiades as she released herself from Kallias' hand and said, "You appear well loved by your friends. I'm told they flutter around like butterflies trying to please you. What do *you* think of love?"

Alkibiades held her eyes as he sipped his wine. "I think love is a caressing of the ego," he began. "Everyone longs to be loved by beautiful people, to possess them. But it is only so they can parade before their friends and make them jealous."

"I don't believe you, Alkibiades," said Timokles.

"Seriously, I think the best lovers are those who think they do not deserve you, because they will do anything to earn their good fortune. Do you remember Anytas, Timokles? I took his silver treasures to give to a friend in need, and all he did was thank me for leaving him anything at all. He thanked me. What a fool! If he had had any sense he would have had me beaten and taken to the courts."

"He must have been besotted with you," said Sellene.

"He was. But only because he thought everyone else would envy him. The triumph of ego."

Timokles laughed. "You'll have them believe you if you're not careful."

Simaetha cleared her throat. "It's time to eat. You! Go find out where the food is." The appointed slave hurried from the room.

"Do you know what I sent, Sellene?" asked Nikolas in a valiant attempt to smile. "Sea bass. Have you tasted the head of a sea bass before? The cheeks are delicious. Perhaps you'd allow me to treat you to the head of mine?"

"That sounds wonderful, Nikolas. Is it a large one?" she asked, her eyebrows raised in a manner that was at once suggestive and innocent.

"Huge," grinned Nikolas, with no hint of innocence.

"Before you settle for sea bass, perhaps you would prefer to taste a Rhodian dogfish," said Kallias with a triumphant smile.

"No! You bought a Rhodian dogfish?" asked Nikolas.

"I... I've never had one before," said Sellene. She leaned close to Kallias, laying a hand on his knee. "They say it's worth dying for."

"Once you have had it, nothing else compares," grinned Kallias.

By the time the food was served, victory belonged to Kallias. Sellene sat beside him, her slender leg brushing against his, feeding him bread and olives as she devoured the fish of dreams. Nikolas, dressed in a becoming scowl, had the Persian girl draped over him in compensation. He did not share the sea bass with her. Simaetha directed the conversation, working to soothe Nikolas for his loss: she did not want Sellene and Kallias to shipwreck on their way out of the harbour.

When the food was finished, the dice came out. Sellene shared Kallias' wine cup, laughed at his stupid jokes, and shouted his name for luck when throwing the dice. Kallias was enslaved.

The wine flowed, and dancing erupted as the music quickened. Nikolas lost some of his glower, aided now by three girls hanging upon him, and Timokles and Samias retired to a room on their own, to Simaetha's evident displeasure. Sellene twinkled beside Kallias, apparently as drunk as he was, but her eyes were sharp. Her hands and lips teased Kallias almost to a state of despair, before she finally led him by his belt from the room. Hades seemed to settle on Nikolas again.

Simaetha whispered her thanks to the gods and to the power of the old crone who had made the wax doll of Kallias, which they had burnt together that morning to inflame his passion. She turned to Alkibiades and fastened her eyes on her lover's face. "And how are your preparations for the Dionysia?"

"The chorus? I am just the money. I have an expert to choose and train the boys. I just ensure he knows that we must win."

"Such a thing can be guaranteed?"

"Money is the prophet of victory. That is why Nikias always wins," said Alkibiades.

"Won't he win this year?"

"He is not competing. He funded a trireme instead."

The oversized doorman lumbered into the room. "Mistress, there are two gentlemen here to see the master and his friend."

Simaetha nodded. "Show them into the blue room. It seems your guests have arrived."

"At last," said Nikolas, standing abruptly and sending a girl tumbling from the couch. "Don't move," he told her. "I'll be back soon."

Simaetha clapped her hands and the remaining girls and slaves followed Nikolas out of the room. She slid along the couch and nestled against Alkibiades, drawing his arms around her. "He'll be okay, no?" she asked.

"Nikolas? He will be fine."

"Thank you for Kallias."

"Consider it my gift." He kissed her neck. "Sellene is certainly an enticing girl."

She elbowed him in the ribs, harder than she meant to. "You have only one lover in this house."

"And that one is plenty. But," he added, patting her on the thigh, "I must deal with my guests." Alkibiades rose from the couch and strode towards the door.

"Hurry back," called Simaetha, a shapely leg making a timely escape from her drapery.

Alkibiades strolled across the courtyard, wondering if the visitors had gotten lost on their way. He had expected them earlier, and he had drunk more wine than he had intended. He shook himself, knocked lightly on the door and entered without waiting.

"Intriguing choice of venue, Alkibiades," said sharp-witted Antiphon from a couch against the far wall. The forest on his face masked his smile but not his penetrating eyes.

"Very picturesque," said Pisander, nodding his hawkish head. Nikolas had taken a seat beside him in a room glowing with oil lamps, the only difference from the previous room seeming to be the blue mattresses on the couches. Pisander glanced at the door. "Is it safe?"

"It is safe."

"You have news for us?" said Pisander.

"Indeed. You have already heard that my family will support the rescue of Plataea. We will use our resources and connections towards that goal. In addition, we will promote Demosthenes and Hipponikus as generals in the next election. We will need them on the Board of Ten if we are to succeed."

"Demosthenes?" said Pisander. "He's not from much of a family."

"No," murmured Antiphon, "but he has an impeccable military reputation. What do you think of him, Alkibiades?"

"He is no politician, but he could make an exceptional general."

"What is he after?" asked Pisander, his eyes locked on

Alkibiades.

"I think all he cares about is making Athens safe from Sparta."

A smile flickered amidst Antiphon's beard. "We can support their election. What about co-operating with Kleon?"

Pisander spat on the floor, shaking his head, and Alkibiades smiled as he recalled the eruption of his own family at the suggestion. "They came to see its utility," he said.

"Excellent," said Antiphon. "Our faith in your powers of persuasion has been justified. Perhaps you can now put them to further use on Kleon."

"I will arrange to meet him."

"One of us should go with you," said Pisander. "To show our solidarity."

Alkibiades tilted his head and smiled. "I would not want to trouble you. I know how distasteful it will be. I am sure I can handle him."

"I have absolute confidence that you can," said Antiphon. "But if Nikolas were with you, it would demonstrate our support, and remind him of your popularity among the young men of the city."

Alkibiades maintained his smile, distrust filling the room like mist. He had assumed their dislike of Kleon would enable him to be the linchpin in any alliance, but now the oligarchs wanted to be in the front ranks, not mere support. "It would be good to have a friend there," he said, and Nikolas seemed to add an inch to his stature. Alkibiades took a sip of water and added, "Kleon may not have the strategic grasp to appreciate the importance of Plataea."

"Make him understand, Alkibiades," said Antiphon. "The rescue of Plataea is vital for the future of Athens."

Alkibiades nodded, but he was worried: Antiphon almost sounded desperate again, and Alkibiades could see no good reason why. "The city will be distracted by General Paches' siege of Mytilene."

"Yes," agreed Antiphon. "But rebellion is evidence of allied disillusionment, and saving Plataea will demonstrate Athens' strength and make other rebels hesitate." He leant back, staring at the ceiling with pursed lips. "To install Demosthenes as general would mean removing Paches," he said. "Could be difficult if he proves capable."

"We will see," said Alkibiades. "I believe he will make himself vulnerable. And as for our allies, ambassadors from Miletus are my guests at the moment. I am sure I can persuade them to spread rumours of possible revolts. Plataean faithfulness is such a contrast with the fickleness of the allies."

"Their faithfulness will be tested. It'll be a while before we can win a damn vote on this," said Pisander.

"Perhaps," said Alkibiades. "But you never know when Opportunity may present herself."

Antiphon fondled his cup and gazed at the table of wine, figs and olives laid out with military precision before him. "You are becoming a force in the city, Alkibiades. Perhaps it is time for you to take a more active role and speak in the Assembly."

"The Assembly?" said Alkibiades. He smiled, but he was disappointed in Antiphon. Could he have misjudged Alkibiades so badly as to attempt such a transparent ploy? To put himself at the head of a coalition of aristocrats and oligarchs would be to invite accusations of tyranny, now or later. Such charges were death in Athenian politics, and without the cover of Kleon or Nikias, the charge would stick. "For the moment I am happy to persuade Kleon to blow the trumpet. This is his time."

Antiphon and Pisander exchanged glances. It was clear to Alkibiades that his response had been unexpected, and he had to suppress his amusement.

"You're such a good orator, Alkibiades," said Nikolas. "It'd be a shame to hide that talent."

"I have no intention of hiding it. But one must choose the right moment."

"That is a shame," said Antiphon. "A great shame. But Kleon's talents may suffice."

Alkibiades felt the heat of Antiphon's stare, and wondered if the older man were wrestling with the common notion that a handsome man must be a virtuous man. Alkibiades had seen such conflict many times. He recognized the mixture of admiration and confusion on Antiphon's face. The bald head was too smart for such things to sway him in the end, however, so Alkibiades decided to remove the doubt. "Remember the story of King Leos? He gave his name to my tribe of Leontis for sacrificing his daughters to avert a famine. People will do much for their superstitions. We should use that." He noted the change in Antiphon's face as if he were recalibrating.

"Take care, young Alkibiades," said Pisander, clenching his shoulders like a nervous owl. "The gods have their favourites. A wise man doesn't cross them."

"Of course. But who is to say that *we* are not their favourites? Nikias has had a monopoly on claims to their favour for too long."

"Playing with people's beliefs," began Antiphon, "is like throwing a lump of red-hot iron into the sea. Lots of steam and noise with no seeing where it will end."

"And whatever we think of Nikias," said Pisander, "he isn't one to *pretend* he honours the gods. The people respect him for it."

Not all people, thought Alkibiades.

"It's a damn shame about him," continued Pisander. "It takes courage to lead your city in a new direction, and Nikias doesn't have it." He leaned forward, his eyes glinting like swords. "Do you have it, Alkibiades?"

"Indeed I do. I will do what it takes to save Athens."

"Whatever it takes?" asked Antiphon.

Alkibiades turned to the beard, not entirely sure what he was being asked, but sure nevertheless of what he felt. "Yes," he said. "Whatever it takes."

Chapter 11

When Khara entered the sunlit room, Hipparete bounded to her. The young girl's smile washed away Khara's memory of Lakon's grumpy farewell as she lost herself in their hug.

"I'm so glad you're here," said Hipparete, leading Khara to a couch. "I'm so bored."

Khara nodded an acknowledgement to Hipparete's Persian maid, Maria, who was feeding red fibres to a spindle spinning slowly to the ground. Sunlight from two unshuttered windows illuminated the colourful hanging tapestries and the sheepskins scattered on the wooden floor. An H-frame loom, bearing a half-completed weaving, leaned against the wall. "I hope I'm not interrupting your work," said Khara.

"Oh, no," said Hipparete. "We're hiding in here, really. Did Alkibiades take Alexias with him this morning?"

"Yes, he did." Khara recalled Alkibiades' amused face in the torchlight as Alexias dashed out of the door to greet him and drag him along the street. They had left before dawn to watch the arrival of General Nikias and his fleet. "It was very thoughtful of Alkibiades to take him."

"Oh, I know. Isn't he sweet? I'm Fortune's favourite."

"Unlike our neighbour, Konstanta."

Khara smiled as Hipparete failed to hide her eagerness. Khara's access to gossip was a crack into the world beyond Hipparete's walls, even if it only referred to a neighbour she barely knew. "What about Konstanta?"

"Her husband, Aristarchus, dropped dead. Just like that."

"No!" exclaimed Hipparete. "Poor thing. Did he upset the gods?"

"He made all the right sacrifices, so I heard."

"Twin Goddesses, you don't think it was the plague, do you?"

"No. We'd know about it by now." Khara had been obsessed with Konstanta's loss, aware of her own husband's vulnerability.

"What will happen to her?" asked Hipparete.

"She has a poor uncle with no surviving son. It's said that he'll divorce his wife and marry Konstanta."

"How long has her uncle been married?"

"Twenty years."

"Twenty years? And he's going to divorce her just like that?" Hipparete stared at the closed door. "Just because she hasn't given him a son?"

"It's not just about a son," Khara said quickly. "He could adopt one of his nephews, after all. But what would they inherit? He needs the estates that Konstanta and her children will bring."

Hipparete rose and resumed her weaving, beating the loose purple weft so that it disappeared into her earlier work. Khara had failed to anticipate how the news would unsettle her friend. Hipparete, like Konstanta, had wealth to ensure her security even after divorce or the death of her husband. Khara and Alexias had no such wealth, balanced on the edge of a precipice, waiting for the push. "Thank the gods you have a rich family, Hipparete."

Hipparete laid aside the weaving sword and plopped onto the couch. Her hands fidgeted in her lap, and Khara noticed her friend's frayed fingernails. "Yes, thank the gods," muttered Hipparete.

"You don't sound too sure."

Hipparete sagged forward, supporting her head in her hands. "Father visited the other day."

"Oh."

"By the Twin Goddesses, he should be married to Deinomache. They'd have plenty to talk about. *Where's my grandson, where's my grandson?* I'm not a goddess. I can't snap my fingers and produce a child at will. I've made sacrifices to Artemis of Childbirth. I've applied ointments of goat fat. What more can I do? And then *she* comes in to have her say. May Artemis rip out her tongue and pluck her teeth like feathers."

Khara hid her face, laughing, and Hipparete, taken aback initially, soon dissolved as well. "She's a toad," she continued between sobs of laughter. "She croaks around the house like she's Queen of the Pond." Hipparete imitated the beast in question, and then sank back as her laughs evaporated. "Why does she hate me? Everyone used to like me. I don't understand what I've done to her."

Khara eased beside her, enfolding Hipparete in her arms. "I'm sure it's not you. Not really. Maybe she's jealous."

"Because Alkibiades loves me?"

Khara stroked her hair. "Yes. Because he loves you."

"I'm his wife. He's supposed to love me. She's so unfair."

Khara kissed her head. "I know. I know. At least you have Alkibiades."

"When he's here."

"He's neglecting you?"

"Oh, no. Not at all. Not really. He couldn't be more attentive. It's just... there's always some cause. A friend. Athens. Plataea."

"I'm glad he still remembers Plataea."

"Oh, he's always going off to do something for Plataea."

Khara knew of Alkibiades' meetings with Plataean elders and of his counsel to them. As a result, they had organized small demonstrations to promote their cause, and targeted wealthy individuals to support them. But these were beetle steps. More promising was that the Council had raised the Plataean siege in the Assembly, and that rumours were circulating in the agora that the allies disapproved of Athens' abandonment of Plataea. But these had nothing to do with Alkibiades as far as Khara was aware, so she assumed his professions to Hipparete were excuses to hide his suspected affairs.

Reaching for a cup of water, Hipparete accidentally knocked it off the table, the terracotta cup shattering on the floor. Hipparete turned white. "Maria!" she whispered. "Quickly. Help me." Hipparete knelt to the ground, grabbing the shards and glancing at the door.

"Hipparete," said Khara, "it's all right. It's just a clay cup. Leave it for Maria." She raised the girl back to the couch as Maria cleaned up the mess.

"She'll be angry," said Hipparete, glancing at the door again.

"Deinomache won't even know about it. Why should she miss one clay cup, no matter how well it was painted?" But as Khara finished they heard steps marching upstairs. Hipparete gripped Khara's hand as the door swung open and Deinomache filled the room, light from the doorway making her golden hair glow as if she were a goddess.

"Oh. Khara. I was unaware that *you* were here." The contempt that laced her words was evident. Deinomache disapproved of Hipparete's friendship with a woman occupying their old slave's quarters, but she would not prevent what Alkibiades encouraged.

"I came to see my friend," parried Khara.

Deinomache's nose seemed to elevate. "I heard something break."

Khara, feeling Hipparete tremble, squeezed her hand. "Yes, I'm sorry about that," said Khara, "I dropped a cup." Hipparete tensed as Khara reflected Deinomache's glare.

Deinomache was statuesque, silent, her eyes releasing clouds of poisoned darts. Finally, she examined the fragments of the cup. "That was one my son's favourites. He will be very disappointed. Do you know where he is, Hipparete?"

"He's gone to see Nikias arrive," said Khara. "It's a pity your son doesn't have the influence of the general. He might be able to do something for my husband."

Deinomache glowered, as if Silence were a stick with which to beat the impudent woman. "My son is young. His time will come." She glanced at the shards of pottery. "It is not good to break the cup that slakes your thirst." She turned to leave, noticed Hipparete's weaving, and paused. "Be more careful, Hipparete. Your mistakes are too obvious." She strode from the room, and slammed the door behind her.

Hipparete released the breath she had held. "Oh, Khara, you're so brave," she whispered.

Khara relinquished her friend's hand to hide her own trembling, and laughed. "Why be scared of a toad?"

"Ribbet," croaked Hipparete.

"It's a shame, though, about the cup. Was it one of Alkibiades' favourites?"

"I doubt he's ever noticed it," said Hipparete.

"Ah. I suspected."

The two friends relaxed again, Khara amusing Hipparete with tales she had heard from slaves at the water fountains and from loquacious shopkeepers. Shouts from downstairs and the patter of feet forewarned them of Alexias' arrival, but when he burst through the door, the force of the gale still surprised them.

"Momma, Momma! Hipparete! We saw so many ships they were crowded like an ant's nest and they had soldiers on board, and there were so many rowers the ships looked like caterpillars and they rowed to pipes and people cheered and clapped and a general talked to them and they cheered louder and I rode on Alkibiades' shoulders and ate an octopus stuffed with cheese, which was so good, and we saw a man that looked like mud and another with a beard that stuck out like this." Alexias paraded with his arm to his chin. Hipparete had already dissolved into giggles.

"Persian," explained Alkibiades as he stepped through the door.

"And I saw a huge fireplace with red liquid in it and it was really hot and there were shops called eyelids and loads of..."

"Eyelids?" said Khara.

"Near Piraeus' agora there are small shops selling food," said Alkibiades. "They have so many customers that their doors open and close frequently, like an eyelid." Hipparete rose, glowing like the moon as Alkibiades kissed her cheeks. They sat beside each other opposite Khara, who had pulled Alexias to her in an effort to calm him.

"I'm grateful, Alkibiades, for taking him with you."

"Not at all. It was fun, wasn't it, Sparrow?"

Alexias laughed. "Alkibiades calls me Sparrow because I jump around everywhere."

"And you are a noisy little thing."

"Did General Nikias impress?" asked Khara.

"He made the most of his little raid," said Alkibiades.

"Will he dominate the Plataea debate now that he's back?" She noticed a spark in his eyes.

"He will try."

"Will you try?" She saw him start.

"You never give up, do you?" he said with an amused smile, taking Hipparete's hand.

"Some things are too important to give up."

"Yes, they are."

His eyes and his voice caressed like silk. Khara held Alexias closer. "I've heard rumours that Miletus is unhappy with Athens. That they think Athens must rescue Plataea. Could you use them?"

"I am close to the ambassadors from Miletus. They are my guests."

Khara frowned. Such an evasive answer was a warning not to push. But did Alkibiades mean to use them, or not? "The Assembly," she continued. "Several debates on Plataea, but no vote. Why haven't you stood up and argued for us?"

Alkibiades helped himself to some water.

"I broke a cup," said Hipparete. "Your mother's upset."

Alkibiades raised an eyebrow and pushed a jug of water off the table, smashing it on the floor. "Oops. So easy to do."

Hipparete's shock transformed into giggles, and Khara was unable to refrain from smiling.

"You're naughty," laughed Alexias.

"I am. As for the Assembly, Khara, it is a hunting ground, and it is better to lay the traps than to step in them. Matters are advancing. You have to trust me."

Trust you? Everything she knew of him cried mistrust and danger, yet it was difficult not to trust that godlike face.

Chapter 12

Legend had it that after Theseus had slain the Minotaur, and escaped the labyrinth with the aid of Ariadne's thread, the future king of Athens had sworn to honour Apollo for his salvation. So was born the Pyanopsia Festival, the day Alkibiades was to try to persuade the demagogue, Kleon, that Athens should rescue Plataea.

The sun had yet to rise when golden Deinomache began to blow through the house. "Hipparete!" she yelled, standing outside the kitchen. "Get out of bed this instant. The Temple of Apollo, remember?" She stepped into the lamp-lit kitchen where a sleepy girl stirred a pot of boiling beans and vegetables. "Watch what you are doing," said Deinomache, and the young girl snapped upright on her stool.

Deinomache strode to a corner table where another woman was slicing bread below the copper pans hanging on the walls. As the mistress approached, the knife acquired a life of its own and the slices became uneven. "How hard is it to slice bread? Concentrate." Deinomache paced beyond the shelves of clay pots, where a girl wound strands of Ariadne's wool around short branches laden with apples for the offering to Apollo. "At least any fool can do that."

Having imparted her encouragement in the kitchen, Deinomache stepped into the courtyard and in the gloom almost collided with Alkibiades' personal slave, Andromachus, hurrying past with an empty cup.

"Ah, Andromachus." He stopped in his tracks, wearing the blank expression of a slave's mask. "Have you prepared my son's bath yet?"

"Yes, mistress."

"And have you made his bed?"

"Yes, mistress."

"So what are you doing now?"

"He wants some wine."

"Then what are you standing here for? Hurry up, man."

As Andromachus scurried away, the sky lightened into swirls of grey, and cockerels alerted the neighbourhood to the new day. Hipparete was still absent by the time Alkibiades appeared.

"Where is your wife?" said Deinomache.

"How should I know?"

"By spending the night with her."

"I do my duty, Mother. If there is no son, it is through no fault of mine."

Deinomache sighed. "I know, son. Are you joining us at the Temple of Apollo?"

"I am meeting Kleon, remember? Andromachus can escort you."

"It is not good to ignore the gods."

"As long as they ignore me, that is fine."

"Tread carefully with that tanner."

"Yes, Mother."

As Alkibiades left, Deinomache's annoyance swelled. The gathering storm rolled up the stairs towards her daughter-in-law's bedroom. Deinomache stomped along the balcony, and Hipparete's maid, Maria, emerged from a door and halted.

"Where is she?" demanded Deinomache.

The Persian's eyes glanced at the door from which she had come as if unsure whether this was a trick question. "In her room."

"I know that, girl. *Why* is she in her room?"

"She feels sick."

"Oh, nonsense. She always imagines herself ill." Deinomache swept past the slave and burst through the door into the flicker of oil lamps.

Hipparete was hunched over a bowl on the edge of her bed, a blanket wrapped around her. She looked up with resignation at her mother-in-law.

"What do you think you are doing in bed at this hour? The cockerels have already started. What example do you think this sets? Especially on a festival day. Do you think you can run a house from bed? It is time you grew up, young lady. You are the wife of an important man. It is time you started acting like one, even if you are unable to give him a son."

Tears crept down Hipparete's cheeks.

"What are you crying for now? How can we talk when all you do is cry?"

Hipparete lurched over the bowl and vomited.

Deinomache hesitated. She poured a cup of water and offered it to her daughter-in-law. "How long have you felt sick?"

Hipparete snuggled into the blanket. "A few days. But it clears up when the sun rises."

Deinomache's eyes narrowed. "Have you bled recently?"

"I missed my last one." Hipparete felt it might be to her advantage to hide that she had always been irregular.

Deinomache smiled. "Well, great is Artemis. I think she has finally blessed us. After we have been to the Temple of Apollo, we will make sacrifices to Artemis for your protection, my dear. Are you feeling any better?"

"A little," Hipparete replied weakly.

"Let me go and get you some boiled beans. And some figs. You lie back and rest and I will bring them to you."

Hipparete lay back on the bed, staring at the stranger in her room. Deinomache walked to the door and chirped, "We must keep your strength up, sweetheart. You could be carrying my grandson."

***

The streets of Piraeus vibrated with the joy of a festival day. Men and women strolled to the temples and shrines of Apollo, and dedicated their fruit-laden branches strewn with wool. Groups of boys hung autumnal wreaths on doors as they sang hymns to the rescuer of Theseus.

"I can't believe we're doing this," grumbled Nikolas, the antithesis of festive, striding alongside Alkibiades.

"Sometimes it is prudent to make an enemy your friend," said Alkibiades.

"Yes, but a *tanner*?"

They reached the tavern, which had ivy painted on its crumbling walls next to a faded list of food prices. Alkibiades pushed through the door without hesitation; Nikolas took a deep breath and followed. For a moment, Alkibiades was blind as he stepped from bright sunshine into the dusky tavern, his ears assaulted by the laughter of drunken sailors, the shouts of dice-players, the cackles of cheap prostitutes. As his eyes adjusted, he noted the brawny arms of the bartender, the tables laden with food and drink, the men playing draughts, the young boys scurrying everywhere carrying plates and pitchers. The room felt alive with possibilities; danger lurked in the shadows, an exciting presence. He edged his way past the crowded tables, and smiled at Nikolas' attempts not to touch or to be touched by anything or anybody.

"Welcome to the real Athens, my friends," said Kleon, a towering, middle-aged man whose smile revealed teeth like weathered tombstones. His cropped hair and beard, and the fine woollen cloth of his himation, suggested refinement; the trenches ploughed into his brow, suspicion.

"Kleon," nodded Alkibiades. Nikolas gave a barely perceptible nod as Kleon sat. They sat opposite him, their backs to the room.

"A drink? Some food, perhaps?" prompted the self-styled Watchdog of the People.

"Not for me," said Nikolas.

"What? Our little establishment not good enough for you, son of Pisander?"

"We will have some boiled bean stew," said Alkibiades. He stood and faced the room, and declared, "A pint of wine for everyone, in honour of Apollo, courtesy of Alkibiades, son of Kleinias."

A cheer blasted the tavern as Alkibiades sat down. Kleon grinned and leant back in his chair. "Nice. To appeal to the gods and to the people. Infallible." The orders given to a tavern boy, Kleon added, "You'll find this a decent place. The measures are fair, the wine well strained and diluted with clean water."

"Are you suggesting," said Alkibiades, raising his eyebrows, "that Kleon, the wealthy owner of a tannery, son of a choregus victor at the Dionysia and married into a distinguished family, is a frequent visitor at this establishment?"

Kleon played with his wine cup. "It's useful to be seen among the people. My friends are here, not displaying their wasted education at the symposia. We must all play our parts, young Alkibiades."

"And you play yours well. You have brought a revolution to our politics."

"Not everyone would see that as a good thing," said Kleon, glancing at Nikolas.

"Not everyone supports you personally," said Alkibiades, "but they can still see the merits of working with someone who, after all, shares their goals."

Kleon's fingers stopped their little dance, and he scrutinized the handsome young man opposite him. A boy appeared and deposited bowls of stew, clay cups, and a jug of wine, but Kleon's eyes never left Alkibiades. "Which goals would they be?"

"We all want Athens to be safe and prosperous."

"So does that fool Nikias," spat Kleon, "but his idea of 'safe' will destroy Athens."

"Indeed," said Alkibiades. "There are many, like you, who feel that he is leading us to defeat."

Nikolas filled his cup, and drank away the dirt of his surroundings. It may have only been one-obol wine, but its taste was less offensive to him than the company.

"What do you propose we do about it?" asked Kleon.

"The board of generals is unbalanced," said Alkibiades. "Too many of Nikias' creatures, all scared to do anything meaningful. Perhaps, if we work together, generals of a more... aggressive temperament could be elected."

"Who do you have in mind?"

"For a start, replacing Paches with Demosthenes, and re-electing my father-in-law."

"Demosthenes," repeated Kleon, the furrows in his head deepening into valleys. "An able man. He would be acceptable. It may be difficult to get him elected, though, if Paches succeeds in Mytilene."

"True enough, but between us I am sure we can do it."

"Perhaps. Of course," continued Kleon, "with the recent death of General Lysikles in Karia, there's an opportunity to put another general on the board."

"Who?"

"Eurymedon, son of Thukles."

"What!" spluttered Nikolas. "That *potter*?"

Kleon glared at the young man. "He owns several workshops, yes. But he's a fighter."

Alkibiades squeezed Nikolas' arm, and said to Kleon, "I know the man. We can support his candidacy."

Nikolas refilled his cup.

Across the room, two men began shouting, jabbing each other in the chest with a finger. The man in a bandanna smashed a pot on the table and slashed it across the bald man's face, who lunged for bandanna's throat as chairs and tables tumbled in their wake. The muscular bartender launched into the sprawling fighters, and in no time, they were out on the street.

"It is better than the theatre here," said Alkibiades, but Kleon's face was stone, and the young man cleared his throat and continued. "We must save Plataea." Alkibiades mined Kleon's face for nuggets, but he could find nothing useful.

"Go on," said Kleon.

"With Plataea in our hands, Demosthenes believes it would provide a base to control Boeotia, as it did in the past. It would spare us from invasion and force Sparta to recognize our control of the empire."

Kleon stroked his neat beard as he looked around the room, though he seemed not to see it. "Tell me, Alkibiades. The rumours circulating about allied dissatisfaction regarding our policy towards Plataea. They're coordinated by you, right?" Alkibiades smiled, but said nothing. "You have promise, son of Kleinias," chuckled Kleon. "But it'll be difficult to persuade the Council to rescue Plataea whilst we bear the cost of the siege of Mytilene."

"There are plenty of Plataean exiles willing to help lubricate such persuasion."

"Hmmm..." Kleon gazed into his wine. "Plataea could be a

useful stepping stone, as you say. And it could sell well in the Assembly, at the right time. Nikias will hate it, of course. Which is as good a reason as any to do it, I suppose." His forefinger drummed the table, and then it stopped, and he looked up. "I can see us working together on this." Kleon raised his cup. "To Plataea!"

"To Plataea!" echoed Alkibiades and Nikolas, taking deep draughts.

"I need a piss," said Nikolas, and he headed for the door.

Kleon jerked his head in the direction of the dark one. "Why are *they* interested in this?"

Alkibiades looked over his shoulder to check on Nikolas' progress before answering. "They are patriots, too. They do not want to see Athens ruined, even if they cannot abide its government."

"Do you believe that?"

Alkibiades leaned forward. "Their dreams are stuck in the past. They cannot possibly overthrow the democracy. It is too entrenched."

"Men always think that, right before governments fall," said Kleon. "They cannot be allowed to endanger the people. I don't trust them, and neither should you, son of Kleinias."

Chapter 13

The oak trees on Mount Kithairon had shed their leaves, and rain shrouded Plataea. The garrison sheltered inside the law court or the shops of the East Stoa, but a few hardy souls huddled outside in the colonnade. Stephanos shivered amidst one such group, mesmerized by the clenched hand that held their fate. As Sémon jostled the dice, grim Skopas wet his lips, long-haired Hybrias gripped his coarse chiton, and even Mikos appeared enchanted.

"Come on, Theo Sémon. We'll be in Hades by the time you roll," said Stephanos.

"Patience," said Sémon. "Anticipation is the greatest of pleasures."

"Is that what you tell Rebia when she's too much for you?" asked Hybrias, a young man with hair hung like curtains that shaded eyes that always seemed ready to sleep. Though he laughed, he did not divert his stare from Sémon's hand, which suddenly stopped in mid-air.

"Take it from an old dog. If you want a woman to beg, make her wait."

Hybrias' gaze snapped to Sémon's face, but the older man simply raised his eyebrows.

"I had a dog," said Skopas, of an age with Sémon, but with a face ploughed with misery. "Followed me everywhere. Randy thing. Must have fathered half the dogs in the neighbourhood. Good company, though."

"Be thankful he's not here," said Sémon. Skopas' face wrinkled like an old grape. "Well, do you think he would survive dinner?" added Sémon.

The circle of eyes darted to Skopas, whose shock gradually fractured into a faint smile. "Must admit, a bit of dog stew sounds good right now."

Mikos, on a stool beside Sémon, smacked the hand of fate.

"Not you as well?" said Sémon. "Given your success with the ladies, I thought you'd learnt to take your time. But let me offer you another thought."

"Two in one day? I may faint," said Stephanos.

They all smiled, but their stares were now fixed on Sémon's face: pretend to understand the secrets of sexual prowess and gain men's undivided attention. "Surprise," said Sémon, "is the best aphrodisiac."

As the words flirted with them, the dice clattered across the stone floor, and they were on their feet, cries of victory strangled by groans. "No winners, pay up," chuckled Sémon, and his pile of pebbles grew as his opponents resumed their seats.

Beyond the sodden remnants of the morning's cooking fires, several women carried amphorae from the water fountain. Stephanos thought of Khara. He should be with her. Plataea should protect his family, not divide it. The town of his ancestors stirred a resentment he dared not admit.

"Talking of surprises," muttered Skopas, "can anyone remember the last one?"

"Well, the other night, Rebia..."

Mikos lurched into Sémon's lap as if stricken by Apollo.

"Well said, Mikos," said curtained Hybrias. "It's depressing when the day's highlight is a story of someone else's sex life."

"That depends on whose sex life it is," returned Sémon.

"I prefer the thrill of seduction, where it's not a sure thing," said Hybrias. Stephanos could not help feeling that, with Hybrias' rough stubble and drowsy eyes, seduction would always be far from a sure thing.

"Then I suggest you give married life a miss," said Sémon.

"Don't listen to him, Hybrias," said Stephanos. "'*A man's best possession is a sympathetic wife*'."

"Oh, no!" cried Sémon. "He attacks me with Euripides. Well, two can play at that game. '*Never say that marriage has more joy than pain*'."

"Euripides. Now there's a man who understands it's better not to have been born at all," said Skopas.

"Oh, my friend," laughed Sémon, "how can you think such things? Listen to the music of the birds. Look at those luscious women over there. Think of the mountains that guard the plain, the oaks of Zeus that cover them. Better not to have been born, indeed!"

"All we do is march along the walls and play dice. What's the point? Why are we doing this?"

"What are you suggesting, Skopas?" said Stephanos, his eyes narrowing.

"I don't know. Perhaps it's time to think about surrendering."

The group stared at him. It was the first time any of them had voiced such a thought, even if they had all considered it. To Stephanos it was at once intoxicating and appalling. To be free of the grinding boredom and the fear of betrayal was attractive, but how could he play traitor to Plataea? The town must live on. Where else would he have land to pass on to his son?

"You're gloomier than a sow's backside," said Sémon. "What about our lively discussions? Our quotations from Euripides? The lovely women?"

Mikos clapped his hands to attract attention, and pretended to wolf a banquet.

"Yes," smiled Stephanos, "let's not forget our wonderful diet."

Hybrias raised his drowsy eyes. "Last time I hunted with my poppa we killed a boar in the forest. Remember, Skopas, the meals we shared that week? Wonder if I'll hunt with him again."

"Who knows what Tyche will dispense from her scales?" said Sémon. "I say Zeus the Liberator has kept us alive this long for a reason. Cast aside your morbid thoughts, trust to your fates, and play dice. Where's your bets?"

Each man extracted a pebble and called out his bet as Stephanos studied Skopas. Would a man ready to surrender be willing to betray?

Sémon chose not to torture them this time, and the dice gambolled across the floor. "Aphrodite!" bellowed Hybrias at the two sixes. "At last, my luck's turned."

"Good morning, gentlemen." The group was jolted by the arrival of General Eupompides, a muscular man whose energy crackled like static. He indicated for them to remain seated. "Sorry to interrupt. I know how hard it is to find a dice game around here. We are passing on a proposal we will discuss at the next assembly."

"Take a seat, general," said Stephanos, dragging a spare stool into the circle.

"I am not going to coat it in honey," began Eupompides. "There is not enough food for the garrison to survive the spring. We see no option but to try and escape. If some choose to remain, we will ensure there are enough left to defend the walls until we can bring Athens to their relief."

Stephanos reeled. From talk of surrender to hope of escape. Could he really be with Khara and Alexias by the spring? To evacuate Plataea was not to desert it, was it? Thoughts flitted like fireflies. "How would the escape be staged?" he asked.

"The plans are secret for the moment as everything will depend on surprise. Any other questions come and ask me or General Arkadius." Eupompides left for the next group of men gathered around their own cold game.

Stephanos looked at his companions. Sémon scratched his nose, Hybrias hid behind his hair, Mikos twirled his thumbs.

"Sounds like suicide," said Skopas.

"Which one?" asked Stephanos. "Staying or going?"

"Going, of course. We're in no immediate danger here. Out there's only death."

"We're not safe here. When our food runs out, we're finished."

"Obviously," said Skopas. "But then we'll surrender, be taken prisoner, and wait out the war on better rations than we get now."

Stephanos recalled the executions of the Thebans who had invaded Plataea three years ago, and the ogre on the siege walls on the day of the Freedom Festival. "Thebans have long memories."

"We can't trust the Thebans," said Skopas. "But Spartans are in charge out there. We can trust them."

"You really think there's a chance of escape?" asked Hybrias. "I mean, if we got over the walls we could get to Athens, couldn't we?"

"My young friend," said Skopas. "If by some miracle we

clamber the walls, fight off the guards, descend the other side, and start for Athens, their cavalry will hunt us down inside a day and we'll be slaughtered."

"When I was young," began Sémon quietly, "my father took my brother Lakon and me to the plain of Marathon, and described to us the battle he had fought there." The unusual stillness of Sémon's voice gave it added authority. "He was so proud of the part he had played in defeating the Persians. He taught us that Plataeans face their responsibilities." He straightened and resumed his normal volume. "I refuse to sit around like an old hen waiting to be plucked. I prefer to fight and die with honour, like my father, than wait to see Plataea destroyed."

Mikos clapped his hands.

"I don't consider throwing my life away a matter of honour," said Skopas. "You make it sound like some glorious exploit, Sémon, but there's no glory in death. I stood next to my father at the battle of Koronea, and I felt every wretched scream of his as he died, wedged against me. Couldn't even fall to the ground. I saw no glory there, covered in my father's blood."

"I remember your father. A loyal man and a good farmer." Sémon reached below his stool for a terracotta cup of water and nursed the vessel as he continued. "Youth has deserted us enough for us to know that war's not glorious, Skopas. But what will we leave for those young Plataeans safe in Athens? Plataea exists because our fathers and grandfathers refused to accept slavery, even when the town was burnt to the ground and they had no hope left. Plataea will only survive beyond our lives if we wrap it in the idea that freedom is worth sacrifice. If we're to die, then our deaths won't be glorious, no. But our legacy could be."

"Pretty speech," said Skopas, "but how will my death feed my children? It's easy to talk of such sacrifice when you have no wife and children waiting in Athens."

Only Mikos could have detected the grasping fingers of the grave that clawed at Sémon, who took a drink, cleared his throat, and continued. "Look at it this way. If some of us escape, it'll leave more food for the rest of you. And if I'm no longer here, you may have a chance with the women. Perhaps the goddess Tyche might then smile on you, Skopas."

Skopas seemed to realize how careless his remark had been, and he struggled to brighten his face. "Given my luck with the dice, she must favour me with something."

"She will favour me, I know it," said Stephanos. "I'm going to take any chance I get to see my wife and son again. What about you, Hybrias?"

"I miss my family. You really think it can work?"

"The generals will figure out how to do it," said Sémon.

Skopas huffed. "Only if the Assembly agrees."

Chapter 14

The days that followed the generals' proposal echoed to the arguments and accusations of both sides. Inured to imprisonment, men found excuses to stay, masking their fear in logic and patriotism, confidently preaching timidity. Stephanos made his decision; it was not difficult. He would abandon his birthplace and go home to his family. Anticipation of escape revived him, transforming a dream into an expectation, but as he climbed the steps of the open-air theatre, he dreaded that the Assembly would wreck it.

The sun was easing towards its rest as the garrison of Plataea, excepting those on guard duty, filed in to the theatre. The tiers of semi-circular stone platforms could seat six hundred, and halfway up, Sémon led Stephanos and Mikos into a partially empty row. Their sombre leaders occupied a wooden bench on the marble-tiled orchestra below. Stephanos studied the faces of the soldiers, and wondered how many minds were set, and in which direction.

"Don't look so worried," said Sémon. "We'll go even if it's just the three of us."

Four hundred Plataeans had remained to defend their home town, joined by eighty Athenians sent at the start of the war to bolster the garrison and show Athens' support for its ally. Cynics suggested that they were there only to ensure Plataea's loyalty. As usual, the Athenians occupied the first three rows of the theatre, with the Plataeans crowded behind them. The wicker entry doors closed, and the gaunt herald struck the floor with his wooden staff, the theatre reverberating to the noise, silence following.

The herald offered water and thyme on a stone altar before praying. "Gods of Olympus, who rule the heavens and move the seas, who shake the earth and shape the destinies of men. Hear those defending your shrines and temples in Plataea. Recall our past sacrifices of juicy thighbones and do not disdain the meagre offerings we give you now. Favour this assembly with your wisdom and courage."

General Arkadius received a myrtle crown from the herald, and adjusted it as he rose. The grandfather general had lost some physical vigour, but he still commanded respect. He gazed at the farmers, carpenters, cobblers, and merchants seated before him. "Soldiers," he declared. "Winter is coming. We should be ploughing our fields, but here we are, enjoying our neighbours' farts."

A ripple of amusement spread through the theatre.

"Friends, you know the food situation is critical. Stricter rationing may make it last until summer. Either way, there are too many of us. Keep this in mind as General Eupompides continues."

The herald transferred the crown to Eupompides, and a nervous energy flickered through the audience.

Eupompides, an athletic man bursting with vitality, opened his arms. "Friends. We few have defied the enemy for nearly two years. When they tried to storm the town, we were outnumbered, but not outwitted. What we lacked in shields, we made up in courage. So unable to defeat us, they decided to starve us." He paused and looked around the captive audience before pounding his chest and shouting, "But we are still here!" The crowd stood and cheered, fists pumping the air. Stephanos allowed himself to soar on the wave of emotion.

Eupompides motioned for quiet. "My friends, we have brought honour to our families. Let us consider our future actions in the light of that honour. Do we wait for Athens, or do we grasp the hand of Fortune ourselves? We have all heard the things they shout to us. That Athens is filled with plague; that she is besieged; that Perikles is dead and the city will soon surrender. We do not believe it. Athens and her allies will *not* be defeated."

Further raucous agreement and stamping of feet.

"But Athens has been unable to help us so far. It is time to accept that we must look to ourselves. It is time to take matters into our own hands. It is time to fight our way out of Plataea and make our way to Athens, and to freedom."

Eupompides handed the myrtle to the herald as the chamber exploded into cheering, jeering, arguing. The herald asked if anyone wanted to speak, and an angry young Athenian from the front row grabbed the crown, set it on his own head and glared at the herald to re-establish order, which he duly did.

"By Athena, it's about time," said the Athenian. "What have we been waiting for? Are we all cowards that we sit on our hands, too afraid to use them? Walls are to defend women, not for men to hide behind. Athens has not forgotten us, she's just wondering where we've lost our balls. If there's any courage and honour left in us, of course we must escape."

Stephanos and Mikos jumped to their feet to join the applause as the young man resumed his seat. He was replaced by a humourless colleague from the front row.

"Fellow soldiers. I am also Athenian, and my balls are intact, but also my brain. Why did Athens not order our retreat from Plataea when we had the chance? Because of the strategic importance of this place. We have our orders, our duty is clear: hold the town until relieved. To escape is not heroism, it's desertion, plain and simple. We would return to Athens as shield slingers, cowards, our honour in shreds. My city does not abandon its allies, and it would never fail its citizens. Athens will rescue us. I propose stricter rationing so that we can await our relief."

The Athenian received congratulations from his friends as the herald held the myrtle aloft and asked for any more speakers. Stephanos hated speaking in the Assembly – his tongue would thicken, his mind fog, his legs buckle, but he could not sit and watch a thief steal his dream. He edged along his row and walked down to the stage as Sémon gave him a booming clap of encouragement. The herald placed the garland on Stephanos' head, and he felt the weight of his hopes resting on his tongue.

"I agree with points made by all speakers," he began. "Athens will not want to stand by and watch us starved into submission." A chorus of agreement rumbled from the nearby seats. "If Athens mounts a relief effort in the spring, it has no guarantee of success and would incur great risk to the Athenians themselves. If Athens were to fail, what then would become of us?"

Stephanos looked round the grim faces, his mouth a desert. "We'll be too weak to attempt an escape at that point, and we'd have to surrender to those Theban dogs out there. Surely, Athens would see it as a noble act if we were to free ourselves, with no risk to them? I urge support for the proposal of Eupompides. Let's escape and return to our families."

Stephanos allowed the herald to remove the token of authority as the assembly delivered a mixed reaction. Arguments rocked the theatre, and Damon, the oak-legged tanner, stomped to the orchestra to take his turn as Stephanos resumed his seat, Mikos beaming and slapping him on the back.

The herald brought order, and Damon became the focus of attention. "Breakin' out without no Athenian army'd be like suicide. So, honourable plan? I don't think so. Getting over that wall'd be hard enough, but how would we get past them mounted patrols?" Here was a concern that united the garrison. "Give Athens more time. Make the food last 'til summer and don't weaken ourselves by no silly adventures. And don't reduce rations, let the women go. They eat like gannets."

The chamber dissolved into uproar. Cries of 'Who's going to cook our food, mate? You?', 'Just because *you* can't get a ride!', and 'I'll be in Hades before I wash my own clothes', swirled around the assembly with the force of a winter storm. Starvation or no, going without women was unbearable.

When the noise finally abated, a lanky young man, whose angular face was a geometrist's dream, stumbled to the stage and received the myrtle, fidgeting and clearing his throat. "I have, er, a question? I was wondering how safe this might be? We've been betrayed once to those Theban bastards. What if someone tells them we're going to escape? Where would we be? In a sty full of pig's shit, that's where." He started to blush, his fingers playing with the folds in his chiton. "Seeing my babies again sounds great, it sure does, but I want to know if I climb that wall that some sneaky, mangy, flea-infested fox won't make a present of me to those Theban bastards."

The young man relieved himself of the burden on his head and hurried back to his seat. Stephanos wondered again how many traitors remained in Plataea, and whispered to his uncle, "Do you think the boy has a point?"

Sémon nodded. "Everyone thinks it, no one admits it."

Eupompides rose to answer on behalf of his colleagues. "Our young friend makes a brave point." The angular soldier grinned. "It is hard to voice your fears. Once betrayed, it is easy to imagine treachery lurking in every corner, to believe that Theban collaborators remain among us. We will be prudent, but it is time to trust one another. We have survived and battled long enough to have earned each other's respect, and trust. There are only patriots here. Have faith in your generals, vote to escape."

As debate animated the chamber, Sémon commented, "Those that betrayed us last time considered themselves patriots."

"I can't believe we may actually lose this chance," said Stephanos. Athens began to feel as far away as Mount Olympus.

Others spoke, and the Assembly's mood swayed with the wind. Finally, when there was no sign of anyone else willing to argue, cries of "Vote! Vote!" crowded the air.

The herald banged his staff, called out the proposition, and asked for those in favour. Stephanos' hand arrowed upwards, but he saw others' arms remain earthbound, fettered by fear. They were stealing his family. He wanted to throttle them, to throw them down the steps and mangle their bodies in a heap of wasted earth.

"We did it," shouted Sémon, hugging his bemused nephew.

"What?"

"We did it, you thick cow turd. We only needed a third, we got half."

It was true: half the garrison had voted to escape. It was going to happen. He was going to see Khara and Alexias.

Chapter 15

Khara stood before the bronze mirror, gazing at her hair, at the long tresses falling gracefully over her shoulders, the symbol of her womanhood. The scissors in her hand trembled. She had only ever cut her hair when loved ones had died, and now she was to cut it once more in mourning.

She braced herself, raised the scissors, hands shaking, and closed her eyes as she made the first cut. Tears threatened as she held the clump of black hair before her, but she released it, and attacked the rest, channelling her anger and frustration into every thrust of the scissors.

"Momma! Momma! What are you doing?" cried Alexias, running into the room and looking as if someone had stolen his favourite toy.

Khara leant over and kissed his head. "It's okay, baby. It's for the funeral."

Alexias perused the battleground of lost hair. "But your hair, Momma!"

"I know. It will grow back. Go and see if pappu needs any help getting ready."

Alexias left the room, glancing over his shoulder in bewilderment. Khara soldiered on, and when she had finally finished, a stranger stared from the mirror and she felt bare and ugly. She spun away and stepped into the harsh sunlight. "Come on, you two! Time to go," she called.

***

The PanAthenaic Way flowed with black robes like the river of Hades. Professional mourners tore their hair, wailing, clawing their cheeks. Wax death masks glided like daemons as two black oxen dragged a cart draped in black cloth and bearing the dead. Lakon shuffled amidst the ocean of men, his face grim. Behind the men, shorn women cried, ripped their robes, and coated themselves in dust like shades from the Underworld.

Among them, Khara released her grief, free from the daylight mask she wore for Alexias, knowing her son was at the rear of the procession with the other children. She glanced at the bemused onlookers and envied them their safe families.

Not since the death of Perikles had Athens beheld such a funeral, and Khara noted with satisfaction the Athenians' amazement turn to fear as they wondered which general and his army had been massacred. The answer hung on the funeral cart, where a sign proclaimed, "Mourn for the dying of Plataea". The body was an effigy.

The Plataean demonstrations had grown more desperate as winter hardened. The siege of Mytilene on the island of Lesbos consumed Athenian attention, and the fog of politics shrouded Plataea. People needed reminding. The Plataean exiles and their friends wanted to shock Athens into action, but for Khara and the other wives the funeral procession felt like a prophecy, and their grief was genuine. Khara saw her home destroyed, Stephanos lying dead with no coin in his mouth to pay Charon for his passage across the River Styx, his face struck from the world forever. Forever. She branded her mind with his image; she would never forget him.

Her fears for Alexias rose again. He was happy today; what boy wouldn't be? He was playing a trick on Athens, and he had implicit permission to throw dust into the air. Khara could imagine the missiles of dung that would happen to mingle with it. But a fatherless boy growing up in exile was in a perilous position. Poverty, starvation, and slavery salivated with open maws. Khara would not allow that to be his destiny. She muttered another plea to Apollo to rescue her husband.

***

The procession eased past stoas and temples, avoided sheep droppings and cowpats, and finally entered the agora. The swell of noise from the market ebbed away as heads turned to watch the black cloud climbing the slope. Alkibiades and Nikolas joined the fringes of the procession, together with a majority of the shoppers, who seemed mesmerised by the spectacle.

"I didn't see Timokles," muttered Nikolas. "I thought he was going to join them. Do you think he's really with us on this?"

"I thought it best he stayed away so as not to jeopardize his chances of Nikias approving his marriage." Alkibiades smiled at Nikolas' evident disappointment. He listened to the rumours eddying among the crowd that ambassadors from Miletus, Chios and Lemnos were among the mourners. He was pleased: his followers had done their job. The city would talk about this for days.

The procession halted and pressed around the statues of the Eponymous Heroes. The wailing subsided, and the effigy was removed from the cart and carried to the base of the statues. The Athenians craned their necks to see what was happening.

A Plataean grandfather mounted the platform, his cheek scarred with the memory of a spear thrust. "People of Athens," he began in a clear, resonant voice. "The gods have blessed your city above all others. They have brought you wealth and empire, and you have honoured them with homes to rival Mount Olympus. Who could deny that you deserve such blessings? You are the champion of Hellas, freeing all Greeks from the yoke of the Great King."

A field of eyes was fixed upon the speaker's face. Trade had halted, and the only sounds were the bleating of penned animals and the orator's voice.

"But may I remind you," he continued, "who stood beside you on the plain of Marathon? Who has been your loyal ally for over eighty years? The people of Plataea. We are here before the statues of the tribes of Athens, but there is one missing. We are your family, too. We are your eleventh tribe. Will you allow a tribe of Athens to be cut down, its root to wither and die? Will you allow the Spartans to litter the fields of Boeotia with the bones of Athenians? Will you let your enemies accuse you of deserting your brothers?" He paused, and the man's delivery gripped even Alkibiades. "Show the world what it means to be Athenian. Honour the gods and free Plataea."

The orator stepped down to loud applause. "Good choice of speaker," said Nikolas. "Nice speech."

"Thank you," replied Alkibiades. "It should add some pressure to Nikias and the Council." The two of them monitored the reactions around them as the crowd dispersed. Alkibiades noticed Khara leaving with her family. Her hair was short, very short. But it exposed her captivating face, and her dust coating gave her an otherworldly appearance. Stephanos was a lucky man.

"Gentlemen," announced Kallias, arriving with the bejewelled Sellene wrapped around him. Under Nikolas' fierce scrutiny, Kallias pulled his prize closer to him. Sellene's curled hair was uncovered, and a gold butterfly hung from a chain around her neck.

"Did you enjoy the show?" Alkibiades asked Kallias.

"Oh, wasn't it wonderful," burst Sellene. "So solemn. So clever."

"That is a pretty pendant," said Alkibiades, tearing himself from her gaze.

"Oh, yes. Kallias bought it for me. It's a beautiful present. Don't you think so, Nikolas?" She held the butterfly for Nikolas to see, brushing lightly against his arm.

"Not bad, if you like trinkets," mumbled Nikolas.

"I also have the most lovely ankle bracelet. See?" Sellene hitched up the yellow folds of her himation, revealing a delicate gold chain around her ankle.

It was evident to Alkibiades that Nikolas wanted to devour the ankle, and who could blame him? He glanced at Kallias. His brother-in-law was a peacock, and Sellene the stars in his feathers.

"Never mind, Nikolas," said Kallias. "I am sure you will find a real woman of your own one day." Chuckling, he led Sellene away.

Nikolas seemed about to pounce on Kallias, but then Sellene smiled over her shoulder and mouthed, "Visit me!" Nikolas frowned, but as the impact of her words registered, he laughed. "I knew that fool had nothing more to offer than jewellery."

"Be sure he does not catch you," said Alkibiades.

Nikolas snorted. "What's he going to do? Cry to daddy?"

Chapter 16

The sun peeked through the leaves as Timokles strode through the undergrowth of the forest. The fresh morning enlivened his lungs as a squirrel bounded ahead of him and birds vented their joyful songs. He felt excited, free, starting a journey to... somewhere.

Another squirrel leapt onto a nearby tree. He loved those rusty creatures, with their nervous hands and spectacular agility. A squirrel on a branch above him vibrated its tail. A rustle in the heather revealed yet one more, standing and staring at him.

A lot of squirrels today, thought Timokles, smiling as they seemed to follow him.

More rustling. More soldierly squirrels playing a silent anthem with their tails, staring, staring. Timokles' skin began to crawl as the eyes, those unblinking eyes, fastened upon him.

His breathing became laboured, the rustling a waterfall of sound as an army of squirrels infested the undergrowth and swarmed amongst the trees. Timokles tried to run, willing his legs forward, but they were lead. The animals smiled. They actually smiled. A squawk; a sudden rush. They were at him, biting, scratching. He ran. Harder. His arms flailed, hurling the creatures away. He was on a grassy plain teeming with squirrels. He struggled towards the sea. A ball of venomous fur landed on his face, biting. He threw it off, noticing that it had the face of his mother. Others had faces: his uncle; his sister; Alkibiades.

He must escape to the sea. A funerary stele sprang out of the grass, tripping him. Pursued by the excited animals, he tumbled down the hill, coming to rest on his back. A cloud of squirrels rained upon him, paws ready to claw, teeth to bite, his mother in the lead. He screamed. He woke.

It was dark. He was sitting upright, panting, the remnants of the scream echoing in his mind. Had he really made any sound? The house was silent. No rustling.

He took a long breath and lay back down, pulling the blanket around his neck and staring into the blackness. He knew the dream was about the coming day, of course, from which there was no escape.

He longed to wrap his arms around Samias, to hear his soothing breathing, to feel his warm skin. No one was going to come between them.

When the house stirred, Timokles washed away the night's terrors in a bowl of cold water, and headed down for libations and breakfast. His prayers were perfunctory, his food tasteless, his mother and Leaina annoyingly animated. Their blessings chased him out of the house. He had sworn by Hera, Queen of licentious Olympus, and incestuous Protectress of Marriage, that he would deal honourably with Nikias, that he would not sabotage a possible marriage contract. The family had made a significant investment, after all: they knew Nikias relied on his ancient seer, Stilbides, and Timokles' uncle had silvered the hand of prophecy.

Rather than meeting with his uncle, General Nikias had insisted on discussing the marriage proposal directly with Timokles, and so now his traitorous feet led him to a door in a clean white wall. A marble herm stood guard, and Timokles touched his hand to his lips and then to the herm. Hermes may be forgiven his uncertainty as to Timokles' motive for doing so. He knocked, the door opened and Nikias' young assistant, Hiero, ushered the supplicant through the courtyard and into a sunlit room that served as an office. Shelves stuffed with scrolls lined the walls, and wax tablets, styluses, and sheets of papyrus littered two low tables. A white beard was nesting in a corner; it was Stilbides. General Nikias and his younger brother, Eukrates, stood abruptly as Timokles entered.

"Welcome, Timokles. I knew your father. He was a fine man," said Nikias. The general was a stout man whose glowing cheeks contrasted with his sad eyes. He appeared to sag under some enormous load, and Timokles wondered whether his visit was the cause, but Nikias smiled and invited him to sit.

"Good to see you again, Timokles," said Eukrates, a handsome man only five years older than Timokles. Eukrates seemed to be Nikias' counterpoint. Where his brother was vital, the general appeared weary. Eukrates' blue eyes danced, whereas Nikias' drooped. The younger brother was impatient for honour and glory, but the general seemed to accept them as a duty. Timokles sat opposite the brothers, before a low table laden with a silver plate of olives, figs and apples.

"So Timokles, why do you want to marry my daughter?"

The abruptness of the question paralysed Timokles. He had to say something: they were staring at him, waiting. His face burned and he longed to flee, but the rehearsals with his mother and uncle forced themselves upon him. He cleared his throat and found his tongue.

"Your accomplishments, General, make you one of the great Athenians of our day. You have carried the mantle left by Perikles with dignity and honour. Your benefactions to the city have been many and generous, and your family is well respected. These facts make an alliance with your family highly desirable." *A perfect delivery*, he thought.

"The fact that my brother's as rich as Kroesus has nothing to do with it, I suppose," said Eukrates.

Timokles bit his lip. He wanted to melt into the ground.

Nikias smiled and grabbed several olives. "Please, help yourself." Timokles obeyed and gingerly picked an olive. "Marriage finds us all in the end," continued Nikias. "I knew a man, swore by Artemis he would never marry. Ended up marrying three times."

"Really?" said Timokles. "Why?"

"Couldn't hold his drink. Got tricked into it each time, swearing by Dionysus." They all laughed lightly. "Your family must have put quite a bit of pressure on you for this marriage."

"Yes, they did," started Timokles, and then halted, wanting to smack himself. The brothers dissolved into laughter, and Timokles released a sigh. He had done his best. He had not tried to fail, but failed he had. A weight lifted from him.

"You're somewhat young to be in the marriage market, aren't you?" said Nikias.

"That's true, General, in the normal course of things," said Timokles. "But with our losses from the plague there's a duty to raise strong Athenian citizens as soon as possible."

Nikias nodded slowly, studying the young man before him. "There are some men," he began, "who find it difficult to let go of boyish ways and embrace their adult responsibilities."

Timokles had known that Nikias would investigate him, and so he was aware that the general was alluding to Samias. His uncle had told him to lie. Alkibiades had told him to lie. To lie well was a virtue, but Timokles hated deception, and now that the moment had arrived he felt his pride at war with his duty to his family. Like most wars, its outcome was predetermined. "I can assure you, General," said Timokles, gripping the chair cushion, "that I understand and welcome my responsibilities as a citizen of Athens."

"Good." Nikias chewed his olives, and his eyes flicked to his brother.

Eukrates cleared his throat. "Changing the subject, did you hear about the mock funeral yesterday? What did you think?"

The interview was clearly over, and Timokles wondered how his family would react. He would not tell them about his blunder if he could help it. "The funeral was an ingenious way of getting everyone's attention," said Timokles.

"Really?" said Eukrates. "I thought it a rather cheap show."

Timokles wondered if they knew that Alkibiades had organized it. "What do you mean?"

"It's one thing to debate an issue on the basis of its merits, in the Council or the Assembly. But to resort to such a flagrant emotional appeal is…"

"What?"

"It's cheap and manipulative, rousing support for a cause that can't be justified rationally."

"Is that necessarily a bad thing?" Timokles could not let an attack on Alkibiades pass, yet he knew he must remain calm: it made no sense to alienate one of the most powerful families in Athens. "Don't you think that sometimes a logical choice is a heartless one? That as people we should accept that we're as much emotional beings as rational ones?"

Eukrates leaned forward, his right hand emphasizing his points. "That's fine for personal choices, but we're talking of the state. How can a state decide to save one citizen when it would risk destroying all of the others? It can't. And that's why this sort of appeal is so dangerous. It mobilizes the mob, which can be swayed by empty rhetoric and showmanship. They care nothing for nuances. They just want to know whether it's good for them so they can get on with their squalid little lives. They don't care whether it benefits the city."

"Do you really have such a jaundiced view of our citizens?" said Timokles. "They can make highly informed decisions, although I admit there are times when they're swayed by baser instincts. As are we all."

"We can't trust the people to vote for the good of the state. At such a dangerous time, doesn't it make sense for a group of well-informed, impartial citizens to run the government, for the good of everyone?"

Timokles was astonished to hear such a viewpoint in this household, as if they had been coached by the little oligarch, Nikolas. Perhaps the city had misjudged Nikias and his family. "I don't think so," he said. "That would be bad for the city."

"How so?" pressed Eukrates.

"Selfishness and greed aren't limited to the poor or uneducated, and you'll find it hard to find a group of 'impartial' men. An elitist government allows decisions to be made on the basis of a few people's selfish ambitions, whereas now it's hard for an unscrupulous few to dominate the many."

"But not impossible," said Eukrates. "Wouldn't you say that those with the most money have the opportunity to, how shall I put it, enhance their voting potential?"

This was one of the richest families in Athens. Were they deliberately provoking him? He reached for an olive, chewing slowly while he framed his answer. "In theory there is that possibility, but how would they keep such large-scale bribery secret? Once the Assembly found out, the man's influence would be destroyed."

Eukrates smiled and reached for his water, cradling the silver cup, exchanging a fleeting glance with his brother. "You think they'd be stupid enough to use their money so blatantly, Timokles? Think of the lavish entertainments we provide at festivals. Are they not a form of bribery? And as for individuals, imagine a man in debt, about to lose his farm, his birthright. A friend loans him the money. For the sake of friendship, you understand. The wealthy friend hasn't only bought his vote, he's bought something far more powerful. His loyalty."

"Of course I know that. I'm not an idiot. But there's no-one in Athens who could afford to pay off the debts of enough people to make a significant difference."

Eukrates laughed lightly. "They don't need to, Timokles. They can hold out promises of favour, threaten withdrawal of patronage, make life easy or difficult for people just through their network of influence. They don't have to spend ruinous amounts of money."

"Are you advocating such a position? Would *you* buy the city?" snapped Timokles.

Eukrates grinned. "Appealing to people's self-interest wins almost any vote. If we are to save the city, we must make that more difficult. We need people to remember that the city's more important than any individual, and persuade our rising politicians to avoid the methods of men like Kleon. Especially people with talent. Like Alkibiades. You know him well, I understand."

"He's my best friend."

"So you trust him."

Timokles glared at his inquisitor. "With my life."

Eukrates smiled but his eyes remained cold. "I know of him, of course. He's rather young, though, to be meddling in politics already, don't you think?"

"Alkibiades is one of the most talented men I know. His youth shouldn't count against him."

"Hmm... It's not his youth as such, but his...inexperience. His current enterprise, for example. Supporting Kleon's programme is unworthy of an Alkmaeonid."

"Alkibiades is as worthy of the Alkmaeonid family name as Perikles was. It's true that, like Kleon, he supports an aggressive war strategy, and rescuing Plataea is part of that," said Timokles. "He wants to save the city. That doesn't mean he supports Kleon's programme wholesale."

"Perikles, my boy," said General Nikias, folding his arms on his chest and slouching in his chair, "was an exceptional leader. He controlled the Assembly through his wisdom and honesty. With him gone, the scum has floated to the surface. I fear for the future of our democracy."

"Why? You cannot think people want a return to aristocratic rule, General?" asked Timokles.

"Want? No. But that's where we're heading. We have leadership by slogans, government by those who shout loudest, ability secondary to popularity. These men will destroy Athens with their mad schemes and in its ruins our enemies will force us to dismantle the government."

Timokles nodded but said nothing. This was a bleak picture coming from the city's leading military commander. Was he right?

"But we seem to have digressed, somewhat," continued Nikias, leaning forward and glancing at Eukrates. "You came here to discuss my daughter, not the state of Athens." Timokles flushed with the remembrance of failure. "Stilbides over there considers the omens for a connection between our families to be good."

"Yes," croaked the old frog in the corner. "As Apollo's chariot raced towards its nightly rest, I was in the agora by the command of Zeus, and saw an eagle, messenger of the King of Olympus, land on the statue of your tribe, Leontis. It was a clear blessing of the gods."

Timokles hid his disdain during the silver-fed prophecy. Eukrates did not.

"I never make a decision without consulting the gods," said Nikias. "You young people would do well not to forget them. I've made enquiries into your circumstances, Timokles. I wouldn't want to hide that from you. You're from a distinguished family and I believe you to be an honourable young man." He hauled himself to his feet, and the others followed suit. "Timokles, I give you Aristeia that she may bless our families with children in a virtuous marriage."

Timokles stared at his new father-in-law, bewildered. How had this happened? He managed to stammer, "I accept her."

Nikias continued calmly, "I agree to provide her with a dowry of ten talents."

Timokles felt the breath sucked from his chest. It was a huge sum, fit for a princess. Nikias was declaring the value of his love for his daughter in the expectation that Timokles would treat her accordingly. After all, if the marriage failed he would have to return the whole amount. "That's most generous. I accept that, too," he replied.

Nikias grunted his satisfaction at the deal and added, "It's the winter solstice. I suggest she transfers in a couple of weeks. It'll be the middle of the month of Gamelion, very propitious for new couples."

They shook hands. Before Timokles could gather his wits, Hiero had been called and led him, dazed, back through the courtyard and out the door. He stood marooned in the middle of the street. He had a wife, a wife he would not recognize if he met her in the agora. And a dowry of ten talents. His family's future was secure. But at what cost?

***

"Congratulations. You have a son-in-law," said Eukrates, biting into an apple.

"Yes. A little idealistic and naive at the moment, but I believe he'll do." Nikias clasped his hands and leaned back in his chair. "So, Alkibiades really is involved with Kleon and Plataea, as we suspected. It's not good that the Alkmaeonids side with that tanner. They should be with us. We'll have to consider what to do."

Nikias threw two more olives into his mouth, knowing that this was not the time to worry about Alkibiades. That would be just an excuse to delay a task he had dreaded for years: he must tell his beloved daughter she was to leave home. It was long past time, of course. Aristeia was nineteen, and had his wife lived he was sure his daughter would have been married several years ago, but the thought of a house devoid of her kindness and laughter emptied him. He sighed and dragged himself towards the door. "I must talk to my daughter."

The front courtyard was stark, two storeys supported by wooden columns, a stone altar, hard-packed earth, a mirage of frugality. Yet even here his daughter, confined to the rear of the house most of the time, had made a mark: potted plants, climbing ivy, a wooden bench from which her father could enjoy the sun.

Nikias paused by the altar, recalling Aristeia's giggles as she took her first steps from her mother's arms to his, not two yards from the spot where he was standing.

He passed through the connecting door and entered the sumptuous second courtyard. It was surrounded by Ionic columns and plants hung from every balcony. The tiled floor was dazzling in the sunlight, and a finely carved marble altar sat in the centre. Three female slaves carried jars of onions and leeks, and an amphora of water, from the storeroom on the far side to the kitchen. An image flashed across his mind: Aristeia, six years old, striding round the house, her two younger brothers tripping after her as she imitated Thea Glukera's control of the household. The children had been motherless for three years at the time, and the boys had already fallen under their sister's spell, as if she had been their mother. At six.

They're not the only ones under her spell, he thought, pausing in the shade to take a deep breath. He had argued in the Assembly, stood trial in the courts, seen friends die beside him on the battlefield, but nothing prepared him for this. How was one supposed to sell your child as if she were a goat, and not the most precious treasure you had?

Nikias cleared his throat and stepped towards the closed door of Aristeia's workroom. He hesitated on the threshold, listening as she sang a popular hymn in praise of Aphrodite. He tasted every note, waiting until she had finished the entire refrain.

He entered the room, and Aristeia looked up from her weaving. "Father! What a lovely surprise." Aristeia's ocean-green eyes and ready smile outshone the sun for Nikias. She rose to meet him but stopped short when she saw his face. "What's the matter?"

"Nothing's the matter, my child." He smiled and kissed her on the forehead. "Sit down. There's something I have to tell you." Aristeia lowered herself gracefully on to a couch and folded her hands neatly in her lap. Nikias raised his eyebrows at her maid, Armina, who rose and left the room. "You've grown into such a lovely young woman. Your mother would have been very proud."

Aristeia smiled. "Thank you, Father. I wish I could remember her."

"I know you do. I know. And you must also know that I wouldn't allow just anyone to marry you. They must deserve you." The colour drained from her face. She trembled, clasping her hands, but he had no choice. It had to be done. He blurted, "I've received an offer of marriage from a young man of note and I've decided to accept it. I've given you to Timokles, son of Alkisthenes, of the tribe of Leontis."

The world was broken, he had broken it. He had sold her like a slave in the market.

His daughter was silent, her eyes cast downwards. A ragged sigh escaped her, but after a moment she shook herself, straightened, and said, "I'm honoured to do what you think best, Father."

Nikias released the breath he had held, and raised her by the hands. "My heart sinks like iron to think of your absence from this house. But I believe he'll be a kind husband."

Aristeia squeezed his hands. "I'll miss you and my brothers, too." She looked to the ground for an instant before meeting her father's eyes. "I know Timokles' sister, Leaina. Her husband was a cousin of yours, remember? She adores her brother, so I'm sure your judgment is right."

Nikias clasped her hands to his chest. "You're such a good girl." He kissed her, turned, and escaped to his work, leaving Aristeia staring at the closed door.

Chapter 17

Being pregnant, Hipparete should have been overjoyed like the rest of her family, not scared out of her sleep. She ached for a child, for a son that would seal Alkibiades' love and fulfil her purpose in life, but the birth stalked her, waiting with a grim smile for her approach. Aunts, cousins, friends had died giving birth, as if the breath of a mother was life's price of admission.

She pulled her thick himation around her neck and glanced up at the dazzling full moon. Deinomache stood beside her, entombed in a brown tunic. Her friend, Leaina, and Nikopatra completed the party, which was illuminated by the torches surrounding the shrine of Hekate. The goddess glared upon them from her pedestal, her three faces watching each road of the intersection, her jet-black hair crowned with flowers. She held a sword before her as snakes writhed in the folds of her black peplos. The goddess unnerved her, but Hekate must be placated for the sake of the baby.

In her arms she cuddled a whining puppy, as black as Hades, with large, begging eyes. Deinomache, encouraged by Hipparete's father, Hipponikus, had insisted not only that they sacrifice to Artemis of Childbirth, but that every conceivable god and goddess must be bribed to avert evil from the child. Tonight was Hekate's turn.

Hipparete did not mind. It was one more sign of her own importance, which would continue to grow with her belly. In recent days Alkibiades had been even more tender, her father solicitous. Even Deinomache had treated her with respect and kindness, and Hipparete revelled in the attention. Deinomache still ruled the house with a clenched fist, but when Hipparete's son was born, *she* would run the house with kindness, and the courtyard would no longer echo with Deinomache's screeching.

Leaina blew warmth into her hands, her face partially obscured by her cloak's scarlet hood. A basket of cakes sat on the ground before her. Hipparete liked Leaina. She was clever, but honest and straightforward, and never talked down to her – traits not shared by Nikopatra. Nikopatra was Deinomache wrapped in less expensive cloth. The two older women had sparred since childhood. Their mothers had been friends, their husbands had been friends, their sons were friends, but Hipparete did not believe Deinomache and Nikopatra to be friends. They were two scorpions manoeuvring to sting each other.

The puppy was restless, and Hipparete calmed it with a kiss, tickled its ears, and held it closer. Deinomache picked up a jug of water and purified their hands. She replaced the jug and raised her hands to the goddess. "Lady Hekate of the three roads, granddaughter of the mighty titans Koeus and Phoebe, accept these offerings."

Leaina handed over the basket of cakes, and Deinomache lit the miniature torches on the cakes one by one before placing them on the pedestal steps. She raised her hands once more. "Powerful Hekate of the three faces, we ask your special favour. Protect my unborn grandchild and bring him to a safe birth. Shield him from evil. To show our gratitude we offer you a blood sacrifice."

Deinomache sprinkled water on the puppy's forehead. The dog whimpered and writhed in Hipparete's arms until she soothed it. Deinomache held out her arms, a smile grazing her eyes. They had bought the puppy that morning as a gift particularly pleasing to Hekate, but Hipparete held on to him.

"It has been promised to the goddess, Hipparete," said Deinomache.

Hipparete knew it. There was no choice. A goddess could not be disappointed. She clung to the black bundle a few moments longer, smelling its freshly washed coat, before allowing Deinomache to take him. Hipparete fastened her eyes on the ground, struggling to close her ears to the whines. Leaina squeezed her arm.

Deinomache carried the offering to the stone altar, and allowed it to stand and sniff the dismembered head of a red mullet, before jerking the pup's head back and slashing a knife across its throat. She held the dog until its struggle ended. She left its body on top of the altar as she turned to her companions. "Let us get out of this awful cold."

Hipparete did not look back as they hurried from the shrine, accompanied by three slaves bearing torches. They were soon safely quarantined in the family room of Alkibiades' house, huddled around the flames of the central hearth as they removed their outer garments and replaced their leather shoes with house slippers. Paintings adorned two walls: harvest workers; Dionysus sailing, surrounded by dolphins; all illuminated by oil lamps on bronze stands in the form of palm trees.

"I love the paintings in this room," said Leaina, as she sat on one of the chairs around the hearth and held her hands to the fire.

Deinomache fingered her ruby necklace and golden hair comb, and then carefully arranged the folds of her sky-blue peplos as she nodded acceptance of the praise. "I have probably told you before that the famous painter, Agarthakus of Samos, was kind enough to spend time with us and furnish several of our rooms with his work."

Nikopatra's stern eyes dissolved into a smile. She knew Alkibiades had imprisoned the poor fellow until he had finished, although Alkibiades had amply compensated the artist afterwards. She had never understood how Alkibiades got away with such scandalous behaviour. "It must've been difficult keeping Agarthakus here when he was in such high demand," she said.

Deinomache's eyes were cold. "He was well rewarded."

"Still, they are good paintings," continued Nikopatra, "though I hear Zeuxis of Heraklea is better. Apparently he painted a bunch of grapes so realistically that birds came to peck at them."

"Really?" said Hipparete, her cheeks still flushed from the cold. "That's wonderful."

"Whose is the armour?" asked Leaina, indicating the bronze breastplate and helmet that dominated one wall.

Deinomache visibly thawed. "That, my dear, is the prize that General Phormio awarded to my son for outstanding bravery at Potidaea. He was only twenty at the time, yet no-one could compare with him."

"I heard that the philosopher Sokrates saved Alkibiades' life on that campaign," said Nikopatra sweetly.

"Such nonsense. The boasts of a filthy, godless man," returned Deinomache.

"How many moons before the birth?" Leaina asked Hipparete hurriedly.

"We think it is five or six to go," said Deinomache. "And how healthy she looks! Are you quite comfortable, my sweet?"

Hipparete smiled. "Yes, thank you. Although some grapes would be nice."

Deinomache broke a sprig of grapes out of a silver bowl and handed them to Hipparete. "Here you are, darling."

"So early summer, then," said Nikopatra. "I always think that's a good time to give birth."

"Yes," said Deinomache. "The temperature is always pleasant. And boys born in the month of Skirophorion grow up to be so much stronger."

"Is that so?" said Nikopatra.

"Oh, yes. You know that. Perikles was born then, Themistokles, and even Achilles, I believe." She ignored Nikopatra's dubious look and turned back to Hipparete. "Would you like something to drink, Hipparete? Are you sure you are comfortable? I can get one of the slaves to bring you a bigger cushion."

"No, thank you, Mother." Hipparete felt the phrase choke her: Mother? Perhaps Supreme Toad-in-law would be more appropriate. She smiled and added, "I'm perfectly comfortable, for the moment."

"Alkibiades was born in the winter, wasn't he?" asked Nikopatra, tilting her face.

"Yes, but you know Alkibiades is exceptional," said Deinomache. "The gods would have favoured him no matter when he was born. He is becoming one of the most important men in the city already, working for the good of Athens. Quite a political impact he is having." Deinomache picked an olive, precisely, transferring it smoothly to her mouth in a manner suggesting that this, and only this, was the way to eat an olive. "Still," she continued, smiling, "politics can be a dangerous game in Athens. You must be relieved that Timokles has no ambitions."

A muscle in Nikopatra's cheek twitched for an instant. "My son's young. As with all men, he must learn to rule himself before having the audacity to lead others."

"That's a lovely material, Hipparete," said Leaina. "It looks very soft and warm."

Hipparete beamed, stroking the folds of her purple himation, the colour of royalty. "Oh, it is. Feel it. Woven in Ekbatana itself, Father said. He visited recently and was so sweet. He gave it to me as a present to keep the baby and me warm."

"It's gorgeous. And I don't remember seeing that necklace before. Is it new?"

Hipparete stroked her delicate new treasure, a waterfall of gold and silver. "Yes. Isn't it lovely? When I'm in the sun it glows. Alkibiades bought it for me. He's so good to me."

"And are you hoping for a beautiful baby daughter?" asked Nikopatra.

Hipparete glanced at Deinomache before answering. "I'll be glad to have a healthy baby. Although I know it will make lots of people especially happy if it's a boy."

"Of course it will be a boy," announced Deinomache, leaning towards Nikopatra as if to impart some great confidence. "I consulted a seer. I asked her about the baby and she said, 'He will bear arms like no other.' You see? He is going to be a great warrior and continue our family's fame." She sat back, exalting in the unassailable nature of her evidence.

Nikopatra nodded, frowning, seemingly dazzled. "That's impressive. What will you name him?"

"Kleinias, of course," said Deinomache, "after his grandfather. And talking of impressive, I am very glad that Timokles has finally found someone who will marry him."

"My son never felt the need to rush into an imprudent marriage. When a man marries too young, it never ends well."

"That depends on the man, dear," said Deinomache. "My son is about to provide an heir already. I think some men just grow up more quickly than others. Are you worried that Timokles may not be ready to give up his boyish desires?"

The allusion to Samias struck at the heart of Nikopatra's own fears, and she struggled to maintain her outward composure.

"Oh, it's wonderful that Timokles will marry Aristeia," burst

Leaina.

"Do you know her?" asked Hipparete.

"Yes, quite well. You'll like her. She's very sweet and loving. I think she'll make Timokles happy."

"And of course," added Nikopatra, "she's the daughter of the richest and most influential man in Athens. And she comes with a huge dowry. Ten talents! But I think happiness is also important in a marriage, don't you? When a man's devoted to his wife and enjoys her company, life's so much easier for everyone. No need for deceit or sneaking around."

The smile on Deinomache's face belied her volcanic eyes.

"I so agree," said Hipparete. "I'm so lucky to have Alkibiades for my husband. He's completely devoted to me and our family name. He's always busy on our behalf. He even helps my friend, Khara. He's so active all the time."

Nikopatra gave her a sympathetic look. "Yes, dear. Very active."

Chapter 18

One more day to go. One last exercise. Stephanos was elated at the prospect of escape. The hollowness of their existence was now filled with purpose, and the possibility of seeing Khara and Alexias again filled him with a strength and power that he had forgotten. Yet he was grieved to abandon the land and graves of his ancestors, and haunted by guilt at deserting men he had fought beside.

Stephanos pounded the twisting streets of Plataea in the midst of two hundred soldiers armed only with daggers and spears, shields slung over their backs. A sliver of moon lit their way. Speed and stealth would be needed for tomorrow's escape, and for the past week they had trained in the moonlight, colliding and cursing, but they could now manoeuvre smoothly. However, tonight would be different. To prepare them for the real flight, General Eupompides would lead them over the partially cleared ground of the burnt southern quarter, to simulate the fields outside.

Stephanos glanced to his left where the smoothness of Mikos' stride and the power of Sémon were unmistakable. Conical felt caps crowned their heads in place of bronze helmets, for the sake of speed. Stephanos was in the middle of a rank of five soldiers, and his stride stuttered as they entered the broken ground. The pace slowed, and the soldiers struggled to avoid noisy clashes. He strained to see the ground, but the men in front obscured it. His ankle turned and he sprang to avoid injuring it. His shin banged against a piece of masonry, and he winced but made no sound as he stumbled and picked up the pace again, silently cursing the exercise, trying to tread like a mountain goat.

A veil of cloud extinguished the moon. Mikos grunted and veered to his left, colliding with Sémon. Stephanos grabbed Mikos' arm to keep him from falling as Sémon switched his spear and caught his friend's other arm. Between them they hauled Mikos along, remaining in formation but continuing to stagger and slip, crashing into each other, their clanging shields betraying their predicament. An angry "Quiet!" accused them from ahead.

The pace increased when they reached the dirt road once more, and by the time they arrived at the fire-lit agora, Stephanos and Sémon were breathing heavily. The company halted, and Eupompides addressed them. "Well done, men. Get a good day's rest tomorrow. Dismissed."

The soldiers dispersed, removing their armour and weapons as they headed for the warmth of the law courts. Mikos collapsed onto the cold steps and removed his shield before grasping his ankle, his head buried in his chest.

"Let's see," said Sémon, frowning as he knelt down.

"Let me have a look," commanded Eupompides. He took over from Sémon and examined the ankle. "How is it? Not so good?" The general gradually twisted the ankle, and Mikos grimaced and tensed. Eupompides gently released the leg and sighed. "I am sorry, Mikos. You cannot come with us."

"What do you mean?" exploded Sémon. "Of course he can come with us. His ankle will be fine tomorrow."

"I am sorry, Sémon, it won't. He will slow us down and we cannot afford that. I am sorry, Mikos."

Mikos shrugged, and Eupompides turned to leave, but Sémon stopped him with a hand on his shoulder.

"He won't slow us down, General. Stephanos and I will help him. We can keep him going at the same pace as everyone else. We did it tonight."

"You did it for three hundred yards. We will be on the road for up to two days. It is not possible."

Sémon stooped beside his friend. "If Mikos isn't going, then neither am I." Mikos thumped Sémon on the arm. "Ow! What was that for?"

Mikos stabbed a finger at Sémon and then repeatedly jabbed towards the mountains, his face flushed with anger.

"No, Mikos. You chose to stay with me. I swear by Apollo I'm not leaving here without you."

"It is your decision, Sémon," said Eupompides. "I will be sorry to lose you. If you decide to stay, report to Arkadius who will assign you to the diversion." Sémon nodded and the general left.

Stephanos held his head in his hands. It was one thing to desert comrades, but how could he possibly abandon his uncle and Mikos? He could not. But Khara and Alexias waited for him in Athens. How could he stay behind? He could not. His fingers curled and gripped his hair, and a groan escaped him. "If you two are staying, then so am I."

Mikos glared at Sémon, who smiled, patted him on the shoulder, and stood. He placed his hands on his nephew's shoulders and gazed into his eyes. "Stephanos, the three of us are brothers, but you can't stay here. Our ancestors' blood runs in your veins. It's your duty to me, and to your father, to make sure our family lives on. We can't be the reason you don't see Khara and Alexias again – it wouldn't be fair. My wife isn't to be found in Athens, but yours is."

Stephanos started at the mention of his uncle's dead wife. "I... I can't leave you."

Sémon hugged him tightly and whispered into his ear, "You must."

Chapter 19

It was a perfect night for an escape. Olympus was in turmoil, and in their frustration with each other, the gods hurled their malice at the Earth. The wind howled as it ripped through the mountains, and thunder and swirling snow rolled down the plains.

Stephanos waited in the street among the mass of men facing the North Gate. He was damp and cold, but he barely noticed: at any moment the gate would open and release him to death or to freedom.

A soldier stooped beside a clay water clock, watching by the light of an oil lamp for the flow to stop. Coordination with the diversion was crucial. At last, the stout gates began to move, complaining softly, but they did not betray those they had protected for so long.

The small army jogged through the gate and turned left onto boggy ground, each man wearing only one shoe so that he could grip with at least one foot in the ice-encrusted mud. Their senses strained to penetrate the darkness to ensure that no spears clashed nor shields banged. After a hundred yards, they turned towards the enemy wall, aiming for a section between two guard towers, within which the sentries would be cocooned beside their fires.

They raced to the walls, and erected five ladders against the battlements. There was no sound of alarm, and the first two rows of men clambered up. Stephanos' muddy feet had little grip on the ladder, and his free hand was stiff with cold, but he climbed steadily, his shield bumping against his back. He jumped over the battlements at the top, slung his shield round to his front, and ran towards the enemy guards huddled beside their comfortable fire.

The sentries barely had time to register their shock before spears and daggers extinguished them. Stephanos looked back to the tower beyond the ladders, a hundred yards away. Its guards were also dead and there was still no sign of alarm. Three of the men with him splashed through the blood to hide from the enemy soldiers at the next tower. Down the open stairwell in the middle of the tower, Stephanos could hear shouting and laughter. Plataean archers climbed to the top of the flat-roofed towers and more men swarmed onto the wall, a larger unit joining Stephanos.

General Eupompides directed operations on top of the battlements. The men pulled up ladders and lowered them on the far side of the wall, and then climbed down towards freedom as fast as others came up. Eupompides strode from one side to the other. Everything was going well.

Epaphras, a young iron worker with Heraklean shoulders, reached the top of a ladder and grinned at the smell of liberty. He leapt onto the battlements, but as he stepped down onto the wall, the tile beneath his foot began to slip. He jumped off and reached for the loose tile, but it was too late. The siren scraped across the bricks before crashing onto his comrades below.

Everyone stopped.

Stephanos cursed but did not look around for the source of the noise; his eyes were riveted on the enemy soldiers in the tower ahead. Two sentries emerged without their helmets, holding swords and torches uncertainly before them. "How goes it?" shouted the fat one in front when he was less than thirty yards away.

"Bloody cold!" replied Stephanos.

The sentry kept coming, warily, squinting against the snow. Stephanos willed him to turn back, and muttered a prayer to Apollo.

"What's the watchword, friend?" called the guard.

Stephanos looked round his companions and shrugged, and as they gripped their weapons tighter, Stephanos yelled back, "Traitorous Thebes, betrayers of Hellas!"

The sentry turned to raise the alarm, but an arrow sliced open his thigh and another pierced his neck, releasing an arc of blood as he fell to the ground. The soldier twenty yards behind him yelled, "Attack! Attack! Man the walls." Arrows struck his calf and then his shoulder before he dragged himself to safety.

Suddenly there was a riot of activity in the stairwell below Stephanos, and he signalled his men to take positions around the opening. Feet pounded up the stairs, and two hoplites emerged, only to be sent tumbling back with ravaged faces. They did not try that way again. Instead, soldiers poured out of the tower ahead, forming a wall of shields and spears, cursing and shouting as they adjusted their hastily donned armour.

"Four shields deep! Four shields deep!" cried Stephanos. He joined the front rank of four men to block the tower exit, another three ranks behind him, and braced himself. Now it began.

***

On the south side of Plataea, the wind had a new rival. Sémon bellowed his fury as he rushed through the South Gate with the remainder of the garrison. His anger at the Fates had lashed him in to a rage that he could only express in battle. The beating of shields and the roar of the soldiers around him carried swiftly to the Theban sentries, whose torches floated eerily above the enemy wall. Archers on the flanks of the attackers halted and took aim at the targets. Panicked shouts emanated from the wall.

The driving snow stung Sémon's eyes, increasing his murderous rage. Someone was going to pay for Mikos' misfortune. To be responsible for trapping his friend beside him at the start of the siege was burden enough, but to have the opportunity of redemption stolen by a sprained ankle was going to be avenged.

Ladders clattered against the enemy wall, and a flood of soldiers rushed up. Sémon raised his shield above his head and followed Pasikles, a boy with faster legs. The sentries had rallied, and missiles flew at the ladders. An arrow thumped into Pasikles' thigh, and he cried out as he swivelled, lost his grip, and fell to the ground.

Sémon's pace did not change. His roar reached a crescendo as he scaled the battlements and launched himself into the cluster of enemy soldiers. With two swipes of his shield, he created a momentary retreat by those who opposed him. He brought his shield firmly before him, looked over its rim through the tunnel vision of his bronze helmet, and jabbed with his spear. Comrades quickly joined him, forming a solid line of spears and locked shields that forced back the few enemy soldiers that had mustered.

More Plataeans hurried over the battlements behind the front spreading along the wall in both directions. The increasing numbers of

Thebans fought desperately, but struggled to stand their ground against the impenetrable barrier that pushed them backwards.

Sémon was a breath away from the enemy, glaring into the panicked blue eyes of the boy before him, unable to reach him – his long spear jabbed at the necks of men three rows back. Weapons probed his own weak spots from unseen hands beyond the Theban front ranks, and iron spear heads crashed against his shield, his helmet, his breast plate.

The men behind him pressed forward, their added weight forcing the Thebans back. Sémon's helmet muted the clamour of battle, and his own yells and grunts dominated other sounds. He did not think – there was no time. His mind and body united. There was him, there was everything else. No inner conflict, no inner tension. Everything hurled outwards at those trying to destroy him.

Fear infected the eyes of the soldiers before him. They had been relaxing around a warm fire only minutes earlier. Now they were fighting for their lives, retreating ever faster before the beast rolling upon them.

The ground beneath Sémon's feet became slippery, and the smell of excrement and urine mingled with their sweat. His spear sliced an exposed neck, and blood cascaded on to those nearby. The Thebans at the back began to melt away. The mischievous god Pan rushed to the front and the Theban line disintegrated.

The Plataeans surged forward. An enemy guard tripped and fell onto his back. Sémon's spear ravaged his groin, the man's screams cut short by a further spear thrust to the throat, his blood spattering Sémon's legs. He moved on, hunting for more targets.

The Thebans fled along the wall, but a new sound joined the night's chorus, and the Plataeans halted and reformed their lines to prepare for the real battle. Compact ranks of the enemy garrison, now led by Spartans, marched towards them from both directions, beating their shields and singing a paean to Apollo. The fleeing soldiers turned around, either heartened by the reinforcements or cowed by their friends' bristling spears.

"Stand firm, men," General Arkadius' voice rang out from the midst of the Plataeans. "We just need to hold them awhile."

Sémon stood braced within Ares' temple of shields, and watched the disciplined ranks of soldiers approach as a tingle ran down his spine. A light from north of the town broke through the wintry gloom. An enormous fire was burning on the enemy wall. The alarm had been raised. The beacon was a signal to the city of Thebes, less than eight miles away, to send their army. It would end any chance of a successful escape.

It was time for Mikos to act.

***

On Plataea's wall, Mikos wrapped his fleecy coat around himself and bobbed up and down. His torch defied the angry weather as he scanned the glow of the fires inside the enemy watch towers. He bent into the wind and limped along the wall. Out of the dark, a tower emerged, and Mikos climbed the internal ladder to the roof. He ducked as he passed underneath the tent that provided token protection from the damp for the mountain of wood on top of the tower. He assured himself that the kindling was dry, and hobbled outside again to resume his watch. He strained his ears, but heard only the thunderous wind. Was that a good sign or bad? Shouldn't the escape have started by now?

Mikos wondered whether he would ever see either of his friends again. They were his only family. He had but shadowy memories of his parents. He had been snatched into slavery as a young child, and the brutality of a Corinthian mistress had left him capable only of incoherent noises. He refused to make such a racket, and so he lived in silence. After a bitter young life, he had been sold to Sémon and found himself in a home for the first time. Although a slave, little time passed before he had needed no commands to fulfil his duties. His one-time master had become his dearest friend and longed-for father. He knew Sémon would be at the forefront of the action, avoiding arrows and dodging spears. But could he evade them all? In battle, skill and bravado were never enough. A soldier needed the favour of Ares and Apollo to survive, and the favour of the gods had been lacking recently. Mikos' stomach churned in an echo of the wind.

He would never see Stephanos again. Even in the unlikely

event that Stephanos reached Athens, Mikos felt little optimism for those left behind. Though Sémon laughed and joked about it, Mikos knew him well enough to know that he agreed. Their one chance of survival had disappeared as Mikos' ankle had swelled.

There was a new sound, snatches of banging and shouting, and Mikos looked up the hill towards the South Gate. The diversion had started. He imagined showers of arrows rising into the air and starting their descent towards Sémon's exposed face. How could he possibly escape Death? Sémon would fall into the bloody mud, left to stare blindly into the night. Mikos gripped the wall.

There was still no sound from the northern wall, yet they must have started their escape, so why couldn't he hear anything?

Two hundred yards away a light burst into life on the enemy wall, a raging fire throwing back the darkness. The warning beacon. Mikos rushed to his own pile of wood, ignoring the pain in his ankle, and ducked beneath the tent and poured oil over the logs and branches. He threw aside the jar and lit the oil in several places before thrusting his torch into the heart of the pile. His beacon began to roar its own battle cry, consuming the tent.

Mikos glanced around the rest of Plataea and saw similar fires take hold, a glowing necklace around the town visible through the veil of snow. He looked northwards towards Thebes, and prayed they had sown enough confusion to delay the dispatch of the Theban army.

***

The Plataean archers on top of the towers maintained a deadly fire on the northern wall, causing the soldiers attacking Stephanos' unit to hesitate. More hoplites reinforced Stephanos' men as the enemy ranks raised their shields against the arrows and charged noisily over the broken bodies of those already fallen.

Stephanos was in the front rank, his shield locked with his neighbours' in the exit of the tower. He launched a drawn out yell, and the enemy's spears surged past his head as they crashed into the Plataeans with a deafening roar. His shield scraped against an enemy shield as he shoved with all his strength, spearheads clattering against his breastplate, wails of pain surrounding him, the wind and swirling snow pelting him.

He could smell the ugly breath of the man straining against him, could see the hatred in his eyes. A spear from the third rank jabbed towards him, and Stephanos jerked his head aside, the weapon grazing his felt helmet. His neck was wet – blood, but the scream from behind him told him it was not his own. There was no time to think of his narrow escape, or the loss of another friend as the supporting pressure from behind slackened briefly.

The two forces maintained their deathly embrace as Plataeans continued to escape over the wall. There was a shout from the archers above – the beacon had been lit, Thebes had been summoned. Eupompides urged on the men still climbing the wall as he maintained a close watch on the status of the two towers. A break in either line would require rapid action. He breathed a little easier when the Plataean fires began their deceptive displays. Everything depended on avoiding detection by the main army in Thebes and any cavalry that supported the siege.

The general stepped to the inside battlements and peered down again. Two dozen men left. He ordered the archers on high to withdraw, and they rushed down from the towers and descended the wall into the muddy ditch below. The first of them had clawed their way out of the steep-sided ditch when a warning cry arose, and Eupompides darted to the outside battlements, shielded his eyes against the snow, and spotted the danger. His heart sank.

Several hundred yards away, a massed column of torches approached from outside the wall. The plan had failed. The Thebans had not been fooled. His men below awaited slaughter.

Eupompides prepared to order a retreat to Plataea, but he noticed that the column was approaching more slowly than he expected. He strained his eyes, and realized they were not cavalry, they were foot soldiers, around three hundred men trotting towards them. Where had they come from? Had they been betrayed? Trapped between the Thebans on the wall and the force outside, should they go forward or come back?

Eupompides yelled at the soldiers assembled in the dark beyond the ditch. "Form up! Five shields deep! Archers and javelins in front, aim at the lights. Spears wait for close contact." At least they had the advantage of the darkness.

A quick check on the other side of the wall confirmed that only a few soldiers remained. "Slow retreat!" he barked at those holding the towers.

Stephanos and his comrades slowly gave ground, withdrawing from the tower, the ranks extending the full width of the wall. The thinning line started to buckle. The controlled retreat was in danger of becoming a rout.

The general bellowed orders to those below. "Give cover to the walls!"

Some of the archers and javelin throwers beyond the ditch released their missiles into the compacted Thebans, easing the pressure on the Plataean lines.

Young Hybrias was one of the last to clamber on to the wall. He sprinted to the far side, grasped the ladder, and froze when he saw the mass of light and noise approaching the men below. *The cavalry was here.* He wheeled around as a javelin pierced Eupompides' neck. The two men stared at each other, trapped between lines of battle in an eternal moment of horror, until the general tumbled backwards over the battlements. Hybrias stared at the empty space the general had occupied. "We're all lost!" he screamed. He darted back across the wall and hurtled down the ladder, followed by the two men with him, fear snapping at their heels as they bolted back towards the gate, back towards Plataea.

Stephanos heard Hybrias' cry behind him, but he could not turn to see the cause. Was the cavalry here? Was his end really at hand? The thoughts flashed like lightning across his mind as he continued to be forced back, step-by-step, not totally under his control.

"The ladders!" cried a voice from the rear of the unit.

Stephanos waited for the command from Eupompides. It did not come. They were out of time. Stephanos gave the command. "Charge!" The Plataeans surged forward with a supreme effort, forcing the Thebans back several paces. "Disengage!" The Plataeans ran for the ladders, their archers below giving cover for their escape as the enemy hoplites faltered for a few critical moments.

Stephanos flung his spear aside, leapt over the wall and slid down the ladder, burning the skin from his hands. His arm was still through the bands of his shield as he crashed into the mud and fell backwards in the ditch. Enemy soldiers peered over the battlements as he struggled to release himself from the clutches of the mud. Stephanos never saw the approach of the spear that punctured the snowy camouflage. As he turned onto his side to push himself up, the spear thumped into his shield, burrowing through the layers of wood and bronze to graze his arm. He struggled to his feet and raised the shield above his head as he scrambled to escape the shooting gallery.

The bank disintegrated wherever he attempted to gain a foothold. He wrenched the spear from his shield and used it to propel himself upwards, but his feet continued to slither and slide. Arrows and javelins thudded into the mud around him. His feet kicked into the bank, but still he was unable to find the freeing grip. Torches appeared on the wall to light the targets below. Stephanos tensed for the enemy missile that would end his struggle.

"Here," an urgent voice shouted from above, "hold out your spear."

Stephanos raised the enemy spear and gripped tightly. A powerful lift gave wings to his feet as his saviour hauled him over the bank. "Thanks," breathed Stephanos through his covering of mud.

"No problem. Come on, let's join the others." Stephanos followed him away from the dangerous walls, but he had no time to savour his freedom. His comrades were in the midst of another battle. In ranks five deep, the hoplites waited behind the row of archers, who continued to unleash their arrows into the midst of a blaze of torches fifty paces ahead of them. Stephanos' heart skipped, expecting cavalry to ride them down, but then he realized that it was a troop of lightly armed Thebans. As he watched their hesitant advance, the body of torches started to evaporate as individuals escaped from the pack like shooting stars.

"Hoplites, prepare to charge." The order echoed along the ranks, and Stephanos took a deep breath. When the enemy's disarray had reached a critical point, the shout arose, "Charge!"

Stephanos raised his battle cry once more, ran past the archers, and appeared in the full light of the enemy torches. Those Thebans who had had the courage to continue the march towards an unseen enemy, now broke as it came into full view. Their lines collapsed as they threw torches aside and flew into the night. Stephanos sprinted after them, a hound baying for blood.

"Halt! Ranks of five!" The command halted Stephanos and his comrades, and they jostled into a snaking line five soldiers wide. "Where is General Eupompides?" Silence greeted the question from Ammias, the second-in-command. He strode further down the line. "Has anyone seen the general?" Still no answer. Ammias did not falter. There was no time for conjecture or grief. "We continue the plan. Fast march!"

The column jogged across fields they had once tended, and headed towards Thebes. They fell into a steady rhythm, and Stephanos had a chance to think. They were outside! For the first time in two years he felt open ground beneath his feet. The air seemed purer, his limbs freer. But where had that troop of soldiers come from? Did it mean the diversion had failed and the cavalry was on its way? Stephanos listened for pounding hooves, but all he heard was the drumming of feet and the rushing wind. There was no sign of an army marching over the plains from Thebes, so perhaps they were safe from that direction. But where was the cavalry?

***

On the southern wall of Plataea, the Spartan-led force had smashed into the Plataean lines, and a struggle of strength and discipline had ensued. Sémon was in the front line, face to face with men bred for warfare. He knew that this enemy would not turn and run, but he knew that if Stephanos was to have a chance, they must keep fighting.

The wall overflowed with soldiers shoving and stabbing. The clash of shields, the thud of javelins hurled into enemy ranks, the hollow screams of the dying, and the ferocious cries of the living blended with the wind and the snow. This quiet land of farms and olive trees, this town of cobblers and barbers, boiled with the futile fury of war. There was no room for compassion, no time for second thoughts, when your enemy was but a sneeze away.

The heaving and thrusting was relentless. Neither side showed any sign of weakening. How long had they grappled? It was impossible to say. For Sémon, Time had been the first to flee the battle. A shout rippled through the Plataean ranks – enemy cavalry had arrived outside the walls. Sémon felt a fleeting surge of satisfaction. At least Stephanos and the others had a chance. Now they had to give them as much time as possible.

Unseen by Sémon, the disorderly pack of Theban cavalry stood illuminated by its own torches. They watched the battle unfold above them, daring anyone to escape to their domain. Another light appeared out of the darkness, and a lone horseman rode to the head of the cavalry. After a few moments, they all turned and galloped down the hill to the north.

A command from Arkadius released a hail of missiles on the Theban hoplites supporting the front rank of Spartans, and Sémon felt the force of his opponents ease. A mighty shove by the Plataeans, followed by a sharp withdrawal of a few paces, left an uncertain space between the front lines. The Plataeans at the rear scrambled down the ladders towards the town, and the Spartans hungrily eyed the thinning ranks before them. On reaching the ground, the soldiers picked up javelins and bows that lay ready and began to provide cover for the dwindling number of men facing the enemy.

Sémon knew that his battle was almost over; it was now just a matter of extricating themselves. But he also knew that it meant the cavalry had left. It seemed too soon. He prayed to Apollo that they had given his nephew enough time.

***

The running was easy now that they were on the main road to Thebes, and Stephanos' mind began to wander. His arm smarted but he gave it no notice. He felt a repressed joy, afraid to give it full rein until he knew they had escaped, trying not to think of Khara yet. She seemed so close he could taste her, the thought more tortuous now that they were outside Plataea.

The hoplites ran past the shrine to the hero Androkrates as the snow eased and the wind settled to a breeze. There was still no sign of activity from Thebes as they turned onto a track heading east, the fire-lit walls of Plataea under a mile away to their right. Stephanos scanned for signs of the cavalry. There was nothing, and he relaxed a little.

Theo Sémon would be thrilled for him. He felt a surge of affection for the older man. "Zeus the Liberator, protect him," he muttered. He had left him behind, but Stephanos swore by Apollo that he had not abandoned him, that he would return with an Athenian army at his back.

Athens. Stephanos could see Khara waving, encouraging him to hurry, and Alexias by her side beaming, jumping up and down. Stephanos loved Alexias' mischievousness. He hoped his son had not lost it, or gained an excess of it. He longed to reach out and take Khara by the hand, and...

"Halt!"

The command from Ammias brought the soldiers to an abrupt stop, and attention focused on Plataea. Stephanos' dreams burst when he spotted the source of interest. A river of torches moved rapidly towards them along the eastern wall of the town. The cavalry. Stephanos watched the lights drift through the air, a beautiful harbinger of their destruction.

He prayed to Zeus the Liberator again. The cavalry reached the northern section through which Eupompides had led the escape, and then stopped. From their screen of darkness, Stephanos felt his world held in Tyche's scales. If the cavalry found them in the open plains it was over. His own death held little fear for him anymore, it was the effect it would have on his family that tortured him. Alexias without a father, Khara without protection. How would they survive in a brutal world without a strong man to shield them?

The horses began their gallop, and Stephanos groaned as they took the road to Thebes, the route that led straight to them. The bluff had been read, they had failed. But then Mighty Zeus the Liberator intervened. The cavalry turned away towards the south, heading for Three Heads Pass through the mountains, starting their search on the logical escape route, the quickest way to Athens, the road the Plataeans had avoided. Now they had a chance. Now there may be time to reach the mountains cloaked in night's disguise. Hope was still with them.

At a signal from Ammias, the men headed east with lighter feet, and a smile invaded Stephanos. A long night of running lay ahead, but if they could make the mountains they would be safe. They would be free.

***

The South Gate was open, and General Arkadius led his tired troops back into town. Mikos waited by the side of the road and scanned the faces that glowed in the torchlight. There was no sign of Sémon, and the panic he had controlled fought back. Where was he? As the ranks filed through the burned southern quarter towards the fires of the agora, Mikos started to reckon the decreasing chances of Sémon's survival. Each passing soldier was one less chance that he was alive. The gates began to close on Mikos' hopes as the last ranks reached them. A few soldiers were carried in on their shields, but none of them was Sémon. Bile rose in Mikos' throat.

Dead.

Alone again.

But then he appeared, lumbering out of the dark in the last line, his face splattered with blood, his breastplate caked with dried crimson streams, a gash on his calf. Sémon spotted his friend's relieved face, and stepped out of formation and embraced him.

"Come on," said Sémon gruffly, "let's go see if there's news of the others."

The agora was a flood of light. The cooks had worked hard during the battle to prepare dinner. The army disbanded noisily amidst the now tender snow, sharing their tales of bravery as they discarded their weapons, the stories expanding as they queued for their food. A hand clapped Sémon on the shoulder from behind.

"You had the courage of Ares on you tonight, my friend." It was one of the remaining Athenian soldiers.

"That's how Plataeans fight," said Sémon. "We like it face to face and up close," he added, wiggling his eyebrows.

The Athenian laughed. "Well, with so few of us left, there'll be ample opportunity for that."

The slave women served the food until a wave of silence eased its way through the agora, and heads turned to the law courts. Beside a fluted column on the top step, Hybrias and two companions sat eating, conscious of the growing multitude of stares in their direction.

General Arkadius strode to the bottom of the steps, empty bowl in hand, and motioned Hybrias and his friends down. The three men set their bowls aside and ambled down the steps like naughty schoolchildren. The rest of the soldiers congregated around the general. All knew that these three had been part of the escape.

"What news?" prompted Arkadius.

Hybrias cleared his throat and brushed aside his curtain of hair. "Bad news, General."

The agora held its breath. "Tell it all, lad."

"Well, it went good at first," began Hybrias. "Many got over the walls before they raised the alarm, and then most of the others while we held them at the towers. But when the defensive lines started to withdraw, the cavalry showed up. And a load of infantry, too. The men outside the wall had no chance. We saw General Eupompides killed ourselves. Those of us left on the wall tried to fight our way back. We're the only ones who made it."

Hybrias flushed as two hundred and fifty faces stared at him in horror.

"We lost over two hundred men?" Arkadius put voice to the awful truth, as he noted the absence of any injuries on Hybrias. The men remained in shocked silence. A shout rang from the northern end of the agora, and a pale-faced soldier sprinted towards them, the men parting to let him through to the general. "What is it?" asked Arkadius.

"General, sir," spluttered the messenger. "The Thebans have stuck the head of General Eupompides on a stake by the North Gate. They say they've plenty more where that came from, but they're gonna' let them rot where they fell so the dogs can have their fill." Grief swept through the assembly as Hybrias and his friends concealed their relief.

Sémon broke away, strode past the cooking fires, dropped his bowl on the ground, and stared at the dirt as he hurried towards the temple of Athena. They had not given him enough time. They should have engaged the cavalry themselves. He saw the terror of the soldiers trapped against the wall as horses and hoplites bore down on them. He saw Stephanos fighting desperately. He saw the agony of his death.

He walked past the temple, into the lonely streets, and wept.

Chapter 20

Monsters everywhere. They stomped and growled as they searched for him, but they couldn't see him, not when he was using the invisible powers of Hades' helmet. Alexias crept between the giants – the Athenian agora was full of them, but like Herakles he was patient. He could wait his chance. He had, after all, already been there several minutes.

Alexias hesitated before the honey seller's cart. The pots called tempting songs to the young hero. Perhaps honey would do, though he hadn't come for honey. He remembered his pappu's stories of the temptations of Odysseus, and he dragged himself onwards.

At the livestock section of the market, he paused to watch two goats locking horns. The market inspector, his white himation bordered with purple, prowled nearby, gripping his thick staff. Alexias gave him a wide berth and sneaked towards the stalls covered with fruit, searching for an opportunity. A tattered blanket on the ground was covered in piles of figs that he thought looked like sheep poo. Figs might do, and the old woman sitting behind them would be slow, but they looked evil.

He continued down the alley formed by the stalls until he reached a busy shopkeeper, whose table was loaded with fresh figs, blackberries, cherries, apples, and raisins. Alexias sidled to a corner of the table. He watched the giants haggling, and leaned on the table as he pretended to examine the cherries, kicking its leg until the table finally crashed to the floor. The fruit rolled amongst the feet of the startled shoppers, and while they gathered their wits, Alexias scooped blackberries from the ground into the folds of his sackcloth tunic and sprinted away.

He heard the angry shouts behind him. Giants were quick, but they couldn't dart between crowded legs and disappear into thin air. Alexias flew out of the market, past the Council chambers, and out of the agora into the winding side streets. He paused to catch his breath and listen for pursuit. Nothing. He was safe. *Those dumb monsters*, he laughed.

The precious cargo stained his tunic purple; his momma would not be impressed. He placed a blackberry in his mouth and savoured its delights, but his quest was unfinished – he had yet to rival Herakles. Alexias wrapped his arms around the fruit and hurried onwards, the stone herms at each street corner and the endless shrines seeming to watch him. He gave each of them a nod of acknowledgement – it was best not to annoy the gods too much in one day. He laughed at a charcoal drawing on a wall of a head vomiting bodies. The name 'Perikles' that appeared next to the face meant nothing to him.

Finally, he reached his destination, the Temple of Apollo of Pestilence and Healing. The sanctuary was surrounded by ramshackle huts squeezed between the god's courtyard and Athenian homes. The garish statues on the temple's pediment mocked the old men and careworn women sitting before their shacks. After the first outbreak of plague in Athens, the poorer Plataean refugees had rushed to Apollo for protection and had stayed there ever since.

Dirty children chased each other between the huts, but when they saw Alexias and his bounty, they screamed sufficiently to startle Apollo himself. Alexias fought to hand out the blackberries, but despite his heroic stature, food was more important than reverence. Little hands grabbed and clawed at his tunic until most of the fruit fell to the ground and the children scrambled in the mud.

The mothers smiled and called out to Alexias to thank him, and the youngsters' adulation gave great satisfaction to the hero, who acknowledged it with a modesty appropriate for one likely to be granted a place beside the gods.

His enjoyment was cut short, though, when a teenage boy bolted into the square, shouting, "They're coming! They're coming! Quick!" He motioned everyone to follow, but nobody moved.

"Who's coming?" one of the old men asked.

"Our fathers, our brothers!" Still they did not understand. "Your sons, your grandsons, your husbands! They've escaped the siege. They're coming towards the Sacred Gate."

The camp erupted. Mothers dumped little children on grandmothers and discovered unknown energy. They sprinted out of the settlement, older children running alongside them, old men hobbling as fast as they could. Those left in the quiet shadows of the temple stared into space, fearing to dream that families would be whole once more.

Alexias stood immobilised as the dwellings disgorged their inhabitants, and only slowly did he understand.

Poppa was coming.

Poppa was coming here.

Poppa was coming home.

His legs exploded and he hurtled back towards the western quarter, willing his feet to fly like Hermes, and as the streets led downhill, he felt like he really was flying. He approached alleys he played in all the time. His home was not far out of the way. Should he stop to tell momma and pappu? They were slow and he might get to the gate too late. He reached a crossroad where he had to make a decision. He jogged on the spot, glancing down one street and then the other. The shoemaker in his shop on the corner smiled at him. *Which way? Which way?* Alexias made up his mind, darted up the street past the shoemaker, and burst through the door.

"Momma! Pappu! Poppa's coming!"

Khara walked out of the kitchen into the courtyard, her bare arms covered in flour to the elbows, a few rogue patches on her cheeks. "What?"

"Poppa's coming!"

"Alexias! What have you done to your clothes?!" exclaimed Khara, seeing the ugly stain on her son's abdomen. Lakon sat up on his couch to see the offending garment and chuckled.

Clothes? Clothes? What do clothes matter? "Momma! Poppa's coming. A man came and said they're coming to the Sacred Gate. Hurry," he shouted, hanging on to the door, refusing to enter the yard.

"Who's coming, Alexias?"

His momma was unbelievably slow this morning. "He said that poppas and husbands, and, erm," he thought hard, "and brothers and, er, poppas and sons, and some other people. But they're coming *now*. Come on!"

"Sweetheart, will you please calm down and tell me what's going on."

"He said they've escaped and they're coming now. Poppa's with them. *Come on*, momma."

Khara frowned. "Do you mean they've escaped?"

"Yes!" shouted Alexias. What did she think he'd been saying?

Khara stared at her son, unable to move. Another command from Alexias jolted her into action, and the two of them rushed out of the door and along the street, followed more gingerly by Lakon. The shoemaker's eyebrows raised at Khara running through the streets covered in flour.

Khara's mind was airborne. Was he really here? Could it possibly be? What if it was just another false rumour? She struggled to keep her hopes in check – to return to earth after such thoughts could not be borne.

The Eleusis Road was crowded. Soldiers embraced crying women, as screams of joy competed with desperate shouts for those yet to be found. Hoplites, their shields still slung over their backs, knelt in the dust and sobbed on discovering that the plague had wiped out their families. Wives drifted away in confusion on finding that their husbands had remained in Plataea. Young children cried in the middle of the street, temporarily forgotten.

Khara searched every face with rising desperation. She held Alexias' hand and pushed into the crowd, struggling towards the gate, searching, searching. Where was he?

"Stephanos!" she cried, but her voice cracked and only Alexias could hear her.

"Poppa!" shouted Alexias, but there were many poppas, and Alexias' voice was swamped.

"Stephanos!" Khara tried again, weakly, barely able to fight the sobs. She waded through the crowd, calling as best she could, her torture reflected in the faces of other wives.

"*Poppa!*" Alexias' voice had changed colour and his hand slipped from Khara's. She turned to see her son fly into the arms of his poppa. Stephanos whirled him around, and crushed him to his bloody armour as tears flowed down his muddy cheeks to the accompaniment of Alexias' laughter.

Khara was rooted, shaking as sobs racked her body. Stephanos saw her. He put Alexias down, stabbed his spear into the dirt, strode to her and enveloped her in his arms as she finally gave in to the sea of tears.

They did not speak. They held onto each other, afraid it was a dream. Never again would they let go. Never again would the gods part them.

Oblivious to the noise around them, they eventually loosed their grip enough to look into each other's face. Stephanos wiped the tears from her eyes, smiling, kissing her with two years of lost love. "I see you've been busy," he said finally, indicating her face and arms. Khara noticed the flour and her face filled with horror. Stephanos laughed and held her to him. "I've never seen anything so beautiful in all my life."

Khara giggled, revelling in the feeling of home that had returned.

"Pappu! Over here!" cried Alexias. Lakon approached slowly, his face flushed, breathing hard, fat tears rolling down his face. Stephanos released Khara and hugged his frail father.

"My son. My son," muttered Lakon over and over, choking on the words. Finally, Lakon looked around. "Where's my brother? Where's Sémon?"

Stephanos winced. "Still in Plataea with Mikos. They couldn't join us." Lakon frowned, and his face, on which spring had dawned, seemed to shrivel again.

"Let's go home," said Khara, wrapping herself around her husband. "The gods have returned *you* safely to us. We'll find a way for Sémon and Mikos to follow."

Chapter 21

"Have you seen the new girl at Dionusia's?" asked Nikolas, his eyes sparkling as he glanced around the men in the barbershop.

"No, but five minutes with you is enough to get her life story," said Alkibiades, laughing carefully as ancient Sporgilus scraped the oil from his neck with a crescent blade.

"Stay still," the old man sighed, smoothing his own few remaining strands of grey hair. "Want me to cut your throat?"

Alkibiades grabbed the popular barber gently by the wrist. "My dear friend, I was only trying to compensate for your shaky hands."

The barber smiled sadly. "With each passing year, Poseidon gains on me. Soon I'll be shaking like one of his earthquakes."

"Then we will just have to laugh all the harder when we are here," said Alkibiades.

A chill breeze wafted through the two open sides of the shop. Footprints stained the clay floor, and half a dozen customers waited on the benches against the walls and listened to the music of scissors. A barbershop was a good place to hear the latest rumours, but Sporgilus' place was renowned. At a crossroad near the agora, with the wealthy flitting into the perfume shop on one corner, and a procession of slaves and the poor collecting water from the public fountains on another, here the gossip of Athens was gathered, digested, and dispersed.

"I'm thankful that Artemis granted me two healthy sons with steady hands," said the barber, looking across the room at his little boys, two immense, middle-aged men.

"And excellent barbers they are, too," said Nikolas, seated on the bench facing Alkibiades, "but we were discussing the new fruit at Dionusia's. Eustathios, have you seen her?"

The sturdy councillor hiding in the corner shook his mass of tight curls. "No, I haven't."

"Well, you should," said Nikolas. "Believe me, there's no

pleasure like it. She's Persian but brought up in Corinth, and has eyes deeper than the sea, skin smoother than Aphrodite's, and breasts like Mount Olympus."

"She would make a good sculpture, then," said Alkibiades.

"Even Phidias could never match her artistry."

"Oh, she is a painter?"

"Very funny, Alkibiades. I'm not talking of mere dyes and pigments, but of the highest art. Sensuality." Nikolas looked smugly around the eyes fastened on him. "She makes it seem that the whole world of sense and feeling is concentrated on you alone. Where else could you experience that?"

"With your wife?" suggested the hairy councillor.

"An Athenian wife knows nothing of the arts of love," said Nikolas. "All she's brought up for is house-keeping and popping out new citizens."

Alkibiades smiled. "Our loyalties are spread among many goddesses. It is impossible to find everything in one person. Do you not agree, Eustathios?"

Eustathios' thick eyebrows furrowed. "Simple farmers like me can't afford the flesh at Dionusia's. We must be content with what we have."

Alkibiades turned to face him, causing his old barber to appeal to the heavens. "It is unfair that men with your excellent qualities cannot sample such simple pleasures," said Alkibiades.

"Especially when you're serving the city," added Nikolas, "carrying the heavy burden of the Council, deciding on what the Assembly will vote." He snapped his fingers, his face flashing a smile. "I know. Why don't you come to Dionusia's as my guest? I'm sure she'll accommodate a friend of mine for a gift, er, more in keeping with your circumstances."

"That's mighty kind of you," said Eustathios, trying to smile but wincing in pain.

"Not at all. I like to help a friend whenever possible." Nikolas paused and exchanged a glance with Alkibiades before continuing. "It reflects the greatness of Athens that honest farmers such as yourself can have such influence over the affairs of the city."

"May be great for Athens," said the councillor, "but I'd rather have my farm back."

"This war must be difficult for you. Financially," said Alkibiades.

"Mighty difficult," said Eustathios. "A councillor's pay isn't enough. I've had to help out at the docks as a hired hand." He rearranged himself in his seat. "No free Athenian who's served as a hoplite should have to do that."

"No, indeed," said Alkibiades. "I think this war will last a long time yet, and I am afraid that as long as Sparta invades Attika each year, your farm will remain desolate. If only there was some way we could safeguard it."

Eustathios nodded. "Yes, but how?"

Alkibiades paused as Sporgilus offered him a bowl of water to wash away the remaining oil, and the end of a towel to pat his face dry. He eased himself from the chair and swapped places with Eustathios.

"Toothache?" asked Sporgilus as the councillor sat down holding the side of his face. "Let's have a look." The old man bent towards the open mouth and shot upright. "Hephaestus, God of Fire! You have the breath of Hades. Here, swill this." He handed him a cup of cypress berry juice from a tall table littered with the tools of his trade.

"Many men are eager to take the fight to Sparta," continued Alkibiades. "Life is too easy for the Peloponnesians. They march here, destroy our crops, and then go home to harvest their own. Every year the same. We are not hurting them, and they have no fear of hurting us."

"That's right," said Nikolas. "All we do is put down rebellions, because our allies think we're weak, hiding behind our walls."

"And they see us abandoning such a staunch friend as Plataea to her fate," added Alkibiades. "It makes them wonder if we will protect our other friends."

"Especially with the rumours of a Peloponnesian fleet preparing to sail to the relief of Mytilene in the spring," continued Nikolas.

"It's hopeless!" cried Eustathios, spitting out the juice. "What are we to do?"

Alkibiades shook his head. "It is a difficult problem."

"Yes, it is," said Sporgilus as he examined the mouth. "The tooth must come out." Eustathios' face turned to marble as Sporgilus prepared the fish resin that would fill the hole left behind.

"Perhaps it would help if we could deprive the Spartans of their cavalry," suggested Nikolas.

Eustathios seemed to welcome the distraction. "The Spartans have no cavalry," he said. "They use Boeotian cavalry led by Thebes."

"You are right, Eustathios," said Alkibiades. "We do not need to attack Sparta. We should defeat Thebes first."

"The Spartans would find it difficult to ravage Attika without cavalry support," added Nikolas. "Our farms would be safe."

Eustathios frowned, nodding slowly. "Makes sense, but how would we do it?"

Alkibiades looked towards the wooden beams of the ceiling, knowing the farmer's eyes were on him. "Perhaps if we found a town in Boeotia where we could put a strong garrison, we could use it to harass the enemy. You know, threaten Theban crops and encourage other cities in Boeotia to break away from Thebes and join us instead. But where would such a stronghold be?"

The room went quiet and Alkibiades studied the farmer. He seemed distracted by his imminent ordeal, and so Alkibiades provided an extra prompt. "It would have to be somewhere loyal and well-fortified." He waited, but only the clatter of carts outside and the constant chatter at the water fountain invaded the shop. "And having soldiers there already would help." Alkibiades began to despair of Athenian farmers. "We would want it close to Attika so we could supply it. And close to Thebes, of course."

"I've an idea." Eustathios sat forward, glancing at the barber-cum-dentist's preparations. "What about using Plataea?"

"What a good idea, Eustathios," said Alkibiades. "And what propitious timing, with you taking your turn on the presiding board of the Council. It is almost as if the gods had planned for you to proclaim their desire to your colleagues."

"It is," agreed Eustathios. "I must make a thank offering to Zeus of the Council."

"But how will you convince your colleagues?" asked Nikolas. "Perhaps you should ask some Plataeans and other allied representatives to make their case before the Council."

"I don't know any," said Eustathios.

"Oh, that is no problem," smiled Alkibiades. "We can round up some people for you."

"That's very kind. Most helpful."

The conversation halted as the bald son of Sporgilus gripped the councillor's jaw, his brother ripping out the offending tooth with a pair of pliers. Eustathios had instant rigor mortis, his eyes exploding from his face, but he made no sound. The surgeon mopped up the blood, and Sporgilus moved in with his resin. The other customers watched in tense fascination.

"Have you heard what happened to Iophon?" asked old Sporgilus as he filled the hole.

"Iophon the wrestler?" said Nikolas.

"Yes. The man who's won the last two PanAthenaic games, and can wrestle a bull to the ground just by breaking wind."

"No. Tell us," said Nikolas, reflecting the consternation of his companions at news of one of their sporting heroes. "What's happened?"

Sporgilus squinted into the open mouth to admire his handiwork. "Well, it's not for me to say what's good behaviour for an athlete we hope will one day glorify our city at Olympia." He started to comb Eustathios' curly hair, allowing his listeners' anticipation to peak. "It's said that the Scythians picked him up off the street last night, so drunk he couldn't find his way home."

"No! That's outrageous," said Nikolas, thumping the bench. "To waste his strength drinking himself into such a state."

"And to have the ignominy of public slaves taking him home," mused Alkibiades, suppressing the urge to mention Nikolas' frequent encounters with the city's night patrols.

"And he wasn't very cooperative," added the barber, happy to shed the pollen among his bees. "They had to keep calling for help, and in the end twenty of them surrounded him."

"Twenty men!" laughed Nikolas.

"But what do you think of a potential Olympian behaving like that?" asked Councillor Eustathios in a much distorted voice, cradling his cheek.

Alkibiades was well aware of his own reputation, but was unsure whether it had reached the councillor. He grinned. This was Athens; of course it had. "We all have our weaknesses, Eustathios. Fortunately for me, mine do not impair the performance of my horses, which will run at Olympia one day. As for Iophon... His skill and strength have given us much pleasure in the past. Perhaps we should refrain from jumping to unfavourable opinions of him. It was, after all, only one night."

"Yes, but he represents Athens," said Nikolas. "What image of our city does it present?"

"We all represent Athens, Nikolas," said Alkibiades. "Some people more prominently than others."

A roar from the agora surged like a wave through the streets, and their heads turned in its direction. The perfume shop released its curious clients onto the street, and amphorae stood unattended in the fountain house. Eyes and ears strained to interpret the momentous sound. Was it joy or despair? Their salvation or destruction?

"The Plataeans have escaped! They've escaped, they're in Athens!" cried a young messenger sprinting into the crossroads and immediately disappearing again.

"Did he say the Plataeans have escaped?" asked Eustathios.

Alkibiades nodded, frowning. Escaped? Was it possible? If Plataea was no longer captive, his scheming may have been wasted. He stepped to the open walls, his fists clenched.

They did not have to wait long for the main body of the news to wash through the city. Two hundred had escaped; the rest remained in Plataea.

"Great news, eh?" said Sporgilus over Alkibiades' shoulder.

"Yes, great news," he answered softly. Plataea was still in play, and with new impetus. He turned into the shop again and sat down. "Yes, wonderful news," he said. "I think this is an event that should be celebrated by all of Athens. What do you think, Eustathios?"

The councillor nodded. "Sounds like Athens is already celebrating."

"No. I mean a real celebration. These men have broken free from the grip of the Spartans. They have shown us the gods are on our side. We should honour them with sacrifices, a feast, games." Eustathios nodded but was frowning. "And we should not burden the public finances with this," continued Alkibiades. "I will pay for it as a sacred honour, together with some of my Plataean friends, to thank the gods for the safe return of our allies."

The councillor's face lightened. "Mighty generous of you, Alkibiades. It won't be cheap."

"We cannot put a price on bravery and the favour of the gods," said Alkibiades. "I am deemed too young to serve Athens in many ways, but I can serve her in this. We should hold it as soon as possible, while the memory of their achievement is fresh in our minds."

"How about in two days?" said Eustathios.

"A good suggestion," began Alkibiades, "but it will need some organizing, so we should give ourselves a few more days. Perhaps we could hold it the day before the next Assembly?"

The councillor nodded, and Alkibiades smiled. Not cheap, indeed. But Tyche, goddess of Fortune, had provided a gift, and after all, what price a city?

Chapter 22

The stench of rotting leaves and animal faeces assailed the hunters' nostrils as they crept through the undergrowth, the morning light filtering through the canopy and fighting the cold air. To Alkibiades every bush seemed to twitch, every piece of ground rustle, as he strained to pierce the camouflage from where the animal might burst.

In front of him, Kallias gripped his short spear, both hands protected behind the bronze hand guard that protruded from the shaft. Behind Alkibiades, General Hipponikus licked his lips, his eyes darting from side to side, followed by Alkibiades' clumsy uncle, Axiochus, and Olympian Megakles, who sauntered at the rear. Their numerous slaves carried spare javelins and spears, and calf-skin sacks full of food, nets, and snares.

Kallias stumbled over a root and cursed. "Careful," whispered Hipponikus, "you never know what wood nymph you may be upsetting."

Alkibiades sneered at his father-in-law's superstition but said nothing. One of the Spartan hounds barked excitedly and dragged his handler along at a run. "What is it, Tracker? What've you got for us?" The party began to jog. Bushes scratched their bare legs as the other dogs picked up the scent, and a chorus of barks removed any need for stealth.

They fell into a clearing and the dogs paused, circling the area with their sniffing. A handler pointed to the ground marked with boar footprints, and his nervous eyes scanned the brush as the hounds searched for the boar's route out. Hipponikus was breathing hard; Axiochus was in need of a drink, preferably not water; Megakles stood majestically alert.

A squawk in the bushes. All weapons pointed its way in an instant, but it was merely a squirrel. Behind them, one of the slaves staked out a net to block the path by which they had entered.

"Carthaginian flax," said Hipponikus, nodding towards the net. "Best there is."

"The ones ahead the same?" asked Megakles. Hipponikus nodded.

In a moment, they were off again, Tracker living up to his name. "Go Tracker!" yelled Kallias as he hurtled after the excited pack, his spear held ready for the attack.

"Let them go!" shouted Hipponikus, and his slaves released the hounds, which bounded ahead. Their masters picked up the pace, but the dogs were quickly out of sight. Tracker's handler, followed closely by Kallias and Alkibiades, sprinted after the barking. The older men failed to keep up, and Hipponikus yelled for the youths to slow down, to not abandon their support. But when blood is up, it flows not to the ears of the young. Kallias and Alkibiades continued at full tilt behind the slave, who pointed to a tree whose bark had been gored by the upturned tusks of a boar.

The noise changed. The excited barks became deep growls. Kallias burst through a bush in time to see a huge boar snort and charge the dogs, impaling Tracker on a tusk before bloodily tossing him aside. Tracker's whimper was masked by the anger of his companions, who started to make fake attacks under the whistled and shouted directions of the slave. They slowly shepherded the boar towards the nets, which had been set before daybreak. Kallias and Alkibiades braced themselves, blocking potential escape routes.

The boar turned to face each attack, at first only moving a few steps at a time, but when Hipponikus and company arrived, the pig turned and ran towards the nets. The dogs followed, keeping their quarry on track. The young men tore after them and left their elders behind again. The boar crashed into one of the nets a hundred yards ahead, the impact ripping the stakes out of the ground and allowing the animal to break free. The slave responsible for the net held a dagger ready to kill the victim, but he froze when he saw the trap disintegrate. The boar charged. The slave roused himself and raised his dagger. A tusk speared his groin, evoking a scream to chase Pan from the forest as the dagger dropped from the slave's hand.

The dogs circled the pair, growling, the howling slave unable to free himself. Kallias burst into the circle and thrust his spear into the back of the boar, but missed the kill and only succeeded in rousing its anger. The animal cast the slave aside and turned to face the defenceless Kallias, his weapon embedded in the animal's back. Their eyes met for an immense moment, a shared knowledge of Kallias' imminent death.

"Get down!" yelled Alkibiades, racing to join the fray. The boar attacked just as Kallias obeyed the command and hit the ground, lying as flat as possible. The boar's head crashed into his shoulders, but its upturned tusks were unable to reach down and harm him. Kallias held his breath as the animal's exhalations clouded over his head.

The boar stamped on Kallias' back as Alkibiades noisily offered a new challenge. It accepted immediately and charged. Alkibiades braced as the huge beast pounded towards him. Rage had settled on the boar, and as it reached the spear, it turned its head aside to thrust the iron tip away, exposing Alkibiades to its deadly tusks. But Alkibiades was a practiced hunter and evaded the move, piercing the boar's chest. It squealed but did not stop. The stout-hearted animal careered towards Alkibiades, burying the shaft deeper within its body until it hit the hand guard of the spear and knocked Alkibiades from his feet. The boar landed on top of him, struggling to turn its tusks towards its killer, its legs pounding the trapped body. Alkibiades held grimly on to the spear to keep the tusks away from him, feeling the strength draining from the crushing weight. His uncles and Hipponikus arrived, and they applied the final dispatch.

"I told you to wait," panted Hipponikus as they rolled the body off Alkibiades. "You were lucky we got here in time."

Alkibiades laughed, almost maniacally. He felt giddy, intoxicated. "He was already all but dead. You could have killed him with a kiss."

"He saved my life," said Kallias, brushing himself down and looking pale. "You should have seen how he stood up to the charge. It was magnificent."

"You should not have missed with your own spear," growled Hipponikus, noting the shaft in the boar's back.

"It was a glorious foe," said Alkibiades, stroking the animal. "What bravery. What strength." He nodded towards the dead slave. "You lost one of your men. He panicked."

"Hades!" exclaimed Hipponikus. "He cost me a good two minas." He motioned to several of the slaves that had caught up. "You there! Bury him and pour libations." The slaves set to work, saying goodbye to yet another friend.

"I'm afraid we also lost Tracker, Father," said Kallias.

"I know. Damn shame. I cannot replace *him* so easily. Trained him from a pup, I did. I left a couple of slaves to bury him." He examined the boar and broke into a grin. "Still, as you say, a magnificent animal. The gods have been good. Let's walk to the clearing with the altar. It is just up the hill."

While some of the slaves dealt with burials and with the boar, others followed the dogs and their masters to a grassy clearing surrounded by a broken wall of stones, an altar at its centre. Hipponikus poured libations of wine to honour Apollo, Lord of the Silver Bow, and his sister, Artemis the Huntress, for their aid in the chase, before they sat down to receive their Euboean apples, dried figs from Rhodes, and pickled slices of dolphin.

"So," began Hipponikus, "we are to have a celebration for the men from Plataea."

"Smart thinking, Alkibiades," said haughty Megakles. "People remember a good party. It will raise the issue in everyone's mind and help us in the elections, I am sure."

"Perhaps," said Hipponikus, dropping a dolphin slice into his mouth. "Seems rather theatrical."

"Are not politics and theatre as brother and sister?" said Alkibiades, as Axiochus resumed his life's purpose in draining the wine.

"I will grant there is an element of theatre in our politics nowadays with the likes of Kleon," said Hipponikus. "But this seems excessive. It is going to be expensive."

"Well," replied Alkibiades, "as Euripides has said, 'what is the use of gold if it doesn't bring fame?'"

"Fame?" snapped Hipponikus. "Notoriety, perhaps."

"They are the same," laughed Alkibiades. "But Theo Megakles is right. People remember a celebration. They will also remember that I helped pay for it."

"I know that," said Hipponikus. "You know that. Everyone with an ounce of political sense will know that. You could not have announced your ambitions any clearer than if you had proclaimed them in the Assembly. You should have consulted us first. You are young and inexperienced. There are plenty of hunters in the Assembly who will treat you no better than that boar if you give them a chance. More than ever, you cannot afford for your chorus to fail at the Dionysia. If you lose, they will ridicule you and charge you with cheapness. Then see how quickly the people forget a party."

"I appreciate your concern," said Alkibiades, amused by his father-in-law's discomfort.

"My concern is for the family."

Of course it is, thought Alkibiades. He glanced at his uncles and Kallias, who followed the conversation as they consumed the victuals. "You need not worry. I will win," said Alkibiades. "As you know, I volunteered for the chorus when there was a shortage of sponsors, even though my age would usually preclude me. People know this. They appreciate such generosity. Together with the celebration, the judges will understand how much I am able to benefit those who help me. I will spend enough owls to make sure they understand."

"You have to be equally careful, young man," began Megakles smoothly, delicately lifting a strand of hair from his face, "that you are not seen to spend too much on the chorus. Extravagance can lead to charges of tyranny, something Athenians are all too ready to believe."

"Especially taken with your excesses," shot Hipponikus. "Everyone knows of your women, parties, and horses. A charge of tyranny will lead to exile quicker than the desertion of a shield flinger."

"Our family has a great tradition of exiles," noted Megakles.

"Who have often returned to greater power," added Alkibiades. "I am not afraid of the mob, or those who manipulate it. People expect their heroes to be larger than life. Athens is ready for a change, for a new voice that will improve our fortunes in the war. Kleon will give words to it before the people, but I have smoothed the path in the Council. A friend will propose a motion for the generals to take all measures to rescue Plataea."

"What?" said Hipponikus, sitting up. "Nikias will never allow it."

"Probably not," said Alkibiades, "but I am betting that the prospect of a huge gathering to celebrate Plataean bravery will make him think twice. Rather than killing the motion, perhaps he will just try to modify it."

"Of what use is that to us, then?" said Hipponikus.

"As long as the motion is ambiguous enough," said Alkibiades, "once we have control of the board of generals we can use it to justify Plataea's rescue."

"And you are using the celebration to ensure its passage in the Assembly the next day," said Megakles, nodding. "That is clever, do you not think, Hipponikus?"

Hipponikus' eyes had narrowed and he seemed to be studying his son-in-law. "Yes, not bad," he murmured.

"Choruses, tragedies, comedies," slurred Axiochus, breaking an uneasy silence. "What a waste of money. They're just a means of keeping the mob entertained and the townsmen employed at our expense."

"They are sacred offerings to the gods," muttered Hipponikus.

And a bargaining chip with the people, thought Alkibiades.

Chapter 23

Khara's little courtyard was festooned with plants, and rang to the laughter of Alexias and the animated talk of his elders. The sun had risen on a glorious new day, and Alexias hustled them out into the street, impatient for Alkibiades' party.

Alkibiades had visited the previous day, and after Alexias had bombarded him with questions about the crowns, the food, the games, and the animals, the talk had grown more serious.

"We appreciate your efforts, Alkibiades," Stephanos had said, sitting beside Khara in the sunny courtyard, "but has Nikias destroyed the chances of saving Plataea?"

"Oh, no," said Alkibiades. "He has made a mistake. He should have tried to kill my motion, but he did not have the courage to do so."

"But the words he added to it," said Khara, gripping Stephanos' hand as if he would float into the ether should she let go. "'The generals shall make every effort to rescue Plataea, *if it is in the interest of Athens*'. He can take that to mean anything."

"That is the point," said Alkibiades.

"What point?" said Khara.

"If the motion is passed by the Assembly, it gives the generals the right to march on Plataea without any further vote."

"But Nikias won't allow it."

"True, for the time being," said Alkibiades. "But once we have a majority of the generals on our side after the election, the motion will still be in place, and they will be able to act immediately."

"Nikias seems fairly popular, from what I've heard," said Stephanos. "Do you really expect to unseat him?"

"Not as a general, but some of his allies are vulnerable. Our chances are good."

"You know my Theo Sémon's still trapped in Plataea," said Stephanos. "You only have to say the word, Alkibiades, and I'm at your service."

The look Alkibiades had given in response had unsettled Khara, and now as they hurried through the crowded streets she shuddered at its recollection. It had seemed as if a hole had opened into the young man for a moment, and there was only blackness.

The sunbathed agora was free of the market, but flooded with a sea of colourful himations. Khara released Stephanos to his duty, and pushed Alexias and Lakon towards the altar of Zeus of Freedom. People crowded around the statues of Harmodius and Aristogeiton, filled the Sanctuary of the Twelve Gods, and climbed the plane trees, craning their necks to see the wooden stage near the altar, where the archons, magistrates of the city, stood beside the generals. A trumpet cried, and thousands of voices raised a hymn in praise of Zeus. Khara felt the voices lift her into the air as if she could fly to Mount Olympus.

A procession of bulls was offered on the altar, but Alexias, perched on a friendly giant's shoulders, was more interested in the carcasses distributed to monster cauldrons of boiling water scattered around the agora. Soon he would have a rare taste of meat.

When they had carted away the last bull, and poured libations of wine over the bloody altar, a man with a face whitened with lead paint climbed the stage. His voice boomed like thunder, praising the victory of the Plataeans in a poem that transfixed the people.

Well, most of them. In truth, there is only so much one can stomach of obscure language in praise of dead men and nasty gods, and Alexias had passed that point. He had an excellent view of the boring windbag, and was sure that even Zeus could hear every word. For the first time in his life, he felt a tinge of pity for the King of Olympus.

Alexias' eyes wandered to the people around him, crowded like sheep in a pen, and he considered the amount of meat cooking. He hoped they were not all as hungry as he was. Suddenly everyone burst into applause, and Alexias joined them because he was extraordinarily pleased the poem was over.

The chief archon, Diotimus, a dumpy fur ball of a man, stepped forward. "People of Athens," he cried. "We honour the brave men who broke out of Plataea. To Ammias, son of Koroebus." Ammias strode from the men beside the stage and climbed the steps. The Archon placed an ivy wreath on Ammias' head and declared, "We honour you, Ammias." The men in the crowd clapped and cheered, and the women ululated their joyful bird song as Ammias rejoined his comrades. "To Naxios, son of Paideros." Another man sprang from the ranks and was soon sporting his own garland. One by one, the men of Plataea received their rewards to the approval of Athens.

Khara rejoiced to see neighbours honoured, men from whom she had bought bread, had shoes made, had seen ploughing fields. She strained on tiptoe to see her husband, and at last, the moment for which she had waited arrived.

"To Stephanos, son of Lakon." Stephanos was before the Archon and the wreath on his head. "We honour you, Stephanos."

Joy erupted from Khara, and fresh tears rolled down her cheeks. The gods had rescued him and made her whole. Beside her, Lakon trembled, a smile cracking his face, and Alexias clapped so hard that he nearly fell from his perch.

Once they had honoured all the Plataeans, the tall figure of Kleon climbed the platform. He surveyed the huge gathering and revealed his crooked teeth in a smile. Not even in the Assembly could he speak to so many people; Alkibiades was smart. Kleon waited for the many-eyed monster to focus upon him.

"My friends, we've witnessed the work of Zeus, and it's right to be grateful. But let's not forget the honest old men of Plataea who've been marooned with us throughout the war, and Alkibiades, hero of Potidaea, son of Kleinias, who together have generously provided the means for this spectacular celebration." A powerful swell of appreciation swept through the agora.

Kleon motioned for silence. "Only in times of danger do we see a man's true worth. Theseus confronting the Minotaur. Harmodius and Aristogeiton refusing to bow to the tyrant. We revere these heroes, but they're not alone. Every man here," Kleon swept the crowd with his arm, his voice crashing ever more powerfully over them, "has a father or grandfather who faced the hordes of Persia but stood firm, like the heroes before them, and against all odds they struck their blow for freedom." Cheering swamped the air, and Kleon stirred it with a clenched fist until finally allowing the gust he had raised to blow itself out.

"They knew," he continued, "they knew that to *win* a war, you have to *fight* a war. Hiding was not an option in their eyes. And now we have more heroes in the men from Plataea, who were surrounded by the armies of Sparta and Thebes. Season upon season trapped inside their walls, seeing their land devastated. Yet they did not allow the fear that stalks every man's heart to master them. They did not tremble to face the foe; they did not seek to hide from death. Disdaining the protection of their walls, they knew that to *win* their war, they had to *fight* their war. And their reward from the gods was freedom. Freedom!" he shouted amidst the tumultuous applause, his arms spearing towards the sky.

Again he waited until he could hear the fat spitting on the altar fires, and the angry mutterings of the generals behind him. "This, my friends, is an example to emulate. You've named me the Watchdog of the People, for I look out for your interests, unlike the wolves who seek to enrich those who already own so much of our city. I speak for the labourer breaking his back in the dockyard, the poor farmer whose land has been ruined by the invasions, the baker rising in the middle of the night to scrape a living to feed his children, all of whom leave their families every summer to sit on the rowing decks of our triremes and risk their lives for the good of Athens. These are the men fighting this war, while our brave hoplites stand idle, our generals too afraid to try their valour. The mettle of the Plataeans has been tested in the furnace of battle, and they've been shown to be strong as iron. Can anyone doubt Athenian hoplites would show such courage given the chance?"

"No!" thundered the assembly.

"Then together we must declare that to win this war, we must fight this war. Let Plataea be our standard bearer, our rallying cry as we rise as men to become heroes to our children and grandchildren." He stepped down from the stage to the excited applause of the people, and the barely suppressed fury of many of the generals.

The crowd drained from the stage and collected in eddies around acrobats, clowns, dancing bears, comic jugglers, stalls of Attik pastries and watery wine. A poet recited Homer and reduced his audience to tears with his quivering intonation and tragic face.

Alexias dragged his family to them all, running circles like a sheepdog around his flock, and pointing out every attraction they could see perfectly well for themselves. In the broad avenue running down the centre of the agora, a group of boys were whacking a ball with any handy piece of wood they could find. Alexias was soon in their midst, having conjured up a bat from who-knows-where, shouting, running, swinging, and occasionally hitting something, sometimes even the ball.

His family stood and watched, laughing at Alexias' wild swings. "What will you do now?" said Lakon, gazing in Alexias' direction.

"I don't know," said Stephanos. "Some of the others talk about rowing in the fleet, with the sailing season approaching."

"Earns reasonable money, I suppose," said Lakon.

Stephanos turned to face his father and placed a hand on his shoulder. "I promise you, Poppa, I will bring them back. I'm not going to leave Athens while Theo Sémon and Mikos are still trapped."

Meanwhile, the ball game had come to an abrupt halt due to the intervention, of course, of Alexias. He had achieved a glorious hit, one to make the gods envious, but in a random direction that sent the ball hurtling into a group of men sitting underneath a tree. He had been ordered to retrieve it. As he approached, his eyes fixed upon a tall, middle-aged man in a dirty sackcloth chiton, who held the prized ball in his large hand. His flaring nostrils and bulging eyes suggested he might be a Fury, and Alexias thought his face looked like a squashed pig's, but as he reached him, the man smiled.

"Wow, you're ugly," said Alexias.

Fortunately for the future of the ball, and Alexias, the man roared with laughter, as did the handsome young men around him. "Do you think being ugly makes me a bad person?" the strange man asked with a smile twinkling in his bulbous eyes.

Alexias recalled the handsome bully who lived with the carpenter. "People with nice faces can be bad, so maybe not."

The man nodded as he raised his eyebrows at his followers. "Good answer, my little man. Perhaps you can help us. Who do you think *is* a bad person?"

Alexias gazed down, his foot tracing patterns in the dirt. Eventually he looked up and said, "Someone who won't give a ball back?"

The group burst into laughter once more and the man returned the ball, saying, "By the dog, you are a philosopher, my friend."

Alexias returned triumphantly to his playmates. Stephanos had witnessed the scene from a distance. "Who's that remarkable looking man over there?"

"Sokrates," said Khara.

"He's an ugly fellow."

"Yes. Strange man. Some of the wealthiest people adore him, and yet others think him godless and annoying. They say the Delphic Oracle declared him the wisest of men."

"Not wise enough to make much of a living, it seems," said Stephanos.

"Stephanos, my friend!"

Distracted by Sokrates, they had failed to notice Alkibiades and his entourage sweep through the crowds towards them. He wore a deep red himation dragging ostentatiously in the dirt, a crown of flowers woven with bright ribbons on his head.

"Great Zeus, he looks like a king," whispered Lakon.

"Alkibiades," called Stephanos. They embraced amidst Alkibiades' courtiers.

"How do you like my party?" said Alkibiades, his arm sweeping the agora.

"It's wonderful," said Stephanos.

"And how about you, mistress Khara?"

Khara blushed. "It will be a glory if it leads to the rescue of Plataea."

Alkibiades laughed and turned to his followers. "She is like a Cretan hound, this one. Once she gets her teeth into something she never lets go." Khara's blush deepened and she half stepped behind Stephanos. "But do not misunderstand me," Alkibiades continued, slapping Stephanos on the arm, "I love Cretan hounds."

Alkibiades swept on, a great smile greeting and being greeted, a river of wine flowing in his wake. A trumpet announced the foot races for the young men and boys of Athens, and Alkibiades shepherded his court to a position alongside the dirt track that cut through the heart of the agora. Kallias paraded Sellene to a spot in the front row. Nikolas stole into a position behind her, locked against her by the crush of bodies. He blew gently on her neck as he pretended to crane his own, pressing his body against her while she stroked Kallias' hand, her face flushed.

Alkibiades allowed the deluge to swallow them all before breaking away and striding towards the statues of Harmodius and Aristogeiton, heroes of the democracy. Clusters of people hovered around stalls and displays, but Alkibiades was only interested in the group by the statues. "Good morning, gentlemen," he said on reaching them.

"Good morning," said Antiphon, through his bushy beard.

"Morning," added Pisander, sunning his hawkish face. A few steps away, a lady examined Alkibiades from the security of her hooded himation. Alkibiades noticed her, and his eyes met hers playfully for an instant, but she glared and looked away. From her step towards Pisander, and the fat old maid beside her, Alkibiades took her to be Pisander's wife.

"It is rather symbolic, do you not think," began Alkibiades, "that we are meeting by the statues of the liberators of Athens, the heralds of democracy?"

"More ironic," said Antiphon. "So they killed a tyrant's brother because of a lover's tiff. Why have we made them heroes of democracy?"

"I agree, of course," chuckled Alkibiades. "But people have short memories and heroes bind them together."

"Yes, they do, as Kleon was at pains to point out," said Antiphon. "It appears you have the ruffian fully behind us. It was quite a speech. I think he forgot he was not in the Assembly."

"You never get to speak to twenty thousand people in the Assembly," said Alkibiades.

"True enough," replied Antiphon, stealing a glance at Pisander. "The motion you pushed in the Council was an... interesting move.

What if Nikias had stamped on it?"

"Nikias does not know how to stamp on anything," said Alkibiades. "I knew that, and it worked admirably."

"Yes, it did," said Antiphon. "It will be beneficial to our cause once it passes the Assembly tomorrow. Still, we are partners and you should have consulted us beforehand."

"I agree," said Alkibiades. They did not like his initiative, but were unable to argue with its results. He loved to pose dilemmas. "We must work together. But there are moments when Time presses hard upon us and forces us to take responsibility. I am sure you understand." He knew from the glint in Antiphon's eyes that he understood fully. Partners they may be, but they were Athenian, after all: they may grasp each other's hands in friendship as they hide knives behind their backs.

Excitement exploded behind Alkibiades as the first race began. Antiphon and Pisander looked towards the source of the uproar. Pisander's wife turned to whisper to her maid and dropped her hand so that her face was momentarily exposed. Alkibiades savoured the dark features and elegant neck. She hurriedly covered her face again, her eyes aflame.

"All this," said Antiphon, sweeping his arm, "and the resolution for the Assembly. Nikias must feel like a phalanx has run over him."

"We can ask him," said Pisander, pointing his beak towards the Sanctuary of the Twelve Gods, from where General Nikias was heading in their direction, accompanied by his young brother, Eukrates, and several ambassadors from Chios.

As they neared, Antiphon called, "We were just telling Alkibiades what a surprise all of this is."

"I never doubted," began Nikias, smiling at Alkibiades, "that Alkibiades could throw a good party."

"I do have that reputation," laughed Alkibiades.

"And congratulations on the Council motion," said Nikias, who continued to focus his attention on Alkibiades. "A most stunning achievement for one so young."

"A victory for me? Surely you mean Kleon? It was he who

swayed the Council."

Nikias raised his eyebrows. "Modesty, too. I can understand and admire, Alkibiades, the work that underpinned the motion, even if I disagree with it."

"Thank you," said Alkibiades. "You did well, too, to get your amendment added. You did your best to dull the teeth of the lion."

"There's more than one 'Watchdog of the People' in Athens," said Nikias. "Another who claims that title is the wolf he deprecates."

"Surely," said Alkibiades, "all our statesmen have the best interests of Athens at heart, even if they disagree on policy."

Eukrates snorted, and for a moment Nikias was silent, before replying, "I admire your idealism. You're like your friend, Timokles. Perfectly understandable in young men. But I eagerly await the day when experience crowns you a true Athenian statesman, like your illustrious ancestors."

Alkibiades controlled the urge to lash out, and after a few pleasantries, he left with the Chian ambassadors in tow like captured triremes.

"He learns quickly," muttered Nikias, watching him go.

"Too quickly," growled Eukrates. "First the Council. Now this." He nodded towards the acclamations for another victor in the races.

"And he's entered in the Dionysia, of course," added Pisander, etching concern on his craggy face.

Nikias frowned. "It's not good for any of us that he hitch his chariot to Kleon. We must remove him from the tanner's influence before it's too late. He could become impossible to work with. The city can't afford a split between the Alkmaeonids and the rest of the nobles."

"I am sure you are right," said Antiphon. "But perhaps we could use his relationship with Kleon to provide Alkibiades with the experience to which you allude."

"How?"

"They are clearly bent on a course of recklessness to which the Assembly and generals will never agree. You know that. The people trust your judgment. Let Kleon blare his trumpets of war and break himself on the rock of their rejection. He will be discredited as a failed bully, and Alkibiades will be caught in the wash, enough to learn his lesson and rejoin his own."

"Sounds dangerous to me," said Eukrates. "We've had Milesians telling us about the symbolic importance of Plataea, and Chians ranting about the inconsistency of democratic government. They say they can't trust the Assembly to protect them. It's as if someone coached them. I could almost believe they'd read your speeches, Antiphon."

Antiphon darkened. "You see conspiracies everywhere, my friend. The Milesians are in the pay of Alkibiades' family, of course, but the Chians?" He looked up to the sky and shook his head. "They have cause to distrust us, when the Assembly smashes treaties with the excuse that only an ambassador agreed it, not the citizens. Anyway, the allies are always complaining."

"Are you suggesting they won't influence our war policy?" asked Nikias.

"I am suggesting that once we crush Mytilene, no ally will dare question us and these mutterings will disappear."

Nikias nodded. "Perhaps. These are certainly things to ponder." Another high-spirited wave crashed through the agora. "What's all this nonsense about fighting a war to win a war? By Apollo, what does Kleon think we've been doing all this time? Dancing around Megara? Partying on the Peloponnese?"

"Kleon may belong with the clowns," said Antiphon, "but he is skilled in serving the people what they want to hear."

"Governing is about serving them what they *need* to hear, not what they want to hear," snapped Nikias. He took a deep breath and gazed into the clear sky, exhaling slowly. "Still, I have more pleasant things to think about."

"Ah, yes," smiled Pisander, "your daughter's wedding."

Chapter 24

Aristeia removed the covering from the basket and examined the treasures of her childhood: a wooden pig her mother had apparently given her; a doll from her father; a spinning top, a gift from her great-aunt. She had considered hiding them and sacrificing toys that meant less to her, but Zeus of the House would know, and the prospect of tomorrow's marriage was fearful enough without antagonizing the gods.

She restored the cover and glanced around the room. Everything was prepared: the empty terracotta bath; the lamp stands; the glowing hearth; the scissors. Her eyes rested on the scissors, a reminder that everything was about to change. She was only moving across the city, but it was a world away. No longer under her father's loving protection, she would be entrusted to a man she did not know. For life. What if he disliked her? There would be no escape, no freedom to go riding with her friends or to wrestle in the gymnasium like *he* could. For her, there would only be the house.

At least Leaina was a ray of hope. They had spent many enjoyable afternoons together. She could count on one friend in her new home.

A slave knocked on the door and announced the arrival of her guests. Excited aunts and cousins chattered and laughed as they entered, and applauded when they saw Aristeia robed in an ankle-length silver-grey himation and her long hair adorned with ribbons. Her great-aunt, Glukera, a matriarchal woman bearing a permanent glow of wine and mischievous merriment, led the group.

"My dear, few are beautiful, and the Twin Goddesses know I've never been so myself," said Glukera, patting her own ample waist, "but you, my young nymph, make a good stab at it." She smiled, cracking her white makeup, kissing Aristeia on the forehead.

"Thea Glukera, the sight of you always makes the world a more beautiful place for me."

Glukera threw her head back and laughed. "My, aren't we the one with the pretty tongue tonight? Just like your grandmother used to be." She glanced around the visitors and then back at Aristeia. "Where's the loutrophorus, child?" Aristeia motioned towards the door, beside which stood the narrow-necked vase, its bulbous white body painted with scenes they were about to imitate. Glukera clapped her hands. "Come, ladies. Let's put this ship to sea. Aristeia, did you remember to put a drachma in the offering box at Aphrodite's Sanctuary?"

"Yes, Thea," said Aristeia. She turned to the young woman who had slipped beside her and beamed, "I'm so glad you could come."

"I'm happy you invited me," said Leaina, taking Aristeia's hands.

"I was afraid it might be difficult for you to get away."

"Well, if mother had her way, I'd be helping rearrange things for the thousandth time. But I was determined, and Timokles was on my side."

Aristeia blushed. "Timokles wanted you to come?"

"Of course. Once he knew that both you and I wanted it, then so did he."

Aristeia threw her arms around her friend. "I'm so glad you'll be living with us."

"It'll be all right. You'll see."

The women, led by a flute-girl and followed by a mass of torch-bearing slaves, marched through the cold to the sacred spring to collect the purifying water, singing hymns to Hymen, Goddess of Marriage and Hot Desire, before returning to the warmth. Aristeia sat on a tall stool beside the empty bath, and the women gathered round her as the flute caressed their ears and the hearth fought the cold.

Glukera picked up the scissors. "Mighty Hera," she began, "Preparer of Weddings, honoured wife of Zeus. Your daughters witness that Aristeia, daughter of Nikias and Agné, is ready to shed her old ways and be planted in new fields. Honour her."

Aristeia freed her long hair from the ribbons, and slowly ran her fingers through it. Glukera eased Aristeia's hand away and began to cut away the tresses. Aristeia sat rigid, staring at the yellow wall. There was no escape now.

The debris of the past littered the floor, and her stick-like teenage cousin, Isias, could bear it no more. "It's not fair. Why should we lose our hair?" she demanded.

"Tradition," said Demetria, a severe, sparrow-like aunt whose hands fluttered in her lap. "She will grow a new crop of hair in her husband's home."

"But it's so silly," insisted Isias. "It makes her look like a boy."

"Perhaps that's the real reason," smiled Glukera, winking at Isias' mother, Theodora.

"What reason?" asked Isias.

"Shhh," soothed Theodora, a slightly plump but elegant woman who seemed to float everywhere. "Now is not the time." Isias scowled. "Does Timokles have any, er, special friends?" Theodora asked Leaina.

A roomful of eager eyes pierced Leaina, who looked down, blushing. "Timokles has lots of friends, but there *are* those that," she paused, fingering the edge of the bath, "he's closer to than others."

"Humph," grunted Glukera, squeezing Aristeia's shoulder. "Don't you worry, my sweet. You know what they say? 'One night is enough to destroy any man's indifference'." She laughed so heartily that Aristeia could not help smiling.

The flute and scissors continued their duet until at last Glukera announced, "There!"

"Nice job, Thea Glukera," said Demetria, her head tilting from side to side like a little bird's.

They refused Aristeia the silver hand mirror from the table. Glukera raised her to unwrap her himation, folding the rectangular material on the oak table. They lifted her peplos over her head, leaving her naked apart from the linen band wound around her chest. She was soon relieved of this and stepped into the empty bath, shivering and hugging herself.

Glukera and Theodora eased the full loutrophorus closer to the bath, examining the trembling figure. "Good hips," said Theodora. "It's always been said our family have good hips."

"But not enough meat," said Glukera. "You need to eat more, child. Where will your husband grab hold of you?"

"Not all men like big women," said the fibrous Demetria. "But she has good breasts. Plenty to satisfy any baby."

"And her husband," said Glukera, winking at Isias, who giggled and mentally compared her own. Aristeia was still blushing as Glukera prayed again. "Mighty Artemis, Virgin Goddess of Marriage. Aristeia is a virgin pure who asks your blessing. She washes away the past and embraces the future."

Glukera and Theodora raised the loutrophorus between them and released a stream of water over Aristeia, who gasped at the cold. The aunts raised the loutrophorus higher so the water covered Aristeia's head as the rest of the group cast white petals into the tub.

"This sacred water purifies and frees you from your childish life," pronounced Glukera, ensuring the water splashed over Demetria, who she suspected needed it more than Aristeia. The loutrophorus emptied, Glukera picked up a small vase of perfume and removed the stopper, releasing the aroma of roses as Aristeia fought to control her shivering. Her great-aunt prayed again. "Heavenly Aphrodite, Goddess of Love and Sex. Aristeia is about to embark on your journey. Let her scent inflame her husband." She poured the perfume over her niece, and the old lady winked and whispered, "You can get dressed now."

Aristeia jumped out of the bath, and dried and dressed in a flash. Glukera picked at the shorn hair and asked, "Do you have the toys, my sweet?"

Aristeia nodded, and grasping the basket of treasures, she followed the troop outside. Torches bathed the courtyard with light, wreaths festooned the balconies, roses and ivy entwined the columns. Slaves had lit a fire upon the marble altar in the centre of the yard, and Aristeia stepped towards it, hugging the basket to her chest. In the flames she saw her final wrench from the past, a parting she did not want to make.

Leaina whispered to her, "The future will be even better than the past."

Aristeia tried to smile, wondering how Leaina seemed to know what she was feeling. Perhaps Leaina had felt the same before her own wedding? Perhaps she was not the only woman to feel she was stepping into quicksand.

"Come here, child," said Glukera gently. Aristeia took her place beside her aunt at the altar. "Great Zeus, Protector of this House," cried Glukera, "we dedicate the hair of your unblemished daughter to you." She threw a handful of Aristeia's hair into the fire. "Great Zeus," continued Glukera, "we give you these tokens in thanks for your protection of this child in the household of Nikias, son of Nikeratus. Protect this woman in her new household of Timokles, son of Alkisthenes." She lowered her arms and looked eagerly towards the basket. "So, Aristeia, what do you have?"

Aristeia extracted the small wooden pig from her treasure trove. "I...I had this as a ba...baby," she smiled, her shivers making her stutter. "It... it makes a noise. S...see?" She shook the pig and it duly rattled.

"Very cute," clucked Demetria, "although I've never heard a pig make that sound before." Her amused cackle dissolved into a scowl as her joke failed to evoke a laugh.

Aristeia caressed the little creature. It was her only link to the mother she could not remember, and her hand trembled as she dropped it into the fire.

Glukera squeezed her hand. "What else, sweetheart?"

Aristeia produced a doll twice the length of her hand, dressed garishly and with long, wiry hair. "I think I must have spent half my life p...playing with Helen. Her... her legs and arms move, too," she demonstrated. "I can even m...make her dance."

"It's time to set aside childish things, Aristeia," said Glukera softly.

Aristeia held up the childhood gift from her father and studied her one last time, before sighing and dropping her into the flames. One by one, she relinquished her childhood treasures, hoping that the gods would reward her for such sacrifice.

When the toys had gone, Glukera announced, "One more goddess to placate, and then we can get down to real business." She bustled towards the family room in the corner of the courtyard, followed by the others except for Leaina and Aristeia.

Leaina watched her friend's melancholy face still contemplating the small fire, and allowed herself a moment to remember her own wedding, a lifetime ago. A lifetime. Some may say a mere five years, but death and suffering can make a moment last forever. She tried to picture her beautiful babies before the plague. Only before. The talons of the past gripped her, and she closed her eyes. Eventually she spoke, with a slight crack in her voice despite herself. "You'll soon have new memories, Aristeia." Her friend turned her head towards her. "And happy ones. I'm sure of it."

Aristeia whispered, "I hope so."

"As Homer said, may the gods grant you a life that your heart loves." They embraced, clinging to each other before turning in silence to join the noise emanating from the corner room.

"Where have you two been?" demanded Glukera, a merry smile lighting her face as they entered the warm room. "I thought you were right behind us. I'm afraid we didn't wait for you," she said, holding up a black cup decorated with red figures. The elegance of the vessel was not what held Glukera's attention, but the red liquid within that slipped down the throat with such ease. "Has it ever struck you as rather odd," she continued, "that Artemis, being the goddess of virginity, is also the goddess of childbirth? Do you think she ever gets confused?"

"You should wait before drinking the wine, Thea Glukera," fluttered Demetria. "We must sacrifice to Hestia first."

Glukera shrugged and took her place on a soft-cushioned chair, forming a circle with the others around the fire in the centre of the room as she fondled her wine cup. "Why don't you continue?" she asked Demetria, who gave a loud "tut" before settling herself and clearing her throat.

"The pomegranate," began Demetria, addressing Isias and her young cousins in particular, "is a gift of the gods. Its red flesh represents the joining of the blood of two families, and its seeds are the blessings of fertility." She held a hand up and a slave appeared from the shadows with a knife. Demetria sliced a piece from the pomegranate half on her table and declared, "Hestia, Goddess of the

Hearth, Protector of this Home. We thank you for your care of Aristeia. Remain her protector at her new hearth." She tossed the slice into the fire.

"At last," cried Glukera. "Let's eat." She devoured her own pomegranate.

Demetria pecked, complaining, "It may represent fertility, but these seeds are a nuisance."

"Oh, Demetria," said Glukera. "You pick at your food like a little hen. How will you get to be as robust as Theodora, or me?"

Silver bowls of pastries, sweet fritters, finches, and slices of tuna appeared on each table. "I believe my husband would not want me to be any different," said Demetria as she delicately picked up a slice of tuna.

"Ah ha!" exclaimed Glukera, taking another swig of wine. "Now we get to the real business of the evening. Sit down, children," she said, motioning vaguely to the young cousins, already seated. "You too, Aristeia. It's our duty, as your elders, to teach you," she looked around the room conspiratorially, "about men."

The cousins beamed their delight, and Leaina tried to conceal her amusement.

"Men, young ladies, are like trierarchs, the ship masters. They may pay to equip the ship and think they are captains of it, but it's the helmsman who determines where it goes." The old lady nodded at her audience. "We, ladies, are the helmsmen."

Demetria almost choked on her tuna.

"Too many pips there, too, dear?" asked Glukera.

Demetria glared her answer before turning to the younger members of the party. "Don't listen to her. Let a man be, and he will take care of you. Put food on your table, warm clothes on your back, and children in your belly. What more could you want?"

"Take care of you?" scoffed Glukera. "Take care of his mistresses, more likely. If you give him the chance, he'll be putting gems on her while putting sackcloth on you. And he'll only do that for you provided you give him an heir."

"Now, now, Thea Glukera," chided Theodora, gracefully raising a fritter from her table. "Men like to sail the seas with experienced captains, so they will have their mistresses. About that, we can do little. Besides," she added, twinkling at Demetria, "it can be to our advantage. After all, young men may have the equipment, but no one told them how to use it."

"Yes, yes," laughed Glukera, sloshing her wine. "Now *there* would be a Council motion everyone could get behind. Free lessons in love."

Demetria perched stiffly, glaring at the laughing women. "I do not think you should encourage your husbands to sail into every whorehouse in Piraeus. It is not seemly."

"Perhaps not," agreed Glukera, wiping away a tear, "but Theodora is right." She turned her attention to the unmarried. "Men may swear by Aphrodite, but the bedroom is like the gymnasium. If he hasn't had a good trainer he's unlikely to perfect his technique."

"He will not get that training in the brothels of Piraeus," snapped Demetria, "where they work to time."

"Quite true, Demetria," soothed Theodora. "Which is why a knowing mistress can be such a help. If a man's only experience is of prostitutes and young boys, where else will he learn?"

Demetria spluttered, but was unable to summon any coherent words. Leaina assumed an innocent face and asked, "Won't all these prostitutes and mistresses wear him out?"

"Oh, when men are young they don't wear out," cried young Isias. Glukera and Theodora glanced at each other and dissolved in laughter.

"You have been listening to your brother boasting too much," said Theodora. "You should listen to our slave girls more. Young men pump their egos up so high. All that air has to come from somewhere. Other things must deflate."

Glukera clapped. "Very good. Yes. Quite so. Young men have such fine bodies, though. Firm and muscular. What a shame that Time has such an appetite for the young."

"But as we age together, we learn to appreciate other qualities," said Demetria.

"Really?" asked Glukera. "Do men have any other qualities?"

"Thea Glukera, you are too hard on them," laughed Theodora.

Glukera turned to the younger women as she took another draught of wine. "You see, their lack of other qualities helps us. A little nudge here, a promise there. A word of encouragement, a refrain from rebuke. Pretty words sway their hearts like linens flapping in the breeze. Men are very simple, and there are so many ways to train them. It's no different from dogs, really."

"Moving in with a new husband is as simple as that?" asked Aristeia.

Glukera's face turned more serious. "Simple? Oh no, not simple. His mother, there's your problem. Men marry young women because they think they'll train us to run the house in the way *they* want. But it's really their mother's way, and she will try to mould you into a new version of herself. Wresting control from your husband is easy. Taking it from his mother is much more difficult. After all," she said, taking another gulp, "she's a woman."

"So how do you do it?" asked Aristeia.

The older women looked at each other and nodded their agreement. "Providing a son," said Demetria. "That is, after all, our highest duty. And to raise them to be good citizens."

"What is Timokles' mother like?" asked bright-eyed Isias.

"Well, Leaina?" asked Glukera, when an answer was not forthcoming. "What can you tell us about the fight that lies before our Aristeia?"

Leaina smiled. "Aristeia is a gem that would sparkle in any household, and all women adore precious stones. What mother could help but love her?"

There was loud approval, and Aristeia leaned across to hug her friend.

"What a diplomat," winked Glukera.

"And what about Timokles?" prodded Demetria. "Is he also being religiously prepared this evening?"

Leaina thought about her brother out with his friends at Simaetha's, determined to worship Dionysus and Aphrodite. "I'm sure that he and his companions are having what they consider to be a thoroughly religious evening."

Chapter 25

Timokles had a headache, and the singing and the midday sun were not helping. The wedding was upon him, and the procession of uncles, aunts, cousins, and friends that crowded in the street behind him was a yoke around his neck. No matter that their songs were so joyful, Timokles was a prized bull led to sacrifice for the sake of a new source of wealth and patronage.

Alkibiades strolled beside him, evidently enjoying the festive atmosphere, but Timokles was hardly aware of the blessings of onlookers, the laughter that mingled with the hymns, the hammering from a sculptor's workshop, or the spontaneous dancing of a tavern's clientele. He tingled with the awareness of Samias behind him, somewhere, lost in the crowd. Lost.

The procession passed through a crossroads and evaded a string of mules like a river navigating boulders. When it approached Nikias' house, the general stepped into the street, smiling and holding his arms open wide as his brothers and sons filed behind him. The crowd slowed to a halt and Alkibiades eased Timokles forward.

"Welcome, all of you," shouted Nikias. "Timokles' family is my family, and my family is your family." He hugged Timokles. "And a special welcome to you, my son."

Timokles blushed. "Thank you. Father."

Music and singing from within the house drifted on the air as Nikias presented his family. "Timokles, Nikeratus and Strettipus are Aristeia's brothers. They are now your brothers." The two teenage boys greeted Timokles awkwardly. "Diognetus and Eukrates," continued Nikias, "are Aristeia's uncles. They are now your uncles." Timokles shook hands with the two men, only half a dozen years or so older than himself. Nikias indicated the open door with a sweep of his arm. "Please. My house is your house."

The crowd bustled into the outer courtyard, surveyed from the balconies above by a host of slaves whose owners were already at the party. Timokles offered a libation of wine on the altar and watched his future drain away.

He blindly followed Nikias through to the main courtyard, where an animated throng of new family and friends cheered their welcome. Bearded men in long tunics and young boys in colourful chitons congregated in the sunshine, slaves buzzed back and forth with cups and pitchers, musicians played on the balcony, women and young girls chattered in the shade. The clans mingled, armies clashing in the plains: the lightly armed women skirmished in the shade, the broad-shouldered men faced off in the sunshine, clever words and ingratiating smiles their weapons. The courtyard hummed with the battle.

Timokles tried to smile but only succeeded in making a strange grimace, raising a degree of sympathy among the young women for Aristeia, who was not yet present.

Nikias gave a signal and a trumpeter succeeded in bringing silence. The general sacrificed a white ox and two sheep, poured their blood on to the altar, and then moved aside to allow ancient Stilbides to examine their entrails. The old seer declared the omens favourable, removing Timokles' last hope, and slaves hauled the carcasses away for cooking.

The music and jollity resumed, and Nikias prepared to take Timokles on a tour of his new family, but Alkibiades caught the general by the arm and smiled. "May I say what an excellent match you have made, General? Not only because of his family, but especially because of the man you are gaining as a son-in-law."

Timokles cracked into his first genuine smile of the day.

"I believe it," said Nikias, patting Alkibiades' arm. "There are many who wanted a connection with my family, but like Odysseus, I believe it's important to lash oneself to the right mast and resist the temptations of the sirens. As true in politics, Alkibiades, as in anything else."

"Indeed," said Alkibiades, "but when a ship is damaged, the mast may need changing, and perhaps sometimes there is wisdom amongst the sirens."

"Not to my ears," said Nikias. "A damaged ship is better than a shipwreck."

"But a damaged ship sailing for the rocks *is* a shipwreck. Only the timing is in question."

"The seas are a dangerous place, son of Kleinias. Rocks and shallows, storms and pirates. An experienced helmsman sees the dangers and avoids them."

"Experience of past calamities can make a helmsman overly cautious. Perhaps younger voices, though they may sound rash, can chart a surer course to safety."

Nikias' good mood seemed to be evaporating. "Take care, Alkibiades. Kleon isn't one of us. He cares nothing for Athens. Only power interests him, and it blinds him to the city's needs. His rhetoric may dazzle, but his course leads only to ruination. The Assembly accepted your motion on Plataea, and you have added lustre to your name. Now return to those trusted by your own guardian."

"Perikles had wisdom and courage," said Alkibiades. "He would have recognized when a change in course was necessary."

Nikias straightened and looked away; Alkibiades shook his head. When the general finally turned back to them, he had resumed his smile. "Shall we?" he said, inviting them onwards.

Timokles struggled to reciprocate the greetings of men he had no urgent desire to know, hiding behind Alkibiades, who made love to them all. The handshakes were endless, and all the while Timokles felt the eyes of Samias upon him, and longed to turn and meet them. The joy of those around him was mockery.

Admiring stares arrowed at Alkibiades from the safety of the shade, but he was not afraid to meet them, and amidst the buzz of women, he held the eyes once more of Pisander's wife, whose name he had learned was Elené. This time her turn of the head was coquettish, and Alkibiades knew he had not been mistaken at the celebration: here was a woman who knew what she wanted.

Pastries, Syracusan cheese, and Phoenician dates circulated with the wine. The party sang with increased exuberance whenever the musicians chose a particularly popular song. Little boys and girls darted between two worlds, between light and shade, ignoring the invisible barrier that separated the men from the women.

Nikolas and Kallias watched jealously as Alkibiades paraded his friend. Nikolas smiled darkly and said to Kallias, "You know he calls you 'Snake', don't you?"

"Who?"

"Timokles."

Kallias turned in surprise, his curly locks glowing in the sun. "Timokles?" He stared for a few moments at a group of jugglers that had started performing. "Why snake?"

"When your name is mentioned he hisses, 'sss', his shorthand for you as sssuperstitious, ssspoilt and ssstupid." Nikolas marvelled at the colour of Kallias' face. Perhaps he should add sssunset. "Now, you know I'm a tease, but it's always harmless fun. No malice. But Timokles worries me. He's been with Alkibiades from childhood and I think he envies our influence. Yours especially. Makes me wonder what he says about us behind our backs." Nikolas noted that Kallias had controlled his anger and was listening attentively. "We should be on our guard against Timokles. For both our sakes."

"Thanks, Nikolas. I appreciate it."

"Think nothing of it." Nikolas nodded in Timokles' direction. "Say, do you think we should suggest to the bride that she wear a false beard like they do in Argos? It might help Timokles perform." Kallias laughed, but Nikolas detected an edge to it, as if Kallias took pleasure in his jab at Timokles. "Ah, here's someone who needs cheering up," added Nikolas as Samias sauntered towards them.

"I'm fine," said Samias, standing beside Nikolas and looking back towards Timokles again.

"Your problems," said Nikolas, "would all be solved if you gouged out your eyes."

"How so?" said Samias.

"Have you not heard? They say that love's an illness of the eyes. Remove the eyes and you're cured."

"Who wants to be cured?" said Kallias. "Especially if one's love is the most beautiful creature on earth."

Nikolas smiled. "You'll want a cure when Sellene rips you apart."

"She will never do that," said Kallias.

"Let me guess, she's vowed her undying love."

"She has. And I am going to buy a place for her so that even when I have to marry, we can still be together."

Nikolas laughed. "Kallias, Kallias. You're so naive. You can't believe a lover's promise. Love is more transferable than money."

"I hope for your sake you don't believe that, Nikolas," said Samias.

"You've no fear, then, that Timokles' wife will steal his love from you?" said Nikolas.

Samias shifted uncomfortably, and Nikolas knew he had struck a chord. "No more than Alkibiades can fear Nikias stealing Timokles' loyalty," said Samias.

Nikolas shook his head and turned his attention back towards Timokles' progress with Alkibiades and the general. Congratulations swamped them, but Nikolas noted Nikias' gaze repeatedly drifted to a closed door on the upper floor.

***

Aristeia sat in her room, hunched over and feeling sick. The hubbub from the courtyard delivered no cheer. Glukera stroked her great-niece's hand, fighting back her own tremors on seeing the fear that gripped Aristeia. The Egyptian maid sat on the bare bed, having stripped its pillows and blankets for the last time.

"What if he hates me?" muttered Aristeia.

"Shh, not possible, my sweet. He'll adore you. And you'll have Leaina right with you."

Aristeia stood and walked around the room, her eyes to the ground, her hands writhing. Golden owls clasped her saffron peplos at her shoulders and her waist was pinched with a thick red belt tied in the traditional knot of Herakles, the first test of manhood for her husband. She strode back and forth, and every crescendo in the music outside raised an echo of dread within. "Oh, Thea Glukera. What if he's mean to me?" She burst into tears and Glukera bustled to her and enfolded her in her arms.

"There, there, child," she murmured. "Now look at me. See these hands? They may be old but they can smite your husband as well as mine, so don't you worry." Aristeia gave a little sob and a faint smile. "Now let's dry those tears and get your veil ready."

They had only just repaired Aristeia's face when there was a light tapping on the door. "Aristeia?"

"Come in, Father," she called with more calmness than she felt.

Nikias entered and was overwhelmed at the sight of his daughter dressed to leave home. The strained smile and slightly wild eyes looked so foreign on her face, and raised a shudder of sadness within him. He squeezed her hands. "You look very beautiful. The gods must smile on Timokles."

"Thank you, Father." She did not feel beautiful. She did not particularly care if she looked beautiful. Standing in her room, stripped of everything that made it hers, she felt abandoned, homeless. She wanted to curl into a ball in the corner and hide from the noise outside. But she was her father's daughter, so she forced a smile. "The daughter of Nikias needs only to avoid appearing ugly for everyone to pronounce her beautiful. And even if they don't think it, today, at least, they'll have to say it."

"It'll take far less effort for them to say so than in most cases," said Glukera, fitting the veil to her niece's head.

Nikias hesitated, on the precipice of saying something, but unable to take the leap. Instead, he sighed and led her by the hand from the room into the bright sunlight. She lowered her veil, and as they appeared on the balcony cheers and ululations greeted them, before morphing into the wedding hymn to Hymen. "Sing Hymen, Hymenai O! Hymen, Hymenai O!" The song enveloped them as they stepped down the stairs, followed by Glukera.

The army of men opened a pathway to the altar as Aristeia searched the faces, wondering which one was her husband. She was dimly aware of the hymn, the raised drinking cups, the bearded faces. She sensed the high pitched singing of the women coming from some ethereal world, but all she looked for was a kind smile from the man she was to marry.

Two men stood their ground before the bloody altar. The first was handsome and confident; the second, shorter, with curly hair and a smooth face, blushing, constantly adjusting his garland and glancing away. Nikias stopped his daughter before the shorter man and raised her veil. Timokles' blush deepened, and she noticed Alkibiades step on his foot, at which Timokles seemed to remember to smile. Aristeia had not considered that he, too, would be nervous, and a smile rose to her face.

Timokles met her eyes fleetingly, and then handed over the gifts he had for her: a marble pestle and a carved weaving sword, symbols of her new role.

Nikias raised his hands, and the hymn petered out. The men cleared a space in the centre of the courtyard, to where Nikias led his daughter. A dozen young girls, in brightly coloured knee-length chitons and wispy veils, appeared from their mothers' care and danced around Aristeia, singing a hymn to Artemis, Goddess of Marriage. The bride stood motionless, lonely amidst the crowd, trying to watch her young cousins and ignore the eyes upon her. Her husband had been embarrassed and awkward, unable to make eye contact. Nervousness was a good sign, wasn't it?

The dance ended to loud applause, and Aristeia escaped with Glukera to the comfort of the shade and the safety of her female relatives and friends. She huddled amongst them, hiding in the crowd. She had not yet exchanged one word with her husband.

The musicians resumed, a troupe of acrobats burst in to entertain the company, slaves circulated with plates of food and pitchers of wine. The entertainments continued through the afternoon. Aristeia shivered in the cool air, surrounding herself with Leaina and Glukera as a stream of women provided advice that Aristeia did not hear: her attention was focused upon her husband across the courtyard, but the dense crowd frustrated her efforts.

The afternoon faded and slaves lit the torches fixed to the marble columns. When the moon had risen above the roof, Nikias ushered the newlyweds to the family room, to the main hearth of the house. Aristeia gripped Glukera's hand, and Timokles sheltered in Alkibiades' shadow as they followed. The little party stood silently around the fire in the centre of the room, listening to the noise outside.

Aristeia watched her father and saw his reluctance to perform the final act. She wanted to run to him, to say that she didn't have to go, that she could stay with him. He glanced up and their eyes met. He looked so sad that she almost burst into tears.

Nikias sighed, and raised a handful of grain from a basket beside the hearth and cast it into the flames. Aristeia and Glukera repeated the offering as Nikias prayed, "Gentle Hestia, Queen of Homes, thank you for bringing my child safely to womanhood." He turned to his daughter and whispered huskily, "We named you well. You truly are an excellent daughter."

Aristeia stifled a sob as her father lowered her veil, a door closing on her home. He took her by the hand and led her around the hearth, and on their third circuit, Timokles gently grabbed her wrist and pulled her towards the door, starting the ritual abduction. Loud cheers and encouragement greeted them as they entered the courtyard, Aristeia alive to the hand encompassing her wrist, her breath catching at the first touch of a man who was not her father.

Timokles led her to the outer courtyard, cluttered with slaves bearing torches, and out into the dark street. Aristeia looked around for her father and brothers but could not spot them amongst the crowd spilling out of the house. A chariot awaited the couple, decorated in bright ribbons and streamers, two impatient black horses yoked before it. Glukera assumed her place ahead of the chariot, carrying a torch to frighten away evil spirits, and joining in the hymn to Hymen that the musicians in front of her had started.

Timokles turned to Aristeia and gave an apologetic smile, before sweeping her from her feet and lifting her onto the chariot. Aristeia felt his strength and trembled.

Alkibiades jumped up beside them, took the reins and looked back to the revellers, crying, "Away!" He prompted the horses into a walk and nudged Timokles, nodding towards Aristeia. The groom obediently took the bride by the wrist again.

As the procession moved away, Aristeia looked back over the bobbing heads. Her father stood alone in the doorway to his house. She smiled, and held his gaze until they turned the corner and the last thread to her home was broken. A tear escaped, and she glanced up at Timokles. He was a post, staring straight ahead.

Blessings showered them as they passed doorways of curious

heads. Slaves at fountains watched sullenly as another world passed by. "Hymen, Hymenai O!" The jubilant voices rocked the streets, and Alkibiades added his own interpretation: "Hymen, oh hymen, whither go you?" Aristeia's face burned.

The clamour approached Timokles' home, where his weighty mother, Nikopatra, stood before the open door. Behind her the house slaves raised torches, the doorway crammed with the craning necks of her friends, including Deinomache and Hipparete.

The sight of his mother reminded Timokles of a conversation they had had two days ago. Nikopatra had been overseeing the wedding preparations, Timokles content to fade into the background until he was jolted by a comment he overheard.

"I just hope she doesn't have ideas above her years," said Nikopatra.

Timokles was leaning against a wall in the sun and looked up sharply. "What do you mean?"

Nikopatra glanced at Leaina. "I run this household. This girl had better not try to change everything. Dowry or no."

"Mother," said Leaina, "Aristeia's an excellent young woman. She's run her father's house for at least five years and I'm sure she'll be anxious to please you. But she *will* be rightfully the lady of the house."

Nikopatra grunted, and Timokles had wondered if the war with the Peloponnesians was not the only conflict on the horizon. And now, as he watched his mother bask in the torchlight, he knew that she was already assessing the girl he was bringing home.

The procession halted and Timokles lifted Aristeia to the ground, taking her by the wrist and leading her into the house, sweeping through the outer courtyard and into the second, the rest of the party tumbling after them.

Aristeia struggled to breath, suffocated by the crowds, the laughter, the singing. She had been sure that entering her new home would be a momentous event, but once she stepped over the threshold she barely had time to notice the balcony, the wreaths, the statues. She was bustled into the family room and stood before the hearth, much as she had done with her father.

Nikopatra, Leaina, and the household slaves stood with them

as the singing outside grew louder, and the young couple each tossed a handful of barley into the fire. Timokles moved his grip from his wife's wrist to her hand and walked her around the hearth, praying, "Hestia, welcome Aristeia, daughter of Nikias, into my house. Protect her, make her prosperous and make her fertile."

It was the first time she had heard his voice, and Aristeia felt it was a gentle one, a promise of a kind future.

As Timokles prayed, Nikopatra, Leaina and the slaves tossed dried dates, figs and nuts over them, echoing his prayer. Three times they circled, throwing grain and renewing the chant, showered by the fruits of fertility.

Finally, Timokles turned to Aristeia and looked at her closely for the first time. He saw the fear in her eyes through the veil and felt the tremble in her hand, which he squeezed gently. "I... I hope you'll be happy here."

Aristeia returned his gaze. "I hope I will make you happy."

"Aristeia, this is my mother. She is your mother."

Aristeia lowered her head, and Nikopatra recited, "Welcome, Daughter."

"And this is my sister. Your sister."

Aristeia smiled and lowered her head to Leaina, who ignored the gesture and threw her arms round her, whispering, "Welcome, oh, welcome, Aristeia." The bride lost herself in Leaina's hug, not wanting to surface.

"We should see to our guests," said Timokles, indicating the commotion outside. The family parted, Timokles to the men, Nikopatra with her two daughters to the clusters of women. Music, dancing, wine, and food ensured that the guests would not forget such a wedding, Nikopatra pleased to highlight to her new daughter the excellent manner in which she had prepared the house.

"Thank you, Mother. It was very kind of you to take such trouble," said Aristeia.

"Oh, my child," laughed Nikopatra. "It was no trouble. When you have my experience, such trifles are easy."

"Aristeia prepared Nikias' house beautifully," grinned Leaina.

"Really?" said Nikopatra. "Good for you. Though I expect

your Thea Glukera did most of the preparation."

"Thea Glukera has been like a mother to me. Always ready with kind advice when I've asked for it, but happy to trust me to do what I think is best."

Nikopatra frowned, but she had no opportunity to respond as Deinomache burst upon them, demanding, "Well, Aristeia? Did you like the chariot and pair that my son provided?"

Aristeia stammered, "S... sorry? Oh. Oh, yes. They were wonderful, thank you."

A golden himation bordered with purple robed Deinomache, a gold band around her head and another round her throat, gold bangles tinkling on her wrists. "That is quite alright. You will find my son always helps out Timokles."

Before any seismic activity could assert itself in Nikopatra, Leaina smiled at Hipparete. "You're looking beautiful, Hipparete." Alkibiades' wife sidled alongside Leaina and squeezed her hand. "I hope you can have the chance to know Aristeia and we'll all be friends."

"That would make me very happy," said Hipparete, leaning past Leaina to smile at Aristeia.

"Of course, there is no happiness like bearing a child," smiled Deinomache, patting Hipparete's stomach. "I wonder if Timokles and Aristeia will manage that."

"You mean 'when'," said Nikopatra, but Deinomache simply raised an eyebrow. Nikopatra's jowls rippled, and she beckoned the nearest slave. "Go tell Alkibiades it's time to get Timokles upstairs." The slave disappeared into the crowd, and Nikopatra turned to Aristeia. "Are you ready, my dear?"

Ready? Absolutely. Ready to run home, ready to run to the Temple of Athena, the fields, anywhere away from the crowd's expectations. She answered with a slight quiver in her voice, "Yes, Mother."

Nikopatra strode into the mass of drunken men with Aristeia in her wake. Timokles and Alkibiades were prepared. Samias had retreated into the background, and amidst bawdy innuendoes and ribald jokes, Alkibiades led the couple to the outer courtyard and up the stairs. The guests thronged the ground below them, singing, chanting, shouting, laughing. Aristeia's breath deserted her.

Outside his bedroom door, Timokles removed Aristeia's veil. She was exposed, to him, to everyone. She noticed his eyes scan her face briefly before he opened the door and led her inside, Alkibiades remaining on guard outside. The house breathed hymns of fertility, and laughter at shouted jokes.

Inside, the oil lamps gave a soft glow to Timokles' room, dominated by a bed covered in a red blanket. The room was sparse apart from two low couches and a large oak chest. Several tapestries hung from the walls, and rugs softened the floor. Timokles released her hand as he closed the door behind them.

"Did Leaina make these?" asked Aristeia, indicating the hangings.

"Yes."

"She's very talented."

"Yes."

The two of them stood listening to the singing, blushing at the words.

"You have a very nice house," said Timokles.

"Yes." Aristeia's smile was a soft light upon her face. "This is my house now."

"Yes. Of course." Timokles' eyes fixed upon her face as if he were studying an interesting flower. He cleared his throat. "You're very beautiful."

"Do you really think so?" Aristeia felt his eyes upon her and her blush deepened. "What do you find beautiful?"

"Your eyes."

They stood in heavy loneliness for several minutes, listening to the singing, glancing at the intimidating bed. Timokles finally fixed his gaze on Aristeia's fiendish knotted belt, and said, "I guess I'd better get to work."

Chapter 26

How was it possible? Could it really be two weeks already?

Sémon opened his eyes and stared at the wooden beams of the ceiling. Beside him slept Rebia, her ample bosom keeping time with her light snoring, a soothing sound that he associated with this safe haven. The morning light crept under the door and ushered in images of his nephew's mangled body. Sémon had seen the carrion gather above the walls, could picture too vividly their ghastly meals. The Thebans had finally buried the dead to prevent the smell, but the sacrilege was a brand burning inside him.

"Zeus will pay them back," he growled. Rebia stirred but then resumed her sleep. Sémon studied her chubby face and smiled: she was no beauty, there would never be a statue in her likeness, but she was good for him. She demanded nothing but the enjoyment of the moment, and for a short time he could forget past and future. She needed no cheering, and after their love-making he could sleep or muse peacefully, content in her companionship.

Did he love her? He had known love, long ago with Ana. She had been a flame of happiness granted by the gods and then extinguished. Now he dared not think of her for more than an instant, lest loss of the past overpower hope for the future. No, he could love no woman in the same manner, yet he was glad Rebia was here.

Angry shouts from the courtyard disrupted his contemplation, two men arguing over the right to one of the rooms. Sémon grinned at the thought of this traitor's house being the garrison's favourite haunt in which to satisfy their needs. The argument grew hotter and Sémon's smile dissolved. Since the failed breakout, tempers had frayed. Something had gone wrong, so someone must be at fault. General Arkadius had maintained his grip as leader simply by the lack of any credible rival, but suspicion accompanied every meal as each man wondered who had betrayed their friends and brothers.

Sémon threw aside the blanket and grabbed his chiton,

embracing the freezing air. But by the time he had wrapped his leather belt around his waist and slipped into his sandals, someone else had acted as mediator.

"Going already?" a sleepy voice enquired from beneath the blanket.

Sémon was tempted to rejoin her, but the day had started. He wrapped himself in his thick tunic and opened the door. "Yes. See you later." He passed under the balcony into the courtyard, and a head poked out of a window.

"You finished, Sémon? Where's Rebia?"

"Sleeping."

"What?!" As Sémon stepped over the threshold in to the street, he heard irate banging and the man shouting, "Get up, you lazy cow. There are people waiting."

Sémon marched along the alley towards the agora, revelling in the cold, energized and ready to face his comrades again. He nodded to the shivering guard on duty at the entrance to the agora. "Sakos."

"Sémon."

"Wonderful weather."

"Yes, if you're inside next to a fire."

Sémon smiled. "No, my friend. Perfect weather for guard duty. Who can fall asleep when it's like this?"

"Well, there is that, I suppose," chuckled Sakos. "See you later."

Sémon waved his hand and continued into the desolate agora. The cold had driven everyone indoors, and Sémon jogged up the steps and into what had once been the law courts. They had cleared the large hall and made it into living quarters for a hundred men. The murmur of muted conversation and the overpowering smell of smoke and sweat filled the court. Sémon edged past the small groups huddled around fires, avoided stacks of shields in their stands, slapped the occasional back, and thundered a friendly greeting. He saw Mikos near a fire in the corner and bellowed, "Mikos! Are you winning?"

Mikos shrugged and rocked his hand. Sémon put his hand on his friend's shoulder as he reached him and watched him roll the dice.

"Yeaah, that's me," muttered grim-faced Skopas, scooping the pebbles towards himself.

"That's me?" mocked Sémon. "Don't get too enthusiastic, will you?"

Skopas mobilized his furrows. "Come on, Sémon, we're not in the mood."

"Not in the mood?" said Sémon.

"We've been talking about the breakout," explained Hybrias, looking at the few pebbles in his hand and brushing his long hair from his boyish face.

"You surprise me," said Sémon, patting Hybrias on the thigh as he sat on a low stool beside him. "And have you been talking about the shock and fear our diversion caused?"

The group was silent until Phelix, a large muscle of a man, replied, "No, Sémon, we haven't. We know what happened there. But we were wondering how some people on the other side of town returned unscathed while all their companions died." He glared at Hybrias.

"I told you," said Hybrias, gritting his teeth, "I'm no shield slinger."

"Hmmm," continued the muscle, watching the young man through half closed eyes. "Perhaps that's because you didn't have a shield with you."

Hybrias flung his pebbles down and braced as if he were about to jump to his feet. Sémon restrained him, but Hybrias continued to snarl and struggle against what he must have known to be an insurmountable force. Phelix stood menacingly and scowled at the youngster.

"Sit down," said Sémon. Phelix's eyes remained nailed on Hybrias. "Phelix!" The warrior's head snapped to Sémon. Whatever it was he saw there, his body relaxed, he shook his head at Hybrias, and sat down. "Hybrias!" barked Sémon. The young man immediately stopped struggling, returning Phelix's stare. "How does this help?" said Sémon. "How can we survive if we don't trust each other?"

"Trust?" coughed a bug-eyed man next to Phelix. "What trust? Why do you think the breakout failed? They knew about it. Someone squealed."

"That's right," said Phelix. "After all, whenever you have this many Greeks together, betrayal can never be too far away."

"Oh, come now, Phelix," said Sémon. "Do you really think that? Greeks are the most loyal people on earth. Once they've figured out what to be loyal to." His companions chuckled.

"But Sémon," said Hybrias, "Phelix is right. Remember the traitors who sold us to Thebes at the start of all this? Perhaps some of them are still here. Waiting." He looked around the hall as if seeing Furies beside every fire.

"I understand how you feel," said Sémon. "But really, is it likely? If anyone was going to betray us, they've had plenty of opportunities throughout the siege. Especially when the whole Peloponnesian army was camped outside. Why wait 'til now? No. I think we're too eager to see evil where there is none. Sometimes bad things happen that are no one's fault."

"Hmph," grunted the muscle. "I don't see that. Do you think a troop of well-disciplined men could be cut down so easily? At night? With no warning? No, by Apollo, of course not. They had to know they were coming to kill them all so close to the walls."

"They were brave men, Phelix," said Skopas, his face a cloudy day, "but perhaps foolish as well. Oh, I know, Sémon, don't get upset with me, but why do you think I opposed the breakout? I always said it was suicide. Perhaps there was betrayal, perhaps not. But really, the Thebans needed no warning. They had cavalry. They could've picked them off one by one with our men unable to land a single blow."

"But how could they leave them unburied so long?" burst Hybrias. "Have you ever heard of such a thing?"

"Not by the Spartans," said Sémon.

"Ah, but Sémon, there you have it," said Skopas. "This is no work of the Spartans. This is those turd-munching Thebans. Their hatred would chase us down to Hades, and no wonder when they remember their comrades we executed. What will become of us when they realize how few we are and bring their full army to crush us?"

"What they did to our friends was an abomination," replied Sémon. "The gods will punish such sacrilege."

"But when?" asked Hybrias. "Skopas is right. If it isn't soon, we may go the same way."

Sémon looked around the expectant faces, feeling the weight of their hopes again. "Athens will dispense the gods' justice. Their army will march like locusts into this plain and destroy Thebes. And as for crushing us, the only crushing that'll happen is when Rebia decides to be on top." His audience gave a faint echo of his laughter as he tore at a half-eaten loaf. "Come the summer," he continued, "we'll be free and we'll see our families once more."

"My wife will have forgotten what I look like," said Skopas.

"When you look like we do," said Sémon, "that can only be a good thing. And I'll bet you think she looks like that minx, Alkia, whose company you're so fond of these days."

"Alkia provides a distraction, I'll admit."

Sémon grinned and they started to play dice again with a little more enthusiasm, buoyed by Sémon's roars of joy or disappointment. His spirit infected the whole hall as each group's conversation rose in volume to match their neighbour's. The noise disguised the tramp of feet entering the court, and at first, no one noticed the rattle of swords and shields as five soldiers scanned the room. They marched towards the far corner, leaving a bemused hush in their wake and a trail of eyes watching their progress. The soldiers arrived at Sémon's dice game and brought an abrupt halt in play.

"Skopas, son of Xenokles," the steely man at the head announced, "you must accompany us."

Skopas looked at him and the armed guards in bewilderment. "What for?"

"Does it matter? I gave you an order. Get to your feet at once and come with us."

Sémon stood and turned to face the guards. "What's this about, Satorus? Why the guards?"

Satorus said quietly, "This is nothing to do with you, Sémon. Please sit down."

Sémon continued to stare at Satorus as Skopas rose. "It's okay, Sémon. I'll see what the fuss is about," said Skopas. He walked in the midst of the guards to the door, watched silently by every man in the hall.

As Skopas passed through the door, Satorus turned to face the room and declared, "Skopas, son of Xenokles, is charged with treason, with the betrayal of our friends into the hands of our enemies. He is to be tried for his life this afternoon in the Temple of Athena."

Chapter 27

The goddess on her throne glared at the thunderous crowd of men gathered in her chamber. The torches that usually granted a mysterious light had been supplemented with dozens of oil lamps, whose light bounced off the dedications of shields and armour and flooded the temple with an unforgiving brightness. Athena, like many of her age, did not enjoy scrutiny under such well-lit conditions – her painted face was flaking.

General Arkadius, having poured a libation and asked for Athena's wisdom, turned his back on the goddess and sat on a chair facing the length of the temple. His restless soldiers stood in menacing groups around the hall, and Skopas fidgeted on a stool near the general.

"I remind you," the general began in his patriarchal voice, "that you have sworn to hear this case without prejudice. May Athena destroy anyone who fails to keep his promise. We are under... unusual circumstances. Given the seriousness of the charge, I will allow anyone to speak and will use my own judgment, not the water clock, to limit speeches as necessary." He nodded to Satorus, who extricated himself from the crowd and stood beside the general, facing his peers.

Satorus was a barrel-chested man, with a scar slashed across his forehead and eyes as hard as iron. "Gentlemen," he said, "I need not recall by name all those who made the heroic attempt to break free and raise Athens to our aid. They were our brothers, our nephews, our uncles, even our sons. All were our friends. Brave men deserving respect and honour. But what did they get?" He posed the question to each angry face. "Dishonour. Left as food for dogs, unable to make the dark journey to Elysium. Is that what they deserved?"

Cries of "No!" echoed around the chamber.

"Is that what they fought for?" Satorus continued amidst more vigorous denials. "In war, preparation is all. Our generals planned everything so well. Yet it failed. Why?" He paused before shouting,

"Because we were betrayed!"

The men's response thundered in the temple, with many a curse shot at Skopas. Mikos bit his lip and looked up at Sémon. His friend was a statue amidst the noise, absorbing the men's reactions but seemingly unmoved by them. Mikos knew better. They both felt sadness and fear at the violent emotions tearing the garrison apart.

Satorus raised his hands to quiet the storm. "We are used to betrayal. The traitors that tried to make this a Theban town nearly four years ago lie dead or hide in Thebes. But did we get them all? How many were left behind?" He allowed a few moments for the suspicion to infect them. "A betrayal of family, of friends, is worthy only of death and *this*, my friends," he jabbed at Skopas as his rhetoric gained pace, "*this* is the man responsible. When we were shocked by the escape's failure, this man," his voice rising in volume to compete with the increasing clamour, "this man was the only one among us who was not surprised. Why? Because he knew it would fail. This is a man whose sister married a Theban." Outrage filled the hall, and Satorus' voice rose louder still. "This is a man whose farming skills are a disgrace. Much better, then, to be paid for betrayal than to fight for a failed farm."

Cries of "Traitor!" flashed like lightening.

"This man," continued Satorus, shouting, "was unable to hide his friendship for our enemies during the Freedom Festival a few months ago. I'm sure you noticed his cosy conversations, but did you know he throws messages to them? This man is a traitor. The shades of our dead demand his death."

Satorus melted into the boiling hatred, and Skopas shuffled forward to plead for his life, his miserable face white. He looked already half way to Hades. He coughed before raising his voice above the din. "Gentlemen! Gentlemen, please." The audience settled to a low simmer. "Gentlemen, I've lived in Plataea all my life, as did my father and grandfather. My father fought the Persians, and I've fought beside you on many occasions. You can't really think I'm a traitor."

He looked around and saw his fate written in the faces staring at him, as stony as Athena's.

"But, but…how can you? I'm as appalled as you are about the

fate of our friends."

"But are you?" asked Phelix the muscle. "As Satorus said, you weren't surprised were you?"

"Well, no, I wasn't surprised." The room exploded once more, forcing Skopas to shout. "I wasn't surprised because I thought the plan was flawed."

"Oh, you would blame the general now, would you?" said iron-eyed Satorus.

"No, of course not. I only mean I thought it risky and likely to fail. Many of us did. Many of us decided to stay behind because we feared for the chances of their success."

"Now he would call us all cowards," cried Satorus. "They died, I suppose, because we were afraid to join them."

Mikos knew that this was an insinuation too close to home for many, and in their determination to hide from their own weaknesses, there was a near mutiny, the men barely restraining themselves from tearing Skopas apart immediately. The grandfather general bellowed for silence, and the tumult subsided, leaving many flushed faces and sore throats.

"I'm not making that suggestion at all," continued Skopas. "If we'd joined them, we'd be dead, too. Look, we all fought on the walls to give them a chance. That's not the action of cowards. It's also not the action of a traitor, is it?"

"Then how do you explain what happened?" demanded Satorus. "Hybrias himself said that it appeared as if the enemy expected them."

All eyes turned to Hybrias, who blushed, cleared his throat, and mumbled, "Yes, it did look that way…"

"Well, there you are," declared Satorus. "A trap. Laid by your treachery."

"What treachery? I swear by Athena of Plataea that I've never betrayed our town and never would." Satorus' supporters broke into exaggerated jeering. "It's true. On my honour, I've never been a traitor to you." More jeers. "Where's your evidence? This is all lies…"

"Oh!" cried Satorus. "Now he's going to try and shift the blame. Excuse away the weaknesses in his case."

"Shame! Shame!" called the gallery. Skopas struggled to regain their attention, but the clamour drowned his appeals, and eventually, with head bowed and tears of frustration, he crept back to his stool, staring at the floor, surrounded by the sound of his doom.

Mikos looked around and barely recognized the distorted faces. The Furies had invaded the temple. Was Skopas to die to satisfy the garrison's feelings of guilt? He felt angry and helpless, but then Sémon strode before the mass jury. The noise abated. Mikos held his breath.

"That night," Sémon began quietly, shaking his head. "Remember the storm? And we created our own storm, didn't we?" He pointed to a bearded man with an oversized head. "Pausanias, I remember you beside me, and very brave you were. Xenophanes. I saw you like a mountain in the front rank." The men in question straightened before the admiring looks. Sémon had no need to remind them of his own exploits. "Well, let me tell you," he added, raising his voice, "I didn't risk my life to see my nephew and friends dishonoured."

He paused to allow the noisy agreement to defuse.

"And if there's someone to blame, I'll be the first to rip them to pieces." More vicious agreement. Sémon waited for them to settle again before asking, "But do you expect me to believe we should blame Skopas? Could Mr. Misery be so important? Satorus is right, Skopas is a poor farmer. But that is a crime against the land, not against the town. And who among us can control our families, eh? Polukrates, your uncle married a woman from Thebes, didn't he? Even moved there?"

Red-faced Polukrates looked around nervously at the narrowed eyes aimed at him. "Yes, and the family hasn't forgiven him."

"But the rest of your family remains loyal to Plataea, don't they? Then we shouldn't let one black sheep taint the whole flock. Even my own family has its dark secret, a notorious womanizer who causes major embarrassment to everyone." He paused, musing in an exaggerated manner before adding, "Oh, hold on. That's me."

A few peals of laughter and rude comments forced Sémon to wait again. "As for our friend throwing messages…well, I've seen him throw. Not a pretty sight. As you know, I myself have perfect aim." Exaggerated guffaws caused Sémon to raise his voice. "I have… almost perfect aim. Our friend here has joined us to target the guards with our stones, and I can assure you that if he threw at the sky, he'd miss."

Sémon paused for the sniggers and comments to disperse before assuming a more solemn tone. "Friends, the loss of our brothers was a disaster. Let's not add to it by condemning an innocent man to death. We've heard no evidence of guilt. Such a case could be made against any one of us. Now, I don't blame Satorus for accusing him. We all feel guilty. Would they have escaped if we'd created more of a diversion? What if we'd gone with them? We'll never know. It's easier to blame another than to face our own failings, our own fears. But it's time to be men and face those fears. The Thebans have angered the gods by their treatment of our dead and will be paid back for it. Let's not give the gods cause for anger against ourselves. Skopas is a pessimist, but that's a betrayal of hope, not of Plataea. You must find him not guilty."

The hall was silent as Sémon resumed his place beside Mikos, who beamed with pride. When no one moved to make another speech, the general directed the urns to be passed around. An unusual stillness accompanied the vessels on their journeys. Mikos said a silent prayer as he put his solid disc in the bronze urn and the holed disc in the wooden one.

Finally, the urns returned to General Arkadius, who ordered the bronze urn emptied. He glanced at the multitude of solid discs, with very few holed interlopers, glanced in Sémon's direction and nodded, smiling, before announcing, "Not guilty."

Chapter 28

It was the first festival that Stephanos had spent with his family in over two years, and strolling through streets festooned with flowers, he savoured the touch of Khara's hand, laughed at Alexias' exuberance, and smiled at his father's caustic remarks. Yet the knowledge that he should be doing something for Sémon haunted him. When they paused to allow Alexias to play on the swings, which had been erected as a propitiation for the hanging of an ancient heroine, Stephanos noted the laughter of the crowd around him, but the absence of Sémon's roar was deafening.

The Anthesteria, the Festival of Flowers, celebrated the god Dionysus' rebirth and his gift of wine, which made it particularly popular, and yet it was a family occasion, when children received presents. Alexias' loot was a wooden sword, which he had tucked into his belt. His wreath of flowers remarkably still crowned his head, though it was still early.

They shuffled with the crowd towards the Phaleron Gate, and joined the procession heading out of the city towards the Sanctuary of Dionysus in the Marshes. Ahead of them, a team of mules pulled a cart draped in red blankets and bearing an erect tree trunk adorned with ivy, to which a mask of Dionysus was nailed. It represented Alexias' favourite story: not realizing he was a god, pirates tried to capture Dionysus, but he had thrown them overboard and turned them into dolphins, which even today continued to chase ships in an attempt to get back aboard. Families sang and laughed along the rutted road that stretched towards the peaks of Mount Hymettus, following carts of revellers who shouted and jeered like pirates.

Stephanos suspected Alexias wanted him to be a pirate, or a sailor at least, but Stephanos had settled into work at the docks. Settled. He did not want to settle, not yet. It had only been a week since the celebration of their escape, but Athens had moved on and Plataea seemed like the whispers of a half-forgotten dream.

But even in sleep, Stephanos could not forget. When he lay down each night, his heart raced, his eyes stared into the dark. Every dog bark, every rattle, every murmur heralded betrayal. And yet this was Athens. This was safety. He was ashamed that fear still stalked him.

Stephanos' family stood with the Athenians amongst the olive trees outside the low wall marking the sanctuary's boundaries. The ancient sanctuary of Dionysus had a path to the Underworld, and silence settled as the god was removed from the cart and placed in the grounds. The priestess mixed the new wine with sacred water as young women danced around Dionysus to the gentle beat of tambourines. After libations, prayers, and hymns the jostling began. The crowds struggled to be served and to hail Dionysus with the first fruits of the vineyards.

The futility of it overwhelmed Stephanos. It may have been just the next festival on the calendar for the Athenians, but to him it was a reminder of the hallowed places around Plataea that remained untended. Although he could now offer libations at his mother's grave, his grandparents lay abandoned.

They walked with the crowds back to the agora, where vendors dispensed wine, men tried to balance on inflated goat skins greased with oil, a chorus sang hymns near the Altar to the Twelve Gods, and street performers vied for an audience. Khara was laughing at the comical efforts of the skin walkers when Nikolas staggered into Stephanos.

"Ah! Steph…Steph…Stephos, isn't it?" said Nikolas, an idiotic grin at odds with his dark features.

"Nikolas," said Stephanos. "Have you been at the drinking races?" Each year the Basileus, the chief magistrate, held a solemn drinking contest to honour Dionysus, which never ended as seriously as it began.

Nikolas nodded gravely, swaying a little. "I won!" He held up his half-empty cup of wine. "Hail Dionus…Dionisss…Dioneee… You know. Have you seen… hic…," he put a hand to his mouth and said, "Hermes." His grin dissolved into a giggle.

"Have I seen…?"

"Ah! Alki…Alki…"

"Alkibiades? No I haven't."

Nikolas huffed and resumed his Odyssian wanderings through the agora, colliding with people every few steps, leaving a wake of stained tunics and angry mutterings. He paused as a young man careered off one of the inflated skins, and he decided to show the crowd how to do it. Moments later, after flailing limbs, his jug broken on the ground and never actually mounting the greasy surface, Nikolas lay prostrate in the dust, fancying the hoots of laughter to be the cawing of crows and wondering whether this would be a good place to sleep.

"Let's get you up, you drunkard."

Nikolas was yanked to his feet. "Alki…Alki… It's you!"

"Yes, it is me," chuckled Alkibiades. "You know, if you are going to enter the races, you should eat something first. It slows the Dionysian madness."

"Damn right," agreed a gruff voice behind Alkibiades' shoulder.

"Greetings, Pisander," said Alkibiades.

"Father," smirked Nikolas. "I won."

Pisander the Hawk shook his head and could not help smiling. "I know you did. Come on, you need water." He supported his son, and added to Alkibiades, "I hope your chorus is training hard for the Dionysia Festival, young man." His eyes held Alkibiades' for an instant before he moved away bearing his charge like a wounded soldier. Behind them, Pisander's wife and her maid appeared from the crowd. Elené held her sea blue tunic across her lower face, but to Alkibiades her eyes seemed inviting.

"Is he alright?" a soft voice asked beside him.

"What?" said Alkibiades, startled by Hipparete. "Oh. Oh, yes, he will be fine. Just too much ambrosia."

"He did look funny," giggled Hipparete. "Like a helpless, newborn puppy. It would be nice to have a puppy in the house, don't you think?"

"I already have lots of dogs."

"But they're hunting dogs. I meant one just to play with. A

cute one."

Alkibiades took her gently by the arm. "What could be cuter than you?" Hipparete blushed and squeezed against her husband.

"Perhaps it would be better to wait until after the birth," said Deinomache, planted behind her daughter-in-law. "We do not want you over-exciting yourself."

Hipparete nodded. "You're probably right. But then can I have one?"

"If that is what you still want," said Alkibiades, aware it would probably be more a question of what his mother wanted her to want.

They wandered around the agora, tasting wine, listening to the chorus, greeting aunts, uncles, cousins as Hipparete chatted like an excited sparrow. A festival meant an escape from the house, and she clearly delighted in the noise, the colour, the smells.

Alkibiades charmed everyone as usual, but he was distracted. His popularity had increased, and in Athenian politics popularity was the great persuader. But it would not be enough to change the board of generals. The elections were less than two months away. Alkibiades held great sway among the young men of the city, but many of his elders distrusted him, as they did all things young. If his chorus won at the Dionysia Festival, he would gain credit with the more conservative elements within the city. It might be enough to make the difference in the elections.

Hipparete's brother, Kallias, appeared before them with Sellene on his arm, and Alkibiades hid his amusement at his mother's Medusan glare. Sellene had covered her face as if she were a wellborn lady rather than a whore parading her captured fly in public.

"Ladies," nodded Sellene, scanning Hipparete.

Hipparete recognized all too well Deinomache's hostility to the young woman, and she blushed and turned to Kallias. "How are you, Brother?"

"Splendid," said Kallias. "Is it not a fine day?"

"And how are you, Hipparete? I understand you're with child," said Sellene.

Hipparete's eyes flicked to Deinomache. "I... I, er..."

"My wife is very healthy," said Alkibiades, squeezing

Hipparete's hand. "I understand your father is looking for you," he added to Kallias. "Perhaps he would like to meet Sellene." It was Kallias' turn to blush as Alkibiades led his wife and mother to safety.

The sun melted into the sea, and torches appeared around the agora. "It is time to leave before the spirits roam," said Alkibiades. Hipparete started to pout, but thought better of it and removed her garland. Alkibiades noticed Elené's matronly slave hovering a few paces away. He met her eye and nodded imperceptibly. "Now, Andromachus will see you both home. I will join the procession and offer our garlands to the priestess." Hipparete opened her mouth to object, but Alkibiades raised his hand. "No. I do not want you out when there may be evil spirits abroad. Remember to get the slaves to smear the doorway with pitch, and be sure to chew buckthorn leaves on the way home to protect you."

"Will you chew them, too?" asked Hipparete.

"Of course," said Alkibiades, holding out his hand for Andromachus to give him some leaves. "Now, hand me your garlands, and I will see you in the morning." They exchanged their offerings for his cup, and torch-bearing Andromachus led them away. Hipparete turned to look back every few steps, and Alkibiades remained in place with a smile painted on his face until they were lost in the crowd.

The chorus had moved towards the top of the agora in the rapidly fading light, and the tipsy crowds joined in the hymns as the procession formed to return to the sanctuary. Alkibiades allowed the buckthorn leaves and garlands to fall to the ground as he nodded to Elené's slave and followed at a discreet distance. They were quickly out of the agora and into the dark, narrow streets, where drunken partygoers staggered to their next host, flute girls draped around their necks. Twisting and turning, Alkibiades strode to keep pace with his surprisingly nimble guide, straining his eyes to penetrate the dark, listening to the heavy footsteps ahead.

The slave disappeared into a doorway, and Alkibiades' breath quickened as he approached. He knew the house, of course, having been to many of Nikolas' parties. He reached for the door, but revellers burst into the street up the hill and headed towards him.

Alkibiades made as if drunk, weaving past his destination. Several of the party greeted him by name, inviting him to join them. He declined incoherently, convincingly. When they had turned the corner, Alkibiades straightened and made for the door again.

He stood before it, listening. He could hear nothing. He tapped, and the door opened. The courtyard was dark, only the area around the door faintly lit by the moon racing above the roofs. Alkibiades stepped past the slave, who closed the door and whispered, "Wait here." She scurried into the dark and Alkibiades saw a burst of light as another door opened and closed. And then silence. His heart was thumping. Where were Pisander and Nikolas? What if they came back? No, she was not stupid. They would be safely away.

He heard the same door open and close, but without the accompaniment of light. The slow, soft tread of feet came towards him, hidden in the moon's shadows. Gradually an ethereal figure appeared, transforming into a shimmering apparition as Elené stepped into the moonlight. She strolled alluringly, her brilliant white peplos draped to her ankles, her black hair hanging loosely over her shoulders, a smile dancing on her lips, her dark eyes examining Alkibiades.

"I see divinities really do walk the streets tonight," she said as she reached him. Her fingers played with the folds of his chiton, standing so close he could almost feel her against him, her perfume tantalizing. He raised his hands to stroke her bare arms, but she took a step back. Her eyes smouldered as she released the clasps at her shoulders and allowed the peplos to fall to the ground. The moonlight endowed her naked body with a statuesque quality, and she stood without embarrassment as Alkibiades drank her shadowy, curvaceous figure. He removed his chiton and flung it aside. Elené strode forward and pressed against him, her mouth searching for his, her hands exploring the young, firm body. Running footsteps in the street, but they no longer heard. Alkibiades whipped her around and pressed her hungrily against the moonlit wall.

Chapter 29

Samias was the root of her problems. Aristeia slept with her husband most nights, but they had lain together only on their wedding night. At first she had thought she had done it wrong, or that she repulsed him, but he had assured her otherwise. Yet each night there was a valid reason they could not lie together. Timokles was kind to her, but he was an unbreachable fortress that made her feel like she was trampling on occupied territory, and her husband's conversation was unguarded enough for her to identify her enemy.

But Samias was not her only problem. Nikopatra waddled around the house like a Queen Goose, and her pecks could be vicious. Her only treasure in her new home was Leaina. Aristeia had confided in no one about Samias, although she suspected that Leaina had guessed. Only to Hestia of the Hearth had Aristeia blurted her problems, but the goddess of her new home seemed deaf to her.

Aristeia shivered, despite the woollen himation she hugged to herself, and she glanced at Timokles placing a corn cake on the altar. Nikopatra, Leaina and the handful of house slaves had gathered with them for the usual early morning ritual, and Timokles raced through his monotonic prayer to Zeus, Protector of the House, before promptly turning towards the family room. Aristeia had resigned herself to this borderline sacrilegious performance, at least for the time being, but she was still shocked as the household scattered like a flock of pigeons.

"Timokles?" she called after her husband's retreating back. "You've forgotten the incense. Today's the new moon."

"Oh, we don't bother with that, child," said Nikopatra, turning to face her daughter-in-law, who failed to hide her horror at this affront to the gods. "I tell you, it's unnecessary. The gods have always been good to this house. I know your father feels the need to placate every possible deity, but you'll learn there really is no need."

Aristeia flushed as Nikopatra turned away, and Leaina

shrugged and smiled sheepishly before joining her. "Orontas," Aristeia called after a limping slave. He was her favourite: an educated Persian captured in the Egyptian war more than thirty years ago, and beloved tutor of Timokles and Leaina. "I need to tell you what we shall have for breakfast."

Orontas brushed aside some of his tight curls. "But Miss, breakfast is laid out."

"What?"

"Mistress gave instructions."

"Oh... oh, yes, of course. I'm so forgetful this morning. Thank you, Orontas."

"Thank you, Miss."

"Oh, Orontas." The slave, who had turned to leave, looked back at the young woman. "Would you get some incense out of the stores for me later?"

Orontas hesitated, a slight smile hidden behind his curly beard. "Of course, Miss." He ambled away, nursing the old war wound in his leg.

Aristeia strode to the family room, closed the door behind her, and sat beside Leaina on a couch. Nikopatra was enthroned on her chair, and Timokles reclined on his own couch, the fire in the hearth the centre of attention. The head of the household broke off a piece of bread and tossed it into the fire, offering a mechanical prayer to Hestia, before the family attacked the onion and garlic soup, bread, goat cheese, and figs on the tables before them.

"I'm sorry I wasn't able to help you direct the slaves this morning," said Aristeia.

Nikopatra smiled. "Oh, that's quite all right. I was up early and I know how you young people like your sleep."

"That's very kind of you," said Aristeia, "but I've appreciated being beside you as you run the house. I've learnt so much. Tomorrow I'll rise earlier so I don't miss the chance to benefit from your experience."

Nikopatra slurped her soup before answering. "Don't you worry about that."

"Oh, but I do. The household is grateful, Mother, for the

manner in which you run things. And I'm sure that even with the experience of running my father's house since I was a child, I couldn't run this house in the same way that you do." Nikopatra gave a condescending nod, and Aristeia felt a twinge of guilt at the disguised barb she had released, but felt justified nevertheless. "I fear for your health carrying such a burden."

"My health's fine, child." Nikopatra looked a little suspiciously at the newlyweds. "Besides, you must save your strength for giving us a baby."

Aristeia blushed and glanced at Timokles, who stared into the fire as he chewed his bread. She looked away, gazed at the bronze Hestia on the nearby table, and offered a silent prayer.

Nikopatra's beady eyes did not leave the couple, her brows lowering, and her foot mindlessly tapping the floor. A young house slave broke the awkward silence, asking Nikopatra, "Cook wants to know what to buy for today's meal, Mistress."

Nikopatra straightened. "I believe our guest likes grey mullet, don't you?"

"Aristeia isn't a guest, Mother," said Leaina.

"Of course," said Nikopatra. "Just a slip of the tongue. Grey mullet, then. Tell him to get a good price, five obols at the most. I'll be checking when he gets back." The slave bowed and left. "You see, my dear," she said, turning again to Aristeia, "you have to be careful with slaves. They have no morals at all. They'll steal your bread from under your nose."

"Mother, really!" cried Leaina. "You've been listening to too much gossip again. Ours are very trustworthy."

"I'm sure that their honesty is a reflection of the care you give them," smiled Aristeia.

"Perhaps," said Nikopatra, frowning.

"And having so many good slaves in the house," continued Aristeia, "makes the job of running it much easier. Maybe even I could manage."

"Oh, my child," said Nikopatra, "you have too sweet and gentle a nature. Even good slaves will take advantage of you. Best you leave it to me and watch and learn."

Aristeia wanted to wrap her fingers around her mother-in-law's throat, but she smiled and clamped her lips. There was no point in open warfare.

"Mother," said Leaina, "I'm sure Aristeia can run our house, and it'd be good for you to have more rest." Aristeia squeezed her friend's hand. Timokles continued to eat his breakfast and fidget on his couch.

"I'm sure the household of an old man who's hardly ever there is a good starting point, but that's nothing compared to this household," said Nikopatra. "This is one of the oldest families in Athens, not a newly sprung one. Oh, my dear," she rushed, half-laughingly, to Aristeia, "I don't mean that as an insult. Your father's a great man and his achievements more than make up for a lack of nobility."

Perhaps his money makes up for even more, thought Aristeia.

"A family's defined by the nobleness of its present members," declared Leaina, "which makes Aristeia's family among the best in Athens." Aristeia bumped shoulders with her sister. "How do you like my new tapestry upstairs?" continued Leaina, the work in question hanging half completed on its loom in the women's room above them.

Nikopatra rubbed her hands in the warmth of the fire. "I wish you'd put some red in it. You know I like red."

Leaina smiled. "Yes, Mother. I know you like red." Nikopatra eyed her daughter, who continued without hesitating, "But I like it."

"So do I," said Aristeia. "It seems very... serene."

"Thank you," beamed Leaina. "I wanted it to look peaceful."

Her mother frowned as she grabbed a fig. "Peaceful? What do we want with peaceful? An Athenian doesn't know what to do with 'peaceful'."

Timokles looked up. "You might be right, Mother. There's pressure in the Assembly for heavier fighting. Your father is resisting it, Aristeia. For the moment, I think he's winning."

Aristeia brightened. It made her happy that Timokles respected her father. "Kleon's methods are repugnant, but Father has faith the people will disown such rhetoric. Unfortunately, we cannot save Plataea. He's more concerned that Alkibiades is working with

Kleon, and rejecting the legacy of Perikles."

"Yes, how can he allow himself to befriend that tanner?" demanded Nikopatra.

"Alkibiades remains loyal to Perikles' legacy," smiled Timokles. "He thinks Perikles would have abandoned a failed policy."

"Failed? We haven't lost," Aristeia pointed out gently.

"No," replied Timokles, "but we haven't won, either. The city's finances are severely strained and there's no end in sight."

"So perhaps there's an opportunity to renew the treaties with Sparta," interjected Leaina. "It seems that neither side can win. Why is Alkibiades so intent on stirring up yet more fighting? Has he not won enough glory already?"

"Alkibiades does what he believes is best for Athens. As I'm sure Nikias does," said Timokles. He took a sip of wine, glancing nervously at his mother. "Which brings me to some news. Alkibiades has persuaded me to serve in the cavalry. I've talked to the registrars and they foresee no problem with my scrutiny. I will be accepted."

"That's wonderful!" cried Leaina and Aristeia in unison, aware that a cavalryman's chances of surviving a battle were significantly greater than a hoplite's: horses can run away faster.

"You're leaving the hoplite lists?" said Nikopatra. "Our family has always fought as hoplites. In the front ranks, face to face like men. Cavalry! Huh!" She spat into the fire. "They do nothing but watch the fighting and run away."

"Mother!" said Leaina. "You can't doubt Timokles' bravery, or that of the other young men."

"I thought you don't even like horses," continued Nikopatra.

"I don't," said Timokles. "But the plague has killed many cavalrymen, and others have had their farms destroyed and can no longer afford the expense, so Athens is short of cavalry. It's my duty to respond."

"But how are we to afford the upkeep of a horse?" said Nikopatra.

"Two horses."

"Two horses? Why two?"

"I have to have an attendant to carry equipment, food, spare weapons and so on. You know that, Mother."

"So we'll have to pay to train one of our slaves?"

"Alkibiades is going to train us. Don't worry. We all have to make sacrifices these days. We can afford it."

"I think it's great news," smiled Aristeia.

"Thank you," said Timokles. "And, of course, I'll be in the Leontis regiment with Alkibiades and Nikolas, as well as Samias, who's just joined."

Aristeia's smile melted, her breathing ceased.

"Speaking of whom," continued Timokles, starting to rise, "I've promised to meet them at the Lykeum this morning." Timokles left the room, leaving his wife staring at the door.

Nikopatra noticed Aristeia's reaction. Her son had shown surprising strength of will in recent days. That was good. But something had to be done about Samias.

Chapter 30

Spring arrived as if late for a lover's tryst. Flamboyant weeds battled for every spot of earth, birds flirted, and grandfather trees awakened. It was Aristeia's favourite time of year, and her most feared: it was the season Greeks went to war.

She pushed the thought aside and smiled at the dirty children playing in the street. "What's the rush?" she asked, nodding in the direction of Nikopatra scurrying ahead.

"Mother likes to charge into battle," said Leaina, and Aristeia raised her eyebrows. "You'll see," continued Leaina. "If it wasn't for Hipparete being there, I'd rather take a boat ride with Charon across the Styx."

"If it's so unpleasant, why is she so keen to go?"

"You must know by now that mother enjoys a good fight. She and Deinomache live to compete against each other, and she has a new daughter-in-law to show off. And I'm sure Deinomache would like to make more cheese out of Hipparete's pregnancy."

Once they had passed Sculptors Row it was not long before a slave ushered them in to Deinomache and Hipparete. The air retained chill memories of winter, but after showing off Agarthakus' paintings to Aristeia, they sat outside in the sun, wrapped in their himations.

"It's good to see you looking so healthy, Hipparete," said Leaina.

"Thank you," said Hipparete. "I'm so glad you've come to visit. There's so much I want to ask you about babies, midwives, doctors..."

"I'll do my best to help," said Leaina.

"We have access, of course," said Deinomache, "to the very best doctor, should we need him. But unfortunately old Antigone died a few years ago, and so a recommendation of a midwife would be appreciated."

"Your midwife was called Antigone?" laughed Aristeia, knowing the ancient heroine to be the subject of numerous plays.

"She delivered your husband, dear, so do not be quick to make fun of her," said Deinomache.

"It was a nickname," explained Nikopatra, settling her ample frame. "She was stubborn and set in her ways, but she knew what she was doing."

"Delivered most of the best men in Athens," added Deinomache.

"What was her real name?" asked Aristeia, trying to redeem herself. Deinomache and Nikopatra exchanged glances and shrugged.

"Well, my midwife was like a gentle titan," said Leaina. "I'll give directions to your slaves and they can arrange a meeting."

"The best midwives, of course, advise giving birth during a northerly wind," stated Nikopatra.

"That is a southerly wind, actually," said Deinomache.

"No, no. I'm sure it's northerly, to bring the cooler, cleaner air."

"No, a northerly wind brings dangerous chills. A southerly brings soothing warmth."

"Perhaps," ventured Leaina, winking at Hipparete, "an easterly wind would be best to avoid extremes."

"Did you have any prophetic dreams when you were pregnant?" burst Hipparete.

Leaina sat back. "No. Why, have you had any?"

"No, I haven't," said Hipparete, glancing at her mother-in-law.

"Our family has a history of such dreams," said Deinomache. "Agariste dreamt she gave birth to a lion before having Perikles. I had a similar dream when I was carrying Alkibiades."

"I never heard you say that before," said Nikopatra. Aristeia tensed at the sharpness in Nikopatra's voice.

"Well I cannot remember to tell you everything," said Deinomache.

"You don't need a dream, though," said Leaina, "to tell you that children are the greatest gift."

Hipparete whispered, "Were you at all... worried before you gave birth?"

Leaina took her hand between both of hers. "I was, a little. It's only natural, Hipparete. But a good midwife will keep you safe."

"My cousin, Nikostraté, thought she had a good midwife, but she still died."

"Yes, yes," said Deinomache, "but she was a scrawny little thing. You are bursting with health, my dear. Tell them about the toys."

"Toys? Oh, oh yes, the toys." Hipparete melted into a smile. "Alkibiades has bought presents for the baby already. A set of painted soldiers. He was so thrilled when he showed us their legs and arms moving, I didn't have the heart to tell him they were far too old for a baby. We'll have to lock them away for years."

"That's very sweet, my dear," said Nikopatra, beaming at the expectant mother before turning to the more expectant grandmother. "Strange. I wouldn't have guessed your son to be so fatherly. Fathering, yes. But fatherly?"

Deinomache glared, but the appearance of Hipparete's pretty maid, Maria, caught her attention. "Has cook returned?" she barked.

Maria hesitated as she looked questioningly at Hipparete. There was a momentary pause, enough for Aristeia to notice Deinomache almost burst into flame.

"Has cook returned, Maria?" asked Hipparete sweetly.

Aristeia thought she detected a triumphant smile held back by the slave. "Yes, Mistress," said Maria. "She have bread and fish, and perfumed oil for hair." She opened her hand beside Hipparete. "Two drachmas and three obols."

Hipparete scooped the owl-faced coins into an ornate box on the table beside her, and Aristeia smiled at Deinomache's evident battle to keep her smile fixed and her tongue silent: she knew as well as Hipparete's mother-in-law that it should not have cost more than two drachmas.

"Something more, Mistress?"

"No, thank you, Maria, that will be all," smiled Hipparete.

Nikopatra's smile was wider than Aristeia had ever seen it, and the words of her aunts came back to her: babies were the key to a mother-in-law's heart. She wondered if the same were true for a husband.

"It's such a coincidence," said Leaina, "that both Hipparete and Aristeia have fathers who made their fortune from the silver mines."

"The mines have been good for us all," agreed Deinomache. "Of course, Hipponikus is from one of the most ancient families in Athens, so in his case it is not so surprising."

Nikopatra bounded into the fray. "Nikias is one of the most respected men in Athens and has far more sway in the Assembly than other generals like, oh, I don't know, Hipponikus, for example."

Aristeia was a fishing boat caught in a sudden squall, reeling at Deinomache's surprise attack, equally unnerved by her own mother-in-law's support.

"It is only natural Nikias is respected," said Deinomache. "He had the good fortune to serve Perikles and bask in the reflected glory. If only today's leaders had my cousin's wisdom."

Aristeia's face burned. "My father serves Athens faithfully. People respect his honesty."

"Perhaps," said Deinomache, her golden head tilting as if assessing a new plaything. "But an honest fool is still a fool. Not that I am suggesting your father is a fool, by any means. I just feel more comfortable with leaders, like Perikles, who have the bright eye, who understand nuances and calculate the right course, rather than stumble upon it by chance."

Aristeia was speechless. No one had ever spoken of her father with such disrespect in her hearing before, and the accusation seemed so absurd that she was unable to respond. Nikopatra came to her rescue. "Nikias' war record is impeccable, and it's hard to imagine getting elected general year after year without sharp wits."

"And besides," continued Aristeia, feeling herself coil as if ready to strike, "I wonder how many nuances Alkibiades' friend, Kleon, understands." She noticed Nikopatra smile at her.

Deinomache played with the folds in her gown, a sharp eyebrow raised. "Let me try to explain politics, my dear. Good leaders must have the humility to recognize when someone else has the skills to benefit Athens, even if you would normally oppose them. In these turbulent times we cannot restrict ourselves to the obsolete ideas of any particular leader."

"It doesn't concern you that your son may be thrust into reckless ventures, such as rescuing Plataea, because of Kleon's rhetoric?" asked Aristeia.

"There is no greatness without risk," replied Deinomache.

"Not everyone seeks greatness, yet they're equally endangered," said Aristeia.

"If they do not seek renown, they are not truly Athenian." Deinomache paused, staring pointedly at Nikopatra. "Though I understand why you might think that way."

"There are other ways to achieve greatness," pressed Aristeia. "Raising Athenian children, for example."

"Legitimate children," added Nikopatra.

"Of course, I agree," smiled Deinomache, reaching to stroke Hipparete's belly. "Changing the subject, how are Timokles' friends these days? I especially like what I hear of young Samias."

Aristeia and Nikopatra blanched, and even Leaina flushed as she said, "Timokles is fortunate to have friends like Alkibiades and Samias."

"Yes, I'm so glad Alkibiades persuaded Timokles to join the cavalry," said Hipparete quickly. "The thought of having someone with him that he trusts as much as Timokles is a great comfort."

"It is important for leaders to have loyal followers," said Deinomache.

"Alkibiades isn't a commander," shot Nikopatra.

"No, not yet. He is second in his squad, and he selects who rides behind him, so I am sure he will choose Timokles to be in his shadow, as usual."

Aristeia's antipathy towards Deinomache grew with every sentence, and in proportion so did her sympathy for Hipparete. She even felt a new attachment to her own mother-in-law.

"I'd heard Leaina talk of Agarthakus' paintings," said Aristeia, nodding towards the family room that housed some of them.

"Yes, they are wonderful," said Deinomache.

"They're fine works," agreed Aristeia. "Although personally I find them too ornate for a home. For a stoa, or a temple, perhaps. I prefer more personal items, like Leaina's beautiful tapestries, for instance. Provided a family has someone with her skill."

Deinomache half smiled, studying Aristeia as she replied. "Everyone has their own tastes, however quaint, but our paintings are universally admired. Alkibiades has many guests for dinner, of course, now that the allies are arriving for the Dionysia, and they fall over themselves in their praises."

"I hope Alkibiades is taking the chorus seriously," said Nikopatra. "Our tribe expects victory. His name will be in the pit if he loses."

"They sing beautifully," said Hipparete. "He took us to hear them."

"I am certain Leontis will be celebrating his victory," added Deinomache.

"Did you know," began Aristeia, "that my father has never lost as choregus? Whether for the hymns, tragedies, or comedies. His victory tripods crowd the monuments. Don't you think that remarkable?"

"I think it outstanding, Aristeia," beamed Nikopatra. "A very difficult act to follow."

"Nikias never started as young as Alkibiades, of course," said Deinomache. "But my son knows what it takes to win."

Chapter 31

Hipparete, Khara and Maria purified their hands in the sacred water beside the gate into the sanctuary of Artemis-in-the-Fields. They left Alkibiades' slave, Andromachus, to hover outside as they breezed through the opening in the low wall and began to browse the monuments that adorned the enclosure: stele carved with reliefs of babies; female genitalia in bronze to combat infertility. Swaddling clothes and tiny pairs of sandals offered in thanks blanketed the base of one statue.

"Do you think Artemis answers every prayer?" said Hipparete.

Khara glanced at her young friend, but she could not lie to her. "She's a goddess and does as she pleases, but I think we're noisy enough to make her hear us."

Hipparete nodded and adjusted her crown of vine leaves and berries, symbols of fertility. Although they were only three hundred yards outside the city walls, it felt like immense freedom to stand in this garden sanctuary, to watch sparrows play among the gnarled olive trees, to feel the lush grass tickle their toes. "Do you really think it will be a boy?" asked Hipparete.

"The gods have been known to reveal the future to those who can see," said Khara.

"The seer told Deinomache that he'll bear arms like no other. She thinks he'll be a great warrior, but I'm not sure I want him to be a warrior. Is that wrong?"

"He'll be what the gods want him to be, and that will make him happy."

"I suppose."

Khara smiled at Hipparete's maid standing behind them. Khara liked to include Maria because of the slave's loyalty to Hipparete, and because she felt sorry for her. Maria had been eight or nine when the caravan was attacked, her recollections were not exact. Her father and older brother had died trying to protect the family, and Hipponikus had bought her at the slave market on Delos to be his daughter's maid and companion, the last time Maria had seen her mother and sisters. Slavery was only ever a conquest or an accident away, and Khara saw her family's vulnerability in the faces of the slaves that filled Athens. If she was kind to unfortunates now, perhaps the gods would requite her in the future if necessary. "Do you think Deinomache is right, Maria?" asked Khara.

"Deinomache know everything, she think," said Maria, "but people who know, don't see." She tapped her nose with a finger.

"You're a wise girl, Maria," said Khara.

"At least The Toad is less bossy these days," said Hipparete.

"To you only, Mistress," said Maria. "Hear how she shout at slaves?"

"Well, when I've had my child, people will be nice to each other and there'll be no screaming and shouting," said Hipparete. "When my son's running around the house and calling for 'momma', she won't dare order anyone around. Her generalship will be ended," she added with a giggle.

"House will cheer," smiled Maria. "This tribe has new leader," she proclaimed in as deep a voice as she could manage. "Time to put old horse out to field."

"Well past time," said Hipparete. "It'll be a happier house with my children running around in it. I'll have to tell them, 'Now boys, don't tire out grandmother, she's too old to be running around '. And they'll shout for me to play with them instead, and we'll rush around the courtyard."

"And Deinomache?" asked Khara.

"She'll be watching from the shade," twinkled Hipparete.

They strolled to the altar in front of the temple. Along the Sounion road, a mile away, families streamed towards the mountains to tend their beehives. Hipparete stroked the grasshopper amulet that hung round her neck, a present from Alkibiades to protect her from evil, and raised her hands to the sky and prayed. "Artemis, Virgin Goddess of Childbirth, I am Hipparete, wife of Alkibiades of the Salaminioi. Lady of Light, remember the juicy goats' thighs I've offered in the past, the libations I've poured, the incense I've burned.

Now use your bow to protect me from evil. Deliver my child safely. I promise you a bronze offering and a succulent sacrifice in thanks, most generous goddess."

Hipparete placed her offering of grapes, figs, dates, and apples on the altar and poured a libation of wine. Khara watched as Hipparete stared at the mountains, and felt a prayer exude from the young girl that expressed far more than the ritual they had performed. She knew Hipparete was scared. "Just think, Hipparete, how much they'll all dote on you once it's over."

Hipparete smiled slightly. "We should go."

They sauntered out of the sanctuary and crossed a wooden footbridge over the Ilissus River, where they noticed a young man in prayer before the altar of the Muses. Khara wondered if he were a poet whose work was to be performed at the City Dionysia. "There's lots of talk about the Dionysia," she said.

"Yes," said Hipparete. "Alkibiades has to win it. Everyone tells him so."

"The elections follow soon after. They're Plataea's and Theo Sémon's only chance. Is he worried he'll lose?"

"I don't think so. Though he's snapped at the slaves once or twice. I'm sure he's doing all he can, Khara."

Khara nodded, but she was worried even if Alkibiades was not. Time was passing and she saw how it tortured her husband. Stephanos had returned to them, but he had left a part of himself in Plataea, and Khara wanted him whole.

They approached the open city gates, and the young hoplites on guard appraised the women. Hipparete and Khara raised their himations across their faces, but Maria's flirtatious smile and swaying hips threatened army discipline.

"You are a tease," said Hipparete.

"What they do?" laughed Maria. "They have long time on guard before relieve themselves, all while think of me."

They wound their way through the city, Hipparete muttering a prayer and kissing her amulet as they passed each shrine and temple. "Once the baby's born, I think Alkibiades will spend much more time at home. What do you think?" Hipparete's doe-like eyes buried into

Khara, who was relieved when Hipparete added rapidly, "Not that he doesn't spend plenty of time now. As much as he can. He's so busy. Everyone wants to be with him."

"You enjoy his company when he's home, though, don't you?" said Khara.

"Oh, yes. He's so kind and generous. And he has such a gentle touch." She blushed and whispered, "You've no idea how his hands feel against my skin."

Khara noticed Maria look away, and wondered if the slave girl knew exactly how his hands felt against her skin.

On entering Hipparete's house they swept into the sanctuary of the second courtyard, giggling before the statue of Dionysus in a final savouring of their expedition.

"Ah! There you are," barked Deinomache from the gloom beneath the balcony. "We thought bandits had carried you off."

Khara glanced at Maria, suspecting Deinomache's choice of words was deliberate. The slave showed no reaction, but it was evident that Hipparete was vexed on her behalf. Her annoyance evaporated as Alkibiades emerged from the shade, crossed the yard and kissed her cheeks in the bright sunlight.

"Hello, Hipparete. You look more beautiful each passing day."

Hipparete glowed. "Thank you, Alkibiades. It's such an unexpected pleasure to see you home at this hour."

"I am only here briefly. I just came back to bring you a fish for dinner. A doctor in the agora suggested white fish was beneficial for pregnant women."

"You came home just to bring me food. What sort of fish is it?"

Alkibiades shrugged and smiled sheepishly. "A white one."

Hipparete giggled. "Why is it good for mothers?"

"I don't really know that, either," he laughed, "but it might help. Anyway, I have given it to Cook. I must be off." He bent down, kissed his wife's stomach and turned to go. "Khara."

"Alkibiades," nodded Khara.

"I appreciate you accompanying Hipparete."

"It was my pleasure. May Dionysus smile on your chorus."

"He will have cause to." Alkibiades strode to the door.

"Thank you, Alkibiades," Hipparete called. "It was very thoughtful of you." She smiled as she glanced across at Deinomache, watching from the shade.

Chapter 32

The Street of Tripods was a monument to the pomposity of victory. Every successful choregus, whether he had sponsored a chorus, a tragedy, or a comedy, erected a marble memorial to display the bronze tripod awarded by the city. Alkibiades' victory monument was designed, his panegyric ode commissioned, his celebratory parties planned. Only winning remained.

His purple robe embroidered with golden ivy, and the gold crown on his head, drew gasps from the crowds that bustled along the street towards the Sanctuary of Dionysus the Liberator. The precipitous rock of the acropolis loomed above them as hawkers stalked the herd, carrying baskets of bread and figs on their heads and skins of wine over their shoulders.

Alkibiades stepped aside from the river of men and halted beside a cylindrical monument, his followers taking his lead and extricating themselves like the desertion of a regiment. Family, friends, and supporters were under his command, many among the most important men in Athens.

"What is the problem?" asked Hipponikus.

"Too many people," said Alkibiades. "I want the theatre nearly full when we make our entrance. So they can see my support."

Hipponikus nodded, and they watched the deluge surge past, giving and receiving warm greetings. "So what has your poet got in store for us?"

"Melanippides of Melos. He has written an amusing little story of Athena throwing away her aulos in disgust. Quite understandably, in my opinion."

"Alkibiades, it is supposed to be a hymn in praise of Dionysus. This is not the day for comic relief but for reverence. I thought I made clear the importance of today."

"Indeed you did," smiled Alkibiades. His family was worried: even with Kleon's support the electioneering was not going as well as they had hoped. They were desperate for a win at the Dionysia to boost their chances. Without a win, there would be no election victory, no rescue of Plataea, no saving of Athens. Alkibiades was the fulcrum, and he loved it. "No need to worry. He weaves in enough praise of the drunken old sot to satisfy most people's religious sensibilities."

Hipponikus acknowledged the hail of two old men wearing wide-brimmed hats to protect them from the sun. "What order did you draw?"

"Ninth."

"Second to last? That is not bad. It will still be fresh in their minds when they vote."

When the stream of people began to ebb, Alkibiades marshalled his forces once more. At the open gate to the sanctuary, they handed over their lead tickets stamped with an impression of an aulos, and strode towards the tide of noise from the Theatre of Dionysus. The semicircular rows of wooden benches that climbed the slope of the acropolis swarmed with excitement. In the front row, the priest of Dionysus lounged in the seat of honour beside the Basileus and the rest of the year's archons, magistrates of Athens. Much higher up the hill swirled the ebullient chatter of Athenian wives and dazzling mistresses. The eyes of the city were upon him, and Alkibiades revelled in it.

The theatre could hold twenty thousand people and was mostly full when they entered. Alkibiades sensed his costume capture attention, and immediately began his performance, extravagantly greeting his entourage: Hipponikus, richest man in Athens; Ariphron, brother of Perikles; Megakles, Olympic hero; Demosthenes, popular military leader; Kleon, Watchdog of the People. Alkibiades paraded his connections and made his case to the Hydra.

His initial mission accomplished, he glided out of the theatre to the nearby Odeon. Perikles had built the Odeon to memorialise the Athenian naval victory over the Persians at Salamis. The roof beams and internal columns were the masts and spars of captured ships, the low stage and benches constructed from the hulls. As Alkibiades entered the hall the choruses of the ten tribes, each comprising fifty boys, appeared anything but reverential as their excitement boiled. Smuggled frogs slipped down the scarlet chitons of an opposing tribe, ink blotches appeared mysteriously on yellow robes, clasps disappeared exposing shoulders, taunting rhymes were exchanged, and all to the melancholy tune of the aulos as the musicians stood aside preparing for battle.

"Where have you been? Where have you been?" said Melanippides, a gaunt, nervous man hiding behind his scrawling beard.

"I told you I would be attending to business," replied Alkibiades. "Don't look so worried. How is our little songbird?"

The poet glanced across at their chorus adorned in sparkling white chitons, purple belts and golden crowns. "Dareios is fine. I have him focused. They say Kinesias has written a fine hymn for Taureas." There was a quiver in his voice.

Alkibiades happened to catch the eye of the choregus in question, who seemed to be smirking. "I am sure it will be nothing to match yours," said Alkibiades. "Tonight you will be crowned with ivy and ribbons and being led in triumph to every party in Athens. Courtesans will queue to mount you."

"I hope you are right," said Melanippides, hugging himself and rocking back and forth. A trainer bawled at an opposing chorus that by Herakles' balls, if they did not start behaving he would have them castrated.

"Master!" Alkibiades' slave, Andromachus, burst upon them, his face full of anxiety.

"Yes, what is it?"

Andromachus hesitated before the inquisitive stare of Melanippides, before leaning to whisper in Alkibiades' ear, "There's a man outside who insists on talking to you about Pisander's wife." The colour drained from Alkibiades.

"What's wrong? What's happened?" demanded Melanippides.

Alkibiades cleared his throat. "Nothing for you to worry about." He followed Andromachus outside, where the noise from the theatre laced the air, and the slave led Alkibiades away from the theatre to the far side of the Odeon, where a short man leant against the wall. His features seemed to betoken hidden sinkholes, and his bloodshot eyes narrowed as he examined Alkibiades' royal robes and fingered the coarse sackcloth that hung loosely from his own shoulders.

"Yes? What do you want?" demanded Alkibiades, facing the little man before him and dismissing Andromachus.

The man straightened. "Nice outfit. Cost much?"

"Say your piece."

He looked up into Alkibiades' handsome face and scratched his own bristly skin, tilting his head to one side. "I'm just a poor man, no denying. Out for hire at the docks, on great lords' farms, wherever there's work to be had. I bet you haven't known no hunger, have you?"

"Get to the point or I am leaving."

"I'm a citizen, like you. Fortunate enough to have worked for some great lords. Like Pisander, for example." He paused, waiting for a reaction that was not forthcoming. "Strange thing. The second night of the Anthesteria, I see you enter his house, though him and his son weren't there."

"This is what you have to say? You saw a shadowy figure on a dark night enter a house?"

The man smiled. "I waited to be sure. You're difficult to miss, Alkibiades. And, er," he added, chuckling, "so were the noises I heard over the wall."

"Well, what of it?" said Alkibiades. "There is a pretty young slave in the house."

This elicited a grin. "Adultery's a serious crime, ain't it? Which punishment do you prefer? Death? A radish up the arse? From what I hear I guess you'd prefer radishment, wouldn't you?" Alkibiades' eyes blazed and his fists clenched, but he remained silent. The man chuckled. "But of course, I've no wish to see one as high and mighty as yourself humiliated. To ruin your political career when you're just starting, eh?"

"Go on."

"And I certainly don't want to see my patron, Pisander, made to divorce his wife, and his sons lose their citizenship. So perhaps there's some agreement we can find."

"You think I could come to an agreement with *you*?"

"I'm a good man, struggling to feed my wife and children. You, a mighty lord, able to wear such princely robes."

Alkibiades glared, but the little man did not falter.

"Twenty minas would make me your loyal servant."

Alkibiades flinched and gave himself a moment to control his voice. "Where can I find you?"

"In Piraeus, east side of Kantharos harbour. Ask for Red Maron at Hera's Tavern, they'll point you right."

Alkibiades nodded and strode away, incinerating the ground with his stare. He re-entered the Odeon and bumped into Melanippides, who had been pacing back and forth. "What is it? Is everything okay?" blustered the poet.

"Yes, fine," snapped Alkibiades, his dark looks forbidding further enquiries.

The herald entered to announce that the theatre was ready, but found it impossible to make himself heard, forcing him to entreat the poets one by one to control their charges.

"Reverent, boys. Reverent," cried Melanippides clapping his hands. His chorus quieted, though this may have been due to the glowering looks of Alkibiades, who had promised them such rewards if they won.

The herald called the choruses by tribe and they filed out of the Odeon to the theatre. With only three choruses left, Alkibiades' smug rival, Taureas, led out the boys from the tribe of Erechtheis, grinning at Alkibiades. "Good luck, Alkibiades. You are going to need it."

Alkibiades ignored him. Who cared about taunts from someone you were about to crush? But what should he do about Maron? Twenty minas was a significant amount of money, fifteen years wages for a man like Maron. And would it really silence him? And how dare such a worm threaten *him*, Alkibiades, Alkmaeonid, descendant of Zeus?

He led his chorus into the theatre, deafening applause engulfing them as they climbed behind those already lining the stone stage. Between them and the audience was the circular orchestra of hard-packed earth where they would perform, an altar to Dionysus draped with ivy and berries in the centre. The inexperienced chorus boys were paralyzed by the wall of sound: the hill was a living being, laughing, applauding, shouting. Alkibiades was indifferent.

The priest of Dionysus shuffled to the altar, wrapped in a fawn-skin cloak and holding the thyrsus, the emblematic wand of Dionysus sprouting ivy and ribbons. He raised the thyrsus and poured a libation of wine to Dionysus the Liberator, before the Basileus called the first tribe to perform, and the young boys of Kekropis encircled the altar, trying to spot fathers, mothers, friends. Their aulos player stood outside the circle, flanked by the agitated poet and choregus. The notes of the aulos rose like the cooing of a dove, and the boys sang and danced around the altar, their libation of song washing the theatre, the people listening in silence.

Alkibiades was oblivious to the proceedings, wondering whether he could face down the blackmailer. Which of them were people likely to believe, after all? A noble, or a nobody? And anyway, what was Maron doing in Pisander's neighbourhood at that time? Obviously, he had fabricated the whole story. Yet nobodies filled the courts, waiting to cut nobles down to size.

What would happen if people believed Maron? He was right: the city viewed adultery very seriously in light of the fact that only sons born of parents of true Athenian blood could become citizens. His political career could be ruined, and with it Plataea and the future of Athens.

The hymn ended, the boys filed back on stage, and the audience burst into evaluations of the performance, refreshing themselves with the bread and wine peddled by merchants along the rows. The next chorus took its place, and the crowd settled until the nervous aulos player missed his notes and several boys stumbled in their overly intricate choreography. Catcalls and jeers accompanied the rest of the hymn, and several figs whistled past the choregus' head.

Each tribe performed their dedication to Dionysus, mostly competent and attended courteously by twenty thousand experts on dithyrambic hymns. Taureas' boys thrilled the audience with their athletic dancing and clever song.

Finally, Alkibiades led the boys of Leontis down on to the

orchestra to ripples of applause for the boys' golden crowns that glowed in the sun. Alkibiades shook himself and smiled at the judges, fingering his robe embroidered in gold.

The boys were assembling round the altar when Taureas jumped down from the stage and shouted, "Wait! There is an interloper here." He bounded to Alkibiades' songbird, Dareios, and grabbed him by the arm. The young boy looked up at him in astonishment. "This boy is not of Athenian parentage. He is not eligible to sing in the chorus." Consternation at the possible sacrilege swept the theatre. Taureas winked at Alkibiades and grinned.

Alkibiades charged him, bounding like a wild animal, smashing a fist into Taureas' nose. "How dare you? How *dare* you?" cried Alkibiades, his fists pummelling the shrinking figure of Taureas. Amidst noisy jeers and encouragement, archons jumped from their front row seats and pulled Alkibiades away.

"Alkibiades!" shouted the Basileus, towering above Alkibiades, who in his fury was struggling to free himself. "Alkibiades!" repeated the archon. "Taureas has a perfect right to make such a challenge, as you well know. He deserves to be respected."

"Respected," spat Alkibiades. "He knows Dareios is of pure Athenian stock. He is just playing games, trying to disrupt our performance."

"That's as may be," replied the archon, "but you'll prove it with words, not with fists. It's disrespectful to Dionysus."

Alkibiades became conscious of the dangerously noisy crowd, the archons gripping his arms, Taureas cowering on the ground holding his bloody face. He relaxed, and the archons released him.

The theatre simmered as Dareios was questioned, his family identified, and members of his father's brotherhood made to testify to their citizenship. The Basileus was convinced, and he ordered the performance to continue. The aulos began, accompanied by hoots and jeering, whistles and missiles. Melanippides looked ill, but Alkibiades was back in control and smiled as if enjoying the show, making eye contact with the judges. His boys performed gamely before an audience part determined not to hear them, part annoyed they could not hear them. The chorus left the orchestra amidst a cacophony of boos and applause.

Alkibiades did not listen to the final chorus, but he noticed the livid face of Hipponikus among the generals. He had been foolish, he knew it. To lose control in battle or in private was one thing, but to do it at a religious festival... Hipponikus would probably not forgive him, but that was of little moment. More importantly, would it outweigh the owls he had laid down with the judges?

The final hymn ended and the Basileus called each tribe in turn for the audience to cry out their approvals and disparagements. The ten judges etched their decisions on wax tablets, which they dropped into an urn. The Basileus pulled out five at random, and the theatre became silent.

"Leagros of Antiochis," began the archon, reading the first tablet, "votes for Erechtheis." Exuberant cheers greeted the news.

Beside Alkibiades, Melanippides shook his head and groaned. "No, no. Taureas is going to win and that braggart Kinesias with him." Alkibiades said nothing, feeling the sting of Hipponikus' glare from across the orchestra.

"Kallipos of Aiantis," continued the archon, "votes for Leontis."

"That's us! That's us!" cried Melanippides, jumping up and down. The crowd's reaction was not quite as favourable, and when the next two votes also went Alkibiades' way, granting him victory, the theatre erupted into angry shouts, and half-eaten apples, figs and bread rained upon the judges.

Alkibiades led his chorus to the orchestra to receive their crowns of victory and his bronze tripod. The theatre was on the verge of a riot as he turned to Melanippides, grinned, and said, "I told you we would win."

Chapter 33

Plataea in the spring is a wondrous place: the fields sing with colour, the air is ambrosia, mountains shed their blankets, and water nymphs gambol into the plain. But the joyful awakening of Mother Earth failed to penetrate Skopas' breastplate of depression as he trudged along the top of the wall. Behind him, Mikos slumped in exaggerated imitation like a weary monkey. Sémon glanced back, saw the performance and began to laugh.

"What?" demanded Skopas, catching the tail end of his portrait. He was on the point of sharp words, but Mikos straightened, laughed, and threw an arm round Skopas' shoulder. "I don't see why you two are so cheerful."

"It's better than the alternative," smiled Sémon.

"Aren't you just hiding from reality?" muttered young Hybrias behind his hair.

Sémon halted his little troop and swept his arm over the countryside beyond the enemy wall. "How can you not be cheerful when you see that?"

"You mean the flocks we can't tend? The trees we can't prune?" said Skopas.

"Skopas, Skopas," said Sémon, tracking a swallow's adventurous flight, and drinking the air like a purifying libation. He turned to face the town below and his smile faded. As the world around them sprang to life, Plataea was dying. True, it was still inhabited by over two hundred men and the slave women, but they were bodies, empty shells whose spirits seemed to have dwindled under the crush of disappointment. Passions regarding the calamitous breakout had calmed, but boredom had returned, bitter whispers had invaded minds: no chance of escape; no chance of rescue. "The gods will punish the Thebans for the sacrilege against our men," said Sémon. "We have to give them the time to act."

"Perhaps it's us they are punishing," said Skopas. "Face it,

Sémon, the Athenians aren't coming. They don't even know about the loss of our men." He slapped the top of the wall. "Hermes' dick, we've resisted long enough for there to be no dishonour in surrender."

Sémon raised an eyebrow. "Perhaps, but it's not only dishonour that concerns me. We can't trust the Thebans. It's our safety that should persuade us to resist to the very last morsel of our strength."

"The men are tired," sighed Skopas. "Weary."

"I know," said Sémon. "Look, in battle our blood is up, we summon our courage, roar at the top of our voices, and fling ourselves into the fray in a frenzy that we call bravery, the 'true test' of a man. But it's a fleeting moment, a pause in life. A man's courage should be judged on all his life, not just one instant."

"Absolutely," agreed Hybrias.

"To show bravery through each moment in life," continued Sémon, "is much more difficult. With no battle, there's time to think, and our minds are the true enemy of manhood, their conquest our greatest test."

In the fields beyond the encircling wall a young shepherd had stopped on the brow of a hill and stared at the town as if it had mysteriously risen from the depths of the earth, a dog sitting beside him as their goats drifted around them. Mikos waved but the shepherd did not respond, his stern face fixed on the little war intruding on the plains.

Suddenly shouts rose from the town. Sémon turned, and his heart skipped: there was smoke. "Quickly," he shouted as he ran along the wall to the steps that led down to the town. The group sprinted through the streets, joining men converging from every direction, but when they reached the fire it was already too late. The wooden rafters were ablaze, and all they could do was to protect the surrounding buildings.

"Zeus the Liberator save us," muttered Hybrias, staring at the fire. "It's one of the granaries."

Everyone knew it. In the midst of the water chains to the nearby buildings, the men avoided each other's eyes and said little. Even Sémon was grave. Half of their grain supply was being destroyed. The spectre of starvation rose with the smoke, and all they could do was watch.

Chapter 34

"You realize you have finished Plataea, don't you?" growled Hipponikus, looking back at Alkibiades. The accused held his glare calmly, unruffled, causing the general to spit on the stone steps. He looked down the slope beyond his son-in-law to the rest of their procession climbing the path between the olive trees. The party atmosphere jarred with his mood. He nodded towards his daughter, the centre of attention of their brood of women, and grunted, "At least you can do something right." He waved at Hipparete and cried, "Daughter! You are a blessing to our families!" The women around her ululated their agreement.

Hipponikus shook his head and muttered, "Thank the gods that *one* of my children is not a disappointment." In his trail, beside Alkibiades, Kallias flushed but said nothing.

"Hipponikus," soothed Ariphron, his broad forehead reflecting the morning sun. "This is a day of celebration, remember? Don't be so hard on the boys."

"Hard? Hard? Alkibiades' childish antics at the Dionysia cost us the election. If not for him, we would have gained a majority of generals."

"We made progress," said Alkibiades. "The board is split evenly now."

"Only because your man, Kleon, got his puppy elected. And I succeeded, of course, no thanks to you." Hipponikus paused and a smile touched his mouth. "Or to Perikles."

The colour rose in Alkibiades' cheeks, and Ariphron touched him on the arm and shook his head, before himself engaging the general. "The Dionysia was an exceptional circumstance. To win it when so young is a great achievement. Most people appreciate that. It would be unfair to disregard Alkibiades' excellent work with Council members, the Plataea celebration, the..."

"That is all very well," interrupted Hipponikus, "but with the generals equally divided there is no hope of rescuing Plataea. His foolishness cost Demosthenes a place on the board and condemned the Plataeans. The Dionysia was a Cadmeian victory, too costly by far."

"Alkibiades may have overreacted, but he was provoked and under a lot of pressure," said Ariphron.

Alkibiades mused on Red Maron: they had no idea what provocation had struck him. Still, at least he had settled *that* issue in his mind. "We only need to overturn the result for one general and we would be free to act on Plataea," he said aloud.

"What do you mean, 'overturn'?" said Hipponikus. "We have had enough of your recklessness."

They continued in silence, listening to the aulos and the bleat of the sacrificial sheep ahead, climbing the steep steps to the Propylaea, monumental gateway to the acropolis. Emerging from the shadows of the Propylaea was to enter a world of treasures. The bronze Athena Promarchos[2] towered over them, a reminder of victory over the Persians; a bronze chariot and horses commemorated an ancient war with Boeotia; a replica ship immortalized the defeat of Samos. War trophies abounded, testament to the military prowess of the young democracy and a source of pride for all Athenians.

But for Alkibiades the greatest trophy was his family's monument, the one Perikles had built: the Temple of Athena Parthenos[3], treasury of the Athenians and symbol of beauty and strength, a wonder throughout Hellas.

The procession eased along the pathway that snaked beside the Parthenon and then fell away to the huge altar of Athena of the City. The heart of Athens' religious life, the marble altar could cater for the holocaust of over fifty bulls simultaneously. Before it stood a simple temple housing the goddess's ancient statue venerated by the Athenians. It always made Alkibiades smile. It had been fifty years since the Persians had destroyed the original temple, but argument still raged over the design of a permanent new home for the most important cult of Athens. *There is nothing quite like a religious dispute*, thought

---

[2] Athena Who Fights in the Front Ranks
[3] Athena the Virgin (from Parthenos we get the Parthenon)

Alkibiades.

The family and friends watched as the Priestess of Athena prayed for Hipparete and her unborn child, and offered a lock of wool on the altar fire. An attendant grabbed the sheep by the head and slit its throat, accompanied by the ritual screams of the women, blood dousing the feet of the butcher as he cut away the thighs to be burnt in offering.

"Euthyphron!" called Deinomache from beside Hipparete. The old man in question, resting on his staff after the hard climb, noted the invitation and hobbled forward, easing down to examine the sheep's liver, the source of life. "Well?" pressed Deinomache. "A boy that will bear arms like no other?"

The diviner's face was a mask of sincerity as his trembling hands held the liver. He heard Deinomache's demand again. "Er. Yes. Yes. They will indeed have a boy who bears arms like no other," he said. Congratulations raced around the party, and Alkibiades smiled, knowing the seer had guaranteed himself an additional fee.

Slaves prepared the sheep for transportation to the feast to be given at Alkibiades' house, and the priestess hovered, awaiting her payment of the sheepskin. Deinomache herded the women towards the Parthenon to admire the reliefs and point out the members of her family that had fought at Marathon, not so secretly represented there. Hipponikus talked with Ariphron as Alkibiades led his friends inside the claustrophobic Temple of Athena of the City. The torchlight revealed the seated Athena, saffron robes draped over her, her life-size wooden features cracked with age. At her feet lay the jewel-encrusted sword ripped from the lifeless hands of the Persian general, Mardonius.

"What are we doing in here?" whispered Nikolas.

"Keeping my mother happy," said Alkibiades.

"Not an insignificant task," muttered Timokles.

Alkibiades looked over his shoulder to ensure they were not overheard, before assuming a prayerful voice and calling out to the goddess,

"Oh Athena, fair and wise,
Give my child big brown eyes,

Grant him arms, strong and brave,
And all the women he might crave."

Kallias took up the chorus.

"Great Athena, pure and strong,
Give him a penis that's very, very long!"

Nikolas continued:

"Give him looks as fair as yours,
Not like Kallias, full of sores."

"They are only temporary," shouted Kallias above their laughter, touching the spots he had recently acquired.

Hipponikus cleared his throat behind them. He was not laughing. Alkibiades settled his friends down and put on a show to please the old man.

"Great Athena, grant me a healthy child. If it is a son, make him strong and brave. If it is a daughter, make her pure and fair." He turned to his companions. "I think we have fulfilled our obligations here."

"It won't go down in history as the most eloquent of prayers," said Timokles.

"But in length, the most welcome," said Nikolas.

Alkibiades led his friends outside, ignoring Hipponikus' glare and acknowledging Theo Ariphron's amusement. They wandered past statues of heroes, leaders, and athletes, until Alkibiades paused before a marble Tolmides, the general who had led his father to his death at Koronea. He gazed into the stony blue eyes of the thief. Only shadows of his father remained, and *this* man had stolen him.

"Why do you think Demosthenes failed to get elected?" asked Kallias quietly.

Alkibiades broke free of his reverie. "Paches is leading the siege in Mytilene. People are reluctant to make a change in the midst of an active command unless the general is truly inept."

"Plus Paches had the support of Nikias," added Nikolas.

"Yes," said Alkibiades, "but he is vulnerable. I think we can reverse the decision."

"Really?" exclaimed Nikolas. "How?"

"I have heard he has been heavy-handed with his men, and that there is jealousy regarding the money he is making. Charges of bribery and corruption could easily be arranged."

"It's not unusual for a general to make money on the side," said Nikolas.

"Of course," said Alkibiades. "But if you lose the trust of your men, even honest corruption can seem like a slight to those making sacrifices."

"From what I've heard, Paches is a good, honourable man," said Timokles.

"That sounds like Nikias talking," burst Nikolas. "Did you marry him or his daughter?"

Kallias chuckled as Timokles flushed.

"It is understandable," began Alkibiades, "that your wife would support her father's confederates, but Paches is an obstacle to the good of Athens. With him in place, this ineffective war policy will continue."

Angry shouts attracted their attention to a sanctuary guardian chasing away a seagull before it could deposit its own offering upon the head of a bronze Apollo. Chatter floated on the wind from the book market on the slopes below, and Alkibiades raised his gaze to the fat merchant ships heading for Piraeus. Piraeus, where his blackmailer was to be found. "Carry on," he said, indicating the path beside the Parthenon. "I will catch up." As his friends moved away, Alkibiades caught Nikolas by the arm to hold him back.

Nikolas looked up questioningly into the handsome face, a match for any of the gods on display, but Alkibiades remained pensive, surveying their surroundings. Once they were alone, Alkibiades held Nikolas' eyes for several seconds before speaking. "Nikolas, I have a delicate problem for which I need the help of a true friend. Someone I can trust beyond doubt, whose loyalty cannot be questioned."

Alkibiades had to hide his smile as Nikolas plumped his feathers. "I am that man, Alkibiades."

Alkibiades nodded, his face sober. "I know that, Nikolas. You are the only man I can trust with this."

"What do you need?"

Now we will see how desperate they are to be close to me, thought Alkibiades. "I have an annoying fly that needs swatting," he said. "Goes by the name Red Maron."

Chapter 35

Fear hunted Nikolas. No shield or breastplate could protect him from it, but he could not turn back, he could not fail his father.

Cloud cloaked the sliver of moon, but when the door to Hera's Tavern burst open, releasing a huddle of stumbling drunks, the street filled with light and laughter. From the shadows, Nikolas examined the faces, satisfying himself that there was none of interest. He adjusted the sackcloth bag over his shoulder as the street plunged into darkness again and the singing to Aphrodite weaved homewards. He blew into his hands – they were not cold, but it was a distraction from the serpent coiling in his stomach. What would tonight mean for *him*? What if the gods really could see all things? He wrapped his arms around himself, standing in the dark heart of Piraeus, an exile from the world.

Nikolas had seen the colour flee his father's face when he told him about Alkibiades' request. Red Maron was his father's man, and Pisander had confessed to Nikolas that he had arranged the blackmail himself to gain a hold over Alkibiades, but he had not counted on Alkibiades' ruthlessness. After some hesitation, Pisander had commanded his son to do Alkibiades' bidding.

That his father might blackmail Alkibiades did not surprise Nikolas. But he did wonder why his father refused to tell him the nature of the blackmail, and why he would place his son so obviously under Alkibiades' power. To be asked to plot and scheme to rescue Athens was one thing, for his father to ask him to kill in cold blood was quite another.

At last his moment arrived. Maron stepped into the street with a wide grin. Nikolas recognized the cavernous face, and felt his own legs buckle. Another man left the tavern to join Maron. How could he deal with two? The tavern door closed and the two men supported each other as they giggled into the darkness. Nikolas crept from his hiding place, stalking them. Could he do it? Kill in cold blood? He had killed in battle, but that was justifiable. How could he defend this to himself, let alone the gods?

They turned down one street, then another. They were not far from Maron's home, the opportunity was slipping away. Perhaps that was a good thing. But he had no choice, did he? A father's command, after all, was like an order from Zeus. How could he disobey Zeus?

Maron's companion turned into a side street, calling farewells over his shoulder. Nikolas increased his pace, half running. He glanced around him. Was there something in the shadows? No. All was darkness. They were alone.

He was within a few yards and called softly, "Hey, Maron."

Maron whipped around, unable to see. "Who's that?"

"Nikolas, Pisander's son," he whispered, concealing his knife.

"Evening, young master. You've instructions from your father?"

"Yes, I do." Nikolas grabbed him by the hair, jerked his head back and slit his throat. Maron grasped his neck, trying to stem the flow of blood, not seeing the glint in Nikolas' eyes as he thrust the dagger into his heart. Maron fell to his knees and slumped to the ground.

Nikolas was trembling, the street swirling around him. He vomited on to the road, a reverberating waterfall of sound. He wiped his mouth, took a slow, deep breath, and knelt down. He felt for Maron's purse, pulling it free of the bloody neck, taking the meagre contents and flinging the empty purse aside. As he focused on his task he began to work more quickly, wiping his blade clean, removing the wine skin from his bag and pouring some of the contents over the body, leaving the remainder beside him. He wiped his hands clean and exchanged his blood-spattered tunic for a spotless one from his bag. For an instant he considered binding the body's hands and feet so that Maron's ghost could not haunt him, but it would spoil the illusion.

The street swam in blood, but it was as silent as the dead when Nikolas slipped away, heading down towards the docks. He hid his face when passing a group of drunken revellers, but as he turned a corner, he stumbled into a squad of Scythian archers patrolling the streets. His heart exploded. Surely their torches would discover remnants of his attack that he had failed to hide, or they would discern his face burning with Maron's blood. Nikolas looked to the ground, waiting for them to accost him, ready to grasp his dagger in one last desperate act. But they passed by, more intent on rowdy drunks and not expecting a lone murderer.

Nikolas hurried on, noting by the light of a tavern a crude painting of a hunting dog with a human face surrounded by the words, "Kleon, watchdog of the people". Beneath it was drawn a puppy on a pile of coins with the logo, "Nikias, lapdog of the rich." Nikolas smiled: people were so gullible.

He continued towards the wharf, where hulls of merchant ships lined the docks, their cables rattling in the wind. He felt better. He had honoured his father, and it had not been so bad in the end. In fact, the thrust of the knife had been exhilarating, now that he thought about it. A burden had lifted, and he could continue his night's work with confidence. Pitiful cries and whimpers escaped from the slave warehouse, and Nikolas sighed, glad that he was his father's son.

***

Alkibiades had stalked Nikolas through the night, uncertain whether the dark one would follow through on his promise, but he had heard the kill, and had smiled in the knowledge that Nikolas was now his tool. But Nikolas had headed for the docks, not Athens, and Alkibiades had smelled intrigue and had continued to follow him.

As he passed the slave warehouse, a lamp appeared on a nearby ship, as shocking as a bolt of lightning. Nikolas had stopped and was in animated discussion with the captain by the light of the lamp. What was Nikolas scheming?

He melted into the shadows when Nikolas finally made his furtive exit, and Alkibiades hesitated. What had just happened? To meet at such a time in such a place invited suspicion. He waited until Nikolas was out of sight, and then strolled to the gangplank of the lamp-lit ship.

"Ho there!" he cried softly. "Captain. I saw you awake."

A barn door of a man rose from the deck, his numerous scars a sea chart. "What d'you want?" he demanded.

"I saw by the light what a fine ship you have, sir. What cargo do you trade?"

"Castor and Polydeuces! What's it to you?"

"I am a merchant, sir, always on the lookout. I noticed you doing business during these hours of Apollo's rest. Very unusual. Must have a special cargo, I told myself."

The captain paused. Alkibiades noticed his hand creep under his tunic as if reaching for a knife, and around him the crew stirred from their blankets. "I make deals when it suits my customers," growled the captain.

"But who would want to do business at this time of night when one could be drinking?" pressed Alkibiades, recognizing the Spartan accent, and acutely aware of the captain's twitchy fingers and the glares of his men.

The barn door raised an eyebrow.

"You are a true businessman, sir," said Alkibiades, "and I wish you Hermes' fortune in your dealings." He beat a hasty retreat to the safety of the shadows, where he turned to watch the ship. Spartans in Piraeus. What was Nikolas up to? His behaviour seemed treasonous. What double game were they playing? As the storm of suspicion whirled around his mind, the lamp on the ship was doused and the mooring lines cast off, and the vessel stole silently into the darkness.

Chapter 36

Aristeia had tried everything: whispered endearments, teasing robes, tantalizing perfume. Nothing had worked. Now, having blurted her unhappiness once more to her aunt, she sat before the hearth, hiding her face in her hands, sobbing. Glukera struggled from her couch to sit beside her niece, wrapping her fleshy arms around Aristeia and clucking soothing tones.

Nikopatra watched them carefully in the lamp light, excited by the opportunity approaching. She had persuaded Glukera, and the old woman was the key to Aristeia.

Glukera sighed, stroking Aristeia's hair. "You know, my sweet, that a child cures many ills."

"Of course I know," blurted Aristeia, laying her head in her aunt's lap. "It's not like Timokles never... performs. It's just," she paused, glancing up at Nikopatra and blushing. "It's just that it's not often, and like he's buying grain at the market. I can't move him. He's not unfriendly, but he seems determined to keep his heart engaged elsewhere."

"You mean Samias," prompted Nikopatra, seeing victory approach.

Aristeia sat up wearily. "Yes, that's where he wants to be, not with me."

Nikopatra nodded with the gravity of a sage and gave Glukera a knowing look.

"We've been worried about you, my sweet," said Glukera, "and have discussed a possible solution to your problems." Aristeia wiped the tears from her cheeks and gazed hopefully at her aunt. "It's time to call upon the gods of the Underworld to remove Samias from Timokles' affections."

"No. Really? I don't want to call a curse on Samias, Thea," said Aristeia. "He's probably not a bad person."

"Whether he's good or bad has nothing to do with it, my dear," said Nikopatra. "If this Samias prevents the birth of a child, it's bad for our families. And for Athens."

"Perhaps we could go back to the Temple of Hera instead and pray for her blessing again," suggested Aristeia.

"My little duckling," began Glukera, her arm round her niece, "we've already made sacrifices to the Queen of Brides and been pecked by her peacocks. We've made offerings to Aphrodite and been pricked by her roses. It hasn't been enough, has it? You're a sweet child, but now we need to enlist the gods of the Underworld as well as those in Olympus."

Aristeia clasped her hands, frowning and glancing round the room. Nikopatra suspected she wanted Leaina's support, but her daughter was safely away with her own aunt tonight. "It's only a little curse," said Nikopatra. "We just want him to stop interfering with your marriage. Trust us, my dear. Your aunt and I know what's best in these circumstances."

"I'm afraid it's our last option," said Glukera.

Aristeia closed her eyes and shook her head. "What kind of curse did you have in mind?"

A surge of triumph washed over Nikopatra and she retrieved a thin lead sheet from the folds of her gown. "I had this prepared by a diviner, just in case." She held the small tablet to the light and read the tiny inscription:

"Let Samias be placed under a spell to Hermes of the Underworld.
Shrivel his heart like an autumn leaf and make it cold like the winter snows on Mount Parnes.
Let his friendships wither and like this lead, be held in no esteem."

"See?" continued Nikopatra. "It will just end their friendship, nothing more. It's a perfectly reasonable request."

"I don't know," said Aristeia.

"What do you have to lose, my dear?" said Nikopatra, holding her breath as Aristeia hesitated.

"Perhaps... perhaps it might be worth a try," said Aristeia.

"Excellent!" cried Nikopatra, jumping to her feet. "Then let's do it now. While the fire burns."

"Now?" said Aristeia. "But what if Timokles comes back? What would we tell him?"

"That we're making offerings for the family. But my son's out for the night. It seems that cavalrymen are required to drink themselves unconscious before they go on campaign."

Glukera rose and between the two of them they shepherded Aristeia out of the house, wrapped in their himations and hurrying behind two slaves bearing torches.

"Where are we going?" said Aristeia.

"The cemetery, of course," said Nikopatra. She saw the uncertainty blanket Aristeia, so she hurried them through the dark streets, past noisy taverns and on to the Piraeus Gate, where a troop of soldiers played dice.

"Where do you think you're going?" demanded a guard whose helmet rested on the back of his head.

"We have business with Hermes, young man, so stand aside," said Glukera.

The guard examined the women and their slaves. "Why at this time of night?"

"Tshh!" exclaimed Glukera. "Don't you know anything? Offerings to Hermes of the Underworld *have* to be made at night."

The guard flushed. "Of course I know that, Lady. You didn't specify which Hermes you were talking about."

"Of course I did," said Glukera. "You youngsters just don't pay attention to your elders. Do you ever listen to your mother? I doubt it. I'll bet she's a wise woman but you just ignore her, don't you? You think age has addled her brain rather than refined it. Don't you? Well?"

"You there!" cried the guard, turning from Glukera and indicating an amused soldier leaning against the wall. "Accompany these women and make sure they return safely."

"Thank you," smiled Glukera. "I'm sure your mother's proud of you."

The group squeezed through the gate and on to Piraeus Road, which was flanked by the graves of the poor.

"Why have we come to *this* cemetery?" whispered Aristeia, feeling exposed outside the city walls and imagining robbers lurking beyond the flickering torch light.

"There's a fresh grave here for a young boy," said Nikopatra. They picked their way along the road, Nikopatra searching for markers that had been easier to spot in daylight. The torches cast an eerie light on the graves around them, and they finally found the freshly turned earth with its simple wooden marker a few yards from the road. "Here we are," said Nikopatra. "They haven't put up a stone yet. He only died yesterday. Six years old."

"That's very sad," said Aristeia.

"Yes, but ideal for us," said Nikopatra, extracting a small doll from her robe. Aristeia glared at the doll, then at Nikopatra. "My dear, we must have a representation of Samias. It's the way these things are done." Nikopatra glanced at Glukera for support, and the old lady nodded with an air of regret. Nikopatra rolled the lead curse and pinned it to the doll, kneeling before the grave and removing some of the soil to bury the impaled doll with the young boy. "You must say the prayer, my dear." Her heart was racing. She could see that Aristeia's misgivings still threatened to rob her of her victory.

Aristeia looked to her aunt, who squeezed her hand, saying, "It's alright, my sweet. It's the right thing to do."

Slowly, Aristeia turned her gaze to the spot where the curse lay buried. Clenching her fists as if they could hold back her words, she said in a rush, "Hermes of the Underworld, take this curse down with the untimely dead and fulfil its promise." She closed her eyes, trembling and fighting back the tears.

"Don't worry," said Glukera. "This will do the trick."

Nikopatra glowed with the torches. Whether it worked or not, the curse was a triumph. To curse Timokles' lover! Her son might expect it of his mother, but of his wife? If he were to ever find out... Nikopatra knew that Aristeia would do anything to avoid such a prospect. There was no question now who would be mistress of the house.

Chapter 37

The cavalry of Athens radiated northwards over farmland and headed for the passes. The Peloponnesian army had invaded, destroying crops and houses, and the families from every village and farmstead in Attika had fled to Athens, leaving only the cavalry to stand in the way.

Samias walked alongside his horse behind Timokles. Their tribal contingent of fifty cavalrymen and their attendants had joined similar units from the other nine tribes of Attika. It appeared to Samias like a mass migration as they headed for the lands of Acharnae, passageway into the heart of Attika, an inviting door between the mountains of Aegaleus and Parnes.

Samias glanced over his shoulder, past Nikolas and on to the city of Athens sparkling in the sun six miles away. His father was there. The shield slinger. Samias' youth had been scarred by the taunts of his peers and the bruises his father had inflicted as if they would relieve his shame. Timokles had been his saviour, and now Samias finally had a chance to clear the stain from the family name, but the possibility that a father's cowardice could infect his son tormented him. He faced the front, reaching up to stroke his horse's ears, which poked through its head armour.

"Hey, Alkibiades!" cried Nikolas from behind Samias. "Help us resolve an argument back here. Nestor thinks we only need fear a wife's sensuality if she's clever. He says that stupidity preserves the virtue of most wives. What do you think?"

Alkibiades walked ahead of Timokles and behind their commander of ten. "Nestor sounds like Euripides," he replied.

"Clever women cause more trouble than the Peloponnesian army," shouted Nestor. "No offence, Alkibiades, but we all know a woman started this war. I swear by Poseidon of Horses that if Aspasia had not stroked Perikles' ego to protect her own Miletus, we'd still be at peace."

Alkibiades shook his head and shouted back, "My dear Nestor, I cannot use the fact that women have befuddled *you*, as evidence that they run the state." The troop chuckled, including Nestor himself.

"When do you think we'll see them?" called Samias.

"The Peloponnesians? Soon enough," said Alkibiades.

Samias gazed across the fields to the other units, five hundred cavalrymen and their attendants, half of Athens' cavalry. To Samias, it was an impressive force, a refusal to cower before the invasion, but Alkibiades had assured him that it was a charade. They would fight and some of them would die, but the damage they could inflict on a hoplite army supported by cavalry was minimal. They were a pretence of Nikias' commitment to protect the farms of Attika. But still, for Samias it was a chance to show his worth, if only he knew what that was.

Two riders raced towards them from the pass and pulled up before the hipparch, leader of the cavalry force. A bugle call followed, and they all vaulted onto their horses. Samias adjusted his position on the cushion sewn into the horse blanket and checked his armour: the white cuirass; the bronze collar around his neck and jaw; the scale armour beneath his chiton that protected his abdomen and groin; the bronze plates clamped to his left arm; the layers of calfskin wrapped around his spear arm. His slave handed him his open-faced helmet, his small shield, and a javelin. Samias' hands trembled: with fear, or excitement?

"Time to give them a bloody nose, by Zeus," growled Nestor as they trotted towards the pass.

"Wait 'till they see how many we are," said Samias. "They'll soon run back home."

"We'll see about that," muttered Nikolas.

The cavalry of Samias' tribe of Leontis urged their steeds up the slope of one of the foothills of Aegaleus, gripping their mounts with their thighs. They halted at the crest, forming a long line on the bare hilltop, gawking into the Thriasian Plain.

"Great Zeus, there's so many of them," whispered Samias.

A plague of men infested the farmland between the mountain ranges of Aegaleus and Parnes, stretching westwards towards Megara.

Smoke from burning farmhouses and crops rose as trophies of victory, hoplites chopped down olive trees, Boeotian cavalry ravaged farms. It was a land of nightmares.

The younger Athenians, seeing such a massed enemy for the first time, lost their bravado like a punctured bladder. Silence settled upon them as they watched tens of thousands destroying the plain little more than a dozen miles from Athens.

Samias' commander of ten, Xenokles, noted their pale faces. He was a political animal, the cavalry his steppingstone to power. "Listen to me, men." He waited for them to wrench their attention from the plain. "By Poseidon, there are a lot of them. More than usual. But so what? We're not here to take on the whole damn army. We're here to stop them taking liberties. See those light-armed men down there? By the stream, near Penelope's well. Those are the men we're after, wandering away from the hoplites and plundering for themselves. We make them think twice about roaming so freely and we'll save a lot of farmland. But we won't be tangling with the hoplites. Got it?" A few uncertain nods greeted his encouragement.

Bugle calls rolled across the broad entrance to the plain and a knot of fear curled inside Samias. What if he failed? What if he really was like his father?

The cavalry of Athens cantered towards the marauders, horses crowding together in a long line, including servants and slaves, javelins aloft to increase their apparent number. Their appearance had immediate effect. Light-armed troops and small groups of enemy cavalry hurried back to the protection of the main body of hoplites, shepherded by trumpet calls that bounced between the mountains. Soon the massed ranks of hoplites marched with raised spears towards the Athenians, Boeotian cavalry protecting the flanks.

The thunder of feet, the whinnying of horses, the blaring of trumpets, the high-pitched Spartan pipes, and the war hymn to Apollo all thudded into Samias' belly like the blows of a boxer. He glanced at Timokles beside him, who smiled and said, "Pay no heed. It's all for show. I'll wager we see no action today."

The words had barely escaped his mouth when three tribal detachments galloped ahead, their attendants following a hundred yards behind. The remaining cavalry continued to trot towards the enemy, now just over a mile away, the army oozing towards them like the inexorable flow of lava.

Hundreds of enemy cavalry rushed from the flanks to form a shield in front of the infantry, and the Athenian advance guard halted three hundred yards from the advancing army. Athenian cavalry from four other tribes galloped for the enemy's flanks. The last three tribes, including Samias' Leontis contingent, remained in reserve. More Boeotian cavalry appeared, countering the Athenian move. The pipes never faltered, and the Peloponnesians continued their march, headed by a line of cavalry facing their Athenian opponents, who gave ground, maintaining a constant separation from the enemy.

Samias kept his horse stepping backwards with the rest of his troop. The army was unstoppable. They might as well stand before a flood of Poseidon and hope to halt its progress. "What happens now?" he asked.

Alkibiades glanced across at him and then returned his gaze to the clamorous beast poised to swallow their comrades half a mile ahead. "If we are lucky," he began, "they will start to probe and we may have some fun. Otherwise, we will have to maintain this dance for the rest of the day."

"But how do we stop them?"

"Weren't you listening, boy?" snapped Commander Xenokles. "We don't stop them, we slow them. We distract them."

An hour passed. Two. Still the forces maintained their order and their creeping momentum. Another hour and Samias looked over his shoulder. Two miles away the Temple of Ares shimmered above the ruined walls of the town of Acharnae. The Boeotians rotated cavalry at the front, bringing in men and horses not wearied by the tension of imminent confrontation. Athenian attendants started to trot forward in ones and twos, bringing drinks to their masters at the front.

"I said no refreshment," shouted the enraged hipparch, the man in charge of the entire Athenian cavalry. Perhaps they were motivated by a desire to please, or from fear of displeasure, but more slaves broke ranks to take water to their masters, and the Athenian forward line became distracted, its formation fractured. Enemy trumpets blared and the Boeotian cavalry charged.

A moment of shock passed before the Athenians wheeled away from the roar and galloped back towards the reserve. A wall of dust chased them and obscured the release of javelins, but could not hide screams of pain and squeals of impaled horses. Samias could not understand what he was watching. It was unreal, a training exercise.

"Extend the line!" shouted the hipparch. "Attendants in the gaps!" The advance forces were routed, and the only way to fight their panic was to block their escape. They were closing. Six hundred yards. Five hundred yards. Samias' breath escaped in short bursts, and he gripped the horse with his legs to stop them trembling. The bugles cried, commanding those fleeing to turn and face the enemy, but the notes were a mere breath of wind. The reserve struggled to rein in their skittish horses as the majority of their own cavalry rushed towards them, hunted by the Boeotians. Three hundred yards. Samias prepared to be trampled by his own men.

"Spears ready!" shouted the hipparch, the order relayed by bugles. Samias adjusted the shield on his left arm and positioned the spear between his horse's ears. Two hundred yards. "Charge!" The tribes of Leontis, Akamantis and Oineis yelled and urged their horses into a gallop. Samias roared as his horse exploded, forgetting his trembles and rising on the wings of exhilaration.

The fleeing cavalry, caught between two storms with nowhere to hide, halted and turned in a disorganized mass, before themselves leading the charge against their pursuers. The Boeotians, chasing a routed enemy through the dusty cloud, had overextended themselves and were now far from the support of the hoplites. The hunters became the hunted. But as the Boeotians fled into the dust, bugles recalled the Athenians and they broke off the pursuit.

Samias was furious: an enemy on the run, and they had let them go. They had snatched away his chance for redemption. "Why have we stopped?" he demanded.

"You do not charge an army of hoplites you cannot see," said Alkibiades, but Samias was unimpressed.

The Athenians regrouped, wolfed rations, and bound the wounded with linen bandages as they waited for the dust to settle. Two bloody men staggered out of the cloud, bereft of their horses. The noise of the unseen enemy was deafening, and Samias was certain the army was about to appear, but the experienced men around him seemed unconcerned. When the air cleared, the Peloponnesians had halted and were making camp, digging ditches, raising a palisade, erecting tents. The size of the force awed Samias again, and his anger turned to relief.

The Peloponnesians remained in camp for the rest of the day, and as dusk fell the Athenians camped on the hillside, maintaining watch over the multitude of enemy campfires. Older men joked around their fires, but Samias sat apart, his eyes restless. Timokles wandered over and sat beside him. "You alright?" he asked.

"Why did the hipparch make our men ride so close to theirs? What did he think would happen?" blustered Samias.

Timokles shrugged. "The mind of a leader is hard to fathom sometimes."

"But he might have destroyed our cavalry. Is he stupid?"

Timokles chuckled and put his arm around Samias' shoulders. "You can never predict a battle. The only thing to do is to fight hard for your brothers."

"I'd like the chance to do so."

"I know," said Timokles. "I know."

Samias was afraid: afraid of letting his troop down; afraid of disappointing Timokles; afraid of being his father. He longed for a battle to test his courage so that he would know, so that the waiting would be over. He stared into the nearest fire, stroked the charm around his neck, and muttered a prayer to Apollo for the morning to come quickly.

***

The size of the invading force unsettled Alkibiades. Nikolas' suspicious rendezvous with the Spartan merchant gnawed at his mind – could Antiphon and Pisander be planning to betray the city to Sparta? The size of the enemy army seemed to augur more than just the destruction of farmland. But to betray Athens? To betray *him*! Anger stirred and he glared across the fire at Nikolas, who seemed perfectly relaxed. Alkibiades took a deep breath. He had taken precautions. He had not been able to tell Hipponikus of his suspicion, of course – he would never have listened. But Theo Ariphron had been receptive and had promised to warn the general. It only remained for Hipponikus to take the appropriate actions.

Another reason for the huge force, of course, may be an intention to storm another town: Plataea. With its depleted forces it would have no chance of surviving, and Alkibiades' plans would be dust. His examination of the enemy's movements was therefore minute.

For the next two days the Athenians kept their distance, never straying closer than half a mile to the enemy. The Peloponnesians continued their march, ignored the route to Athens, and destroyed the small towns and villages to the north. They reduced Acharnae to rubble, returned the mud-brick houses of Kholleidai to the earth, reduced crops to a charred wasteland, and burnt, cut down, and dug up trees and vines. But progress was slow, much of the army remaining on the defensive. Without fighting, the Athenians were achieving their objective of minimizing the damage, but Alkibiades wondered if the Peloponnesians were waiting for a signal, for a message from Athens to attack the city, or from Thebes to march on Plataea.

On the third day everything changed. The Peloponnesian general split his forces, some heading north to Phyle, others south and east towards Marathon and Brauron, a force moving on the fortress of Dekeleia, another to the coast near Rhamnous. Less cautious, they moved quickly, and the black smoke multiplied. Alkibiades was relieved: the splintered forces were no threat to Athens or Plataea.

The hipparch assigned his cavalry, by tribe, to track each detachment. The men of Leontis headed north to the hill fortress of Dekeleia, a stronghold with a permanent garrison that could only watch as the lands around them burned. The tribal contingent of fifty cavalrymen skirted an enemy of five thousand, positioning themselves around the fringes with strict instructions not to engage. Days of endless sitting, standing, and watching, as the lands of Attika burned.

By the evening of the fourth such day, discontent bubbled in the camp. The men of Leontis crammed inside the walls of Dekeleia, with no room to escape each other's grumbles. The slaves fed barley to the horses as the soldiers ate cheese cakes and drank goat's milk around the fires.

"Why are we here?" Samias hissed at his companions. "I mean, what's the point if we just watch them destroy everything?"

"We cannot attack such a large force," said Alkibiades between mouthfuls.

"No," agreed Timokles, "but Samias is right. We have to do something, don't we?"

"The phylarch is no fool," said Alkibiades. "He is also no coward. If I were leading the tribal regiment, I would be doing the same thing."

"And what is that, exactly?" asked Samias.

"Letting them feel confident, hoping they get careless."

"I'll bet the others have seen action," said Samias.

"If they have, let us hope it was under conditions of their choosing," said Alkibiades. The fire crackled and he glanced across at Nikolas. "Of course, you can create those conditions if you know what the enemy is planning, if you have spies in their camp. Do you not think so, Nikolas?"

Nikolas looked up sharply, but Alkibiades was smiling. "Certainly," said Nikolas. "Information wins wars."

"Do you think we could recruit a Spartan spy, given their loyalty to their city?"

"Many noble families have longstanding ties with Sparta, as you know very well, Alkibiades," said Nikolas. "And there's no people with as great a greed for silver as the Spartans."

"Ironically," smiled Alkibiades, "given they refuse to use money. But what about the other way round? Do you think any Athenians would betray us to Sparta?"

"Surely not," laughed Timokles. "What could the Spartans possibly offer in return?"

"Betrayal is a harsh word," said Alkibiades. "Let me put it this way. Do you think there are Athenians who would collaborate with Sparta in order to secure their own interests within Athens?"

Alkibiades' eyes burned into Nikolas. "There's precedent for that, I suppose," said Nikolas.

"Indeed, which my ancestors famously resisted," said Alkibiades.

"True, but though each generation may be tested in similar ways, it's never in exactly the same circumstances, and the honourable path may change with time. Do you agree?"

Alkibiades grinned and looked into the fire. It was a clever response, and he liked cleverness. "You are right, of course. We can never fully know how we will respond to circumstances." He paused and looked up at Nikolas, who was picking his nails and staring into the distance with an air of disinterestedness. "But selfishness is not always the cause of treason," continued Alkibiades. "There is blackmail. A man's dark secrets can always be used against him." Nikolas continued to look away and say nothing, but his face flushed.

Talk around the fires continued until the soldiers fell asleep. Alkibiades pondered every word and look of Nikolas as wolves howled in the surrounding hills.

***

The following day began much the same. Commander Xenokles led his men over the foothills, stopping frequently as the enemy consumed the fields below. Timokles, though, noted that Xenokles seemed tense and excited in a way he had not been for days. At every hint of a foray by small groups of enemy soldiers, he stretched his neck as if willing them to expose themselves.

"Will their discipline never end?" exclaimed Xenokles as the soldiers in the plain stopped for their midday meal. As if in response, a dozen lightly armed soldiers wandered from the plain towards an unscathed farmhouse on the rise of a hill a mile ahead. "There!" cried Xenokles. "Perfect. They're going to plunder that house for themselves." He scanned the terrain that separated them. "We can skirt these hills until we reach them. They'll never see us coming."

"What about the rise behind the house?" said Alkibiades beside him. "Perhaps we should circle it and attack from behind, make sure there are no surprises."

"Oh, there'll be no surprises alright," said Xenokles. "By the time we circled them they'd be gone." He turned to his men and grinned.

"Quietly, boys, prepare to attack."

Timokles smiled at Samias, whose pale features attempted to return the favour. Timokles guessed what he was feeling – a lifetime waiting to redeem his family was about to culminate in a single moment. He was confident Samias would meet the challenge.

They galloped, using the foothills to hide them from the plain, and as they climbed up the final slope, the stone farmhouse appeared before them. Two men sat outside on barrels, drinking wine, as old benches and broken tables flew out of the door. Others destroyed trellises and another drew water from a well.

Xenokles broke their silence with a yell and his men charged up the hill. Timokles saw the years of training rush upon Samias, who hurtled forward with the face of a Fury, javelin poised. The soldiers scattered, grabbing their spears and small shields. The cavalry rode to within twenty yards and launched their javelins. The man running from the well was struck in the chest, and another was pierced between the shoulder blades as he scrambled for the farmhouse door. Three javelins thudded into the door as the soldiers took shelter in the house.

Samias beamed at Timokles, "I got one! Did you see? I got one."

"I saw."

The Athenians were ecstatic, shouting taunts, stripping the dead of anything worth taking: rings, amulets, knives. Their attendants joined them, handing over spare javelins where needed. Beside one of the barrels, a lit torch lay discarded in the dust, and Xenokles pounced upon it. He rode around the building setting light to the thatched roof, and finally hurled the torch into the rafters. He lined his men facing the door and grinned.

The fire embraced the roof, and the smoke spiralled into the clear sky as the horsemen jeered, laughing at each other's baiting. Except for Alkibiades. He frowned, watching the smoke curl upwards like a signal, eyeing the grassy rise of the hill they had not scouted beyond the house. "Xenokles," he called, and pointed to the rise. "I really think we should check what is back there."

"He's right," shouted the experienced Nestor. "You should take a man."

Xenokles glared from one to the other. "Oh, very well. Samias! With me!" He galloped towards the rise, and Timokles saw the disappointment on Samias' face. The young man followed reluctantly, his eyes still ablaze with the fire of battle. They were half way to the top when the men burst out of the house, coughing, eyes streaming, crying for mercy. A shower of javelins was the answer to these destroyers of Attika. The survivors of this initial onslaught flung aside their weapons and sprinted down the hill, the cavalry charging after them.

Xenokles and Samias watched jealously from above, before the commander resumed his progress towards the crest, leaving Samias to watch the slaughter. He saw Timokles run down a man and pierce him neatly with his spear, and Alkibiades reach down and hack a head off with his sword. As the bodies fell amid whooping and hollering, Samias boiled that he was not with them.

Suddenly there was a yell of anguish above him. Xenokles wheeled his horse and shouted, "Run, Samias! Run!" Samias jerked his horse's head and urged him back down the hill, looking over his shoulder in time to see Xenokles' horse tumble in the grass, an arrow lodged in its hind leg. He heard the crack as another leg broke in the fall.

Xenokles struggled to extract himself from the fallen body, rose to his feet, pulled out his sword, and waited. A rumble of thunder surged over the summit, and a horde of enemy cavalry stormed upon him. He dodged the spear thrust of the first soldier and slashed the horse's legs, bringing it crashing to the ground, before he was overwhelmed, battered to death by the onslaught.

Samias sped down the hill, arrows whistling past his head, screaming, "Retreat! Retreat!"

The rest of the troop were half a mile away, and scattered. Alkibiades quickly estimated the enemy to be about fifty and bellowed, "On me! On me!" He started his horse at an easy gallop down the slope, waiting for the others to join him, including the slaves. "We must retreat together," he shouted. "Keep our discipline and we may escape. Let's go."

"Wait!" cried Timokles. "What about Samias?"

Alkibiades glanced to where Samias maintained a fifty yard advantage over the hunters, half a mile away. "There are too many for us to engage them, Timokles. Samias must look to himself for now." Timokles was on the point of turning back, but Alkibiades gave his friend's horse a slap on the rear and they raced away.

Timokles looked over his shoulder, panic crushing his chest as he saw Samias weave to avoid arrows, the pack gaining on him. They rounded the hill and he could see him no more. Alkibiades and Nikolas rode beside Timokles to prevent him from turning back, forcing him to climb the slope and then head back on themselves. They halted a hundred yards above their initial route of escape.

"What are we doing?" asked Timokles, his voice choking.

"Sorry, had to keep you moving," said Alkibiades, before raising his voice to continue. "Listen closely. When they round the hill, we charge as one. Everyone," he added, indicating the slaves. "We form one line and hope the shock scares them away long enough for us to make our escape. With Samias," he added with a smile at Timokles.

They formed a line and waited. The pain of hope swamped Timokles, and he willed Samias to appear, arguing with himself over why he was taking so long. Perhaps he had forgotten his training, changed direction? Perhaps he was already captured, a prisoner of Sparta or of Hades? When Samias finally appeared below them, Timokles' relief was cut short by the sight of five horsemen hard on his tail. A javelin flew past Samias' head, and Timokles implored Alkibiades to give the command.

Alkibiades waited for what seemed a lifetime to Timokles, until the main pack rounded the hill, and then Alkibiades urged his men forward and they charged with spears ready, raging battle cries. The body of the enemy cavalry, seeing an apparently numerous foe suddenly appear from above, broke and ran away into the plain. Alkibiades wheeled his jubilant men around as the pursuers caught Samias, oblivious to what had happened behind them. One of them jumped at Samias and brought them both tumbling to the ground.

Timokles buried his heels into the belly of his horse, desperate for the wings of Pegasus. He watched Samias wrestle and gain an advantage. A second man jumped from his horse. A scream caught in Timokles' throat as a spear plunged into Samias' chest, skewering Timokles.

Sudden recognition that they were pursued scattered the horsemen, Alkibiades killing the dismounted men before they could regain their horses. Timokles leapt down and rushed to Samias' side. The spear stood erect, but he was still alive. Bloody bubbles escaped his mouth, each breath a gurgling struggle. Timokles cradled his head, unable to fight the tears. "Samias," he whispered. "Oh, Samias. Don't leave me."

Samias turned his eyes from the sky to Timokles, a smile touching his lips. His eyes lost focus, and a last rogue bubble escaped into the air.

Chapter 38

From his perch on the Long Walls, Pisander watched the solemn procession taking the ancient statue of Athena of the City to the sea for its ritual wash, the priestess's robes shimmering in the plain like an apparition. He fingered the short grey beard protruding from his face like the weathered ram of a trireme. It was a bad day to do business. Even the temples were closed because all prayers and divinations would be unfruitful until the goddess returned. It was a ritual rooted in the days of heroes, when Athens was governed properly by men such as himself.

"Have you heard from Nikolas?" asked Antiphon, standing beside him.

"Two days ago," said Pisander, gazing into the distance at the ceremony merging with the sparkling water. "He was in good health."

"Good. Good." Antiphon adjusted his sun hat and leaned against the battlements. "And Alkibiades?"

Pisander wakened from his dream and turned to face Antiphon. Below them, in the space between the two walls connecting Athens to the port of Piraeus, the refugees of Attika crowded in huts while the Peloponnesians ravaged their lands. Anxiety was rampant, tempers flaring. "You know that Alkibiades was promoted to Commander of Ten?"

Antiphon smiled. "It has been well publicized."

"He's striving to cover himself with glory, of course. However, I've interesting news regarding the Peloponnesians. King Archidamus isn't in command. It's Kleomenes."

"Kleomenes? The regent?"

"The very one. Archidamus was taken ill, so the Spartans appointed Kleomenes to lead the army." Antiphon frowned, and Pisander saw the calculations in his friend's eyes. Antiphon's intellect was intimidating – Pisander was glad they were on the same side.

"Do you have any contact with Kleomenes?" asked Antiphon.

"No. He's a hardliner, not as amenable as Archidamus. He's determined to destroy Athens, has no interest in sharing power with us."

Antiphon turned his eyes to the ground, his face shaded by his broad hat, his mind recalibrating. "Well that explains why the army has not approached the city walls."

"I guess so," said Pisander. He indicated a group of guards propped against the wall nearby. "Although, with all the extra security that's appeared, it would've been a waste of time anyway. We could never have got our men in a position to let them in." The additional guards on the walls, in the docks, on the acropolis, at the armoury, made Pisander nervous. "Do you think they know?"

"No," said Antiphon. "If they knew, our families would be in prison and we would be dead. They may suspect, but suspicion is the foundation of democracy, the way they ensure no one rules."

"Hmm. Nikolas is worried that Alkibiades knows something of our contacts with Sparta."

"Interesting," said Antiphon. "I wonder if Alkibiades is behind the security measures."

"Perhaps," said Pisander, knowing the moment for his confession had arrived, and feeling his guts squirm like an eel. He cleared his throat. "I may have...underestimated him."

"How so?"

"He's young, inexperienced. I thought the damn bugger could be... manipulated. I tried to bind him closer to us. Have you heard of Red Maron?"

"Sounds familiar. Was he the drunk killed for his purse a few weeks ago?"

"Supposedly. Funny, given how poor he was. I believe Alkibiades had him murdered."

Antiphon gaped. "Alkibiades? But why?"

An image of his wife, Elené, flashed through Pisander's mind. "Maron was blackmailing him. At my behest."

"Blackmail? Over what?"

Pisander's grey face acquired some unusual colour. "That's unimportant. But Alkibiades acted with a ruthlessness I didn't expect."

"Well, it does not surprise *me*," said Antiphon, eyeing Pisander uneasily. "Does he know you were behind it?"

"I doubt it. His ego would never allow it." Pisander watched a guard yawning in the sun. "Do you think we should delay? Wait until suspicions fade?"

"No. We cannot be idle while the mob destroys Athens piece by piece. Athena and our ancestors demand that we save her. We shall just have to be more careful."

"Good," said Pisander. "I can't bear to watch these damn imbeciles destroy the city and do nothing about it."

"Events may still fall our way. If the Peloponnesian fleet relieves Mytilene, the whole of Lesbos will switch sides and other islands will threaten to follow suit. With Kleomenes still in the field, people will panic and we will strike."

"In which case Plataea can go to the crows," said Pisander.

"Yes, but if the relief fails, Plataea will still be our best hope. Your friend, King Archidamus, or one of his minions will *have* to lead the Peloponnesians to trap our troops at Plataea. Only the threat of our army's destruction will create the opportunity we need."

"I know." Pisander paused, tapping the wall. "But the negotiations with Sparta could prove more difficult than we thought. Archidamus wants us to relinquish much of our empire. He wants our allies to be our equals, not our puppets."

"We can tell him we will do that," said Antiphon.

"What?" exclaimed Pisander. "You can't mean that. With no empire we've no money, no fleet, no power. What's the point of taking power in Athens only to let it go?"

"I did not say we *would* lay the empire down, just that we should *say* we would."

"But any treaty will be sworn before the gods," said Pisander.

Antiphon grinned and patted his partner on the shoulder, turning him to face Athens. "Do you not recall your Homer? The scheming of the gods against each other?" He pointed towards the Parthenon, built using protection money appropriated from their 'allies'. "The gods understand political promises."

Pisander was uneasy. The gods may be corrupt and amoral,

but that did not mean they looked kindly on mortals who emulated them. "Even if we did that, won't we just be back where we started at the beginning of the damn war? Sparta would still distrust us if our empire remained intact."

Antiphon gazed at a flock of geese heading out to sea. "Perikles was a traitor to his class, appealing to the masses at our expense and releasing a beast upon the world that swallows everything in its path. We will return Athens to the moderate rule of the noblemen who guarded its interests in the past. Sparta understands such rule, she trusts it."

"I guess you're right." The traffic between the Long Walls was almost non-existent, just two men riding to Athens, and a mule pulling an empty cart to Piraeus. Ragged children played on the empty road while their parents snoozed in the heat. Pisander continued. "Aristokrates has mercenaries quartered on Aegina awaiting our call. But they're expensive."

"We will have money enough when we secure the Treasury. Power without wealth is an illusion, my friend."

"The two do seem to be lovers," smiled Pisander. "We may still need to lubricate the loyalty of some of the citizens."

"Perhaps," said Antiphon, "although ambitious men are often prepared to act on credit. Anyway, control of Piraeus will enable us to squeeze some extra juice from the fat merchants."

"And allow us to control the grain supply," noted Pisander.

"The dirty ones would rather lose their freedom than their fat bellies."

Pisander watched the guards take shelter beneath their shields from the blistering sun. "Do you think we'll need bodyguards?"

"My dear Pisander. Everyone knows that bodyguards are the foreplay to tyranny, and Athens will never accept another tyrant. We must banish such suspicion from their minds. Once the nobles have control we shall run the city so well that the mob will not dream of a return to their failed experiment."

"At the first hint of a threat to the democracy, or a move towards peace negotiations, Kleon will raise all Hades to his aid, of course."

"Of course, which is why we must dispose of him the moment we are ready to move."

"What about his damn bloodhounds, Hyperbolus and Theorus?" asked Pisander.

"When you tear out a weed you must take care to grab its seeds as well."

"Which leaves Nikias."

"Which leaves... Nikias," agreed Antiphon. "Always we come back to Nikias."

"I still can't see him accepting an oligarchy," said Pisander.

"No," said Antiphon. "But he may be useful, nevertheless. Many trust him, and he would provide an appearance of continuity during the transition. If he felt endangered by the Assembly, he would become amenable to us. If he led the expedition to Plataea, for instance, he would be the general forced to surrender and lose the war."

The Hawk grinned. "People love having someone to blame."

"Exactly. We can promise to protect him. At the same time, we will restore his reputation by using his avowed opposition to Plataea's relief."

"Why wouldn't he do that himself and remain loyal to the democracy?" said Pisander.

"I know him. His failure will destroy his confidence. He will believe the gods have abandoned him. We will be his security, and he will be our bridge to the mob."

Pisander was not entirely convinced. "What if he won't do it?"

Antiphon smiled. "He will have no choice."

Chapter 39

Excitement pervaded Alkibiades' house. The slaves glanced up at the closed door, listening for clues before continuing their chores. Deinomache appeared, shooting instructions as she bustled around the courtyard, before scurrying back to the room.

Hipparete only vaguely noticed the tidal appearances of her mother-in-law, being more conscious that a new wave of pain would be crashing soon. She was perched on the edge of the bed, naked and drenched in sweat. The midwife knelt before her, a sturdy, kind-faced woman with a voice like flowers. She finished her latest examination and rose with a smile, winking encouragement at her patient. Maria sat beside her mistress and childhood friend, holding her hand, mopping her brow, and feeling the thunders of pain echo within her own body.

The midwife checked her preparations once more by the glow of oil lamps: bowls of water; a pile of linen; and a terracotta bath for the mother and child's ritual cleansing. Beside a water-filled goatskin in the corner, a slave girl nodded her head to accompany her quiet counting so that she could tinkle her bell every few minutes to ward off evil. Whenever Hipparete's face contorted, the arithmetic stopped and the bell provided a chorus to the cries of pain.

"I want Alkibiades," Hipparete whimpered after the latest attack.

Maria stroked her hand. "He still with cavalry, remember?" Hipparete's hollow eyes met Maria's for a moment, causing the slave girl a pang of panic. Her mistress looked exhausted, almost ghostly. The slave girl whispered a prayer to Artemis.

Hipparete stared at the gold serpent necklace on the bedside table, which Alkibiades had bought to hang around their baby's neck for protection. The necklace reminded her that her ordeal was on behalf of the life fighting to burst from her belly, strengthening her resolve.

The midwife offered encouragements, clucking around the room. Deinomache exchanged a whispered conversation with her before announcing to Hipparete, "Not long now, dear. It will be over soon."

Hipparete nodded, longing to lie back and sleep, free from pain. The bell trembled again to another piercing scream of side-splitting pain that engulfed her.

The midwife made a further inspection and declared, "It's time. Stand up, my dear. Bring the goatskin." In response to her command, the bell slave brought the bloated goatskin, and Deinomache and Maria helped Hipparete stand astride the water-filled sack. The midwife remained kneeling before Hipparete, who hung on the shoulders of her two supporters. "Now's the time to push, my dear. A few big pushes and we'll be done. You ready?" The midwife smiled warmly at the young girl, who bit her lip and nodded. "Okay. Push!"

Hipparete melted in pain, and her fingers clawed the shoulders of Deinomache and Maria as the bell sang and the midwife continued her reassurances. True to her word, after several heroic efforts she cried, "That's it!" and the tiny creature lay in her hands, Deinomache and Maria ululating their ritual cries of joy as the midwife lowered the child onto the goatskin, which she punctured with a knife. The water ebbed away, lowering the baby and gently pulling the afterbirth from its mother.

Hipparete collapsed on to the bed, her body an open wound, her spirit spent but flooded with relief. From a distant world she heard two wet slaps followed by a splutter and an ear-perforating scream. "Let me see! Let me see!" The midwife held up a slimy, wriggling mass of blood that looked more lizard than human. It was the most beautiful thing Hipparete had ever seen. She clasped her hands to her mouth and tears made their happy journey down her cheeks. It was a boy.

The midwife removed him from his mother's sight and Hipparete sank back in ecstasy, holding Maria's hand, whose own happiness matched her mistress's. "It's a boy, Maria. A beautiful boy." Hipparete was filled with a joy that swamped pain, and she revelled in the prospect of showing her husband their wonderful son. She noticed the serpent necklace and struggled to raise herself. "I need to put the necklace around his neck." The bell sang, but Hipparete could not see her child. Deinomache and the midwife were bent over him on the floor, bloody linens cast aside into the puddles of water, little Kleinias boldly announcing his arrival in the world. "What lungs he has," grinned Hipparete, the boy's screams the greatest music.

The midwife turned around and held Hipparete's gaze for an instant before averting her eyes. She was no longer smiling. "What is it?" asked Hipparete.

Deinomache raised herself wearily and turned to Hipparete.

"What is it?" demanded Hipparete, her joy deflating like the goatskin.

"It's…the child," said Deinomache, her voice trembling.

"What?" cried Hipparete, straining to sit upright and inching towards the edge of the bed.

Deinomache took a deep breath, held her head high, and in a voice breathing ice declared, "The child is deformed."

The words haunted the room, but Hipparete was unable to grasp them. The disconcerted slave rang the bell. "What?"

"Your child. It is deformed," said Deinomache. "Its right arm is withered, hardly there. We cannot keep it." She turned away and began to wrap the baby in a white cloth.

Hipparete shook her head. "No. No, it can't be. I saw it."

"I'm afraid it's true," said the midwife gently.

Hipparete struggled to her feet, wincing with the effort. "I want to hold my baby. Give me my baby." She staggered towards her son, but the midwife blocked her path.

"It's best you don't hold him, my dear."

Hipparete glared at her, reaching for her shoulder for support. "No…No." The midwife eased Hipparete to her and held her close. The young girl felt like a rag doll, limp and lifeless, but she suddenly exploded, wrestling to free herself of the midwife's grip. "Give me my baby!" she screamed. "Give me my baby!"

Deinomache held the white cloth bundle, whose own shouts echoed its mother's. "Maria," commanded Deinomache, "take this and leave it outside the city walls."

Maria stood rooted, her eyes wide, staring at Deinomache.

"Maria!" shouted Deinomache. "You will take this, this, this *thing*, outside the city walls or you will find yourself a prostitute before the week is out."

A ferocious scream of "No!" blasted from Hipparete's wasted body.

Maria looked at her squirming, struggling mistress, and tears swam into her eyes. Deinomache repeated her threat, and Maria's feet found their way to the child. Deinomache's eyes drilled into Maria as she handed over the wriggling bundle. The slave girl peered down at the perfect, red face and energetic mouth, and then at the contorted, desperate features of his mother. Hipparete's tear-streaked face met Maria's stare, her wild eyes branding her maid's heart.

"Go!" commanded Deinomache, and shoved her towards the door. Hipparete's fierce screams chased them outside, where Deinomache gave hurried instructions for her two most burly slaves to join them on the balcony. The bell-wielding slave and midwife escaped the room, and the two strongmen leant against the slammed door, which vibrated to Hipparete's feverish banging and the smashing of pots and vases.

"Shouldn't we wait for the father to decide to expose the child?" asked the midwife over the baby's cries and the mother's hysterical shouts.

"He is away on campaign." said Deinomache. "And anyway, he will hardly want a monster for a son. Such a *thing* is clearly hated by the gods, so why would my son want it?"

The midwife nodded and said to Maria, "Place him in the shrine to Heavenly Aphrodite. Perhaps someone will claim him." Their exchanged look acknowledged its unlikelihood.

Maria's tears only encouraged Deinomache's threats, and gradually the slave girl shuffled away from Hipparete's screeching, carrying the bawling baby down the stairs and out of the house.

Hipparete's bellowing, scratching, smashing, hammering became more frenzied as the cries of her son faded. Deinomache banged on the door and shouted, "This is no way for an Athenian noblewoman to behave." Her admonishment had no effect and she turned to the midwife. "You can go now. There is no need, of course, to mention any of this. The child died at birth. I will see you get extra for the service you have given us."

"Thank you. Don't forget to have the house cleansed and propitiate the gods." The midwife escaped, closing her ears to the finger nails tearing at the door, and Hipparete's inhuman screams.

When she had left, Deinomache thumped on the door and hissed, "Shut up, you little taste of Hades. What kind of a woman are you to soil our family with a creature like that?" The courtyard filled with Hipparete's agony as Deinomache cursed the gods. Bear arms like no other, indeed. Very funny.

Inside, hidden from the sunshine, Hipparete gripped to her chest the necklace that was supposed to protect her son, and the bell tinkled no more.

Chapter 40

It was a dazzling afternoon, and Aristeia paced back and forth between the altar and the shade of the balcony, afraid of Timokles' return, afraid that he would not return. The Peloponnesian army was returning home, and the refugee families streamed out of Athens alongside their ox-driven carts. Timokles was due home, and the possibility that he knew she had cursed Samias tortured Aristeia.

Nikopatra sat in the shade sewing flowery patterns on to a blanket. Beside her mother, Leaina sat, tapped her feet, stood, paced, and sat again.

"Will you two calm down?" chided Nikopatra. "He'll be here when he's here."

"But why's he taking so long?" said Aristeia as she began her march back from the other side of the courtyard.

"Careful you don't get too much sun, dear," said Nikopatra. "You don't want to lose that pale complexion of yours."

"But why *is* he taking so long?" pressed Leaina, standing yet again. "Perhaps something has happened," she added, mashing her hands.

"Nonsense. We'd have heard."

"But Mother, it's been three days since we've had definite news of him. What if they had to fight again?" Leaina's question brought Aristeia to a halt.

Nikopatra shook her head. "No. He couldn't survive right to the end and then get hurt. No. My son will be here soon, you can count on it." Her apparent confidence did little to comfort Timokles' wife and sister, and they resumed their tortured vigil.

Aristeia's mind was a whirlpool. What if the gods had revealed to Timokles that she was to blame for Samias' death, that she had spoken the curse that had ended his life? Perhaps that was why he had not come home, because she was there. Aristeia glanced at Leaina and wondered again whether she could admit such a dreadful deed to her friend.

"I wonder whether he's over that young man yet," said Nikopatra, glancing at Aristeia, who stopped in her tracks. "Samias, was it?"

"Hmmm," said Leaina, "I suspect he hasn't had a chance to grieve properly yet." She looked up at Aristeia's taut features, and added, "But I'm sure he's longing to come home."

"Such a shame," continued Nikopatra. "So young. Samias' family must be devastated, losing their only son. The gods of the Underworld are unpredictable." Aristeia turned aside to hide a rogue tear, and Nikopatra put her sewing down and turned to Leaina. "You haven't told us about your visit to Hipparete this morning. How is the poor girl?"

Leaina's face sagged. "She looks like an army has marched over her. So gaunt and pale. She just lies on her bed staring into space."

"Did you share your own experience of losing children?" asked Aristeia, brushing aside her tears and joining them in the shade.

"No. No-one else's pain can comfort someone for the loss of a child. I just held her and stroked her hair."

"She didn't talk at all?" asked Nikopatra.

"Barely a word. I did speak with her maid, Maria. She seemed almost as distraught as Hipparete."

"What did she have to say?" pressed Nikopatra.

Leaina hesitated, pursing her lips. "She was... very upset. She said the baby didn't die at birth, that it had a deformed arm and she had been forced to leave it at the Temple of Aphrodite."

"Oh, poor Hipparete!" exclaimed Aristeia. "How terrible for her."

"A deformed arm," muttered Nikopatra, suppressing a smile as she recalled the prophecy. "And how is Deinomache now that she has no grandson?"

"Maria says she rants at everyone and has not visited anyone or gone to a temple since."

"I wonder how Alkibiades took the news," said Aristeia. They fell into silence and resumed the routine of their vigil. "Perhaps we shouldn't have sent Orontas to meet Timokles," she said finally. "With his limp it'll be hard for him, and slow them down."

Leaina smiled. "You couldn't have stopped Orontas going to meet him if you had lashed him to the altar." A moment later, a door in the outer courtyard opened and they froze. Footsteps moved quickly to the connecting door and Timokles burst through, followed by Orontas, whose Persian face was alight. Leaina launched herself at her brother and enveloped him with happy cries, raising a fleeting smile to his face.

"Welcome home, Son," said Nikopatra.

"Thank you, Mother," said Timokles as Leaina released her grip. Aristeia thought his face strained, as if he wore a heavy mask. She shuffled towards him. "It's nice to see you, Aristeia," he said mechanically.

Aristeia dissolved into tears and inched towards him, finally laying her head on his chest as she wailed, "Oh, Timokles. I'm sorry. I'm so sorry about Samias. I'm sorry. I'm sorry."

"Thank you," choked Timokles, holding her to him, Aristeia continuing to whimper her apologies. "It wasn't your fault," he added, trying to chuckle, but the dam broke and his tears rolled down his cheeks. Aristeia gripped him tighter.

"You won't have to go out and fight again, will you, at Plataea?" asked Leaina, her voice quivering.

Timokles, wrapped around Aristeia, shook his head, wiped away his tears and cleared his throat. "No. There's no chance of fighting at Plataea so long as the siege of Mytilene continues, and Paches is still general."

Leaina and Aristeia smiled at each other in relief: no more tortuous waiting, no longer living a shadow of existence.

A roar from the heart of the city intruded on their reunion, and they glanced anxiously at each other, aware that something of great import must have happened. They dispatched a slave to investigate, and their conversation was muted as they awaited his return, their eyes constantly drifting towards the door.

Finally the slave rushed upon them, declaring, "It's Mytilene! It's Mytilene! The siege is over, they've surrendered!"

Chapter 41

In the dark sanctuary of her room, Hipparete buried herself in the arms of her husband, sobs racking her fragile body. Alkibiades stroked her hair, muttering endearments, gently raising her tear-streaked face to his, gazing into her brown eyes and whispering, "I promise you, Hipparete, there will be others."

Hipparete was imprisoned in her fortress of grief, and as she wiped the tears from her cheeks, she stared again at her son's redundant serpent necklace. "It's my fault. I upset the gods."

Alkibiades held her closer to him. "It is no one's fault, especially not yours. Do you hear me?" He raised her head gently so that she looked into his eyes. "It is not your fault, Hipparete. Such things happen and there is no reason. Can you accept that?" She nodded, but he knew that he had failed again.

He kissed her forehead and slipped out of the room, leaving Hipparete with her shadows. He stepped down the stairs, brooding on his wife's continued distress. The pots of flowers blooming in the courtyard only reminded him of the olive crown missing from the door, which would have announced the birth of a son. Even Dionysus' merry features seemed to mock their disappointment.

"Still the same?" asked Deinomache. Alkibiades nodded, and his mother grimaced. "If she wants to behave like an invalid, we should treat her as one. I will get Doctor Eryximachus to visit and prescribe some hellebore to treat this madness."

"No," said Alkibiades. "Hellebore is too dangerous. I will get some silphium."

Deinomache smiled. "Let us see what the doctor says, shall we? We can try the silphium as well."

Alkibiades nodded and the two of them lingered at the foot of the stairs, listening to the bustle of the slaves beginning the day. "Anyway," continued Alkibiades, "she is not mad, she has lost a child."

"We all lose children, but we do not lock ourselves away from our responsibilities."

"She is young. She has had few of life's bruises." He paused, glancing at his mother before adding, "She feels guilty."

"So she should."

"It helps no one if you continually remind her of it."

"She has a duty to provide a healthy son for us, and she failed. She does not still refer to it as Kleinias, does she? Oh, really," she exclaimed on Alkibiades' confirmation. "We must put a stop to that. It was never introduced to the hearth, how can it have a name?"

Andromachus sidled alongside his master and handed him a cup of onion soup and some bread. Alkibiades ate where he stood, watched thoughtfully by his mother. "You are off to the Assembly?" she asked. "Do you think today's outcome will be any different from yesterday's?" Alkibiades shrugged, seemingly more interested in his soup. "Who would have thought that Athens would condemn an entire Greek city to destruction?"

"Only the male citizens of Mitylene are to die," corrected Alkibiades through a mouthful of bread. "The women and children will be enslaved."

"Unless they overturn the motion today."

"Unless they overturn it," confirmed Alkibiades, noting his mother's frown. "You must understand, Mother, how much anger there is out there. Many feared for Athens' very existence, what with the rebellion, the invasion, and the Peloponnesian fleet cruising Ionian waters. They want to make an example of Mytilene."

"No doubt your new friend, Kleon, stoked the feeling."

"He made use of it for the benefit of Athens, like a good politician should. Even Pisander supports executing all the men of Mytilene and not just those oligarchs who plotted the revolt. Though I am not sure why."

"A lot has happened recently, you are not thinking clearly," said Deinomache. "If Pisander's oligarchic friends in Mytilene are to die, then why not their democratic enemies too?"

Alkibiades paused in the consumption of his breakfast. "Hmm, perhaps. Anyway, unless Nikias and his friends change their tune the motion will stand."

"How do you mean?"

"They spent yesterday's debate talking about 'justice' and 'mercy'. A waste of time in the face of fear and anger. They must frame the argument in the people's self-interest. Mercy is a luxury only the secure can afford."

"Shame about the Spartan, though," prompted Deinomache.

"Salaethus? Yes." Alkibiades recalled the handsome Spartan commander who had marshalled the revolt in Mytilene. In exchange for his freedom, the Spartans had promised to have the Peloponnesian forces withdraw from Plataea. It had been an opportunity to attain Alkibiades' first objective without striking a blow. An opportunity the Assembly ignored.

"Why did Kleon not save him?" asked Deinomache.

"It was impossible. There was such hatred towards Salaethus for stirring the revolt that anyone speaking against his execution would have most likely joined him in the pit."

Deinomache nodded as Alkibiades continued eating. "Do you really think you can unseat General Paches? He will be returning as an all-conquering hero."

"I believe so. There is talk of heavy-handedness and bribery after the surrender. Excellent fodder to feed the suspicion of tyranny. And knowing him, I predict he will return full of self-importance and throw parties to extol his virtues and boast of his success. As Kleon is fond of saying, democracy is like a whore: never get carried away by the ride or you will lose everything that is of value to you."

"Very funny," chuckled Deinomache. "I still think a prophecy in our favour would give the sheep on the Council some balls. Have you spoken to Hierokles the oracle monger yet?"

"I am preparing a draft for him."

"Good." She hesitated, a twinkle in her eyes. "I have an idea of how to bring our opponents along at little risk." Alkibiades looked up sharply, and his mother continued. "No doubt Nikias will continue his opposition to the rescue of Plataea. So be it. Let us accept his fear of encountering the Theban army, and argue for an overwhelming force to be sent with Nikias in command of it."

"*Nikias* in command?"

"Yes," said Deinomache. "It will make his followers happier, and if he succeeds he will get little credit, as with such a force how could he fail?"

"And if by some mischance he does fail," continued Alkibiades, "he will get all the blame. I like it, Mother."

Above the chopping of vegetables, the sweeping of floors, and the beating of blankets, impatient voices rumbled into the outer courtyard. Andromachus returned to Alkibiades to lead him away from Deinomache. The master of the house strode through the connecting door to be greeted, before he had even escaped the gloom beneath the balcony, by the gruff voice of Hipponikus.

"What do you think you are doing?" demanded the general, his aggressive stance reflected in the shallow pool beside him. Ariphron and Megakles bore equally serious faces.

"Having breakfast," said Alkibiades.

"How can you support that rat-infested-goat-faced-fart-breathing-sack-of-leather?" said Hipponikus, the veins on his forehead ready to burst. "He is pushing us to wage a war of terror on our allies, to frighten them into submission. That was not Perikles' way and you know it."

"In a time of war," said Alkibiades, "simply displaying the benefits of our protection is not enough. Otherwise Mytilene would not have revolted. Potential rebels are more impressed by might than by mercy."

"You sound like Kleon," snapped Hipponikus. "Have you forgotten how to think for yourself?"

Alkibiades hid a deep breath behind a gracious smile. "I believe Kleon is right."

"What?" shouted Hipponikus.

"Perikles' policy was fine when we were not involved in a war to the death, but now the whole of Hellas is split in two, either for us or for Sparta. There will be straw friends tempted by the example of Mytilene unless we use it as a deterrent."

"But Alkibiades," said Ariphron, his voice a soothing ointment, "such an attitude leaves no room for manoeuvre, for negotiation that could be to our benefit."

"And whom will it deter?" asked Megakles theatrically, looking up to the balconies as if they were filled with his admirers. "If death was a deterrent there would be no murders. It is a scheme's danger that deters, not punishment for its failure."

"And our ruthlessness in dealing with Mytilene," said Alkibiades, "will make that danger apparent."

"Dealing firmly with enemies is fine," said Hipponikus, "but identify those enemies first. Murdering innocent men along with the rebels is sacrilege."

"They all had opportunities to betray the rebels," said Alkibiades. "It will encourage others not to be so passive in accepting a revolt led by a clique of their own city."

"I fear this is a grave mistake, Alkibiades," said Ariphron. "I pray Athena will sway the Assembly to vote in the interests of Athens."

"I am sure we all do," said Alkibiades.

***

Passions were running high in Athens. It was almost unheard of for an Assembly to re-examine a decision made the previous day, and it had divided the city. Families argued over breakfast, and friends nearly came to blows on the way to the Pnyx, where a scarlet flag hung limply at the crest of the grassy rise that formed the auditorium. Men scrambled over each other to find a space to sit, neighbours shared wineskins as the hillside filled, and the expectant throb echoed off the rocky outcrops. At the foot of the Assembly a wooden platform awaited the councillors officiating at the day's meeting, the ridge falling away sharply beyond it so that those not absorbed in debate could see the agora, the acropolis, and the houses of Athens, to remind them of why they were there.

The officials were last to enter: after all, it is not every day you can make ten thousand people wait for you. A piglet was sacrificed and its blood spattered over the platform and the councillors. The flag was struck and the herald prayed to bless the proceedings, cursing anyone who would undermine Athens, promote tyranny, or plot with the Persians.

The formalities over, ambassadors from Mytilene pleaded for their families' lives, and then the debate began. This was no polite argument over which architects should design the ship sheds, or what doctor they should appoint to minister to the poor. This was a verbal brawl. A fight, as many saw it, for the soul of Athens. Speakers donned the garland and begged, threatened, implored, bullied. They asked for mercy and for revenge, for leniency and for punishment, all appealing to the gods and demanding justice. The crowd hooted, jeered, cheered and clapped, flooding the arena with a deafening chorus. Men stood and argued with neighbours, fights erupted, and the trousered Scythians beat the transgressors into order. Meanwhile, time passed and the ambassadors from Mytilene looked to the sea, knowing that a trireme dispatched with the previous day's execution orders was well on its way.

General Nikias tried to smooth the waters, urging Athens to remain true to the policies of Perikles, but Kleon spoke next. For him there was no attempt at dignity, no reason to soothe passions. He worked his bellows to inflame his audience, thundered around the platform spitting obscenities, cajoled them not to be tricked by clever men who would guilt them into error. His blustering argument, based not on revenge, nor on justice, but on self-interest, won the day, as he knew it would, but not in the manner he had assumed. A young follower of Nikias, by the name of Diodotus, seized the argument for himself, allowing the mask of self-interest to become bedfellow to the guilt felt by many Athenians. The vote was close, so close that hands had to be raised several times, but the previous day's motion was overturned. The people of Mytilene were to be spared.

Another ship was sent, paid for by the ambassadors with promises of great rewards if they reached the city in time to prevent the massacre. They were twenty four hours behind the first trireme, but their silver-powered oars arrived as the sentence was being read. The people of Mytilene were saved.

Most of them. The one thousand prisoners sent to Athens by General Paches were deemed to be oligarchs and most responsible for the revolt. The vote to execute them was nearly unanimous. One tenth of the citizens of Mytilene thus met their fate.

Nikias and his friends celebrated, believing they had defeated Kleon, but Kleon was content. All of the oligarchs in Mytilene had been exterminated, leaving it safely in the hands of loyal democrats. On his motion, farmland surrounding Mytilene was allocated to provide income for Athenian farmers whose own lands had been devastated by war, and so Kleon gained a loyal new following. It was merely a question of where to use it.

He knew, of course: General Paches.

Chapter 42

At fifty, Zeus the Liberator was a few years older than Sémon, if a god can be said to age. The intensity of his stare, his powerful ivory arms, the incandescent thunderbolt, the obstinate stance, all promised the protection of the god who had delivered Plataea and Hellas from the Persians.

And yet.

And yet the gods were prone to tantrums, easily distracted, jealous. Who was to say that Zeus still favoured Plataea? They could offer him no juicy thighbones, not even a libation of wine; he had to suffer their own misfortunes, to settle for water and barley grains. Was Zeus as hungry as they were? What if the Thebans gave more pleasing sacrifices? Whose prayers would then tickle the ears of God?

Sémon felt an elbow in his side. Beside him, Mikos raised his eyebrows. "Oh, nothing," said Sémon, turning away from the statue. "Just wondering whose side he's on." Mikos grinned and pointed back at the statue. "Yes, you're probably right," continued Sémon. "His own."

"But what does that mean?" As usual, young Hybrias' shroud of hair hid his frown as he adjusted his shield on his back. "Will he protect us or not?"

Mikos ran towards the north barricade of the agora and punched his spear into the thick gate. He smiled and turned to Hybrias with his arms wide. Hybrias did not understand.

"I think what he means," said Sémon, as Mikos extracted his spear and they passed through the gate, "is that we must trust to our own strength."

"The strength that leaks away with every stingy meal," grumbled Skopas.

"That will be enough, though, won't it?" said Hybrias.

Sémon shook his head, his tired eyes twinkling. "Hybrias, my friend, take advantage of the opportunities we have here. It would distract you."

"Opportunities? On guard duty for eight hours, standby for eight hours, and reserve for eight hours. What opportunities?"

"You're a young man, surely you have things on your mind other than sleep when we're in reserve?"

"I prefer to sleep. The Furies don't torment us when we're asleep."

Sémon and Mikos exchanged glances. The night of the escape was a topic with which they only ever flirted, a bad dream that for Sémon forcibly evaporated with the rising of the sun. He understood that for Hybrias, who had witnessed the slaughter first hand, it must be much worse.

They reached the North Gate, where a huddle of soldiers played dice in edgy boredom. Sémon led the way up the stone steps to the top of the town wall, where guards on every watchtower had their eyes nailed on the enemy wall.

"They won't attack today, will they?" asked Hybrias.

Sémon looked at Mikos and raised an eyebrow; Mikos nodded. "I think so, too," said Sémon. Every day for a week, small forces of Thebans had attacked points along the town wall, a different area each day, keeping the garrison on edge, depriving them of easy sleep. "At least it gives us good exercise," continued Sémon. "Keeps us on our toes."

Mikos punched Sémon in his side and pretended to lie back, his arms fondling the air.

Sémon roared. "By Aphrodite you're right. I prefer to be on my back, and then with more than my toes up."

Hybrias was unmoved by the hilarity. "The general says they're just probing."

"Or they're as bored as we are," grunted Skopas.

"But what happens when they attack with their full force?" said Hybrias.

Sémon stopped and looked across at the enemy guards patrolling their own walls. "Remember when their whole army filled the plains? The tents, the cooking fires, the men swarming like ants. Remember? We were as flustered as virgins in a brothel. But even then they couldn't beat us."

"There were more of us then, and it was a close thing," said Hybrias. "We can't cover the wall properly anymore. What happens when they work that out?"

"Maybe they won't. And if they do, then by Zeus we'll give them some bruises."

"And sit out the rest of the war as prisoners?"

"Sure. When we..." Sémon stopped, and they all turned back towards the town, looking in the direction of the East Gate: war cries drowned the dusk birdsong. They raced down the steps to their unit's gathering point at the North Gate. General Arkadius was soon with them, satisfying himself that they were ready before climbing to the top of the wall to assess the situation. Sémon and his company remained below, listening to the fever of battle drifting on the air, wondering if it was about to burst full force upon them.

Sémon smiled grimly at Mikos. So far the attacks had been probes, but perhaps this one was different. Perhaps this was a full assault. Sémon banished the thought that this could be the last sun that would set on Plataea.

The Plataean farmers, disguised in their soldier's garb, strained their ears for hints of what was to come. The clash of swords and shields stalked their spirits. They stared at the ground, afraid that their own fear was etched on their friends' faces, or ashamed that it was not. Sometimes it was easier to fight than to wait.

Hybrias was sweating, his hands trembling. After a few minutes the disturbance stilled, to be replaced by cheers. Arkadius came to the edge of the wall and shouted down, "Must have been another probe. There's no sign of activity here. Return to standby."

The men dispersed again in the general area of the North Gate, playing dice, sleeping, talking, walking.

Hybrias pushed his helmet back to his forehead and wiped his brow. "Will this never end?"

"All things end," said Sémon, "but it's not always wise to wish for it."

Chapter 43

Khara strode alongside Stephanos and Alkibiades, excitement and anxiety at war within. General Paches, the victor of Mytilene, was to be tried for gross mismanagement of the Mytilene campaign. If he were to be found guilty, he would be stripped of his generalship, and the road would be cleared for the relief of Plataea. Stephanos would have to go back to war, but Theo Sémon would be rescued.

Alkibiades' prediction had been correct: on his return to Athens, Paches had made his valedictory tour of drinking parties, regaled all with his heroic tales, and condescended to report his unsurpassed exploits to the Assembly. Now he was to pay for his arrogance.

They entered the agora and passed the men and women organizing their stalls amongst the trees. Khara gazed in wonder at the rivers of old men heading up the slope towards the Heliaia, the People's Court. Service in the courts was voluntary, and jurors were paid a small stipend, which meant that those no longer able to work could continue to eat. "Do you really think that these old men will find Paches guilty?" asked Khara.

"I told you," replied Alkibiades, "he is a proud and haughty man. He would not think it amiss to find a crown on his head. Old men can sniff out such attitudes."

"I hear there are others like Paches," said Khara, raising her eyebrows.

Alkibiades laughed. "I swear Stephanos, your wife's words could slice a goat's balls sometimes."

Khara flushed. "Isn't using Kleon as prosecutor a mistake? His antics may upset the old men."

"Not after Kleon just raised their pay by half in the Assembly," smiled Alkibiades. "And besides, Kleon's supporters will pack the audience. It is, after all, a chance to attack Paches' patron, Nikias."

"It's said that Paches has written his own speech," said Stephanos, taking Khara by the hand.

"Of course," said Alkibiades. "It is beneath him to use a speechwriter. He does not even plan to have his wife and children present to excite the jury's pity."

"Sounds confident," said Khara.

"Yes," grinned Alkibiades. "Fatal in a law court. As Simonides once said: 'appearance overpowers reality'. Paint the right picture, and the facts are irrelevant."

"You don't think he's guilty?" said Khara.

"He is guilty of pomposity and self-importance, while lacking the charm to soften them. In Athens, that is guilt enough."

The court stood beside the beautiful South Stoa, but the comparison was not flattering. A functional brick building with orange roof tiles, and surrounded by a wooden fence, the structure was built for the messy affairs of men. Khara felt jostled by the old men as they entered the precinct through a wicker gate. How much did she really want Plataea to be rescued if it meant Stephanos was to be hurled into danger again? And yet she yearned for Theo Sémon's laughter, which she knew would restore the smile to Stephanos' face.

Alkibiades led them to the rear entrance of the building and they surged into the courtroom amidst an excited mob ready to bay for blood. The jurors sat on the long benches that rose from the stone floor like the steps of a temple, five hundred and one men, assigned at random from the thousands on duty, prepared to cast their vote. A wooden barricade separated the standing spectators from the theatre to come, and Alkibiades eased his neighbours to the front, where his family had already gathered.

"I told you we would get him," said Alkibiades to Hipponikus beside him.

"Bringing General Paches to court on a misconduct charge that no-one will believe is not the same as removing him from the board of generals," growled Hipponikus.

"You do not believe so?" said Alkibiades. "Interesting."

Hipponikus reddened and rocked on his heels, but refrained from arguing the point. "I am uncomfortable with the power your manoeuvrings are shovelling Kleon's way. We cannot afford a ship with no anchor to lead the fleet."

"You worry too much, General," said Alkibiades. "Kleon has the ear of the people and that makes him useful, but he is a mouthpiece, nothing more. He has neither the skill nor the inclination to lead men in battle, and in the end that is where real power lies."

"You would think so," rumbled Hipponikus, "yet here we stand, with his Mouthship about to try to disgrace an honourable man who has led a successful campaign."

The lamp-lit court filled around them, and an archon took his seat facing the jury. A clerk sat beside him with a wax writing tablet and a stylus, a chest on the floor holding the documents submitted as evidence, the timekeeper poised before his water clock.

Paches strode into the court beside Nikias, and the room erupted into jeers and obscenities. Paches' expertly coiffed beard framed a square jaw, and his black eyes threatened Hades, the dark waves of his hair breaking suddenly over his ears as if a tempest had raised them. He glanced in disdain at the spectators before looking away. Khara thought he looked impatient, as if this were a waste of his precious time.

A herald banged his staff, and the stone echoed around the chamber. After an offering of incense and prayers to Apollo of Light and Athena the Wise, the clerk read the charges and the archon invited the accuser to begin. Kleon stepped forward from the gang of litigants at the side of the room, his penetrating eyes and warm smile greeting every juror as he turned to face them, pausing to allow the silence to hang in the air like a swing about to begin its downward rush.

"What a shame it is," he began, the stopper being removed from the water clock, "that we have to try the man who led the Mytilene campaign. You might be tempted to forgive his faults and not even listen to the list of his crimes, but I remind you that you swore an oath to listen impartially to the prosecution. No-one should be immune from your justice. Not I, an ordinary citizen like yourselves, nor Paches, a rich general surrounded by his wealthy, important friends."

"Nice," whispered Alkibiades.

Kleon's deep voice owned the room. "No doubt," he continued, "they'll try to distinguish themselves from us. They'll use words like 'honour' and 'decency'. But do you know what their honour really is? It's code for them protecting their own backs as they steal the riches of the empire that belong to you." Rumbling recognition swelled the chamber. "It's an excuse to treat us like dirt, to justify their extravagant behaviour. It's another word for them believing they're better than us." A chorus of agreement from the crowd found echoes in the jury. "They believe their farts are the breath of gods." The room filled with laughter and chatter, forcing the herald to restore order again.

"That's what honour is to them," continued Kleon. "Yet all the time they steal the money needed to pay you for your service here. It's time we stopped their thievery." The audience gave boisterous approval. Kleon drew a portrait of theft, bribery and corruption, with a sprinkling of tyrannical aspirations, sparking outbursts of rage from the crowd. He called witnesses who had been carefully prepared by Antiphon. The clerk read out forged documents, the shocked spectators underlining their truth. It was a performance to admire.

The case was convincing to Khara, and she glanced at the defendant. General Paches seemed ready to explode with anger at every syllable that Kleon conjured, but Khara thought that beside him Nikias was frightened by the reactions of the audience. She noted Alkibiades' smile, Hipponikus' frown. Stephanos appeared elated, as if the freedom of Plataea were assured. Khara's chest fluttered.

Kleon rose to his climax, pacing before the dense rows of jurors. "As a general, Paches wasn't fighting for us but for himself, for his own glorification. He wears his victory like a crown and receives our praise like incense offered to the gods. Like Harmodius and Aristogeiton, we mustn't stand aside and allow the abuse of power to threaten our freedom. You've heard witnesses to his crimes. It's now for you to decide whether his actions were those of someone who believes he's one of us. Whether his behaviour threatens the well-being of Athens. Whether deeds such as his put your pay in jeopardy. The answer is clear to the gods; I pray it is clear to you."

Kleon's supporters erupted into cries of, "Guilty!", "Traitor!"

and "Exile him!" The herald struck the ground with his staff repeatedly, but to no avail as the crowd made their fury clear to the jury. Finally, at a discreet signal from Kleon, the audience settled and the archon invited Paches to make his defence. He strode to the centre of the room, glaring at the crowd who began to taunt and jeer him.

"Silence!" boomed the herald, bringing enough order for the water clock to be started.

"I do not pretend to be an orator," began Paches, ignoring the continuing jibes, "but I believe in facts, and the facts prove my innocence."

"Liar!" cried a voice from the crowd.

"Yes, liar!"

"Thief!"

"Quiet!" shouted the herald.

"For Kleon to imply that I am on a path to tyranny is typical bluster from a man such as him. It is quite ridiculous, I am sure you will agree," said Paches.

Thunderous exclamations of "Tyrant!" enveloped the room, and the archon was forced to ask the timekeeper to stopper the water clock while the herald tried to regain order.

"Only someone without honour," continued Paches eventually, "can speak of it in the terms he did. I am proud to be a man of honour and to have honourable friends. Some of them will bear witness to my unblemished record in the service of Athens." Hoots of laughter, but Paches pressed on. "Their truthfulness cannot be denied. My family is descended from the gods of Attika, and our loyalty is rooted here. I have been choregus three times, a trierarch twice, and a general. It was my honour to lead our men to victory at Mytilene. Is it in your interests to allow an ambitious man like *him* to pack the audience with his lapdogs and pressure you into disgracing one of your foremost men?"

The heckling continued throughout Paches' speech. Nikias pleaded on behalf of his friend, but it provoked only sympathy for himself, not for the accused. The documents proving Paches' innocence were barely noticed, the jurors chatting amongst themselves as the clerk was forced to read ever louder. By the time Paches came to his conclusion, water had run out.

The archon cut him off mid-sentence and called for the vote. The benches emptied as the five hundred and one judges struggled down to the voting urns to cast their pebbles, the audience shouting their advice. The accused remained standing, facing the benches, his shoulders back, his head aloft.

"What happens now?" said Khara, her heart thumping as if the verdict were hers.

Alkibiades indicated Nikias and Kleon in earnest conversation. "They will strike a deal. Paches will be found guilty, no question."

"He doesn't seem to think so," said Stephanos.

"No," chuckled Alkibiades. "He does seem to be displaying his peacock feathers. But he is in for a surprise. Kleon will bargain away exile for a fine and the loss of Paches' generalship."

"Then the route to Plataea is open," muttered Stephanos, gripping the barricade.

"It is open," agreed Alkibiades. "I told you I would do it," he twinkled at Khara, who smiled warmly.

As the jurors resumed their seats, Khara was unsure whether to be happy or terrified. General Paches remained aloof as the archon ordered the pebbles emptied from the two urns, and a flood of pebbles poured from the bronze urn, a mere trickle from the terracotta. There was no need for counting.

"This court finds General Paches guilty of misconduct in his duties as general," declared the archon amidst cheers and backslapping. Kleon could not restrain his grin as he embraced his witnesses.

Stephanos lifted Khara from her feet and spun her around. She could not help but laugh at her husband's joy.

Paches' head began to droop and his shoulders slump. He shuddered as if an enemy shield had struck him, his face white. He looked around in bewilderment at his fellow citizens. Venomous calls for his exile assaulted him. His hand trembled. He reached into his tunic, pulled out a dagger, and stabbed himself in the heart.

A cry of horror accompanied Paches' sinking to the ground in a pool of blood. The taunts stopped, faces blanched, and a shocked silence imposed itself. Nikias rushed to the side of his bloody friend and grasped his hand. A brief twitch flicked Paches' mouth before the lights went out. "Fair journey, my friend," choked Nikias. Around him, eyes searched for explanations, and whispered prayers accompanied the amazement. Nikias stood, his himation stained with blood, and he turned to face the jury.

"This, my friends," he began, the anger rising in his voice, "this is what slander does to an honourable man. Unable to accept even the appearance of dishonour, he has set out for Hades ahead of his time. We have been robbed of one of our best generals because of the petty jealousies of men who would lead you astray with their lies. I pray this will be a lesson." He stormed towards the door of the silent room, glaring at Kleon the whole way. Kleon met his stare, and smiled.

Chapter 44

In the days following the death of Paches, Demosthenes was appointed general in his place, and the Assembly passed a motion to raise a huge army to be placed under the command of General Nikias. The city buzzed with the expectation that Plataea was the target. The names of those drafted into the tribal regiments were posted before the statues of the eponymous heroes in the agora, and the lists were long. All age groups between twenty and forty five were called to form their largest army since the first year of the war. Excitement spread like a disease among the young men, and confidence was extreme. With such a force, what could they possibly have to fear?

And then there was the timely oracle from Hierokles the seer, which seemed to promise conquest. Even Nikias had been impressed.

Almost every household prepared for the imminent expedition. Armour was taken down and polished, swords sharpened, arrows gathered, shields repaired. Alexias watched his father's preparations like an adoring puppy. Lakon regarded his son with a mixture of jealousy and trepidation.

Khara busied herself to mask her anxiety, but there were times when she was unable to bear it, and she escaped to visit Hipparete. To Khara's relief, Hipparete had finally left her room. Now they met in the sunlit work room, where Hipparete's maid, Maria, spun wool while her eyes twitched constantly to her mistress. Hipparete sat on a stool with her hair draped over a bowl, Khara standing over her.

"I'm glad you're letting me wash your hair," said Khara as she poured water over Hipparete's greasy crown.

"It's been a while," said Hipparete. "It must be horrible."

"You have lovely hair, Hipparete."

"I can't remember what colour hair Kleinias had. That's awful, isn't it? I should've looked more carefully. If I'd known."

Khara poured perfumed oil over Hipparete's head and

exchanged an anxious glance with Maria, whose distress for her mistress was evident.

"He was so beautiful," continued Hipparete. "I wonder what I did."

"Nothing, Hipparete. You did nothing." Khara worked the oil into her hair and glanced at the vase she had laid aside. It reminded her of a cup, a broken one, in this very room. "Alkibiades must be busy. Preparing for the expedition."

"Yes. I guess so."

"You don't see him much?"

"I think so." Hipparete paused, and continued hesitantly. "I have... dreams. Sometimes I'm not sure what's real or what I dreamt."

"Is Alkibiades in those dreams?"

"Oh, yes. And Kleinias."

Khara massaged Hipparete's head, and the young girl moaned with pleasure. Maria smiled.

"Stephanos is very excited at the prospect of seeing Theo Sémon again," said Khara. "Alkibiades arranged riding lessons for him."

"Oh? Why?"

"He's going to be a scout for the expedition. Together with some other Plataeans."

"That's good, isn't it?" said Hipparete.

"I hope so. A scout is in less danger than a hoplite, don't you think?"

"Oh, I'm sure."

Khara washed the oil from Hipparete's hair and handed her a towel. "Feel better?"

"I do, a little. You were right."

Khara watched as Hipparete beckoned Maria, who caressed her hair dry. It seemed like an act of reconciliation, a dismantling of an unspoken wall. Hipparete closed her eyes as her loyal maid rubbed the long tresses.

"Are you afraid?" said Hipparete without opening her eyes.

Khara looked at the tapestries hanging on the walls, the abandoned loom in the corner. "Yes, I'm afraid. I've only just got him. Now he's being taken away."

Hipparete reached up to stop her maid's hands and raised her head. Her sad eyes engulfed the room. "I understand, Khara."

"Oh, Hipparete!" exclaimed Khara. "I'm sorry. That was so thoughtless."

"No. It wasn't. You have to accept Stephanos leaving. I have to accept losing Kleinias." Hipparete stroked her child's unused serpent necklace, which she wore as a bracelet.

"Kleinias have plenty of brothers," said Maria from behind her mistress.

Hipparete reached for her hand. "Yes. He will."

Chapter 45

They were all hungry and exhausted. Rations were pitiful, and two weeks of surprise attacks had kept the garrison on edge. Sleep, when it deigned to appear, was a shallow creature.

Sémon sat against the battlements, gazing over the town and up to the oak blanket that covered Mount Kithairon. An eagle of Zeus glided serenely over the sunny peaks. He closed his eyes and felt the breeze stroke his face, smelled the hint of honeysuckle, listened to the industrious cicadas. For a moment he was free, free of the soldiers milling around him, free of the weight of his breastplate, free of the burning hunger, a feather drifting on the air. He started to fall sideways, jolted upright, opened his eyes, and rose to his feet.

"Why do they continue with these pointless attacks?" whined Hybrias, staring at the guards on the enemy walls.

"They're just showing off," said Sémon, rubbing his eyes and stretching. "Like dogs that bark but won't bite."

"You needn't worry," added Skopas, leaning over the wall to watch the rabbits in no-man's land. "It doesn't look like they really want to risk their men."

"Oh, I'm not worried," said Hybrias quickly. "I just wondered, that's all." His fingers drummed against the stone battlements. "Still, we only have a few weeks' rations left. What's the point in fighting now? We'll have to surrender anyway."

Mikos banged his spear angrily on the ground, and Sémon's dark brow made young Hybrias shuffle uneasily. "We must give the gods time to pay back the Thebans," said Sémon quietly, but he knew Hybrias had a point. Sémon had felt his own strength leach away. He was tired, weary, his legs leaden. He had known hard winters with little food, but never had he felt himself so... diminished.

"Time or not," said Skopas, "I won't see my wife and children for a long time."

Sémon smiled: if they could count upon one thing, it was Skopas' gloom. "As long as we have our freedom, there's hope."

"This is freedom?" said Hybrias.

"Freedom is relative, Hybrias," said Sémon. "Compared to what awaits if we surrender, then yes, we're free."

"Great Zeus, look!" cried Hybrias.

Sémon followed the young man's gaze: the enemy wall opposite them had burst into life, soldiers rushing from the towers and lowering ladders to the ground. In the moments the Plataeans had stood frozen, mesmerized by the activity, dozens of soldiers had slid to the foot of the battlements to form a wall of shields that grew with every second. The warning horns blared around the town.

"Our turn today," said Sémon as he grabbed his shield.

"Wonderful," muttered Hybrias.

"Look lively, lads!" called General Arkadius, prowling behind his men near the North Gate.

The number of enemy soldiers continued to grow, banging their shields, singing their battle hymn to Apollo. Suddenly they released an unearthly bellow and hurled themselves at the town wall.

Sémon pulled down his helmet and scanned the approaching line. This was no ordinary probe, there were too many of them. His heart skipped, but he gripped his javelin tighter, pounding his shield with his javelin and shouting, "Zeus Liberator!"

"Prepare javelins," cried Arkadius. The thirty men lining the northern wall reached back, ready to launch their missiles on the charging soldiers below, but before the order could be given a shower of arrows rose from the enemy walls. The Plataeans ducked beneath their shields, in the shelter of the battlements, the hail of arrows thudding and clattering around them.

The arrows stopped, and Sémon jumped to his feet, hurling his javelin with all the hatred he felt for his nephew's killers. He did not pause to see where it hit, but grabbed his spear as the enemy wave crashed upon Plataea with undiminished force, a dozen ladders banging against the battlements.

"Get rid of those things," yelled Arkadius.

Hybrias and Mikos heaved their long staffs against an upright of the same ladder, which vibrated to the pounding feet of hoplites they could not see. Sémon stood at the battlements, jabbing his spear down the ladder at the climbing soldiers. "Come on, you bastards. I'm here."

The lead man clambering upwards deflected Sémon's spear, but when the Theban reached the top of the wall he hesitated as he prepared to jump into Plataea. Sémon thrust his spear between the rungs of the ladder, past the cheek guards and into the Theban's left eye. The man screamed and fell backwards, his momentum giving Hybrias and Mikos the boost they needed to send the ladder crashing back to the ground.

All along the wall, ladders slammed back onto the soldiers below, but the assault did not falter. Ladders rose again and fresh soldiers scrambled upwards. Where they gained a foothold, spears were cast aside and the clash of swords joined the desperate chorus.

"Mikos! Quickly!" screamed Hybrias, and the pair of them lent their shoulders to another ladder, but it was too late. A black mountain appeared before them and slashed his sword at Sémon's neck. Sémon blocked the blow with his shield and lunged with his spear, but the giant was quick. He launched himself with a wild roar and landed on top of Hybrias and Sémon, sending all three sprawling across the wall, Sémon losing his spear. The Theban recovered in an instant and on his knees raised his sword again, but Sémon crashed him aside with his shield and leapt to his feet.

With Skopas and Mikos jabbing desperately at the men on the ladder, Sémon pulled out his sword and lunged at the mountain, catching the counter-thrust with his shield. The two circled like sparring crabs, glaring at each other. They swung and parried, a smile emerging amidst the black beard as the giant felt his advantage. Sémon's breathing shortened, his parries became ragged. He refused to be forced backwards, but his strength was failing, and he knew it.

Suddenly the Theban jolted upright, his eyes wide, a spear buried in his armpit. He sank to his knees, and with one stroke Sémon sent his head tumbling down the steps. He winked at Mikos, who grinned as he freed his spear, and the two turned their attention back to the battle seething around them.

***

General Arkadius paced behind his men and shouted encouragement and commands, but they were lost amidst the clamour. This was the heaviest attack they had faced for several years. He turned to face the rest of the town, and he turned to ice: this was not an isolated fight. All around the town, battle raged. Frantic hand-to-hand fighting had erupted on the walls around the East Gate, ladders were being repelled to the west, and the frenzy of war surrounded the south. This was no probe, this was an all-out assault, and the Plataean lines were as thin as their rations.

Even as Arkadius watched, the eastern commander committed his reserves, which dashed up the steps in a last throw of the dice to eject the invaders. The general scanned the rest of the walls and realized that all reserves had already been used except for his own. He glanced to the street below where two dozen men watched him anxiously, awaiting the command. He met the eyes of his trumpeter: should he order retreat to the agora?

Around him the gods of battle procrastinated as the momentum continued to swing. The defenders were outnumbered three to one, but within the confines of the enemy's entry points, they were just about holding their ground. The general waited.

***

"Hybrias! Over here," yelled Skopas as another ladder crashed against the wall. Hybrias and Mikos rushed over with their staffs to drive the danger back, but there were already too many men scrambling upwards. The first reached the top in time to receive a powerful thrust from Sémon's sword that dented his shield and propelled him backwards, knocking several comrades back to the ground. The next hoplite to emerge had his face destroyed by Skopas' spear.

"Now!" shouted Skopas. Hybrias and Mikos gained the leverage they needed and the ladder leaned backwards, teetered and fell to the ground. Skopas raised his spear in triumph, and an arrow embedded itself in his face.

"Skopas!" cried Hybrias as his friend lurched backwards.

"Not now, Hybrias," bellowed Sémon. A handful of enemy

soldiers had climbed onto the wall behind them, and Sémon launched himself at them.

General Arkadius made his last gamble. The reserve stormed up the steps and into the bloody arena, rushing past a comrade struggling to gather his guts into his gaping belly.

Sémon felt a surge of renewed vigour as the fresh soldiers joined the fray, and suddenly the invaders were scattering and tumbling back over the walls. Sémon picked up a spear from the ground and launched it at a retreating soldier, but it clattered off his armour. A trumpet beckoned, and all around the town the Thebans withdrew, climbing back to their own walls amidst a barrage of arrows and javelins.

"Yes, run. Run, you sulfur-breathing-snake-slithering bunch of pigeon shit!" shouted Sémon, holding his bloody sword aloft. "Still undefeated," he cried, and the cheers rose around him. He grinned at Mikos, standing beside him. "Still got all your limbs?" Mikos nodded and pointed along the wall to where Skopas' body lay among mangled corpses. Sémon's smile faded and he sighed. "I know. I know."

***

As the defenders of Plataea rested and vented their relief, General Arkadius stared across the void at a grim-faced man in a red cloak. The Spartan commander of the enemy garrison stood on the encircling wall with his arms crossed, watching the celebrations. He glanced towards Arkadius and then disappeared below, followed by his staff.

It had been close, and he should be grateful to the gods, but Arkadius remained motionless, unable to share his men's joy. The Plataeans burst into songs celebrating their strength and the gods' favour, but the general was a statue staring over the walls and at the road to Thebes. His heart pounded, longing to be wrong. His men's boasts and their taunts of the enemy multiplied, but Arkadius dared not move, dared not tear his eyes from the dirt track. Amidst the cries of happiness and sorrow, relief and pain, General Arkadius saw the end of Plataea: a solitary rider galloping towards Thebes prophesying their fate clearer than any oracle.

Arkadius turned to look upon his jubilant men. These brave, patient farmers, husbands and sons, had resisted like heroes for over two years, but now their end was here. Should he tell them? No, let them at least have this one night of pleasure. It would probably be their last.

Chapter 46

Aristeia and her new family lounged in the sunshine, watching their slaves prepare Timokles' supplies for tomorrow's campaign. They burnished his small shield, sharpened his javelins and sword, cleaned his armour, folded his riding blanket. They filled sackcloth bags of food, gathered sleeping blankets and cooking equipment, receiving instructions from Nikopatra every few minutes, none of them asking Aristeia.

Her mother-in-law directed the flow like a harbour master organizing a fleet of triremes, and she wore the contented smile of one confident and settled in her authority. Samias was her crown before which Aristeia had no choice but to submit. Each command from Nikopatra elicited an echo of pain in Aristeia, a reminder of her defeat and of the fearful hurt she had caused Timokles.

And yet she did not hate her mother-in-law. She may have been manipulated, but no one had forced her to curse Samias: she had done that all by herself. Aristeia disliked and distrusted Nikopatra, but she could lay that aside for the sake of peace, and her husband longed for peace.

Her submission to his mother was no surprise to Timokles. He thought her young and sweet, his mother experienced and stubborn, and he believed Aristeia had withdrawn from the battle in order to bring the quiet Timokles craved after the loss of his friend. Aristeia's pain over what she had done appeared to Timokles an empathy that comforted him. It had been over two months since Samias had died, but the image of the javelin thrust into his chest seared Timokles' dreams.

Wrapping themselves in each other helped both to chase away the spears of the night.

Orontas had lit a small fire on the altar in the courtyard and was arranging a few items around it. "What's he up to?" demanded Nikopatra, glaring towards the Persian slave.

"I asked him to do it," said Aristeia, rising from the couch she shared with Timokles. "I want to make a sacrifice."

"Would you like me there, too?" asked Leaina, keen to propitiate any and all gods necessary to ensure her brother's safe return.

"Not this time, if you don't mind, Leaina. This one is... personal." Aristeia burned to share it with Leaina, but how could she?

"That girl gets more religious by the day," said Nikopatra as Aristeia walked towards the altar.

"She's just worried about Timokles and her father leaving with the army tomorrow," said Leaina.

Aristeia reached Orontas, who pointed out the incense and the fire burning in the bronze pan on the altar, before discreetly passing a small olive branch to her from his cloak. "Thank you, Orontas," she whispered. She offered the incense, praying for her husband and father's safe return, before secretly burning the olive branch. It was the most pleasing offering the gods could receive to appease guilt, and she so needed to appease guilt. The smoke spiralled into the air and disappeared in the vastness of the sky. Aristeia watched it longingly.

When she returned to sit beside Timokles, she nestled against him and stared at the wisps of smoke still escaping the altar.

"Don't you worry, my dear," said Nikopatra. "Cavalry play no role in an attack on a wall. Timokles and your father will be perfectly safe."

"There's no official word there's going to be an attack," said Timokles.

"Oh, everyone knows you're going to relieve Plataea," replied Nikopatra. "Official or not. And the hoplites and peltasts will do all the fighting, as usual, don't you think? That's what everyone's saying."

Timokles shrugged. "Probably."

"It's horrible to drag men away from their homes," said Leaina.

"Alkibiades thinks this campaign could turn the war," said Timokles, turning towards his sister.

Aristeia rested a hand on her husband's thigh, and Timokles absentmindedly stroked the smooth skin of her forearm. "War kills so many," she said quietly.

"Humph," snorted Nikopatra. "Not Athenians, not this time, not with the number we're sending. Whoever heard of sending the whole army to fight a small garrison? I remember the days when Athenian soldiers didn't hide behind numbers."

"Athenians will still die, Mother," murmured Leaina.

"I still see your father marching to battle. You were only little. His armour sparkling, his shield slung over his back." Nikopatra sighed and smiled; a notable event to Aristeia. "He was a handsome sight. A hoplite, of course, and proud of it. Fighting in the front line, that's the true place for an Athenian."

"And long ago Milesians were brave," said Leaina. "Times change, Mother. Cavalry are important nowadays." She grinned mischievously at her brother. "Are you friends with your horse, yet?"

Timokles screwed up his face at her. "We're just fine. We have an understanding."

"Which is...?"

"That we go where he wants to go."

They laughed and even Nikopatra was unable to suppress a hint of a smile. A slave girl approached her to determine the number of onions to pack and the size of wineskins to fill. She was dispatched with curt instructions.

"The army does seem rather large," continued Aristeia. "My father thinks so, and he's leading it! He wonders why Kleon pushed for such a large force."

"Perhaps he wanted to show that he puts the good of Athens before his rivalry with your father," said Timokles.

"You don't think there was an ulterior motive?"

Timokles' fingers intertwined his wife's. "What do you mean?"

Aristeia looked around the family uncomfortably. Her father was worried about Kleon's connection to Alkibiades, and Alkibiades' motives. He wondered if Timokles knew of his friend's plans, but Timokles and Alkibiades were a single hair that could not be parted, and she was afraid to interfere with another of her husband's friends. "I don't know," she said. "My father wonders if there's something else behind it."

"If there is, it's beyond me," said Timokles.

"War is so wasteful," said Leaina. "How much benefit to Athens could there be if we spent the money here instead of in foreign lands? I worked out that we could have built two Temples of Athena Parthenos for the cost of the siege of Potidaea. Two!"

"Maybe, but you know that if we'd lost Potidaea our hold on the coast of Thrace would have been weakened, which would have threatened our corn supply," said Timokles. "A starving people build no temples."

"We can make treaties to secure our corn," replied Leaina. "The siege only benefited the merchants and their wealthy investors at the expense of ordinary citizens who died for them. War spends the lives of honest men to pay the unscrupulous."

"Perhaps," said Timokles. "But treaties break. We have no choice but to control the corn supply."

"But it leads to endless fighting," said Leaina, her hands orchestrating her speech. "We take some of their land, they steal some of ours. We kill a few soldiers, they murder our sons. Is that it? What's the point?"

"The point," began Timokles, "is that if we don't hit back, they'll take more and more until we're too weak to do anything about it. Athens will be a slave to Sparta."

"But how?" asked Leaina, and Aristeia could not help smiling at her sister's fervour. "Everyone says our walls are impregnable, and Perikles himself thought our safety lies at sea. Our power and wealth come from trade, not from war, and we're sort of neighbours with Sparta, so why can't we just be friends?"

Timokles smiled; Aristeia knew he was enjoying his sister's feistiness. "Neighbours make the most vicious enemies," he said "and our wealth isn't only from trade. Our temples and stoas are the envy of Hellas, but they didn't spring from the earth like Athena's olive tree. War paid for them, as much as it secured our food. And it's our strength at sea that allows trade to flourish."

Leaina sat forward on her chair, a little flushed, her gestures as passionate as her language. "But look at Persia, Timokles. We hear of a wealth there that would make Athens look like a collection of mud huts. Their palaces are lined with gold, and achieved, my friend, by trade throughout their empire."

"Trade and tribute," responded Timokles. "And it's trade throughout a region they conquered. You can't have trade without order."

"Exactly!" cried Leaina. "So Hellas could have much more trade and be wealthier if we weren't always fighting each other. We don't need Persia to wage war on us, we conquer ourselves. Let's agree to be friends and we'll all be happier." She raised her arms above her head. "Yes! I win!"

Timokles laughed and threw a cushion in her direction, which she caught with ease before returning fire and scoring a hit on her brother's chest.

Aristeia, noting her own vulnerable position should full-scale cushion war erupt, prompted further discussion. "My father suspects Persia is secretly supplying funds to Sparta."

Timokles and Leaina lowered their defences slowly, not taking their eyes from each other's grinning face until they were sure an unofficial truce had been declared.

"It wouldn't surprise me," said Timokles. "Why go to the expense of conquering Hellas when a few darics can pay your enemies to destroy one another?"

"You make my point for me!" cried Leaina. "Hellas united."

"A united Hellas. Sounds like Alkibiades' dream. But can you really see Athens uniting with the kings of Sparta?" asked Timokles. "Our citizens wouldn't stand for it."

"Ah, but our women might," teased Leaina. "Men may be freer in Athens than in Sparta, but it's at our expense."

"That may be so," smiled Timokles, "but are you prepared to fight a war over it?"

Leaina returned a haughty look to suppress her smile and retain her air of victory.

"The Plataeans and young men in town have been accusing father of delaying the campaign," said Aristeia, "but he says that Plataea has resisted for over two years, so a few days won't make any difference."

"Well, it's here now," said Timokles.

Aristeia squeezed her husband's hand and whispered, "You'll be careful, won't you?"

Timokles smiled and kissed her lightly on the cheek. "I promise."

They lapsed into silence once more, listening to the busy slaves. Aristeia knew that Timokles was impatient to meet the enemy for a chance to avenge Samias, and yet she felt a sadness in him, a reluctance to be parted from her. It gave her hope as she steeled herself for another anxious confinement with her sister and mother-in-law.

Chapter 47

Officially Alkibiades may be a cavalryman, but there was no way he was going to stand aside and watch others grab the glory of rescuing Plataea. He would be the first over the Theban wall. And so he stood beside his mother in the fading light, watching a slave polish the hoplite armour awarded to him at Potidaea, as another prepared the lighter protection he would need for the cavalry.

"Our family has always been the greatest in Athens," said Deinomache. "Kleisthenes rescued the city from the tyrant Pisistratus and his family. And what would Athens be without Perikles? A trifling town controlled by Sparta. Athens is nothing without us." She paused and looked at her son. "You are from a famous line of heroes, Son. Whatever the Fates throw at you, I am confident you will have the courage to seize every opportunity."

Alkibiades smiled wryly and continued to watch the slave work. He never quite knew whether his mother's pronouncements were expressions of confidence or Poseidon's trident up his backside. They felt the same. The chatter of the kitchen hands wafted into the courtyard, along with the aroma of silphium, which could transform any food into a delight. "Antiphon and Pisander are very unhappy with Nikias' decision to split his forces," he murmured.

"You mean sending Hipponikus with the fleet to the Argolid?"

"Yes. They wanted the entire army at Plataea in case Thebes attacks."

Deinomache considered for a moment, before asking, "Do you agree with them?"

The sun was setting, and Alkibiades looked up from the slave to gaze briefly at the blushing clouds before responding. "No, not really. I would not have sent as many men to the Argolid as Nikias has done, but then he is overly cautious. He is terrified the Spartans will raise an army in our rear, but a few companies of scouts across the isthmus would have been sufficient. Still, Pisander in particular was livid that so many men had been diverted."

"You think his anger reveals something other than strategic misgivings?"

"I wish I knew, Mother, but his son got himself assigned as a scout with Hipponikus at the last minute, rather than accompany us to Plataea. It makes me uneasy."

"Nikolas has sailed with Hipponikus?" said Deinomache.

A gnarled old woman emerged from the kitchen holding a burning taper with which she proceeded to light the torches around the courtyard. When she was part way round, a door upstairs opened softly and Hipparete appeared for her daily pilgrimage, like Persephone escaping the Underworld. She floated down the stairs in her white peplos, her dark hair hanging to her waist, Maria following as if afraid the apparition would vanish into the ether. Deinomache shook her head and scowled as the two girls stopped at the altar in the corner of the courtyard.

Hipparete gripped yet another olive branch to be offered for her guilt: her son had been taken from her, she must have offended the gods, there was no other explanation. She had failed her family, she had failed her husband.

"Hipparete." Alkibiades appeared at her side and gently touched her shoulder. She turned her hollow eyes towards her sun and smiled bravely. Alkibiades saw what it cost her and stroked her cheek. "I leave with the army tomorrow, but I will return soon."

"Will you stay to eat, tonight?" she asked in a barely audible voice.

Alkibiades shook his head. "No. Unfortunately, I have lots to take care of before tomorrow. But I will see you before I leave in the morning." He brushed his lips against her cheek, and then left for his evening entertainment at Simaetha's.

Deinomache turned angrily from her daughter-in-law and marched into the kitchen.

Hipparete laid the olive branch on the altar, begging the gods to forgive her, for Demeter and Kore to help her be a better wife, a better daughter-in-law.

Chapter 48

When the trumpets woke Khara she knew this was no ordinary day. She prepared breakfast by lamplight, raised Alexias from his bed, filled the water jug as she had done a thousand times, and yet every action was tainted by bringing the sun closer to its rise. After waiting so long for her husband to come back to her, Stephanos was going away.

Lakon poured libations and offered prayers at the altar, but Khara did not watch, her eyes consuming Stephanos' visage as if she needed to imprint his image on her mind. His light tunic was cast carelessly over his shoulder, and he blushed slightly as if aware of her scrutiny.

"May Hermes, protector of travellers," continued Lakon, "bring my son back to us. And Zeus Liberator, let my..." Lakon's voice cracked, forcing him to pause, before adding softly, "Let my tired eyes feast upon my brother's happy face again."

"I will bring him home, Father," said Stephanos. "I swear it by Apollo."

Lakon patted him on the shoulder with a strained smile.

"I can't wait to see Theo Sémon," said Alexias. "Will he bring me a present like he used to?"

"I'm sure he'll try, Alexias," said Khara.

"I'll bet he's got cart loads of Theban helmets."

"But he may have to give them to the gods, baby," said Khara.

"What, all of them?"

Khara shrugged and pulled Alexias to her side, holding him tightly against her. The trumpets resounded around the city again, and Stephanos brushed Khara's hand. "I guess we should go," he sighed. He picked up his supplies from beside the wall, slinging the sackcloth bundle over his shoulder on the end of a javelin. Lakon grabbed a torch and led them outside.

Although it was still dark, the streets of Athens were filled with hoplite shields and helmets glittering in the torchlight, slaves shouldering supplies, tents and siege equipment weighing down ox-drawn carts, wine merchants and whores preparing to follow the army, a cacophony of light and noise as if it were a night festival. The Etruscan battle trumpets blared the summons from the fields of the Akademy gymnasium, and the army, in all its forms, pressed through the opening in the massive fortifications of the Dipylon Gate.

Khara squeezed Stephanos' hand as they approached the gate, a cock crowing and the sky quivering at the approach of dawn. The mass pressed upon them as it weaved past the huddles of farewells. Lakon grasped his son's arm to hold him back, his gaze a prayer. "Go get my brother, Son," he croaked.

"I will, Father," replied Stephanos, wrapping his arms around him.

Alexias had been surprisingly quiet on the walk, apparently overwhelmed rubbing shoulders with the army of Athens, as if there were so much excitement he was unable to express it. Stephanos released his father and lifted his son. "Now Alexias, I need your help while I'm gone. Will you look after momma and pappu for me while I fetch Theo Sémon?"

"Yes, Poppa," replied Alexias. "Don't worry. I'll make sure they don't get into trouble." Stephanos kissed him and crushed him against his new leather cuirass.

When he finally let him down, Khara launched herself into her husband's arms, wanting to invade his skin, already feeling the sear of the wrench to come. "I can't believe you're going away again," she whispered through her sobs.

Stephanos stroked her hair and said softly, "It'll just be a few days." But when a day could be forever, this gave Khara little comfort.

The trumpets blared and before Khara knew it, before she was ready, long, long before she was ready, Stephanos was gone, swallowed by the crowd.

"This way, Momma!" shouted Alexias, dragging the two grown-ups in his charge to the stone steps that led to the top of the wall, where they struggled to find a spot from which they could watch the city exude its men. The road to the Akademy was a river of torches as if Athens were shedding a tear of light.

"Can you see him? Can you see him?" sobbed Khara.

"There's too many," replied Lakon.

"Look!" said Alexias. "Do you see those men with fox skins over their heads? They're Thracians. And see the Scythians with their bows?"

But Khara had no interest in other men. Somewhere down there was Stephanos, a soldier off to war again, Alexias' hero. But it was the farmer for whom Khara longed. Peaceful days in the fields, cups of wine under the eaves, family laughing in the breeze. Where had those days gone?

Chapter 49

General Arkadius continued to stalk the wall over the North Gate of Plataea. It was a clear summer morning and the warm air gave a dreamy quality to the lush fields and regal mountains. The gentle clonking of wooden bells around the necks of sheep was the perfect inducement to sleep, but the general could not sleep. Through the sticky night he had not slept. Expecting at any moment to hear the alarm, he had spent the dreary night staring into the blackness and saying his ethereal goodbyes to his wife and sons, and with the break of day he had resumed his vigil for the Theban army.

His men had enjoyed what passed for a celebratory feast after their great victory yesterday, their cares swept away by the relief of survival and extravagant rations. They had eaten well and slept soundly, as they deserved. Today would be another matter.

Arkadius turned and stared again towards Thebes, eight miles to the north and hidden by the grassy ridge that rose under a mile from Plataea. There was nothing: no noise; no dust cloud; no army. He continued his pacing. Perhaps he had misread the situation. Perhaps the Spartan commander had not recognized Plataea's weakness and had not sent to Thebes for reinforcements after all.

He paused and gazed around Plataea, at the walls so sparsely guarded, at the smoke spiralling from the cooking fires in the agora, at the mountain rising above the town. Was it possible that the gods would save this place again? He glanced in the direction of the passes to Athens. Nothing. Always nothing. There would be no rescue from there, not now. He turned towards Thebes and his breath caught. A small stain rose in the distance, peeking over the ridge. He stared, longing to be mistaken, for it to be a trick of the morning light or the product of his imagination. He glared at the dirty cloud, willing it to disappear, but it grew, and quenched his last ember of hope.

A cry rose from the nearby tower and news of the cloud swept the town. Within minutes the northern wall was crammed with men wiping the sleep from their eyes and arguing the significance of the sight. No-one doubted that an army was on the march, but where was it going? North to put down a rebellious ally? South to Attika? To the Peloponnese to rescue Sparta from an Athenian attack? No-one murmured the monstrous thought that besieged every mind.

A dozen horsemen emerged over the ridge and galloped to Plataea, waving their spears and jeering at the besieged before disappearing from view behind the encircling wall. Arkadius felt his men's elation shrivel like Antigone's stream in summer. They drifted away in lonely silence to don their armour.

Arkadius gave them the time he could. The thought of surrender flashed across his mind, but he dismissed it; he was Athenian and he would follow his orders: they must, at least, defend the walls.

He motioned his trumpeter to sound assembly for the North Gate, and when the men had gathered, the general looked down upon them from the wall, his shield bearing the bull of Marathon, his armour gleaming, his grandfather face stern and determined. He had had all night to prepare for this, his men less than half an hour.

"There seems little doubt," he began, "that an army from Thebes is on its way here. If they intend to conquer this town, then by Athena of Plataea they will pay for it." His men did not react. There was defeat in their eyes.

"All I ask of you," he continued, "is to remember your fathers and grandfathers. They stood near here facing an enemy that outnumbered them, and they were afraid. Afraid they would not see their wives again. Afraid they would not see their sons grow to manhood. Afraid of the pain of dying. And yet they stood firm. They fought as one and won a great victory. Today, we will see the fields filled with enemies again and we will all feel the fear that our fathers felt, but if we fight as one, we will survive. We have resisted them for what seems a lifetime. This is our final test. Fight for each other and we will triumph again." He paused, looking over the grim faces and wondering how many would survive the day, how many had believed anything he had said. "Dismissed!"

The trumpet calls filled Plataea and the men jogged to their assigned positions around the town, and waited. The cloud grew painfully slowly, but finally the beating drums and the rumbling thunder of feet announced the imminent arrival of the army from Thebes. A handful of cavalrymen ascended the ridge, their horses walking slowly. Row upon row of hoplites rose behind them and descended towards Plataea in an endless flood, their round shields and bronze helmets a multitude of suns, their spears fields of barley.

"How many do you think?" asked Hybrias, putting on his helmet. His face was white and his hands trembled with the shaking earth.

Enough, thought Sémon. He noted Hybrias' tremors and realized that his own hands were shaking. He clasped them and took a deep breath. "Perhaps they're here for a picnic. You know, get out into the country, sample the fresh air. Probably no-one told them about your farts, Hybrias."

Mikos' shoulders shook, but the butt of the joke had lost his sense of humour. "Would you say four thousand?"

Sémon scrutinized the fields more seriously and shook his head. "No, at least eight."

"Eight thousand!" exclaimed Hybrias. "How are we to resist such a number?"

Sémon smiled sadly. "We're not." He practiced a few sword thrusts and parries with an imaginary foe before sheathing his sword and grabbing his spear. So the end had come. Well, so be it, but those sons of whores would feel the sting of it.

The tide of hoplites marched in a silence that was unnerving, the clank of weapons, the rhythmic drums and the dull thud of thousands of feet the only sound. The soldiers on the walls of Plataea stretched their muscles, checked the sharpness of their weapons, and practiced their murderous dances as the army fanned out around the encircling walls. The Thebans surrounded the town and halted. Suddenly they released a torrent of curses and abuse that the hate of generations had nurtured, the bellowing scaling the walls of Plataea and assaulting the ears and hearts of the defenders.

"You sons of whores!" Sémon yelled back. "You cess-pools of dog shit. You fish-breathed-goat-loving-cockroach-ridden-dunghills. We're gonna' send you to Hades and you can take your fleecy lovers with you!" His fellow countrymen launched their own cries born of fear and hatred, but the immense throat of Thebes swallowed them whole.

As suddenly as the verbal barrage had started, it ended.

"Okay, men, this is it," cried Arkadius. Sémon gripped his shield and readied himself.

The Thebans' ordered ranks dissolved and they began to unload their supply carts, and lead cattle bedecked in ribbons and gold foil around the walls.

"What in Hades are they doing?" asked Hybrias.

Sémon frowned, and then realized that Mikos was laughing. "What is it?" His friend mimed with his hands, and Sémon looked back at the Thebans and roared with laughter.

"What? What is it?" pressed Hybrias.

"Hybrias, my friend," said Sémon, putting his arm around the young man's shoulders, "never doubt the wisdom of your elders again. Look! They're preparing a picnic!"

Sure enough, the Thebans were sacrificing and butchering cattle, building fires, circulating bread and wine.

"But why?" said Hybrias.

"Well, which would you prefer? To fight on a full belly or an empty one?"

"Oh."

"And in any case," Sémon continued, "I'm sure they want to torture us with the smell." An order rippled around the wall: food was to be served; triple rations.

"Triple rations?" said Hybrias.

"Maybe it's to take our minds off their feast," said Sémon, but he saw that Mikos also understood the implications of the order: there was no longer any need to conserve food. *Mikos, Mikos. Why did you have to stay? Now we shall both die.*

By the time the women distributed the meal, the Plataeans had seen the free-flowing wine and smelled the roasting meat their enemies were enjoying, and for men long denied the pleasure of food, the Theban banquet was a spear to the belly.

The Plataeans ate quietly amidst the laughter, music and

dancing that surrounded them. The tasteless meal did not last long, and Sémon sat in the shade of his shield, waiting. For years their lives had been waiting for them, somewhere out there, beyond the walls. His brother, his nephew's child, out there, waiting for him. Had it been worth it, this wait? Was his death meaningful? He shook himself. Plataea would live on. It would be rebuilt on their bones. He wanted the waiting to be over.

Apollo had begun his fall from the sky when trumpets broke the party atmosphere in the fields. The Thebans grabbed their armour and weapons and formed ordered ranks around the town again. Sémon rose and sighed with relief. *At last.*

The surrounding army tightened its grip around the neck of its victim to the music of pipes and drums, advancing to the encircling wall where they disappeared from view, entering the fortifications and climbing the stairs in the towers. All around the town, the Theban hoplites took positions shoulder to shoulder, facing the Plataeans, the fields emptying as the dense ranks crowded the walls.

Sémon looked around at his own comrades, the men whose lives had been grimly intertwined for so long. Their own walls seemed sad and empty, and as he turned back to face the army he muttered, "I think they're serious this time."

It took two hours for the Thebans to fill the wall and then, nothing happened. The two forces glared at each other across the void, that blessed ground of one hundred paces that gave the Plataeans hope and the Thebans pause.

A great rumbling rose from the Thebans and they launched into the paean, a lusty hymn of praise to Apollo, conqueror of the mighty Python of Delphi. Their imprecations rushed to Mount Olympus in a tidal wave, drowning the efforts of the Plataeans to enlist the gods on their own behalf.

When the paean finished, horns blared from the towers, the Theban soldiers lowered ladders to the ground, and the Plataean archers prepared their first volley. Another horn blast and a blizzard of arrows sprang from beyond the enemy walls, forcing the Plataeans to raise their shields and crouch to the ground amidst the whistle, clatter and thud of the projectiles falling in dense clouds. Cries of pain pierced the storm as the arrows swarmed like locusts. It was impossible for the Plataean soldiers to escape their cover for a moment, even though the approaching howls of the enemy below urged their attention.

The arrows ended and Sémon jumped to his feet. Their enemies infested the ground below, and ladders crashed against the town walls. Mikos and Hybrias hurled their staffs at the nearest ladder and pushed for their lives, sending it clattering back on those below. Even as the ladder fell, they shoved on another, this time heavier with the weight of men. This, too, they returned to the ground amidst the shrieks of those falling. Sémon stood nearby, his spear and shield ready, tremors forgotten. All around the town, ladders rose and fell to cries of anguish and exhortation.

"There are too many of them!" screamed Hybrias, as the battlements sprouted ladders. Almost as one, the Plataeans accepted the impossibility of removing the scourge, flung aside their staffs and grabbed their spears and shields. They fought like Furies to prevent the Thebans getting onto the wall, jabbing ferociously at the heads appearing on the ladders.

The clash of weapons and the roar of battle was Sémon's entire existence, his whole life focused on the small patch of wall before him. He had no time to consider whether Mikos had fallen or part of the walls had been taken. All he could see was snarling faces of hated Thebans intent on destroying him. He fought them off with the ferocity of a cornered animal, sending an avalanche of Thebans to form drifts at the foot of the wall.

"Come on, you dogs," he bellowed. "Is this all you've got?" His spear and arrow-studded shield swung in lethal harmony. Mikos, Hybrias, and the rest of their company tried to stem the flow, shoving and stabbing, dodging, swinging, clubbing. But there were too many holes in the dam. The ladders continued to appear, and Theban hoplites began jumping onto the walls of Plataea.

Isolated individuals were cut down, and huddles of defenders drove the initial landings back along the wall, only to find the space behind them filling with Thebans. Larger groups of Plataeans formed barriers of shields and held their own for a time, until the pressure of enemy forces grew. Around Plataea, the defensive reserve was committed, charging noisily to the top of the wall, but all they could do was add to the growing piles of bodies.

"Two lines at the stairs!" yelled Arkadius as the total loss of the northern wall became inevitable.

Mikos, facing several blood-spattered Thebans brandishing swords, stepped backwards towards the stairs but stumbled as he trod on a severed leg. He tried to recover his balance and a sword flashed past his shield, piercing his thigh.

"Mikos!" screamed Hybrias.

Sémon whirled around, aghast to see Mikos with blood pouring down his leg and falling on one knee, his adversaries closing in. Mikos caught the first blow on his shield and thrust his spear into the groin of his enemy. The spear stuck fast, and Mikos unsheathed his sword just in time to receive the slash from another soldier.

Sémon leapt in front of him, roaring like a lion, sweeping away the detritus with his shield and slashing his sword at them. The Thebans hesitated before this monster, allowing two soldiers to rush to Mikos' aid and drag him back to the stairs, leaving a trail of blood.

"Sémon!" shouted Hybrias. "They've got him, get back here!"

Sémon was in a standoff with those in front of him. He growled as the Thebans closed warily on him, and he retreated slowly to the remnant of his unit as the Theban army swarmed on to the walls.

General Arkadius glanced around the town. It had happened so quickly. It was clear that all of the reserves had been committed, and yet they had lost the walls. All around the battlements, soldiers fought in close combat, the continuous thud and clank of weapons a dirge to the screams of agony. He had already ordered the archers to their positions for their last desperate act. The time had come for the last stand.

"Sound the retreat," he bellowed to the trumpeter below. The clean notes signalled the release of Fear from its flimsy prison to rampage through the town. Plataeans who had fought with desperate courage now panicked and broke off from the fight, hurtling down the stairs only for javelins to pierce them in the back of the neck. The more disciplined retreated as a body.

Sémon was in the front line facing the enemy as the thirty Plataeans around him edged backwards down the stairs, the ranks behind raising their shields to protect themselves from the missiles raining down on them. When they were halfway down the stairs, Plataean archers on the roofs of nearby buildings released a handful of accurate arrows into the Theban ranks. The enemy faltered under this unexpected attack, and the Plataean hoplites bolted down the street towards the agora.

Mikos limped rapidly with Hybrias' help, but not quickly enough. The Thebans had recovered and their angry shouts were too loud for comfort. Hybrias dared not look back. They fell behind their fleeing comrades, and Hybrias' chest imploded, his breath vanished. His unblinking eyes darted to his burden. *This was not bravery, this was suicide. Anybody could see that. Mikos would understand.* Hybrias loosened his grip around his friend, and Mikos staggered, but Sémon appeared and virtually swept Mikos off the ground. The three of them tore for the wall that blocked the end of the street, expecting an arrow or javelin in the back at any moment.

It did not come. Sémon shoved his friends through the barricade and then helped to close the stout wooden gate. He climbed the barricade and looked back to see the massed hoplites halted at the end of the street, and the Plataean archers retreating to the roofs around the agora, chased there by enemy missiles. He jumped back down to the panting, bloody soldiers who had made it back.

"You okay?" he asked Mikos, who was wrapping a piece of cloth tightly around his leg. Mikos nodded and winked. "You should get that seen to. An injury like that can seriously affect your health, you know." Mikos smiled grimly.

The remains of the garrison of Plataea were scattered around the agora, close to one hundred and fifty men. Some lay amidst pools of blood in the shadow of Zeus the Liberator, moaning gently as the women tended them. The rest stood on or behind the walls at the four entrances to the agora, waiting for the final attack. From inside the law courts the remaining women wailed at the approach of the multitude of rapists.

General Arkadius paused beside the barricade near the Temple of Athena and leant on his shield, breathing heavily and looking around at the men left to him. About a quarter had not made it back. He sighed heavily and closed his eyes.

"Sir! A herald's approaching."

The general climbed the wall and saw a lone man in a white tunic striding towards them. He carried a tall bronze staff and wore the winged hat of Hermes, messenger of the gods. Beyond him, at the now open North Gate, stood the Theban army.

The herald stopped a few yards in front of the defences. "I have a message for General Arkadius from the commander of the forces of Sparta and Thebes." His clear, sonorous voice swept over the wall and through the agora.

"Speak, herald. I am Arkadius."

"General, you have led your men bravely throughout this siege. The gods have borne witness to the courage of your soldiers. Your resilience is known throughout Hellas." He paused, before adding, "The siege is now over, General. Plataea is ours. To fight on is certain death for you and your men. Such a death will deliver no glory, only an end. We urge you to honour the gods and prevent such senseless sacrifice. You have until Apollo rises to present your unconditional surrender."

Chapter 50

Nikolas dismounted, and Zopuros, the artless youngster riding with him, sprang from his horse and scrambled after Nikolas up the slope. Their slaves sheltered the mounts in the shade of a grove of olive trees as Nikolas approached the crest. He slowed, bending double and keeping his javelin tip low to the ground, throwing himself down flat at the top and gazing into the plain below. His heart raced, and he struggled to hide his excitement.

"Oh, Great Athena!" mumbled his pale comrade beside him. "General Nikias was right."

The range of hills providing their viewpoint rose abruptly from the plain and ran parallel to the Gulf of Corinth a mile away. The carpet of farmland below them was filled with tents, cooking fires, carts, and soldiers, extending to the calm waters and eastwards towards the city of Corinth. Beyond the northern reaches of the strait, the hazy blue mountains that enclosed Delphi stretched to the sky. To Nikolas it was all beautiful; for Zopuros, it was an unnatural disaster.

"Looks like the entire Peloponnesian army," Zopuros whispered. "We must tell General Hipponikus. He's got to warn General Nikias to retreat to Athens. The army's in danger."

Nikolas chuckled. "Not so fast. He'll want to know how many men they have."

"Well, it must be at least forty thousand, wouldn't you say?"

"Perhaps. But we don't know for sure where they're going."

"What do you mean? Has to be Attika. In any case, the general should know they're here. Let's go." Zopuros pushed himself back from the ridge and started to descend.

"Zopuros," called Nikolas, catching up to him and grasping his shoulder to slow him down. "Why don't you stay here to watch their movements and I'll report to Hipponikus?"

"Our orders were to stay together."

"You're right." They bounced down the rocky slope, and

Nikolas nodded to his loyal slave, who had tied their horses to one of the trees. The slave sidled alongside Zopuros' man, and Nikolas pretended to stumble, dropping several paces behind his confederate. Zopuros glanced back as Nikolas gripped his javelin in both hands, thrust his full weight behind the iron tip and skewered the youth's neck. Zopuros' mouth opened in a silent, bloody scream. He clawed at the javelin, his hands dripping blood, choking, dropping to his knees.

At the same moment, Nikolas' slave pulled out a dagger and slashed the throat of the man beside him. The horses stamped as their reins were released, but the slave grabbed them quickly.

Nikolas pulled his javelin from Zopuros' body. There was no nausea: the kill had been easier this time. But then, he understood its importance: the Peloponnesian army must be given time to cross the isthmus and trap Nikias' forces. The later Nikias learned of their presence, the more likely he would be forced to surrender.

Nikolas jogged down the hill calling, "Hold them steady." When he reached Zopuros' two horses he drove his javelin into their chests, bringing them crashing to the ground, kicking and whinnying. "We were ambushed. They didn't make it," said Nikolas, ignoring the cries of the horses and cleaning his javelin. He motioned for his mount. "Come on. Let's go see the king of Sparta."

Chapter 51

There was a time when Plataea's agora blazed with laughter and music, but that seemed another age to Sémon. Now there was only fear, and it filled him with dread. He looked up at the moon, bright, lonely. Would he ever see it again?

Handfuls of soldiers guarded the barricades, and dark silhouettes of archers prowled the rooftops. The fires had burned low, the women sitting quietly beneath the long colonnade, waiting to hear their fate. Sémon listened to the Theban army laughing and singing on the walls of Plataea as the last of his weary comrades found seats on the steps of the law court. They had laid aside shields and weapons, but every man still wore the bloodstained armour he had fought in a few hours earlier. There was little talk and no laughter among them.

General Arkadius struggled to his feet and walked a few paces before turning to face his men. "Gentlemen, we have one last decision to make. Let each speak his mind without fear. Astymachus, son of Asopolaus, has asked to speak first." Arkadius resumed his seat, and a balding man with the air of a philosopher rose to his feet, his nose swollen and misshapen, broken during the battle and giving his voice a nasal quality.

"Friends." He held his arms out and nodded as he gazed around the well-known faces. "It has been a long struggle. Against all the odds we are still here. No-one can say," he said, raising his voice, "that we have not fought like heroes. No-one can doubt that we have brought glory to our families and to our homes. The herald himself acknowledged that all Hellas knows of our bravery. But he is right, suicide is not honourable." A lazy breeze carried an approving murmur through the ranks. "You know that I enjoyed ties with Sparta in times of peace, although my face testifies that I bear them no favours in war. But this I will say: they are honourable men. You know it. It is time to surrender to them. We will wait out the war as prisoners, and when it is done, they will return us to our families. Let us leave our deeds free of pointless gestures."

He resumed his seat, many men nodding in silence. In the flickering fire-light, Hybrias clambered down to the make-shift stage. "Astymachus is right," he began, his face flushing. "We can't hold out any longer, they'll destroy us. No doubt about it. If the Athenians were here we might have a chance, but it's too late. We've no choice but to surrender."

One by one they spoke in favour of capitulation, their spirit finally crumbling, each speech of surrender removing a log in the dam containing the waters of their resilience, their will leaking away to the music of their enemy's laughter.

Sémon could bear it no longer, and marched clumsily down the steps, carrying his helmet, deftly using it to express his displeasure at earlier speakers unfortunate enough to lie in his path. "Make way, coming through. Look out, there. Watch your hea...oh, sorry." He jumped from the last step and turned to face them. "I thought I shared this town with men, not mice." There was shocked silence. The men stared at him, convinced they must have misheard the heretical words. "After all we've been through, you want to surrender to Thebans. A more foul, hateful, treacherous, lying people you could not meet, and you want to trust your lives to them?"

"We'd be surrendering to Spartans, not Thebans," a voice croaked.

"Yes, and Spartans are trustworthy," shouted another. "They didn't trick us at the Freedom Festival." There was a low growl of assent from his comrades.

"There's an army of Thebans out there now, you cow turds," said Sémon. "Have you forgotten that the victory we celebrate in the festival was over traitorous Thebans as well as the barbarians? Treachery spreads like a disease, and the Thebans are infectious. We should die killing them like our fathers did, not be cut down like dogs."

"That won't happen, Sémon," yelled a man at the top of the steps. "We'll be imprisoned and freed at the end of the war. How can you suggest they'll kill us?"

"Because," bellowed Sémon, "a Theban would as soon cut

your head off and spit down your bloody neck as look at you. We can't trust them. Look what they did to those who escaped. How can you risk such a dishonourable death?"

Astymachus stood up beside Sémon, raising his arms to quiet the angry mutterings. "We all know that Sémon is an outstanding soldier and we honour him for it. But the time for fighting is over. Can you imagine Sparta executing prisoners? It is unthinkable. They will return us to our families at the end of the war."

"We'll be a bit smelly by then," replied Sémon. "I doubt our families will insist they empty our graves."

The men continued to shout their objections, and when Sémon finally sat down he was shaking with frustration. Arkadius stood and silenced the men. "It is time to decide," he announced.

"What about you, what do you think, General?" called Astymachus.

Arkadius sighed and looked to the heavens before answering. "It has been my greatest privilege to lead you. I feel fortunate to have served with such brave, resourceful men. Athenians and Plataeans, we have fought as one with no hint of betrayal. Whatever you decide now, it will not change my high opinion of you all." The men watched him silently as he paused once more. "I think Sémon is right, that we cannot trust the Thebans, but I believe the Spartans would never allow them to usurp their authority. It is safe to give ourselves up to Sparta, and I do not wish to lose any more men. I believe it is time to surrender."

Sémon hung his head, and the vote that followed showed only a handful supported his view. When Arkadius officially announced the decision to surrender, the soldiers remained in their places, staring into the void, the merry music from the town walls clashing with their acknowledgement of final defeat. Gradually they dispersed to their stations around the barricades, a few going to sleep, others playing dice, many stealing a last visit to the women. Zeus the Liberator stood proudly in the heart of the agora to share their last night of imprisoned freedom.

Sémon felt as if a great tailwind had stopped blowing. He was powerless, and foreboding overwhelmed him. He glanced at Mikos, sitting beside him on the steps of the Temple of Athena. "I'm sorry you're a part of this," he said softly, fingering his shield resting on the step below. "If you hadn't got it into your foolish head to stay with me, you could've been chasing some buxom lass around a farm right now."

Mikos elbowed Sémon in the ribs and started gesturing as Sémon tried to translate. "You're...sad? No, what then? Sorry? Yes, you're sorry... for one thing. What's that?" Mikos pointed to his ankle and twisted it. "Ah, yes. That was unfortunate. Better for us to have died with dear Stephanos." He patted Mikos on the knee. "It wasn't to be. But you give great comfort to a silly old fool. You always have." They shared a wistful smile, remembering their sunny days on the farm.

Hybrias ambled towards them and sat beside Sémon. "I thought you'd be with Rebia."

Sémon looked to the ground. "Not tonight," he muttered. Ever since the battle, his wife's image had invaded him and for once, he had not banished it. He saw her long silky hair, the creases around her eyes when she glowed with laughter, the way she glided into a room, the adoring glances turned towards him. Too little. There had been too little time.

Chapter 52

"We have been given the honour of the advance guard," declared Alkibiades, unable to keep the excitement from his voice as he glanced around the men of his troop gathered in the light of the morning's fire.

"Given, or seized?" asked Timokles, a glint in his eye. The troop chuckled.

"Today," continued Alkibiades, "we will rescue Plataea, and we will be the first to its walls." He searched out the man he needed. "Stephanos!"

"Alkibiades," said Stephanos.

"You will take the scouts ahead of us and report directly to me."

To you? thought Stephanos. He was under the impression he should report to the Phylarch, but he did not want to cross the man who had done so much for him, so he said nothing. Alkibiades issued further commands and dismissed them to their duties.

"Alkibiades," said Stephanos. "The camp is still quiet. Few tents have been struck."

"I know. That is Nikias for you. He will not issue a command without the sanction of the gods, and I understand they are stalling on their omens."

"The omens for Plataea would be much better if we began our march now," said Stephanos.

"You are right. But not even Nikias' dithering can stop us now. Stop worrying. Before the end of the day, you will be with your uncle again."

"Zeus Liberator make it so." Stephanos strode towards the wood where the horses were tethered. The hills were gathering a hint of brightness as the cocks crowed, the haunting melody of a shepherd's pipe wafting over the awakening camp. He passed a clock-watcher marking the drops of water emerge from their urn, and wished it would flow more quickly. He brushed aside an old man selling charms for protection in the coming battle, and nearly collided with a prostitute rearranging herself after her last shift of the night. Slaves prepared breakfasts and removed shields from covers, soldiers stumbled naked from their beds, offering prayers to the new day and washing in the stream that meandered through the encampment. Stephanos scowled at the leisurely activity.

A cluster of men laughed as they ate their bread and onions before their tent. "Strike your tent. The sun will be over the mountains soon," Stephanos barked at them.

"Keep your sword sheathed, mate," replied a swarthy man, stretching. "The signal ain't been given yet."

Stephanos glared but hurried onwards. Why had the trumpet not sounded?

Across the camp beside a portable altar, Nikias paced back and forth as old Stilbides struggled to obtain the favour of the gods. They had sacrificed and rejected three goats, their livers having defects that did not bode well at all. The stars had vanished into the clear sky by the time they had made an acceptable offering and spotted an eagle flying towards Plataea. Stilbides pronounced that the army would not be defeated, and began his long prayer to Athena, their Lady Victory, the Golden Helmeted One.

When he had finally finished, Nikias strode back inside his command tent. "Any news from Hipponikus?" he demanded sharply.

One of his staff responded promptly, "No, sir, not since yesterday. There was no sign of an enemy army then, sir."

"Fine," snapped Nikias, gripping the top of the chair he stood behind. "Order the army to break camp. We march on Plataea."

Chapter 53

The sun had crept above the mountains when General Arkadius, clad in full armour, kissed his sword and laid it beside his spear at the foot of Zeus the Liberator. He paused, gazing wistfully at his weapons, before turning towards the demolished barricade at the head of the road from the agora to the North Gate. The roofs of the buildings lining their route towards the gate had sprouted enemy archers, and Theban hoplites lined the street.

Arkadius stepped into the jaws of the enemy. Behind him, the clatter of arms cast to the ground proclaimed the end of Plataea as his men followed in silence. The women wept in the shelter of the stoa as their old masters abandoned them to new.

Sémon reached the mound of weapons and held his sword aloft, breaking the silence with a shout. "All hail Zeus, liberator of Plataea." A weak, "Hail Zeus!" was all his comrades could muster as their final offering to their god. Sémon followed them through the rubble of the barricade and down the street, but he did not see the sneering faces of the spearmen or the taut bows of the archers. He was strolling beside his wife again, greeting old friends in the sunshine as a gentle breeze played with her hair, holding Ana's hand as she chattered happily about nothing in particular.

He passed through the gate into the territory between the two walls, removing his helmet and laying it gently on the growing heap of armour beyond the gate. He unbuckled his breastplate and looked up. Both the town and besieging walls were crowded above and below with hoplites. The silence was as heavy as a sword blow to a shield.

His cuirass removed, guards shepherded Sémon with the rest of his comrades away from the monuments of the Persian victory, and into the grassy space between the two walls. The ground buzzed with wild flowers in their colourful finery, a nation of insects humming within their courts as swallows frolicked overhead.

The Plataeans formed a long line just twenty paces from the enemy wall. As the last of the Plataeans joined the line, the Thebans erupted, the enraged voices assailing the prisoners from every side. Sémon glanced along the line: the men cowered beneath the shower of bread, olives, and stones that fell on them. Beside him, Mikos stared into space, unblinking even as an olive struck his head. A stone thumped Sémon's chest, and he faced the front again. He narrowed his eyes, crushing the panic he felt rise like the tide, itching to grab a sword and rush at those hated faces.

Gradually the angry waves subsided enough for the Spartan commander to make himself heard. "Soldiers of Plataea!" he cried from the height of the wall above them. "Hear your fate." The captives looked hopefully to the respected leader. "In the war for the freedom of Hellas," the Spartan continued, "no-one can serve two masters. Therefore, each man shall be asked whether he has helped Sparta in the war. Any man unable to answer 'yes' will be put to death."

The Plataeans stared, unable to comprehend, until their shock was overthrown by outrage at what was a death sentence dressed in false garments of justice. They hurled cries of disbelief and anger at the commander amidst the hoots and laughter of the Thebans.

Sémon closed his eyes, pain welling like a bubble from the deep. All men die, but to die like a dog...

"They can't do this, can they?" demanded Hybrias, standing the other side of Mikos.

Sémon opened his eyes and indicated the multitude of raucous hoplites. "They can do what they want." He saw the panic envelop Hybrias and added quickly, "But you never know, perhaps they can be persuaded out of it." His friend grasped wildly for this straw of hope and held tight.

General Arkadius stepped before his men and motioned for silence. "Commander," he cried to the Spartan. "I call for justice."

"This is justice, General."

"But is it Spartan justice? This is a despicable act you propose. As one leader to another, I ask that you allow us to plead our case, before you undertake this Theban deed."

The Spartan commander turned to those around him, and a vigorous debate ensued.

"What are they saying?" hissed Hybrias.

Sémon shrugged.

Eventually the commander turned back to Arkadius. "Make your case, General."

"Yes!" cried Hybrias. "I knew it. I knew they couldn't do it."

"Thank you, Commander," called Arkadius. "But I am a man of poor words, and for such a speech I would like a man more skilled in the arts of persuasion to make our defence." The commander nodded his assent and Arkadius motioned to Astymachus.

Astymachus the philosopher ambled forward in obedience to Arkadius' command, his tongue the size of a cedar, his breath stolen. The heavily armed hoplites a few yards away shouted abuse and waved their spears, leering at him as if only his blood would quench their desire. He turned to the anxious faces of his comrades. Their eyes burned with desperate pleading, and he felt the crushing weight of their hopes. All those years of practicing speeches to his sister, how could they prepare for this?

Astymachus took a slow, deep breath and cleared his throat, the Thebans settling as they saw him prepare, as if they were about to hear the prologue of a play.

"Come on, you old git," shouted a lurid scar leaning over the wall. "We want to see some blood." Ripples of laughter and agreement spread among the soldiers.

"Commander!" Astymachus called out. "Never before have I felt such a weight of death in my words. My throat rebels at the thought. I wonder if I may have a drink of water?"

A Theban hoplite ran to the speaker and handed him a skin of water. "Enjoy it, mate," he grinned, "it'll be your last." Astymachus' eyes closed as the tepid liquid soothed his throat. "That's enough," growled the soldier, snatching it away.

Astymachus was left standing lonely.

He licked his lips and began. "When we surrendered this morning, we gave ourselves up to Spartan justice, secure in your honour. Imagine our shock, then, at this sentence. It makes no sense. You are really asking if we have betrayed our ally, Athens, the answer to which is obvious. No-one is deceived; you just sentenced us all to death without trial." He glanced at the Theban generals surrounding the Spartan commander, wondering how strong their bonds were. "I doubt whether anything Apollo himself could say in our defence would make a difference, so eager you seem to please your new ally."

The Spartan commander stiffened, and scowls disfigured the faces around him, but Astymachus continued without pausing.

"I have not the golden tongue of Apollo, and no case to put of which you are not already aware. I only hope that whispers have temporarily blinded you to your interests and to the services we have paid you in the past. Have you forgotten how our fathers stood side by side to face the barbarian storm? Can you fail to recollect that it was to Plataean gods they sacrificed before that battle? Are those same gods no longer worthy of honour? Yet here you stand, beside Thebans, the betrayers of Hellas, who fought with the barbarians. Is this how you reward patriotism and treachery?"

A new storm broke over Plataea as the Thebans unleashed their rage at the speaker. Olives and bread rained upon Astymachus, who held himself calm and aloof, thankful that the interruption gave him time to plan what was to come.

"You bastards!" screamed Hybrias at the Thebans, his face red and contorted, tears streaking his cheeks. "You stinking, filthy bastards!"

The noise enveloped the prisoners, and Mikos strode in front of the line, turned his back on the enemy wall and bent over, raising his tunic and thrusting his bare bottom at them. He smoothed his clothing into place and strolled serenely back to Sémon.

The Spartan leader remained unmoved, holding the stare of the statuesque Astymachus. Unbridled hatred reared amongst the Theban soldiers and fingers twitched at bows, fists clenched spears. Eventually the commander gave instructions, and when a horn finally re-established peace, Astymachus continued.

"Our service to Hellas extends beyond the Persian Wars. We have honoured the monuments to the men who fell here, including those to the Spartan heroes. Would you condemn the tombs of your fathers to lie beneath the feet of a people they considered their enemy? But let us move on from events that should make your inconstant ally blush."

"You're the one gonna' blush, mate," shouted a soldier from the wall. "Blush red all over, and wet, like." He nudged his neighbour and there was muted chuckling around him.

"Let me remind you," continued Astymachus, "that we sent a third of our citizens to crush the helot revolt that threatened your city forty years ago. And yet now you consider us enemies. And why? Because we are allied to Athens? When Thebes first stretched its greedy fist towards us in the time of our grandfathers, you felt unable to intervene being so far away, and you recommended we make an alliance with Athens, instead. Yet now you blame us for staying loyal to our long-standing friend. How could you have any regard for us if we were to betray such a friendship? How could you trust us if we so easily switched allegiance? It is to our credit that we keep faith with our oaths."

"You shouldn't have joined Athens to fight against us," yelled an aide near the commander.

Astymachus was almost oblivious of his surroundings. He was before his sister again, the arguments marshalling themselves in his mind, the words falling from his mouth as easy as morning dew. "We did not leave our town to take arms against you. We simply followed the universal instinct to defend one's home. If a shark drifts into forbidden waters, should you blame the pilot fish that accompanies it and is dependent upon it? Of course not. Neither should we shoulder the blame for being allied to your enemy. We have no choice. Thebes, on the other hand, has committed many wrongs of her own volition. They tried to seize our town in peace time, and we dealt with them as befits an invader, but it has made them mad to avenge their failure. They want the honourable Spartan name to shield their misdeeds. Do not make us suffer on their account."

He looked around towards the mountains behind the town, to the road to Athens and Three Heads Pass where their hope of rescue had lain every day of the siege. Like each one of those days, the road was deserted. He faced his judge again. "Our allies have abandoned us and left us to your mercy. All we ask is for true Spartan justice. Turn back from the shameful influence of Thebes. To kill us is easy enough, but how will you erase the infamy of the deed from the memory of Hellas? Your honourable name will be no more."

Astymachus took a long look at his companions and felt his breath shorten, turning slowly to the commander again. "It is difficult to stop speaking when you know the lives of you and your friends depend on your words, but stop I must. All I will say is that we trust in Spartan justice, not Theban tyranny. We would rather starve or die fighting than be given to an enemy with whom we share a mutual hatred. Stand by your avowed mission to free Hellas, and grant us clemency."

"Good speech, Astymachus," bellowed Sémon, clapping his hands as the Plataean defender shuffled back to the line with his head bowed and lips pursed, the hoots and jeers of the Thebans swamping Sémon's cry of support.

"It was a great speech, don't you think?" pleaded Hybrias. "A great speech."

"Yes, a fine speech," nodded Sémon. "Let's hope our judge agrees."

On the wall above them, an animated discussion between the commander and his Theban subordinates held the Plataeans in a trance. Arms waved and fingers pointed, heads shook and fists pounded the top of the wall. The prisoners watched their fate hang in the balance, barely noticing the boisterous Theban soldiers threatening to charge them at any moment.

"What do you think they're saying?" asked Hybrias, his eyes fixed on the theatre above.

Sémon shrugged. "The commander is saying they should feed us beef to thank us for the sport we've provided. The Theban," he added, as another round of fist pounding ensued, "is saying the beef is a little off today, a bit tough. Lamb would be much better."

Mikos smiled sadly.

"I think they're going to release us," stated Hybrias. Sémon thought his own interpretation more likely, but said nothing. Eventually the Spartan commander calmed the men around him and announced that the Thebans would make a speech of their own. "What? Why? Why should they make a speech?" Hybrias turned his incredulity upon

Sémon. "They're not the ones on trial. This is between Sparta and us."

"Now we're gonna' hear the real truth," sneered a forked beard beneath the wall. "We'll soon see who the real sons of bitches are."

A stick man, who appeared to have swallowed a bag of lemons, pushed through the Thebans on the wall above, his thin smile betraying little humour. Though standing only a few paces from the Spartan commander, he played to the gallery in a startlingly loud voice.

"I did not expect to have to defend my city to an ally. If you knew the Plataeans as we do, you'd make them answer your just question. At least now you know that if there was an Olympic contest for exaggeration, the Plataeans would certainly win with their self-glorifications and slanders."

There was a rumbling murmur of agreement around the walls.

"How can you know the truth when only a liar's mouth is open? They will not deny that our ancestors founded Plataea after driving off the ancient tribes that cursed this land. But what thanks and loyalty did we receive? They refused to accept our rights as founders and ran to Athens like rebellious children."

Shouts of "Traitors!" and "Snakes!" emphasized the point.

"They have an almighty attitude about how they stood against the barbarians." He paused, before adding emphatically, "But it was only because Athens told them to fight."

"That's right," a few men grunted.

The Stick raised his arms in an exaggerated shrug. "How can they now claim innocence on the basis that Athens led them against Sparta, yet glorify themselves for obeying Athens in fighting the barbarians? How can they congratulate themselves on fighting for freedom in the past, when they now struggle to help Athens enslave Hellas? They have shown their true natures. Not heroes, but cruel oppressors and opportunists. They are, indeed, Athenians at heart."

An angry roar rose above the town to be lost in the oaks of Zeus that had watched Plataea's birth and now stood impassively at its death. The Theban army banged their shields and bawled their abuse to remind the Spartan commander of its strength. Eventually the speaker raised his hand for silence and continued.

"They charge us with invading their city, but their own citizens invited us in. We did not enter with massed troops, killing and maiming, but peacefully, to support those Plataeans who realized that this town's interests lay with Thebes and Sparta, not Athens. They wanted sensible government and they welcomed us. Only later did these murderers standing before us attack our men with no warning. And then their prisoners, our brothers, who held out their hands in surrender, they slaughtered without mercy. How can these villains ask for anything better for themselves? We demand punishment for their crimes!"

"Punish them!" echoed the soldiers. "Death!" "Kill them!" The vicious shouts crashed in waves over the Plataeans. Sémon held his head high and puffed his chest like a prize bull; others looked to the ground and tried to close their ears.

"Their pleadings," continued their accuser, "are nothing next to the families of Thebes ripped apart by Plataean butchery. Any past honour only magnifies their present crimes. Athens set the example in this war by executing one thousand men of Mytilene for their desire for freedom." Sémon and Mikos exchanged puzzled looks. "By any standard, all of the men standing before us are guilty of resisting the cause of freedom. We demand that Sparta shows it is deeds and not words that matter. Infamy mates with pleasing words to recommend itself, but honourable actions speak for themselves. Thebes is your strong right arm. Punish our enemy for its crimes, and do not let oratory deny justice. Put your question before them to determine their fate."

The speaker folded his arms and nodded in self-satisfaction as his fellow citizens released a stinging stream of hate and anger. The Spartan commander consulted his staff, while the Theban soldiers continued unabated their own contribution to the decision.

"What do you think?" asked Hybrias. "He won't believe him, will he?"

Mikos closed his eyes and Sémon remained silent, gazing sadly around the spitting, snarling faces, and then looking away. He looked along the walls towards the mountains, the ragged grey peaks glistening in the sun like snow. Beside him, Mikos stooped and plucked a poppy from the ground, examining every detail of its sensual petals.

Movement near the gate caught Sémon's attention, and an ox-drawn cart trundled from the town bearing a heavy load. It was the statue of Zeus the Liberator. Ever since he was a boy, Sémon had looked up in wonder at the god who had saved Hellas. Zeus Liberator was a friend, a constant in a world of chaos, the protector of Plataea. Tears stood on his cheeks as the statue disappeared through the enemy wall.

A trumpet returned order to the Theban ranks, and Mikos rose as the Spartan commander announced their fate. "In this time of widespread conflict, you either stand with us, or with our enemies. You will answer for your crimes in the manner already prescribed."

"Yes!" thundered the Thebans, succeeded by their jubilant shouts like a hymn of victory. The Plataeans stared open-mouthed, slowly turning to face their companions, hoping they would wake from their nightmare.

Sémon turned again to the mountains, towards Three Heads Pass. He stared at the calm trees and the lush grass on the gently undulating hills, willing an Athenian army to appear bearing Zeus' lightning to strike down the sacrilegious Thebans. Gradually he turned his attention back to the hate-filled town and met Mikos' gaze. They embraced roughly, oblivious to the taunts, to the banging of shields.

"Goodbye, my friend," whispered Sémon huskily. "You have been like a son to me."

Mikos clamped his eyes shut, unable to prevent his tears escaping, gripping Sémon closer.

"No. No." Hybrias shook his head as he watched them. "No, this can't be. They're bluffing. They're not going to go through with it."

Sémon gently disentangled himself and looked away into the sky for a few moments, before clearing his throat and meeting Hybrias' wild stare. "Hybrias, it's time to prepare yourself."

"No! They can't."

Hybrias turned to follow Sémon's gaze and saw their Theban

prosecutor and a hoplite standing before General Arkadius at the start of the line. The soldiers' abuse relented so they could concentrate on the drama with savage glee.

"Have you done anything in this war to help the Spartan cause?" the Stick proclaimed.

For a moment, silence swallowed the stage, and then the grandfather general answered in a clear, loud voice, "No!"

"Kill him!" The maniacal cry rose from the chorus, and the hoplite standing before the general raised his sword, pointing it downwards with the tip resting on Arkadius' chest. The soldier grinned and then pressed down hard with both hands. The general groaned, falling to his knees as the soldier removed the bloody sword. Cheers filled Arkadius' ears as he looked up fleetingly at the pitiless features of his executioner, before falling face down in the poppies.

"No!" screamed Hybrias, looking around desperately for a means of escape. "Maybe they'll only kill the general. You know, as an example? He's the leader. He's the one to blame. They won't kill us. Not us." His speech came in short, breathless bursts, and Mikos laid a hand on his shoulder, but Hybrias shrugged him off.

The Theban inquisitor stood before Astymachus and the noise settled once more.

"Have you done anything in this war to help the Spartan cause?"

The philosopher's face was white, his eyes wide. He shook his head and whispered, "No." The sword pierced his chest, blood gushing over the killer as he struggled to free his weapon, pulling entrails with it. Astymachus' legs buckled, blood oozing from his mouth, the audience cheering joyfully.

The ghostly Plataeans waited their turn, kissed the charms that hung around their necks, looked to the heavens to implore the gods, and stared sightless at the grass, remembering better times. They looked down the line of their friends to see death approach as one by one, to the exuberant exclamations of the Thebans, the Plataeans and Athenians died. With memories of heroic deeds extinguished, one hundred and fifty war-weary citizens swayed in the wind waiting to be cut down like wheat. There was no madness of battle to dull their senses, no rush of excitement to conquer their fear. Death approached slowly, inexorably. There was time to torture themselves over the wives they would never hold, the sons whose laughter they would never hear, and the daughters whose smiles they would never see.

"The Athenians are coming. The Athenians are coming," Hybrias chanted to himself, staring blindly ahead.

Sémon looked to the mountains again, towards the pass to Athens. There was a hint of stirring in the leaves, a gentle murmur of hope. But it was merely a breeze. There was no army. Of course there was no army. His eyes caught the sparkle of a flock of gulls playing in the sunlight, flashes of white escaping like lightning from their midst. Ana would have liked that. She loved to watch the birds.

Death was now just a few strides away, and Sémon watched Mikos still examining his poppy. Mikos looked up and they held each other's gaze in a final, silent goodbye, Sémon reaching for his hand. If only Stephanos had succeeded. If only Mikos had not hurt his ankle. If only Athens had sent her army.

If only.

The furrow of dead bodies sown among the flowers had reached the feet of Hybrias. The thin, tight-lipped Theban with lifeless eyes stood before him as Hybrias continued to mutter, "The Athenians are coming."

"Have you done anything in this war to help the Spartan cause?"

Hybrias continued his mantra, his eyes fixed on the bloody sword held by the hoplite standing beside the questioner.

"Are you deaf? Answer!"

Hybrias looked up into the cold eyes and whimpered, "I could. I could. Please don't kill me."

"Just answer the question. Have you done anything in this war to help the Spartan cause?"

Hybrias' eyes swam with tears. He trembled and sobbed, "No." The soldier raised his sword, but suddenly turned away in disgust as the stench of Hybrias' emptying bowels assaulted his nostrils.

"You filthy dog."

"No, please. Please, don't."

The soldier held his breath as he stepped forward again, carefully avoiding the excrement, thrusting his sword deep into the guilty chest. Hybrias stood wide eyed, a silent scream stuck in his mouth, before falling to the ground.

The Thebans moved before Mikos, who still held Sémon's hand. Sémon looked to the everlasting mountains once more, those faithful companions of his life. What a beautiful land this was, with its fields bursting with crops, its exuberant flowers and stately trees.

If only the Athenians had come.

Sémon felt Mikos shake his head in response to the question and his grip tighten.

"Answer aloud, dog."

Sémon glared at the man staring at Mikos. "He can't speak."

The Theban looked coldly at Sémon, then back at Mikos. "Then shake your head again."

Sémon looked over the walls at the all-seeing sky as the question was put to Mikos once more. A pause. A grunt and a tight squeeze of the hand. Sliding. The hand was sliding from his grip but Sémon grasped it tighter as he continued to stare upwards. The body of his friend slumped against him and slowly, slowly, he let go, staring hard into the distance, not hearing the resounding Theban cheers.

"You. Have you done anything in this war to help the Spartan cause?"

Sémon did not hear. He heard the birds' joyful singing, the insects' buzzing excitement, Ana's infectious laughter. How wonderful it all was. How extraordinary she was. And how she delighted in it all.

"Answer! Have you done anything in this war to help the Spartan cause?"

Sémon turned his gaze slowly to the harsh features of the Theban, smiled, and said, "No."

Chapter 54

Stephanos and the six scouts accompanying him cantered warily along the weed-infested track. It was wide enough for two carts to pass, and on either side the land rose sharply, hidden by the forest. The route twisted along the pass within a couple of miles of the plain around Plataea, and this knowledge had suspended their banter and enlivened their senses. When a stag bolted for the depths of the forest, the scouts' heads snapped in its direction as if Zeus had cast a lightning bolt by their sides.

An eagle sat on the upper branches of a fir tree. A resting eagle was a bad omen; Stephanos pretended to himself that he had not seen it. He was restless and impatient, longing to gallop ahead and see his home again, to call out to Sémon and Mikos that they were coming, that Plataea was saved. But who knew what ambushes had been laid along the pass in the aftermath of their breakout?

"Hello. What have we here?" muttered one of his companions. Two horsemen had appeared little more than one hundred yards ahead of them and stopped abruptly. Stephanos and his men tensed, maintaining their pace, the two strangers talking animatedly to each other. Suddenly, one of the men ahead swung something above his head.

"Is that a sack?" said Stephanos.

Before anyone answered, the man had tossed the item to the ground and the two riders had turned and galloped back in the direction they had come.

"After them!" cried Stephanos, urging his horse into a gallop. "They mustn't warn the garrison."

They charged after the riders, who were quickly out of sight round a bend. The pursuers raced up the slope, the pass thundering hooves as they swerved to avoid thorny bushes on the track and hurdled the trunks of fallen trees. Stephanos, riding one of Alkibiades' horses, led the way, and as he neared the spot where the mysterious item had been thrown, he shouted behind him, "Man at the rear, grab that thing!" He faced forwards again just in time to see it: a sack; spherical; bloodstained. Dread strangled his stomach. It could not be. Not now.

Stephanos rounded the bend and there was no sign of the enemy as the track twisted and turned at the whim of the mountains. That they were the enemy he no longer questioned, and that he would catch them, he had no doubt, his horse sailing over the ground, already five yards ahead of his nearest comrade.

He climbed through the trees and suddenly burst over a ridge. The plain of Plataea emerged below him, the heat of Apollo slapping him as he escaped the cool shade of the pass. Stephanos glanced at the fields stretching away like the easy swells of the sea to the encircling mountains. He had always loved the sight, but now he focused on the horsemen only fifty yards away racing along the side of the mountain.

Plataea was still out of sight, but Stephanos knew it was near and began to fear they would be too late to catch the riders. He urged his horse to greater effort, and then he smelt it: burning. The normal cooking fires in the agora of Plataea, had to be. Had to be.

The track headed down and around the side of the mountain, farms spread on the slope below, tall oaks dominating the mountainside above them. Stephanos' horse careered closer. Forty yards. Thirty. He was gaining rapidly as the horses ahead tired. The disturbing smell intensified. Stephanos did not notice how far he had outdistanced his own men, and as the enemy darted glances over their shoulders, a fierce grin twitched Stephanos' lips as he saw their fear rising. Vultures circled high in the sky. Stephanos dismissed them as eagles.

The riders disappeared over another ridge and Stephanos charged after them, but as he reached the crest, he yanked his horse to an abrupt halt. The horse whinnied, but Stephanos remained motionless, his mouth frozen in a silent cry of anguish, his eyes wide with horror. A mile further along the mountainside stood his home town surrounded by its imprisoning wall. But Plataea was burning, black smoke billowing and flames tasting the air above the public buildings in the heart of the town. On the slopes below Plataea, where once a united force of Greeks had fought off a foreign invasion, an army was once more breaking camp after a successful campaign. Only this time, they were marching home to Thebes.

Stephanos dismounted and staggered a few steps along the track, taking no notice of the flies hovering around him. His companions reached the ridge and brought their own horses to a precipitous halt amidst much swearing, one of them calling out that the sack contained the head of General Arkadius. Stephanos barely heard. They were reducing his home to rubble, and he knew that Sémon and Mikos were dead. Too late. They were too late. He sank to his knees, clutching earth that had once been Plataean, and wept.

Two Athenian comrades rode on to the town to discover the full truth and negotiate the return of the bodies, without revealing that an army was on its way. When they finally gave Stephanos their report, it brought no comfort.

The ride back to the army was a living nightmare. Stephanos was drowning, adrift in a hostile sea. To never again see his uncle's face explode into that joyful roar was to face the extinction of light. Laughter had died.

What would he tell his father? They had failed. *He* had failed. He had not persuaded the Athenians to intervene sooner. Even a few hours earlier would have been enough, and those precious hours tormented him. He mumbled an apology to Sémon and Mikos over and over, urging his horse faster as if he could outrun the accusations of his mind.

***

At the vanguard of the army, Alkibiades swayed gently with the smooth ambling of his horse. Beside him, Timokles sat as if perched on a sword, followed by the rest of the troop. The pass overflowed with cavalry, hoplites, engineers and their equipment, a great river of noise and dust. The jovial curses of soldiers, the braying of donkeys and the clatter of carts rebounded from the once quiet mountain slopes.

Alkibiades was subdued, staring into the distance but not really watching where they were going: there was, after all, only one direction. Other matters occupied him. Why had Nikolas gone to the Argolid? Why was Pisander so upset about splitting the force? Whom could he trust?

A shout from Timokles woke Alkibiades from his reverie to see the scouts rushing towards them. In moments, Stephanos had come to a sharp stop before him, the Plataean's pale face foreshadowing his news.

"What is it?" demanded Alkibiades.

"Plataea has fallen," replied Stephanos, his voice trembling. "The Thebans have attacked it and destroyed our men. Their army's returning to Thebes but they've left a contingent that's reducing the town to rubble. I need to report to General Nikias."

Alkibiades stared at him as if he had heard a foreign tongue. "Fallen? All dead?"

Stephanos looked down and said quietly, "Yes. All."

Alkibiades frowned and straightened his shoulders. "No. That is not possible."

Stephanos motioned to one of his companions. Timokles groaned in disgust and horror as a scout held up a bloody head.

"It's the head of General Arkadius, leader in Plataea," stated the scout. Alkibiades stared at the grotesque object.

"Commander, we must inform General Nikias," urged Stephanos.

"Yes, we must," muttered Alkibiades. "Timokles and I will report to the general. The army will continue to march on and you and your men will scout ahead for us."

Stephanos quickly gave Alkibiades his full report before reluctantly turning back towards Plataea. Alkibiades wheeled his horse and led Timokles back through their army.

Progress was slow along the track choked with the armed forces of Athens, and Alkibiades was in no hurry to reach the general. He failed to acknowledge the greetings from the soldiers as he churned over the news. Even if Plataea had fallen, the equation remained unchanged. Athens had to control Plataea even if its people were dead. If the Thebans had taken it, the Athenians must take it back. From where else were they to strike at Boeotia and Thebes if not from

Plataea? And if they were unable to strike at Thebes, where would that leave his war plans? A ruined Plataea may persuade the Assembly that Nikias' conservative approach was right, after all, and Athens would continue its meek path to destruction. He could not allow that to happen.

All too soon, they arrived before a cluster of dusty men riding amidst dense ranks of hoplites. Alkibiades straightened and called, "Hail, General!"

"Commander," acknowledged Nikias warily. "What brings you from your post?"

"One of the scouts brought news that I thought you should hear right away, General."

Nikias looked beyond Alkibiades and Timokles. "And where is this scout? Is he unable to deliver such news himself?"

Alkibiades laughed, and even to his own ears it sounded false. "Not at all, General. Given the nature of his information, I felt bound to deliver it myself and release him back to his duty."

"Very well. What is it?"

"Plataea has been taken by the Theban army, and the garrison is dead. The Theban army has returned home."

For a few moments, Nikias was speechless. "When did it happen?"

"This very morning, General."

"This morning," whispered Nikias, his face turning ashen. "Oh, all the gods and Lord Herakles," he muttered, his head sinking to his chest.

It was as if a door opened on the sun for Alkibiades. He saw the vicious howls of the Assembly filling Nikias' mind: the general had been too slow. Many had urged him to move sooner but he had delayed. Too cautious, always too cautious they would say, and now Plataea was no more. The mob's anger stood before Nikias like a wounded bull, and not only was his political career in danger, his very status as an Athenian citizen was in jeopardy: enforced exile beckoned. It was an opportunity.

"General," said Alkibiades, "we must press on and take Plataea back. We owe it to our friends. It will be easy enough." He paused, before adding, "It's what the Assembly would want."

Nikias looked up sharply and held Alkibiades' stare. "Do they know we're here?" he snapped.

"They only know of a party of scouts. Their entire army has returned to Thebes. Plataea is open to us."

Nikias nodded, his face grim. "There's no point in empty gestures, especially with the Theban army already mustered. The Council gave instructions to relieve Plataea, but the town is no more. That mission is at an end." He turned to one of his staff alongside him. "Halt the column. We shall head back towards Megara and carry out the campaign I urged in the first place."

"No!" exclaimed Alkibiades, provoking surprised looks all around him. "General, you cannot do this. It is a stain on Athenian honour. We must reclaim the town. The Assembly will stand for nothing less."

Nikias' jaw tightened, colour returning to his cheeks. "Commander," he began, quietly but firmly, "I appreciate your enthusiasm, but I've issued my orders. Return to your post and protect the rear of the column with your men."

"You cannot disgrace Athens in this way, Nikias," pressed Alkibiades. "Generals are elected to fight, not to run away."

The men around them gasped. The general's hands clenched white around his reins as he walked his horse next to Alkibiades'. "If you feel unable to comply with my orders," he hissed, "I'll be happy to relieve you."

Alkibiades' eyes buried themselves in the general's skull. "Is this your idea of Athenian greatness? To assemble a massive army just to scare the rabbits?"

The paralyzed soldiers nearby watched the two men in fascinated horror. Nikias met Alkibiades' glare, and his voice rumbled in the young man's ear. "The only reason I'm not ordering your immediate arrest is out of respect for your guardian, Perikles, and the fact you're friends with my son-in-law. One more outburst will find that line of credit cut off. Now, return to your troop."

Alkibiades did not move. The eyes of the soldiers around them pressed upon Nikias, waiting for him to act. Everyone seemed to be holding their breath.

Suddenly, Timokles appeared by his friend's side, grabbed him by the arm and whispered urgently, "Commander! Alkibiades! *Alkibiades*! Let's go."

Alkibiades slowly emerged from the clouds of his fury, tore his eyes from the general's face, and galloped back in the direction of his men, causing a stream of hoplites to leap out of the way.

Nikias was boiling. The man he had hoped to make his ally had tried to humiliate him. Alkibiades had become Kleon. Nikias brought the external world to order and projected an unruffled visage to his men. "These youngsters," he chuckled loudly. "Think they can run the army as soon as they leave their mother's breasts."

His staff relaxed and began to relay his commands. He would order Hipponikus to bring the fleet, and together they would subdue the island of Minoa, off the coast of Megara, as he had argued all along that they should. A tiny piece of land to be sure, but from there they would get early warning of any Corinthian fleet foolish enough to threaten Athens. A certain victory and a sound strategy. Surely enough to keep the wolves in the Assembly at bay.

Chapter 55

When the Athenians marched into Megara, news of the Spartan-led army beyond the isthmus finally reached Nikias. The panicked general prepared to withdraw to Athens, but Hipponikus arrived with the fleet and the report that the enemy force had mysteriously dispersed. No longer threatened, the Athenians captured Minoa, installed a garrison, devastated the fields around the city of Megara, and returned home.

The loss of Plataea caused a wave of mourning throughout Athens. The lone friend that had stood beside them at Marathon was lost. Alkibiades maintained his influence among the survivors by persuading his cousin, Hippokrates, son of Ariphron, to propose the unprecedented measure of making the Plataeans citizens of Athens. The motion passed unanimously.

The presence of the Peloponnesian army so late in the summer justified Nikias' prior misgivings about the Plataea campaign, and his conquest of Minoa added to his aura of invincibility as general. The stain of Plataea did not attach itself to his reputation.

But the city was uncomfortably aware of how close it had come to disaster. Trapped between the armies of Boeotia and the Peloponnese, the Athenians would have been crushed. Speculation was rife as to why the Spartans had raised such a force at that particular time. Few had answers.

***

Pisander the Hawk strolled along the wall near the Sacred Gate towards his friend, Antiphon. The skin beneath Antiphon's eyes seemed to have sagged in recent days, and the furrows in his brow deepened, but his eyes remained lively and his mind sharp. "By Hades, what happened?" Antiphon exclaimed through gritted teeth. "Why did the fools attack Plataea? They destroyed the whole scheme. If Nikias had not turned back, the Spartans would have trapped our entire army."

Pisander smiled grimly and shook his head. His nose had caught the sun and protruded like a beacon. "Turns out Spartan organization isn't what we've come to expect. They raised an army alright, but they didn't tell the Boeotians of the plan. The garrison commander wanted to grab some glory and decided of his own accord to capture Plataea."

Antiphon stared at his companion. "Unbelievable," he muttered. "Foiled by the petty ambition of a would-be hero. And not even an Athenian one at that."

"Yes, though it made little difference in the end. Sparta didn't withdraw their army because of Nikias' retreat."

"What do you mean?"

"King Archidamus died. The rigors of campaign were too much for the old man. The army disbanded so they could perform the requisite mourning."

Antiphon chuckled bitterly. "You would think that our tyrannous gods actually favour democracy." He looked over the city, beyond the agora and to the acropolis, monument to the success of democratic Athens.

"There'll be other opportunities," said Pisander, with more hope than conviction.

"Hmmm. It seems this democracy has the luck of Tyche herself." Antiphon looked up at the approach of Alkibiades and Nikolas. "Still, luck changes," he muttered, "especially when there are those we can use to give it a push."

"Alkibiades!" called Pisander.

Alkibiades acknowledged Pisander's hail with feigned enthusiasm, using the full power of his handsome features to lull them. They had used him, he was sure of it. Nikolas and the Spartan captain, Nikolas in the Argolid, a Spartan army. He was not stupid. Nor was his mother. They had deciphered the code and it spelt betrayal. Betrayal of Athens, betrayal of him.

But the oligarchs' tracks were hidden in fog, and so he would wait, wait and watch. He leaned against the battlements as a guard strolled past them on his way to the nearest tower.

Antiphon smiled and said, "I heard about your disagreement with Nikias. You have made an enemy there."

Alkibiades snorted. "I do not care for him, he is a mouse."

"Maybe, but a mouse with influence."

"His luck will run out," said Alkibiades.

"People say the gods favour him," noted Pisander, earning a disparaging glance from the young man.

"Do not be discouraged, Alkibiades," said Antiphon. "We may have failed to capture Plataea, but our policies will be pursued by the likes of Demosthenes. If he had led the army, you can be sure Plataea would have been recaptured."

Alkibiades needed no reminding of this fact: Hipponikus had helpfully spelled it out numerous times, and pointed out that his manoeuvrings to place Nikias in command had misfired. Alkibiades assumed his genial smile. "You are quite right. Strange that the Spartans raised an army just as we headed for Plataea, though. And how is it that our scouts failed to discover it earlier?"

Antiphon shrugged. "It is a mystery. But lucky for us that the Spartans turned back."

Alkibiades smiled. "Yes. Lucky." Betrayed by the oligarchs, failed by Nikias, frustrated by the passivity of the nobles, he knew there was only one man in a position to save Athens. One man who had consistently espoused action. One man whose motives he understood and trusted.

Kleon.

It had become clear to him that the nobles would not save Athens. Kleon had always known this. Now Alkibiades would stand beside the Watchdog of the People and call the bakers, the dyers, the dockhands, to Athens' rescue.

***

Khara stared into the darkness. It would soon be morning. Beside her Stephanos snored lightly. The warmth of his body soothed her, and her heart swelled with relief that he was there. Life had flowered again. His sleeping whimpers and moans would pass eventually, and his smile would return.

It was quiet outside. So quiet. No soldiers running through the street. No swords striking shields. She smiled into the darkness. They were safe. There was no fear of betrayal here.

THE END

Historical note

Although this is a work of fiction, I have tried to represent as much actual history as possible. Many of the characters are based on historical figures, although the amount of information available on those people varies from quite a lot (e.g. Alkibiades) to very little. The broad outline of events, including Plataea's fate, is based on Thucydides' masterpiece. Although there is little direct evidence for oligarchic plotting within Athens at this time, contemptuous attitudes to the democracy are well attested, and such plotting was rife in other democratic cities and was successful in Athens several decades later. Only snippets about Alkibiades are known for this period of his life, but I have extrapolated from what is known about his later life.

The Aristophanes quote at the front of the book is a famous reference to Alkibiades, whom the Athenians alternately loved and hated.

Printed in Poland
by Amazon Fulfillment
Poland Sp. z o.o., Wrocław